This Man's

George Manville Fenn

Alpha Editions

This edition published in 2023

ISBN : 9789357944786

Design and Setting By
Alpha Editions
www.alphaedis.com
Email - info@alphaedis.com

Volume One—Chapter One.

The New Curate—Christie Bayle's Mistake.

If that hat had occupied its proper place it would have been perched upon a stake to scare the sparrows away from the young peas, but the wretched weather-beaten structure was upon the old man's head, matching well with his coat, as he busied himself that pleasant morning dibbling in broccoli-plants with the pointed handle of an old spade.

The soft genial rain had fallen heavily during the night, thoroughly soaking the ground, which sent forth a delicious steaming incense quivering like visible transparent air in the morning sun. There had been a month's drought, and flower and fruit had languished; but on the previous evening dark clouds had gathered above the woods, swept over King's Castor, and, as Gemp said, "For twelve mortal hours the rain had poured down."

Old Gemp was wrong: it had not poured, but stolen softly from the kindly heavens, as if every fertilising drop had been wrapped in liquid silver velvet, and no flower was beaten flat, no thirsty vegetable soiled, but earth and plant had drunk and drunk during the long night to wake up refreshed; the soil was of a rich dark hue, in place of drab, and the birds were singing as if they meant to split their throats.

Dr Luttrell's garden was just far enough out of the town for the birds to sing. They came so far, and no farther. Once in a way, perhaps, some reckless young blackbird went right into the elder clump behind the mill, close up to the streets, and hunted snails from out of the hollow roots, and from the ivy that hung over the stone wall by the great water-tank in Thickens's garden; but that was an exception. Only one robin and the sparrows strayed so far in as that.

But with the doctor's garden it was different. There was the thick hawthorn hedge that separated it from the north road, a hedge kept carefully clipped, and with one tall stem every twelve yards that was never touched, but allowed to grow as it pleased, and to blossom every May and June into almond-scented snow, as it was blooming now. Then there was the great laurel hedge, fifteen feet high, on the north; the thick shrubbery about the red-bricked gabled house, and the dense ivy that covered it from the porch upwards and over Millicent's window, and then crawled right up the sides to the chimney stacks.

There were plenty of places for birds, and, as they were never disturbed, the doctor's was a haven where nests were made, eggs laid, and young hatched, to the terrible detriment of the doctor's fruit; but he only gave his handsome grey head a rub and laughed.

That delicious June morning as the line was stretched over the bed that had been so long prepared, and the plants that had been nursed in a frame were being planted, the foreshortening of the old man's figure was rather strange, so strange that as he came along the road looking over the hedge, and taking in long breaths of delicious scents, the Reverend Christie Bayle, the newly-appointed curate of St. Anthony's, paused to watch the planting.

He was tall, slight, and pale, looking extremely youthful in his black clerical attire; but it was the pallor of much hard study, not of ill-health, for as he had come down the road it was with a free elastic stride, and he carried his head as a man does who feels that he is young and full of hope, and thinks that this world is, after all, a very beautiful place.

But it was a delicious June morning.

True, but the Reverend Christie Bayle was just as light and elastic when he walked back to his lodgings, through the rain on the previous night, and without an umbrella. He had caught himself whistling, too, several times, and checked himself, thinking that, perhaps, he ought to cease; but somehow— it was very dark—he was thoroughly light-hearted, and he had the feeling that he had made a poor weak old woman more restful at heart during his chat with her by her bedside, and so he began whistling again.

He was not whistling now as he stopped short, looking over the hedge, watching the foreshortened figure coming down towards him, with a leg on either side of the line, the dibber in one hand, a bunch of broccoli-plants in the other. The earth was soft, and the old man's arm strong, while long practice had made him clever. He had no rule, only his eye and the line for guidance; but, as he came slowly down the row, he left behind him, at exactly two feet apart, the bright green tightly-set plants.

Whig! went the dibber: in went a plant; there was a quick poke or two, the soft earth was round the stem, and the old man went on till he reached the path, straightened himself, and began to softly rub the small of his back with the hand that held the tool.

"Good-morning," said the curate.

"Morning."

"Ladies at home?"

"No, they've gone up to the town shopping. Won't be long."

"Do you think they'd mind if I were to wait?"

"Mind? No. Come and have a look round."

"Peculiarity of the Lincolnshire folk, that they rarely say *sir* to their superiors," mused the Reverend Christie Bayle, as he entered the garden. "Perhaps they think we are not their superiors, and perhaps they are right; for what am I better than that old gardener?"

"Nice rain."

"Delicious! By Geo—I—ah, you have a beautiful garden here."

The old man gave him a droll look, and the curate's, face turned scarlet, for that old college expression had nearly slipped out.

"Yes, it's a nice bit of garden, and pretty fruitful considering. You won't mind my planting another row of these broccoli?"

"Not a bit. Pray go on, and I can talk to you. Seems too bad for me to be doing nothing, and you breaking your back."

"Oh, it won't break my back; *I'm* used to it. Well, how do you like King's Castor?"

"Very much. The place is old and quaint, and I like the country. The people are a little distant at present. They are not all so sociable as you are."

"Ah, they don't know you yet. There: that's done. Now I'm going to stick those peas."

He thrust the dibber into the earth, kicked the soil off his heavy boots, and came out on to the path rubbing his hands and looking at them.

"Shake hands with you another time."

"To be sure. Going to stick those peas, are you?"

"Yes. I've the sticks all ready."

The old man went to the top of the path, and into a nook where, already sharpened, were about a dozen bundles of clean-looking ground-birch sticks full of twigs for the pea tendrils to hold on by as they climbed.

The old fellow smiled genially, and there was something very pleasant in his clear blue eyes, florid face, and thick grey beard, which—a peculiarity in those days—he wore cut rather short, but innocent of razor.

"Shall I carry a bundle or two down?" said the curate.

"If you like."

The Reverend Christie Bayle did like, and he carried a couple of bundles down to where the peas were waiting their support. And then—they neither of them knew how it happened, only that a question arose as to whether it was better to put in pea-sticks perpendicular or diagonal, the old man being in favour of the upright, the curate of the slope—both began sticking a row, with the result that, before a quarter of a row was done, the curate had taken off his black coat, hung it upon the gnarled Ripston-pippin-tree, rolled up his shirt sleeves over a pair of white, muscular arms, and quite a race ensued.

Four rows had been stuck, and a barrow had been fetched and a couple of spades, for the digging and preparing of a patch for some turnips, when, spade in hand, the curate paused and wiped his forehead. "You seem to like gardening, parson."

"I do," was the reply. "I quite revel in the smell of the newly turned earth on a morning like this, only it makes me so terribly hungry."

"Ah, yes, so it does me. Well, let's dig this piece, and then you can have a mouthful of lunch with me."

"Thank you, no; I'll help you dig this piece, and then I must go. I'll come in another time. I want to see more of the garden."

There was about ten minutes' steady digging, during which the curate showed that he was no mean hand with the spade, and then the old man paused for a moment to scrape the adherent soil from the broad blade.

"My master will be back soon," he said; "and then there'll be some lunch; and, oh! here they are."

The Reverend Christie Bayle had been so intent upon lifting that great spadeful of black earth without crumbling, that he had not heard the approaching footsteps, and from behind the yew hedge that sheltered them from the flower-garden, two ladies and a tall, handsome-looking man suddenly appeared, awaking the curate to the fact that he was in his shirt sleeves, digging, with his hat on a gooseberry-bush, his coat in an apple-tree, and his well-blackened boots covered with soil.

He was already flushed with his exercise. He turned of a deeper red now, as he saw the pleasant-looking, elderly lady give her silvery-grey curls a shake, the younger lady gaze from one to the other as if astonished, and the tall, dark gentleman suppress a smile as he raised his eyebrows slightly, and seemed to be amused.

The curate thrust his spade into the ground, bowed hurriedly, took a long step and snatched his hat from the gooseberry-bush, and began to hastily roll down his sleeves.

"Oh, never mind them," said his companion. "Adam was not ashamed of his arms. Here, my dears, this is our new curate, Mr Bayle, the first clergyman we've had who could use a spade. Mr Bayle—my wife, my daughter Millicent. Mr Hallam, from the bank."

The Reverend Christie Bayle's face was covered with dew, and he longed to beat a retreat from the presence of the pleasant-faced elderly lady; to make that retreat a rout, as he met the large, earnest grey eyes of "my daughter Millicent," and saw as if through a mist that she was fair to see—how fair in his agitation he could not tell; and lastly, to rally and form a stubborn front, as he bowed to the handsome, supercilious man, well-dressed, perfectly at his ease, and evidently enjoying the parson's confusion.

"We are very glad you have come to see us, Mr Bayle," said the elderly lady, smiling, and shaking hands warmly. "Of course we knew you soon would. And so you've been helping Dr Luttrell."

"The doctor!" thought the visitor with a mental groan; "and I took him for the gardener!"

Volume One—Chapter Two.

Some Introductions and a Little Music.

The reception had been so simple and homely, that, once having secured his coat and donned it, the doctor's volunteer assistant felt more at his ease. His disposition to retreat passed off, and, in despite of all refusal, he was almost compelled to enter the house, Mrs Luttrell taking possession of him to chat rather volubly about King's Castor and the old vicar, while from time to time a few words passed with Millicent, at whom the visitor gazed almost in wonder.

She was so different from the provincial young lady he had set up in his own mind as a type. Calm, almost grave in its aspect, her face was remarkable for its sweet, self-contained look of intelligence, and the new curate had not been many minutes in her society before he was aware that he was conversing with a woman as highly cultivated as she was beautiful.

Her sweet, rich voice absolutely thrilled, while her quiet self-possession sent a pang through him, as he felt how young, how awkward, and wanting in confidence he must seem in her eyes, which met his with a frank, friendly look that was endorsed during conversation, as she easily and pleasantly helped him out of two or three verbal bogs into which he had floundered.

After a walk through the garden, they had entered the house, where Mrs Luttrell had turned suddenly upon her visitor, to confuse him again by her sudden appeal.

"Did you ever see such a straw hat as that, Mr Bayle?"

"Oh, it's an old favourite of papa's, Mr Bayle," interrupted Millicent, turning to smile at the elderly gentleman taking the dilapidated straw from his head to hang it upon one particular peg. "He would not enjoy the gardening so much without that."

The tall handsome man left at the end of a few minutes. Business was his excuse. He had met the ladies, and just walked down with them, he told the doctor.

"But you'll come in to-night, Mr Hallam? We shall expect you," said Mrs Luttrell warmly.

"Oh, of course!" said Millicent, as Mr Hallam, from the bank, involuntarily turned to her; and her manner was warm but not conscious.

"I shall be here," he said quietly; and after a quiet friendly leave-taking, Christie Bayle felt relieved, and as if he could be a little more at his ease.

It was not a success though, and when he in turn rose to go, thinking dolefully about his dirty boots as compared with the speckless Wellingtons of the other visitor, and after feeling something like a throb of pleasure at being warmly pressed to step in without ceremony that evening, he walked to his apartments in the main street, irritated and wroth with himself, and more dissatisfied than he had ever before felt in his life.

"I wish I had not come," he said to himself. "I'm too young, and what's worse, I *feel* so horribly young. That supercilious Mr Hallam was laughing at me; the old lady treated me as if I were a boy; and Miss Luttrell—"

He stopped thinking, for her tall graceful presence seemed before him, and he felt again the touch of her cool, soft, white hand.

"Yes; she talked to me as if I were a boy, whom she wanted to cure of being shy. I am a boy, and it's my own fault for not mixing more with men."

"Bah! What an idiot I was! I might have known it was not the gardener. He did not talk like a servant, but I blundered into the idea, and went on blindfold in my belief. What a ridiculous *début* I made there, to be sure, where I wanted to make a good impression! How can I profess to teach people like that when they treat me as if I were a boy? I can never show my face there again."

He felt in despair, and his self-abasement grew more bitter as the day went on. It would be folly, he thought, to go to the doctor's that evening; but, as the time drew near, he altered his mind, and at last, taking a small case from where it rested upon a bookshelf, he thrust it into his pocket and started, his teeth set, his nerves strung, and his whole being bent upon the determination to show these people that he was not the mere bashful boy they thought him.

It was a deliciously soft, warm evening, and as he left the town behind with its few dim oil lamps, the lights that twinkled through the trees from the doctor's drawing-room were like so many invitations to him to hurry his feet, and so full was his mind of one of the dwellers beneath the roof that, as he neared the gate, he was not surprised to hear Millicent's voice, sweet, clear, and ringing. It hastened his steps. He did not know why, but it was as if attracting—positively magnetic. The next moment there was the low, deep-toned rich utterance of a man's voice—a voice that he recognised at once as that of Mr Hallam, from the bank; and if this was magnetic, it was from the negative pole, for Christie Bayle stopped.

He went on again, angry, he knew not why, and the next minute was being introduced on the lawn to a thin, careworn, middle-aged man, and a tall, bony, aquiline lady, as Mr and Mrs Trampleasure, Mrs Luttrell's pleasant, sociable voice being drowned almost the next moment by that of the bony dame, who in tones resembling those emitted by a brazen instrument, said very slowly:

"How do you do? I saw you last Sunday. Don't you think it is getting too late to stop out on the grass?"

"Yes, yes," said Mrs Luttrell hastily, "the grass is growing damp. Milly, dear, take Mr Hallam into the drawing-room."

The pleasant flower-decked room, with its candles and old-fashioned oil lamp, seemed truly delightful to Christie Bayle, for the next hour. He was very young, and he was the new arrival in King's Castor, and consequently felt flattered by the many attentions he received. The doctor was friendly, and disposed to be jocose with allusions to gardening. Mr Trampleasure, thin and languid, made his advances, but his questions were puzzling, as they related to rates of exchange and other monetary matters, regarding which the curate's mind was a blank.

"Not a well-informed young man, my dear," said Mr Trampleasure to his wife; whereupon that lady looked at him, and Mr Trampleasure seemed to wither away, or rather to shrink into a corner, where Millicent, who looked slightly flushed, but very quiet and self-possessed, was turning over some music, every piece of which had a strip of ribbon sewn with many stitches all up its back.

"Not a well-informed young man, this new curate, Millicent," said Mr Trampleasure, trying to sow his discordant seed on more genial soil.

"Not well-informed, uncle?" said the daughter of the house, looking up wide-eyed and amused, "why, I thought him most interesting."

"Oh! dear me, no, my dear. Quite ignorant of the most everyday matters. I just asked him—"

"Are you going to give us some music, Miss Luttrell?" said a deep, rich voice behind them, and Millicent turned round smiling.

"I was looking out two of your songs, Mr Hallam. You will sing something?"

"If you wish it," he said quietly, and there was nothing impressive in his manner.

"Oh, we should all be glad. Mamma is so fond of your songs."

"I must make the regular stipulation," said Mr Hallam smiling. "Banking people are very exacting: they do nothing without being paid."

"You mean that I must sing as well," said Millicent.

"Oh, certainly. And," she added eagerly, "Mr Bayle is musical. I will ask him to sing."

"Yes, do," said Hallam, with a shade of eagerness in his voice. "He cannot refuse you."

She did not know why, but as Millicent Luttrell heard these words, something like regret at her proposal crossed her mind, and she glanced at where Bayle was seated, listening to Mrs Trampleasure, who was talking to him loudly— so loudly that her voice reached their ears.

"I should be very glad indeed, Mr Bayle, if, when you call upon us, you would look through Edgar and Edmund's Latin exercises. I'm quite sure that the head master at the grammar school does not pay the attention to the boys that he should."

To wait until Mrs Trampleasure came to the end of a conversational chapter, would have been to give up the singing, so Millicent sat down to the little old-fashioned square piano, running her hands skilfully over the keys, and bringing forth harmonious sounds. But they were the *aigue* wiry tones of the modern zither, and Christie Bayle bent forward as if attracted by the sweet face thrown up by the candles, and turned slightly towards Hallam, dark, handsome, and self-possessed, standing with one hand resting on the instrument.

"I don't like music!" said Mrs Trampleasure, in a very slightly subdued voice.

"Indeed!" said Bayle starting, for his thoughts were wandering, and an unpleasant, indefinable feeling was stealing over him.

"I think it a great waste of time," continued Mrs Trampleasure. "Do you like it, Mr Bayle?"

"Well, I must confess I am very fond of it," he replied.

"But you don't play anything," said the lady with quite a look of horror.

"I—I play the flute—a little," faltered the curate.

"Well," said Mrs Trampleasure austerely, "we learn a great many habits when we are young, Mr Bayle, that we leave off when we grow older. You are youngs Mr Bayle."

He looked up in her face as if she had wounded him, her words went so deeply home, and he replied softly:

"Yes, I'm afraid I am very young."

Just then the doctor came and laid his hand upon Mrs Trampleasure's lips.

"Silence! One tablespoonful to be taken directly. Hush, softly, not a word;" and he stood over his sister—with a warning index finger held up, while in a deep, thrilling baritone voice Mr Hallam from the bank sang "Treasures of the Deep."

A dead silence was preserved, and the sweet rich notes seemed to fill the room and float out where the dewy flowers were exhaling their odours on the soft night air. The words were poetical, the pianoforte accompaniment was skilfully played, and, though perhaps but slightly cultivated, the voice of the singer was modulated by that dramatic feeling which is given but to few, so that the expression was natural, and, without troubling the composer's marks, the song appealed to the feelings of the listeners, though in different ways.

"Bravo! bravo!" cried Mr Trampleasure, crossing to the singer.

"He has a very fine voice," said Dr Luttrell in a quiet, subdued way; and his handsome face wrinkled a little as he glanced towards the piano.

"Yes, yes, it's very beautiful," said Mrs Luttrell, fingering a bracelet round and round, "but I wish he wouldn't, dear; I declare it always makes me feel as if I wanted to cry. Ah! here's Sir Gordon."

Pleasant, sweet-faced Mrs Luttrell crossed the room to welcome a new arrival in the person of a remarkably well-preserved elderly gentleman, dressed with a care that told of his personal appearance being one of the important questions of his life. There was a suspicion of the curling tongs about his hair, which was of a glossy black that was not more natural in hue than that of his carefully-arranged full whiskers. There was a little black patch, too, beneath the nether lip that matched his eyebrows, which seemed more regular and dark than those of gentlemen as a rule at his time of life. The lines in his face were not deep, but they were many, and, in short, he looked, from the curl on the top of his head, down past his high black satin stock, well-padded coat, pinched waist, and carefully strapped down trousers over his painfully small patent leather boots, like one who had taken up the challenge of Time, and meant to fight him to the death.

"Good evening, Mrs Luttrell. Ah! how do, doctor? My dear Miss Luttrell, I've been seeing your fingers in the dark as I waited outside."

"Seeing my fingers, Sir Gordon?"

"Yes; an idea—a fancy of mine," said the newcomer, bending over the hand he took with courtly old-fashioned grace. "I heard the music, and the sounds brought the producers before my eyes. Hallam, my dear sir, you have a remarkably fine voice. I've known men, sir, at the London Concerts, draw large incomes on worse voices than that!"

"You flatter me, Sir Gordon."

"Not at all, sir," said the newcomer shortly. "*I* never stoop to flatter any one, not even a lady. Miss Luttrell, do I?"

"You never flattered me," said Millicent, smiling.

"Never. It is a form of insincerity I detest. My dear Mrs Luttrell, you should make your unworthy husband take that to heart."

"Why, I never flatter," said the doctor warmly.

"How dare you say so, sir, when you are always flattering your patients, and preaching peace when there is no peace? Ah, yes, I've heard of him," he said in an undertone. "Introduce me."

The formal introduction took place, and the last comer seated himself beside the new curate.

"I'm very glad to meet you, Mr Bayle. Glad to see you here, too, sir. Charming family this; doctor and his wife people to make friends. Eh! singing again? Hah! Miss Luttrell. Have you heard her sing?"

"No, she has not sung since I have been here."

"Then prepare yourself for a treat, sir. I flatter myself I know what singing is. It is the singing of one of our *prima donnas* without the artificiality."

"I think I heard Sir Gordon say he did not flatter," said Bayle quietly.

"Thank you," said the old beau, looking round sharply; "but I shall not take the rebuke. You have not heard her sing. Oh, I see," he continued, raising his gold-rimmed eye-glass, "a duet."

There was again silence, as after the prelude Millicent's voice rose clear and thrilling in the opening of one of the simple old duets of the day; and as she sang with the effortless ease of one to whom song was a gift, Sir Gordon bent forward, swaying himself slightly to the music, but only to stop short and watch with gathering uneasiness in his expression, the rapt earnestness of Christie Bayle as he seemed to drink in like some intoxicating draught the notes that vibrated through the room. He drew a deep breath, and sat up rather stiffly as she ended, and Mr Hallam from the bank took up the second verse. If anything, his voice sounded richer and more full; and again the harmony was perfect when the two voices, soprano and baritone, blended, and rose and fell in impassioned strains, and then gradually died off in a soft, sweet, final chord, that the subdued notes of the piano, wiry though they were, failed to spoil.

"You are not fond of music?" said Sir Gordon, making Bayle, who had been still sitting back rather stiffly, and with his eyes closed, start, as he replied:

"Who? I? Oh, yes, I love it!" he replied hastily.

"Young! young!" said Sir Gordon to himself as he rose and crossed the room to congratulate Millicent on her performance—Hallam giving way as he approached—saying to himself: "I'm beginning to wish we had not engaged him, good a man as he is."

"Yes, I'm very fond of that duet," said Millicent. "Excuse me, Sir Gordon, here's Miss Heathery."

She crossed to the door to welcome a lady in a very tight evening dress of cream satin—tight, that is, in the body—and pinched in by a broad sash at the waist, but the sleeves were like two cream-coloured spheres, whose open mouths hung down as if trying to swallow the long crinkly gloves that the wearer kept drawing above her pointed elbows, and which then slipped down.

It is a disrespectful comparison, but it was impossible to look at Miss Heathery's face without thinking of a white rabbit. One of Nature's paradoxical mysteries, no doubt, for it was not very white, nor were her eyes pink, and the sausage-shaped, brown curls on either side of her forehead, backed by a great shovel-like, tortoise-shell comb, in no wise resembled ears; but still the fact remained, and even Christie Bayle, on being introduced to the elderly bashful lady, thought of the rabbit, and actually blushed.

"You are just in time to sing, Miss Heathery," said Millicent.

Miss Heathery could not; but there was a good deal of pressing, during which the lady's eyes rolled round pleadingly from speaker to speaker, as if saying, "Press me a little more, and I will."

"You must sing, my dear," said Mrs Luttrell in a whisper. "Make haste, and then Millicent's going to ask Mr Bayle, and you must play the accompaniment." Miss Heathery said, "Oh, really!" and Sir Gordon completed the form by offering his arm, and leading the little lady to the piano, taking from her hands her reticule, made in pale blue satin to resemble a butterfly; after that her gloves.

Then, after a good deal of arrangement of large medical folios upon a chair to make Miss Heathery the proper height, she raised her shoulders, the left becoming a support to her head as she lifted her chin and gazed into one corner of the room.

Christie Bayle was a lover of natural history, and he said to himself, "How could I be so rude as to think she looked like a white rabbit? She is exactly like a bird."

It was only that a change that had come over the lady, who was now wonderfully bird-like, and, what was quite to the point, like a bird about to sing.

She sang.

It was a tippity-tippity little tinkling song, quite in accordance with the wiry, zither-like piano, all about "dewy twilight lingers," and harps "touched by fairy fingers," and appeals to some one to "meet me there, love," and so on.

The French say we are not a polite nation. We may not be as to some little bits of outer polish, but at heart we are, and never more so than at a social gathering, when some terrible execution has taken place under the name of music. It was so here, for, moved by the feeling that the poor little woman had done her best, and would have been deeply wounded had she not been asked to sing, all warmly thanked Miss Heathery; and directly after, Christie Bayle, with his ears still burning from the effects of the performance, found himself beside the fair singer, trying to talk of King's Castor and its surroundings.

"I would rather not ask him, mamma dear," said Millicent at the other side of the room.

"But you had better, my dear. I know he is musical, and he might feel slighted."

"Oh, yes, he's a good fellow, my dear; I like him," said the doctor bluffly. "Ask him."

With a curious shrinking sensation that seemed somehow vaguely connected with Mr Hallam from the bank, and his eagerness earlier in the evening, Millicent crossed to where Bayle was seated, and asked him if he would sing.

"Oh, no," he said hastily, "I have no voice!"

"But we hear that you are musical, Mr Bayle," said Millicent in her sweet, calm way.

"Oh, yes, I am. Yes, I am a little musical."

"Pray sing then," she said, now that she had taken the step, forgetting the diffident feeling; "we are very simple people here, and so glad to have a fresh recruit in our narrow ranks."

"Yes, pray sing, Mr Bayle; we should be so charmed."

"I—er—I really—"

"Oh, but do, Mr Bayle," said Miss Heathery again sweetly.

"I think you will oblige us, Mr Bayle," said Millicent smiling; and as their eyes met, if the request had been to perform the act of Marcus Curtius on foot, and with a reasonable chance of finding water at the bottom to break the fall, Christie Bayle would have taken the plunge.

"Have you anything I know?" he said despairingly.

"I know," cried Miss Heathery, with a sort of peck made in bird-like playfulness. "Mr Bayle can sing 'They bid me forget thee.'"

"Full many a shaft at random sent, hits," et cetera. This was a chance shot, and it struck home.

"I think—er—perhaps, I could sing that," stammered Bayle, and then in a fit of desperation—"I'll try."

"I have it among my music, Millicent dear. May I play the accompaniment?"

Miss Heathery meant to look winning, but she made Bayle shiver.

"If you will be so good, Miss Heathery;" and the piece being found and spread out, Christie Bayle, perspiring far more profusely than when he was using the doctor's spade, stood listening to the prelude, and then began to sing, wishing that the dead silence around had been broken up by a hurricane, or the loudest thunder that ever roared.

Truth to tell, it was a depressing performance of a melancholy song. Bayle's voice was not bad, but his extreme nervousness paralysed him, and the accompaniment would have driven the best vocalist frantic.

It was a dismal failure, and when, in the midst of a pleasant little chorus of "Thank you's" Christie Bayle left the piano, he felt as if he had disgraced himself for ever in the eyes of King's Castor, above all in those of this sweetly calm and beautiful woman who seemed like some Muse of classic days come back to life.

Every one smiled kindly, and Mrs Luttrell came over, called him "my dear" in her motherly way, and thanked him again.

"Only want practice and confidence, sir," said the doctor.

"Exactly," said Sir Gordon; "practise, sir, and you'll soon beat Hallam there."

Bayle felt as if he would give anything to be able to retreat; and just then he caught Mrs Trampleasure's eyes as she signalled him to come to her side.

"She told me she did not like music," he said to himself; and he was yielding to his fate, and going to have the cup of his misery filled to the brim when he caught Hallam's eye.

Hallam was by the chimney-piece, talking to Mr Trampleasure about bank matters; but that look seemed so full of triumphant contempt, that Bayle drew his breath as if in pain, and turned to reach the door.

"It was very kind of you to sing when I asked you, Mr Bayle," said that sweet low voice that thrilled him; and he turned hastily, seeing again Hallam's sneering look, or the glance that he so read.

"I cannot sing," he replied with boyish petulance. "It was absurd to attempt it. I have only made myself ridiculous."

"Pray do not say that," said Millicent kindly. "You give me pain. I feel as if it is my fault, and that I have spoiled your evening."

"I—I have had no practice," he faltered.

"But you love music. You have a good voice. You must come and try over a few songs and duets with me."

He looked at her half-wonderingly, and then moved by perhaps a youthful but natural desire to redeem himself, he said hastily:

"I can—play a little—the flute."

"But you have not brought it?"

"Yes," he said hastily. "Will you play an accompaniment? Anything, say one of Henry Bishop's songs or duets."

Millicent sighed, for she felt regret, but she concealed her chagrin, and said quietly, "Certainly, Mr Bayle;" and they walked together to the piano.

"Bravo!" cried Sir Gordon. "No one need be told that Mr Bayle is an Englishman."

There was a rather uncomfortable silence as, more and more feeling pity and sympathy for their visitor, Millicent began to turn over a volume of bound up music, while, with trembling hands, Bayle drew his quaint boxwood flute with its brass keys and ivory mounts from its case.

It was a wonderfully different instrument from one of those cocoa-wood or metal flutes of the present day, every hole of which is stopped not with the fingers but with keys. This was an old-fashioned affair, in four pieces, which had to be moistened at the joints when they were stuck together, and all this business the Reverend Christie Bayle went through mechanically, for his eyes were fixed upon the music Millicent was turning over.

"Let's try that," he said suddenly, in a voice tremulous with eagerness, as she turned over leaf after leaf, hesitating at two or three songs—"Robin Adair," "Ye Banks and Braes," and another—easy melodies, such as a flute player could be expected to get through. But though she had given him plenty of time to choose either of these, he let her turn over, and went on wetting the flute joints, and screwing them up till she arrived at "I Know a Bank."

"But it is a duet," she said, smiling at him as an elder sister might have smiled at a brother she wished to encourage, and who had just made another mistake.

"Yes," he said hastily; "but I can take up first one voice and then the other, and when it comes to the duet part the piano will hide the want of the second voice."

"Or I can play it where necessary," said Millicent, who began to brighten up. Perhaps this was not going to be such a dismal failure after all.

"To be sure," he said: "if you will. There, I think that will do. Pray excuse me if I seem terribly nervous," he whispered.

"Oh! don't apologise, Mr Bayle. We are all friends here. I do not mind. I was thinking of you."

"Thank you," he said hastily. "You are very kind. Shall we begin?"

"Yes, I am ready," said Millicent, glancing involuntarily at Hallam, who was still conversing with Trampleasure, his face perfectly calm, but his eyes wearing a singular look of triumph.

"One moment. Would you mind sounding D?" Millicent obeyed, and Bayle blew a tremulous note upon the flute nearly a quarter of a tone too sharp.

This necessitated a certain amount of unscrewing and lengthening which made the drops glisten upon Bayle's forehead.

"Poor fellow!" thought Millicent, "how nervous he is! I wish he were not going to play."

"I think that will do," he said at last, after blowing one or two more tremulous notes. "Shall we begin?" Millicent nodded, giving him a smile of encouragement, and after whispering, "Don't mind me, I'll try and keep to your time," she ran over the prelude, and shivered as the flute took up the melody and began.

It has been said that the flute, of all instruments, most resembles the human voice, and to Millicent Luttrell it seemed to wail here piteously how it knew a bank whereon the wild thyme grew. Her hands were moist from sympathy for the flautist, and she was striving to play her best with the fullest chords so as to hide his weakness, when, as he went on, it seemed to her that Bayle was forgetting the presence of listeners and growing interested in the beautiful melody he played. The notes of the flute became, moment by moment, more rich and round; they were no longer spasmodic, beginning and ending clumsily, but were breathed forth softly, with a crescendo and diminuendo where necessary, and so full of feeling that the pianiste was encouraged. She, too, forgot the listeners, and yielding to her love of her art, played on. The slow, measured strains were succeeded by the florid runs; but she never wondered whether the flautist would succeed, for they were amongst them before she knew they were *so* near, with the flute seeming to trip deftly over the most difficult passages without the slightest hesitation, the audience thoroughly enjoying the novel performance, till the final chord was struck, and followed by a hearty round of applause.

"Oh! Mr Bayle," cried Millicent, looking up in his flushed face, "I am so glad."

Her brightened eyes told him the same tale, for he had thoroughly won her sympathy as well as the praise of all present; Mr Hallam from the bank being as ready as the rest to thank him for so "delicious a rendering of that charming duet."

The rest of that evening was strange and dreamlike to Christie Bayle. He played some more florid pieces of music by one Henry Bishop, and he took Millicent in to supper. Then, soon after, he walked home, Sir Gordon Bourne being his companion.

After that he sat for some hours thinking and wondering how it was that while some men of his years were manly and able to maintain their own, he was so boyish and easily upset.

"I'm afraid my old tutor's right," he said; "I want ballast."

Perhaps that was why, when he dropped to sleep and went sailing away into the sea of dreams, his voyage was so wild and strange. Every minute some gust of passion threatened to capsize his barque, but he sailed on with his dreams growing more wild, the sky around still more strange.

It was a restless night for Christie Bayle, B.A. But the scholar of Oriel College, Oxford, was thinking as he had never thought before.

Volume One—Chapter Three.

A Little Business of the Bank.

"Would you be kind enough to cash this little cheque for me, Mr Thickens?"

The speaker was Miss Heathery, in the morning costume of a plum-coloured silk dress, with wide-spreading bonnet of the same material, ornamented with several large bows of broad satin ribbon, and an extremely dilapidated bird of paradise plume. She placed her reticule bag, also of plum-colour, but of satin—upon the broad mahogany counter of Dixons' Bank, Market Place, King's Castor, and tried to draw the bag open.

This, however, was not so easy. When it was open all you had to do was to pull the thick silk cord strings, and it closed up tightly, but there was no similar plan for opening a lady's reticule in the year 1818. It was then necessary to insert the forefingers of each hand, knuckle to knuckle, force them well down, and then draw, the result being an opening, out of which you could extract pocket-handkerchief, Preston salts, or purse. Thin fingers were very useful at such a time, and Miss Heathery's fingers were thin; but she wore gloves, and the gloves of that period, especially those sold in provincial towns, were not of the delicate second-skin nature worn by ladies now. The consequence was that hard-featured, iron-grey haired, closely-shaven Mr James Thickens, in his buff waistcoat and stiff white cravat, had to stand for some time, with a very large quill pen behind his right ear, waiting till Miss Heathery, who was growing very hot and red, exclaimed:

"That's it!" and drew open the bag.

But even then the cheque was not immediately forthcoming, for it had to be fished for. First there was Miss Heathery's pocket-handkerchief, delicately scented with otto of roses; then there was the pattern she was going to match at Crumple's, the draper's; then her large piece of orris root got in the way, and had to be shaken on one side with the knitting, and the ball of Berlin wool, when the purse was found in the far corner.

Purses, too, in those days were not of the "open sesame" kind popular now. The *porte-monnaie* was not born, and ladies knitted long silken hose, with a slit in the middle, placed ornamental slide-rings and tassels thereon, and even went so far sometimes as to make these old-fashioned purses of beads.

Miss Heathery's was of netted silk, however, orange and blue, and through the reticulations could be seen at one end the metallic twinkle of coins, at the other the subdued tint and cornerish distensions of folded paper.

"I'm afraid I'm keeping you, Mr Thickens," said the lady in a sweet, bird-like chirp, as she drew one slide, and tried to coax the folded cheque along the hose, though it refused to be coaxed, and obstinately stuck its elbows out at every opening of the net.

Mr Thickens said, "Not at all," and passed his tongue over his dry lips, and moved his long fingers as if he were a kind of human actinia, and these were his tentacles, involuntarily trying to get at the cheque.

"That's it!" said Miss Heathery again with a satisfied sigh, and she handed the paper across the counter.

James Thickens drew down a pair of very strongly-framed, round-eyed, silver-mounted spectacles from where they had been resting close to his brushed up "Brutus," and unfolded and smoothed out the slip of paper, spreading it on the counter, and bending over it so much that his glasses would have fallen off but for the fact that a piece of black silk shoe-string formed a band behind.

"Two thirteen six," said Mr Thickens, looking up at the lady.

"Yes; two pounds thirteen shillings and sixpence," she replied, in token of assent. And while she was speaking, Mr Thickens took the big quill pen from behind his ear, and stood with his head on one side in an attitude of attention till the word "sixpence" was uttered, when the pen was darted into a great shining leaden inkstand and out again, like a peck from a heron's bill, and without damaging the finely-cut point. A peculiar cancelling mark was made upon the cheque, which was carried to a railed-in desk. A great book was opened with a bang, and an entry made, the cheque dropped into a drawer, and then, in sharp, business-like tones, Mr Thickens asked the question he had been asking for the last twenty years.

"How will you have it?"

Miss Heathery chirped out her wishes, and Mr Thickens counted out two sovereigns twice over, rattled them into a bright copper shovel, and cleverly threw them before the customer's hand. A half-sovereign was treated similarly, but retained with the left hand till half-a-crown and a shilling were ready, then all these coins were thrust over together, without the copper shovel, and the transaction would have been ended, only that Miss Heathery said sweetly: "Would you mind, Mr Thickens, giving me some smaller change?"

Mr Thickens bowed, and, taking back the half-crown, changed it for two shillings and sixpence, all bearing the round, bucolic countenance of King George the Third, upon which Miss Heathery beamed as she slipped the coins in the blue and orange purse.

"I hope Mr Hallam is quite well, Mr Thickens."

"Quite well, ma'am."

"And the gold and silver fish?"

"Quite well, ma'am," said Mr Thickens, a little more austerely.

"I always think it so curiously droll, Mr Thickens, your keeping gold and silver fish," simpered Miss Heathery. "It always seems as if the pretty things had something to do with the bank, and that their scales—"

"Would some day turn into sixpences and half-sovereigns, eh, ma'am?" said the bank clerk sharply. "Yes—exactly, Mr Thickens."

"Ah, well, ma'am, it's a very pretty idea, but that's all. It isn't solid."

"Exactly, Mr Thickens. My compliments to Mr Hallam. Good-day."

"If that woman goes on making that joke about my fish many more times, I shall kill her!" said James Thickens, giving his head a vicious rub. "An old idiot! I wish she'd keep her money at home. I believe she passes her time in writing cheques, getting 'em changed, and paying the money in again, as an excuse for something to do, and for the sake of calling here. *I'm* not such an ass as to think it's to see me; and as to Hallam—well, who knows? Perhaps she means Sir Gordon. There's no telling where a woman may hang up her heart."

James Thickens returned to his desk after a glance down the main street, which looked as solemn and quiet as if there were no inhabitants in the place; so still was it, that no explanation was needed for the presence of a good deal of fine grass cropping up between the paving-stones. The houses looked clean and bright in the clear sunshine, which made the wonderfully twisted and floral-looking iron support of the "George" sign sparkle where the green paint was touched up with gold. The shadows were clearly cut and dark, and the flowers in the "George" window almost glittered, so bright were their colours. An elderly lady came across the market place, in a red shawl and carrying a pair of pattens in one hand, a dead-leaf tinted gingham umbrella in the other, though it had not rained for a month and the sky was without a cloud.

That red shawl seemed, as it moved, to give light and animation for a few minutes to the place; but as it disappeared round the corner by the "George," the place was all sunshine and shadow once more. The uninhabited look came back, and James Thickens pushed up his spectacles and began to write, his pen scratching and wheezing over the thick hand-made paper till a tremendous nose-blowing and a quick step were heard, and the clerk said "Gemp."

The next minute there was, the sharp tap of a stick on the step, continued on the floor, and the owner of that name entered with his coat tightly buttoned across his chest.

He was a keen-looking man of sixty, with rather obstinate features, and above all, an obstinate beard, which seemed as if it refused to be shaved, remaining in stiff, grey, wiry patches in corners and on prominences, as well as down in little ravines cut deeply in his face. His eyes, which were dark and sharp, twinkled and looked inquisitive, while, in addition, there was a restless wandering irregularity in their movements as if in turn each was trying to make out what its fellow was doing on the other side of that big bony nose.

"Morning, Mr Thickens, sir, morning," in a coffee-grinding tone of voice; "I want to see the chief."

"Mr Hallam? Yes; I'll see if he's at liberty, Mr Gemp."

"Do, Mr Thickens, sir, do; but one moment," he continued, leaning over and taking the clerk by the coat. "Don't you think I slight you, Mr Thickens; not a bit, sir, not a bit. But when a man has a valuable deposit to make, eh?—you see?—it isn't a matter of trusting this man or that; he sees the chief."

Mr Gemp drew himself up, slapped the bulgy left breast of his buttoned-up coat, nodded sagely, and blew his nose with a snort like a blast on a cow-horn, using a great blue cotton handkerchief with white spots.

Mr James Thickens passed through a glass door, covered on the inner side with dark green muslin, and returned directly to usher the visitor into the presence of Robert Hallam, the business manager of Dixons' Bank.

The room was neatly furnished, half office half parlour, and, but for a pair of crossed cutlasses over the chimney-piece, a bell-mouthed brass blunderbuss, and a pair of rusty flint-lock pistols, the place might have been the ordinary sitting-room of a man of quiet habits. There was another object though in one corner, which took from the latter aspect, this being the door of the cupboard which, instead of being ordinary painted panel, was of strong iron, a couple of inches thick.

"Morning, Mr Hallam, sir."

"Good-morning, Mr Gemp."

The manager rose from his seat at the baize-covered table to shake hands and point to a chair, and then, resuming his own, he crossed his legs and smiled blandly as he waited to hear his visitor's business.

Mr Gemp's first act was to spread his blue handkerchief over his knees, and then begin to stare about the room, after carefully hooking himself with his thick oak stick which he passed over his neck and held with both hands as if he felt himself to be rather an errant kind of sheep who needed the restraint of the crook.

"Loaded?" he said suddenly, after letting his eyes rest upon the fire-arms.

"Oh, yes, Mr Gemp, they are all loaded," replied the manager smiling. "But I suppose I need not get them down; you are not going to make an attack?"

"Me? attack? eh? Oh, you're joking. That's a good one. Ha! ha! ha!"

Mr Gemp's laugh was not pleasant on account of dental defects. It was rather boisterous too, and his neck shook itself free of the crook; but he hooked himself again, grew composed, and nodded once more in the direction of the chimney.

"Them swords sharp?"

"As razors, Mr Gemp."

"Are they now? Well, that's a blessing. Fire-proof, I suppose?" he added, nodding towards the safe.

"Fire-proof, burglar-proof, bank-proof, Mr Gemp," said the manager smiling. "Dixons' neglect nothing for the safety of their customers."

"No, they don't, do they?" said Mr Gemp, holding on very tightly to the stick, keeping himself down as it were and safe as well.

"No, sir, they neglect nothing."

"I say," said Mr Gemp, leaning forward, after a glance over his shoulder towards the bank counter, and Mr Thickens's back, dimly seen through the muslin, "does the new parson bank here?"

The manager smiled, and looked very hard at the bulge in his visitor's breast pocket, a look which involuntarily made the old man change the position of his hooked stick by bringing it down across his breast as if to protect the contents.

"Now, my dear Mr Gemp, you do not expect an answer to that question. Do you suppose I have ever told anybody that you have been here three times to ask me whether Dixons' would advance you a hundred pounds at five per cent?"

"On good security, eh?" interposed the old man sharply; "only on good security."

"Exactly, my dear sir. Why, you don't suppose we make advances without?"

"No, of course not, eh? Not to anybody, eh, Mr Hallam?" said the old man eagerly. "You could not oblige me now with a hundred, say at seven and a half? I'm a safe man, you know. Say at seven and a half per cent, on my note of hand. You wouldn't, would you?"

"No, Mr Gemp, nor yet at ten per cent. Dixons' are not usurers, sir. I can let you have a hundred, sir, any time you like, upon good security, deeds or the like, but not without."

"Ha! you are particular. Good way of doing business, sir. Hey, but I like you to be strict."

"It is the only safe way of conducting business, Mr Gemp."

"I say, though—oh, you are close!—close as a cash-box, Mr Hallam, sir; but what do you think of the new parson?"

"Quiet, pleasant, gentlemanly young man, Mr Gemp."

"Yes, yes," cried the visitor, hurting himself by using his crook quite violently, and getting it back round his neck; "but a mere boy, sir, a mere boy. He's driven me away. I'm not going to church to hear him while there's a chapel. I want to know what the bishop was a thinking about."

"Ah? but he's a scholar and a gentleman, Mr Gemp," said the manager, blandly.

"Tchuck! so was the young doctor who set up and only lasted a year. If you were ill, sir, you wouldn't have gone to he; you'd have gone to Dr Luttrell. If I've got vallerable deeds to deposit, I don't go to some young clever-shakes who sets up in business, and calls himself a banker: I come to Dixons'."

"And so you have some valuable deeds you want us to take care of for you, Mr Gemp," said the manager sharply.

"Eh! I didn't say so, did I?"

"Yes; and you want a hundred pounds. Shall I look at the deeds?"

Mr Gemp brought his oaken crook down over his breast, and his quick, shifty eyes turned from the manager to the lethal weapons over the chimney, then to the safe, then to the bank, and Mr Thickens's back.

"I say," he said at last, "arn't you scared about being robbed?"

"Robbed! oh, dear no. Come, Mr Gemp. I must bring you to the point. Let me look at the deeds you have in your pocket; perhaps there will be no need to send them to our solicitor. A hundred pounds, didn't you say?"

The old man hesitated, and looked about suspiciously for a few moments before meeting the manager's eyes. Then he succumbed before the firm, keen, searching look.

"Yes," he said slowly, "I said a hundred pounds, but I don't want no hundred pounds. I want you—"

He paused for a few moments with his hands at his breast, as if to take a long breath, and then, as if by a tremendous wrench, he mastered his fear and suspicion.

"I want you to take care of these for me."

He tore open his breast and brought out quickly a couple of dirty yellow parchments and some slips of paper, roughly bound in a little leather folio.

The manager stretched his hand across the table and took hold of the parchments; but the old man held on by one corner for a few moments till Hallam raised his eyebrows and smiled, when the visitor uttered a deep sigh, and thrust parchments and little folio hastily from him.

"Lock 'em up in yonder iron safe," he said hoarsely, taking up his blue handkerchief to wipe his brow. "It's open now, but you'll keep it locked, won't you?"

"The deeds will be safe, Mr Gemp," said the manager coolly throwing open the parchment. "Ah! I see, the conveyances to a row of certain messuages."

"Yes, sir; row of houses, Gemp's Terrace, all my own, sir; not a penny on 'em."

"And these? Ah, I see, bank-warrants. Quite right, my dear sir, they will be safe. And you do not need an advance?"

"Tchuck! what should I want with an advance? There's a good fifteen hundred pound there—all my own. Now you give me a writing, saying you've got 'em to hold for me, and that will do."

The manager smiled as he wrote out the document, while Mr Gemp, who seemed as much relieved as if he had been eased of an aching tooth, rose to make a closer inspection of the loaded pistols and the bell-mouthed brass blunderbuss, all of which he tapped gently in turn with the hook of his stick.

"There you are, Mr Gemp," said the manager smiling. "Now you can go home and feel at rest, for your deeds and warrants will be secure."

"Yes, sir, to be sure; that's the way," said the old man, hastily reading the memorandum, and then placing it in a very old leather pocket-book; "but if you wouldn't mind, sir, Mr Hallam, sir, I should like to see you lock them all in yonder."

"Well, then, you shall," said the manager good-humouredly and taking up the packets he tied them together with some green ferret, swung open the heavy door, which creaked upon its pivots, stepped inside, turned a key with a rattle, and opened a large iron chest, into which he threw the deeds, shut the lid with a clang, locked it ostentatiously, took out the key, backed out, and then closed and locked the great door of the safe.

"There, Mr Gemp; I think you'll find they are secure now."

"Safe! safe as the bank!" said the old man with an admiring smile as, with a sigh of relief, he picked up his old rough beaver hat from the floor, stuck it on rather sidewise, and with a short "good-morning," stamped out, tapping the floor as he went.

"Good-morning, Mr Thickens, sir," he said, pausing at the outer door to look back over his shoulder at the clerk. "I've done my bit o' business with the manager. It's all right."

"Good-morning, Mr Gemp," said Thickens quietly; and then to himself, as the tap of the stick was heard going down the street, "An important old idiot!"

Several little pieces of business were transacted, and then, according to routine, the manager came behind the counter to relieve his lieutenant, who put on his hat and went to his dinner.

During his absence the manager took his place at his subordinate's desk, and was very busy making a few calculations, after divers references to a copy of yesterday's *Times*, which came regularly by coach.

These calculations made him thoughtful, and he was in the middle of one when his face changed, and turned of a strange waxen hue, but he recovered himself directly.

"Might have expected it," he said softly; and he went on writing as some one entered the bank.

The visitor was a thin, dejected-looking youth of about two-and-twenty, shabbily dressed in clothes that did not fit him. His face was of a sickly pallor, as if he had just risen from an invalid couch, an idea strengthened by the extremely shortly-cut hair, whose deficiency was made the more manifest by his wearing a hat a full size too large. This was drawn down closely over his forehead, his pressed-out ears acting as brackets to keep it from going lower still.

He was a tamed-down, feeble-looking being, but the spirit was not all gone, for as he came down the street, with the genial friendliness of all dogs towards one who seems to be a stranger and down in the world, Miss Heathery's fat, ill-conditioned terrier, that she pampered under the belief that it was a dog of good breed, being in an evil temper consequent upon not having been taken for a walk by its mistress, rushed out baying, barking, and snapping at the stranger's heels.

"Get out, will you?" he shouted; but the dog barked the more, and the stranger looked as if about to run. In fact he did run a few yards, but, as the dog followed, he caught up a flower-pot from a handy window-sill—every one had flower-pots at King's Castor—and hurled it at the dog.

There was a yell, a crash, and explosion as if of a shell; Miss Heathery's dog fled, and, without waiting to encounter the owner of the flower-pot, the stranger hurried round the corner, and after an inquiry or two, made for the bank.

"Vicious little beast! Wish I'd killed it," he grumbled, giving the hat a hoist behind which necessitated another in front, and then the equilibrium adjusting at the sides. "Wonder people keep dogs," he continued. "A nuisance. Wish I was a dog—somebody's dog, and well fed. Lead a regular dog's life, and get none of the bones. Perhaps I shall, though, now."

The young man looked anything but a bank customer, but he did not hesitate. Merely stopping to give his coat a drag down, and then, tilting his hat slightly, he entered with a swagger, and walked up to the broad counter. Upon this he rested a gloveless hand, an act which seemed to give a little more steadiness to his weak frame.

"Rob," he said.

The manager raised his head with an affected start.

"Oh, you don't know me, eh?" said the visitor. "Well, I s'pose I am a bit changed."

"Know you? You wish to see me?" said Hallam coolly.

"Yes, Mr Robert Hallam; I've come down from London on purpose. I couldn't come before," he added meaningly, "but now I want to have a talk with you."

"Stephen Crellock! Why, you are changed."

"Yes, as aforesaid."

"Well, sir. What is it you want with me?" said the manager coldly.

"What do I want with you, eh? Oh, come, that's rich! You're a lucky one, you are. I go to prison, and you get made manager down here. Ah! you see I know all about it."

"I do not understand you, sir."

"Then I'll tell you, my fine fellow. Some men never get found out, some do; that's the difference between us two. I've gone to the wall—inside it," he added, with a sickly grin. "You've got to be quite the gentleman. But they'll find you out some day."

"Well, sir, what is this to lead up to?" said Hallam.

"Oh, I say though, Rob Hallam, this is too rich. Manager here, and going, they say, to marry the prettiest girl in the place." Hallam started in spite of his self-command. "And I suppose I shall be asked to the wedding, shan't I?"

"Will you be so good as to explain what is the object of this visit?" said Hallam coldly.

"Why, can't you see? I've come to the bank because I want some money. There, you need not look like that, my lad. It's my turn now, and you've got to put things a bit straight for me after what I suffered sooner than speak."

"Do you mean you have come here to insult me and make me send for a constable?" cried Hallam.

"Yes, if you like," said the young man, leaning forward, and gazing full in the manager's face; "send for one if you like. But you don't like, Robert Hallam. There, I'm a man of few words. I've suffered a deal just through being true to my mate, and now you've got to make it up to me."

"You scoun—"

"Sh! That'll do. Just please yourself, my fine fellow; only, if you don't play fair towards the man who let things go against him without a word, I shall just go round the town and say—"

"Silence, you scoundrel!" cried Hallam fiercely; and he caught his unpleasant visitor by the arm.

Just then James Thickens entered, as quietly as a shadow, taking everything in at a glance, but without evincing any surprise.

"Think yourself lucky, sir," continued Hallam aloud, "that I do not have you locked up. Mr Thickens, see this man off the premises."

Then, in a whisper that his visitor alone could hear, and with a meaning look:

"Be quiet and go. Come to my rooms to-night."

Volume One—Chapter Four.

Drawing a Dog's Teeth.

"I think that's all, Mr Hallam, sir," said Mrs Pinet, looking plump, smiling, and contented, as she ran her eyes over the tea-table in the bank manager's comfortably-furnished room—"tea-pot, cream, salt, pepper, butter, bread,"—she ran on below her breath in rapid enumeration, "why, bless my heart, I didn't bring the sauce!"

"Yes, that's all, Mrs Pinet," said the manager in his gravely-polite manner.

"But, begging your pardon, it is not, sir; I forgot the sauce."

"Oh! never mind that to-night."

"If you'll excuse me, sir, I would rather," said plump, pleasant-faced Mrs Pinet, who supplemented a small income by letting apartments; and before she could be checked she hurried out, to return at the end of a few minutes, bearing a small round bottle.

"And King of Oude," said the little woman. "Shall I take the cover, sir?"

"If you please, Mrs Pinet?"

"Which it's a pleasure to wait upon such a thorough gentleman," said Mrs Pinet to herself as she trotted back to her own region, leaving Hallam gazing down at the homely, pleasant meal.

He threw himself into a chair, poured out a cup of the tea, cooled it by the addition of some water from a bottle on a stand, and drank it hastily. Then, sitting back, he seemed to be thinking deeply, and finally drew up to the table, but turned from the food in disgust.

"Pah!" he ejaculated; but returned to his chair, pulled the loaf in half, and then cut off two thick slices, hacked the meat from the bones of two hot steaming chops and took a pat of the butter to lay upon one of the slices of bread. This done, his eye wandered round the room for a moment or two, and he rose and hastily caught up a newspaper, rolled the bread and meat therein, and placed the packet on a shelf before pouring out a portion of the tea through the window and then giving the slop-basin and cup the appearance of having been used. This done, he sat back in his chair to think, and remained so for quite half-an-hour, when Mrs Pinet came with an announcement for which he was quite prepared.

"A strange man, sir," said the landlady, looking troubled and smoothing down her apron, "a strange young man, sir. I'm afraid, sir—"

"Afraid, Mrs Pinet?"

"I mean, sir, I'm afraid he's a tramp, sir; but he said you told him to come."

"I'm afraid, too, that he is a tramp, Mrs Pinet, poor fellow! But it's quite right, I did tell him to come. You can show him in."

"In—in here, sir?"

"Yes, Mrs Pinet. He has been unfortunate, poor fellow! and has come to ask for help."

Mrs Pinet sighed, mentally declared that Mr Hallam was a true gentleman, and introduced shabby, broken-down and dejected Stephen Crellock.

Hallam did not move nor raise his eyes, while the visitor gave a quick, furtive look round at all in the room, and Mrs Pinet's departing footsteps sounded quite loud. Then a door was heard to close, and Hallam turned fiercely upon his visitor.

"Now, you scoundrel—you miserable gaol-bird, what do you mean by coming to me?"

"Mean by coming? I mean you to do things right. If you'd had your dues you'd have been where I was; only you played monkey and made me cat."

"What?"

"And I had my paws burned while you got the chestnuts."

"You scoundrel!" cried Hallam, rushing to the fireplace and ringing sharply, "I'll have the constable and put a stop to this."

"No, no, no, don't, don't, Rob. I'll do anything you like; I won't say anything," gasped the visitor piteously, "only: don't send for the constable."

"Indeed but I will," cried Hallam fiercely, as he walked to the door: but his visitor made quite a leap, fell at his feet, and clung to his legs.

"No, no, don't, don't," he cried hoarsely, and Hallam shook him off, opened the door, and called out:

"Never mind, now; I'll ring in a few minutes."

He closed the door and stood scowling at his visitor.

"I did not think you'd be so hard on a poor fellow when he was down, Hallam," he whimpered, "I didn't, 'pon my honour."

"Your honour, you dog, you gaol-bird," cried Hallam in a low, angry voice. "How dare you come down and insult me!"

"I—thought you'd help me, that you'd lend your old friend a hand now you're so well off, while I am in a state like this."

"And did you come in the right way, you dog, bullying and threatening me, thinking to frighten me, just as if you could find a soul to take any notice of a word such a blackguard as you would say? But there, I've no time to waste; I've done wrong in bringing you here. Go and tell everybody in the town what you please, how I was in the same bank with you in London and you were given into custody for embezzlement, and at your trial received for sentence two years' imprisonment."

"Yes, when if I had been a coward and spoken out—"

Hallam made a move towards him, when the poor, weak, broken-down wretch cowered lower.

"Don't, Rob; don't, old man," he cried piteously. "I'll never say a word. I'll never open my lips. You know I wouldn't be such a coward, bad as I am. But you will help a fellow, won't you?"

"Help you? What, have you come to me for blackmail? Why should I help you?"

"Because we were old friends, Hallam. Because I always looked up to you, and did what you told me; and you don't know what it has been, Rob, you don't indeed! I used to be a strong fellow, but this two years have brought me down till I'm as thin and weak as you see me. I'm like a great girl; least thing makes me cry and sob, so that I feel ashamed of myself!"

"Ashamed? You?" cried Hallam scornfully.

"Yes, I do, 'pon my word, Rob. But you will help me, won't you?"

"No. Go to the constable's place, and they'll give you an order for the workhouse. Be off, and if you ever dare to come asking for me again, I'll send for the officer at once."

"But—but you will give me a shilling or two, Hallam," said the miserable wretch. "I'm half-starved."

"You deserve to be quite starved! Now go."

"But, Hallam, won't you believe me, old fellow? I want to be honest now— to do the right thing."

"Go and do it, then," said Hallam contemptuously. "Be off."

"But give me a chance, old fellow; just one."

"I tell you I'll do nothing for you," cried Hallam fiercely. "On the strength of your having been once respectable, if you had come to me humbly I'd have helped you, but you came down here to try and frighten me with your noise and bullying. You thought that if you came to the bank you would be able to dictate all your own terms; but you have failed, Stephen Crellock: so now go."

"But, Rob, old fellow, I was so—so hard up. You don't know."

"Are you going before I send for the constable?"

"Yes, yes, I'm going," said the miserable wretch, gathering himself up. "I'm sorry I came to you, Hallam. I thought you would have helped a poor wretch, down as I am."

"And you found out your mistake. A man in my position does not know a gaol-bird."

There was a flash from the sunken eyes, and a quick gesture, but the flash died out, and the gesture seemed to be cut in half. Two years' hard labour in one of His Majesty's gaols had pretty well broken the weak fellow's spirit. He stepped to the door, glanced round the comfortable room, uttered a low moan, and was half out, when Hallam uttered sharply the one word "Stop!"

His visitor paused, and looked eagerly round upon him.

"Look here, Stephen Crellock," he said, "I don't like to see a man like you go to the dogs without giving him a chance. There, come back and close the door!"

The poor wretch came back hurriedly, and made a snatch at Hallam's hand, which was withdrawn.

"No, no, wait till you've proved yourself an honest man," he said.

Crellock's eyes flashed again, but, as before, the flash died out at once, and he stood humbly before his old fellow clerk.

Hallam remained silent for a few moments, and then as if he had made up his mind, he said: "I ought to hand you over to the constable, that is, if I did my duty as manager of Dixons' Bank, and a good member of society; but I can't forget that you were once a smart, gentlemanly-looking young fellow, who slipped and fell."

Crellock stood bent and humbled, staring at him in silence.

"I'm going to let heart get the better of discipline," continued Hallam, "and to-night I'm going to give you five guineas to get back to London and make a fresh start; and till that fresh start is made, and you can do without it, I'm going to give you a pound a week, if asked for by letter humbly, and in a proper spirit."

"Rob!"

"There, there; no words. I don't want thanks. I know I'm doing wrong, and I hope my weakness will not prove my punishment."

"It shan't, Rob; it shan't," faltered the poor shivering wretch, who had hard work to keep back his tears.

"There are four guineas, there's a half, and there are ten shillings in silver. Now go to some decent inn—here is some food for present use—get a bed, and to-morrow morning catch the coach, and get back to London to seek work."

Hallam handed him the parcel he had made.

"I will, Rob; I will, Mr Hallam, sir, and may—"

"There, that will do," said Hallam, interrupting him. "Prove all your gratitude by making yourself independent as soon as you can. There, you see you have not frightened me into bribing you to be silent."

"No, no, sir. Oh, no, I see that!" said the poor wretch dolefully. "I'm very grateful, I am, indeed, and I will try."

"Go, then, and try," said Hallam shortly. "Stop a moment."

He rang his bell, and Mrs Pinet entered promptly, glancing curiously at the visitor, and then back at her lodger, who paused to give her ample time to take in the scene.

"Mrs Pinet," he said at last, and in the coolest and most matter-of-fact way, "this poor fellow wants a lodging for the night at some respectable place, where they will not be hard upon his pocket."

"Well, sir, then he couldn't do better than go to Mrs Deene's, sir. A very respectable woman, whose husband—"

"Yes, to be sure, Mrs Pinet," said Hallam abruptly; "then you'll show him where it is. Good-night, Stephen; don't waste your money, and I hope you will succeed."

"Good-night, sir, good-night," and the dejected-looking object, thoroughly cowed by the treatment he had received, followed Hallam's landlady to the outer door, where a short colloquy could be heard, and then there was a shuffling step passing the window, and the door closed.

"I always expected it," said Hallam to himself, as he stood gazing straight before him; "but I've drawn his teeth; he won't bite—he dare not. I think I can manage Master Stephen—I always could." He stood thinking for a few minutes, and then said softly: "Well, what are ten or twenty pounds, or forty, if it comes to that! Yes," he added deliberately, "I have done quite rightly, I am sure."

Undoubtedly, as far as his worldly wisdom lay, for it did not take long for the news to run round the town that a very shabby-looking fellow had been to the bank, evidently with burglarious intentions, but that the new manager had seized and held him, while James Thickens placed the big brass blunderbuss to his head, and then turned it round and knocked him down. This was Mr Gemp's version; but it was rather spoiled by Mrs Pinet when she was questioned, and told her story of Mr Hallam's generous behaviour to this poor young man:

"One whom he had known in better days, my dear; and now he has quite set him up."

Volume One—Chapter Five.

A Little Bit of News.

Time glided very rapidly by at King's Castor, for there were few things to check his progress. People came to the market and did their business, and went away. Most of them had something to do at Dixons' Bank, for it was the pivot upon which the affairs of King's Castor and the neighbourhood turned. It was the centre from which radiated the commerce of the place. Pivot or axle, there it was, with a patent box full of the oil that makes matters run easily, and so trade and finance round King's Castor seemed like some large wheel, that turned gently and easily on.

Dixons' had a great deal to do with everybody, but Dixons' was safe, and Dixons' was sure. On every side you heard how that Dixons' had taken this or that man by the hand, with the best of results. Stammers borrowed money at five per cent, when he put out that new front. Morris bought his house with Dixons' money, and they held the deeds, so that Morris was a man of importance—one of the privileged who paid no rent. He paid interest on so many hundred pounds to Dixons' half-yearly, but that was interest, not rent.

Old Thomas Dixon seldom came to the bank now, though he was supposed to hold the reins of government, which he declined to hand over to his junior partners, Sir Gordon Bourne and Mr Andrew Trampleasure. It was his wish that a practised manager should be engaged from London, and hence the arrival of Mr Robert Hallam, who wore a much talked-of watch, that was by accident shown to Gemp, who learned what a repeater was, and read on the inside how that it was a testimonial from Barrow, Fladgate, and Range for faithful services performed.

Barrow, Fladgate, and Range were the Lombard Street bankers, who acted as Dixons' agents; and the news of that watch spread, and its possession was as a talisman to Robert Hallam.

Sir Gordon did not exactly take offence, for he rarely took offence at anything; but he felt slighted about the engagement of Hallam, and visited the place very little, handing over his duties to Trampleasure, who dwelt at the bank, had his private room, did all the talking to the farmers who came in, and did nothing more; but everything went smoothly and well. The new manager was the pattern of gentlemanly consideration—even to defaulters; and the main thing discussed after two years' residence in King's Castor was, whom would he marry?

There were plenty of wealthy farmers' daughters in the neighbourhood; several of the tradespeople were rich in money and had marriageable girls; but to all and several Mr Hallam of the bank displayed the same politeness, and at the end of two years there was quite a feeling of satisfaction among the younger ladies of King's Castor at the general impression, and that was, that the much-talked-of settler in their midst was not a marrying man.

The reason is simple—he could only have married one, and not all. Many were vain enough to think that the good fortune would have come to them. But now, so to speak, Mr Hallam of the bank had grown rather stale, and the interest was centred upon the new curate.

The gossips were not long in settling his fate.

"I know," said Gemp to a great many people; "gardening, eh? He! he! he! hi! hi! hi! You wouldn't have thought it in a parson? But, there, he's very young!"

"Yes, he is very young, Mr Gemp," said Mrs Pinet one morning to that worthy, who quite occupied the ground that would have been covered by a local journal. For, having retired years back from business, he had—not being a reading man—nothing whatever to do but stand at his door and see what went on. "Yes, he is very young, Mr Gemp," said Mrs Pinet. "But poor young man, I suppose he can't help it."

"Help it, no! Just the age, too, when a fellow's always thinking about love. We know better at our time of life, eh?"

Mrs Pinet, who was one of those plump and rosy ladies with nice elastic flesh, which springs up again wherever time has made a crease, so that it does not show, bridled a little, and became very much interested in her row of geraniums in the parlour window, every one of which had lately been made more ornamental by a coat of red lead over its pot. For Mrs Pinet did not yet know better. She had known better five years before, when Gemp had asked her to wed; but at the time present she was wondering whether, if Mr Thickens at the bank, where her little store of money lay, should fail, after all, to make her an offer, it was possible that Mr Robert Hallam might think it very nice to have some one to go on always taking so much care of his linen as she did, and seeing that his breakfast bacon was always nicely broiled, his coffee clear, and his dinners exactly as he liked to have them. Certainly he was a good deal younger than she was; but she did not see why the wife should not be the elder sometimes, as well as the husband.

Hence it was that Gemp's words jarred.

"Seems rum, don't it?" continued Gemp. "I went by the other day, and there he was with his coat off, helping Luttrell, wheeling barrows, and I've seen him weeding before now."

"Well, I'm sure it's very kind of him," said Mrs Pinet quickly. She could not speak tartly; her physique and constitution forbade.

"Oh, yes, it's very kind of him indeed; but he'd better be attending to his work."

"I'm sure he works very hard in the place."

"Oh, yes. Of course he does; but, don't you see?"

"See? No! See what?"

"He—he—he! And you women pretend to be so sharp about these things. What does he go there gardening for?"

"Why, goodness gracious me, Mr Gemp, you don't think—"

"Think? Why, I'm sure of it. I see a deal of what's going on, Mrs Pinet. I never look for it, but it comes. Why, he's always there. He helps Luttrell when he's at home; and old mother Luttrell talks to him about her jam. That's his artfulness; he isn't too young for that. Gets the old girl on his side."

"But do you really think—Why, she's never had a sweetheart yet."

"That we know of, Mrs P.," said Gemp, with a meaning look.

"She never has had," said Mrs Pinet emphatically, "or we should have known. Well, she's very handsome, and very nice, and I hope they'll be very happy. But do you really think it's true?"

"True? Why, he's always there of an evening, tootling on the flute and singing."

"Oh, but that's nothing; Mr Hallam goes there too, and has some music."

"Ay, but Hallam don't go out with her picking flowers, and botalising. I've often seen 'em come home together with arms full o' rubbish; and one day, what do you think?"

"Really, Mr Gemp!"

"I dropped upon 'em down in a ditch, and when they saw me coming, they pretended that they were finding little snail-shells."

"Snail-shells?"

"Yes, ma'am, and he pulls out a little magnifying-glass for her to look through. It may be a religious way of courting, but I say it's disgusting."

"Really, Mr Gemp!" said Mrs Pinet, bridling.

"Ay, it is, ma'am. I like things open and above board—a young man giving a young woman his arm, and taking her out for a walk reg'lar, and not going out in the lanes, and keeping about a yard apart."

"But do they, Mr Gemp?"

"Yes, just to make people think there's nothing going on. But there, ma'am, I must be off. You mustn't keep me. I can't stop talking here."

"Well, really, Mr Gemp!" said his hearer, bridling again, and resenting the idea that she had detained him.

"Yes, I must go indeed. I say, though, seen any more of that chap?"

"Chap?—what chap, Mr Gemp?"

"Come now, you know what I mean. That shack: that ragged, shabby fellow—him as come to see Mr Hallam the other day?"

"Oh, the poor fellow that Mr Hallam helped?"

"To be sure—him. Been here again?" said Gemp, making a rasping noise with a rough finger on his beard.

"No, Mr Gemp."

"No! Well, I suppose not. I haven't seen him myself. Mornin'; can't stop talking here."

Mr Gemp concluded his gossips invariably in this mode, as if he resented being kept from business, which consisted in going to tell his tale again.

Mrs Pinet was left to pick a few withering leaves from her geraniums, a floricultural act which she performed rather mechanically, for her mind was a good deal occupied by Gemp's disclosure.

"They'd make a very nice pair, that they would," she said thoughtfully; "and how would it be managed, I wonder? He couldn't marry himself, of course, and—oh, Mr Thickens, how you did make me jump!"

"Jump! Didn't see you jump, Mrs Pinet," said the clerk, smiling sadly, as if he thought Mrs Pinet's banking account was lower than it should be.

"Well, bless the man, you know what I mean. Stealing up so quietly, like a robber or thief in the night."

"Oh! Not come to steal, but to beg."

"Beg, Mr Thickens? What, a subscription for something?"

"No. I was coming by. Mr Hallam wants the book on his shelf, 'Brown's Investor.'"

"Oh, I see. Come in, Mr Thickens!" she exclaimed warmly. "I'll get the book."

"Won't come in, thank you."

"Now do, Mr Thickens, and have a glass of wine and a bit of cake."

The quiet, dry-looking clerk shook his head and smiled.

"Plenty of gossips in the town, Mrs Pinet, without my joining the ranks."

"Now that's unkind, Mr Thickens. I only wanted to ask you if you thought it true that Mr Bayle is going to marry Miss Millicent Luttrell; Mr Gemp says he is."

"Divide what Gemp says by five, subtract half, and the remainder may be correct, ma'am."

"Then it isn't true?"

"I don't know, ma'am."

"Oh, what a tiresome, close old bank-safe of a man you are, Mr Thickens! Just like your cupboard in the bank."

"Where I want to be, Mrs Pinet, if you will get me the book."

"Oh, well, come inside, and I'll get it for you directly. But it isn't neighbourly when I wanted to ask you about fifty pounds I wish to put away."

He followed her quickly into the parlour occupied by the manager, and then glanced sharply round.

"Have you consulted him—Mr Hallam?" he said sharply.

"No, of course not. I have always taken your advice so far, Mr Thickens. I don't talk about my bit of money to all my friends."

"Quite right," he said—"quite right. Fifty pounds, did you say?"

"Yes; and I'd better bring it to Dixons', hadn't I?" James Thickens began to work at his smoothly-shaven face, pinching his cheeks with his long white fingers and thumb, and drawing them down to his chin, as if he wished to pare that off to a point—an unnecessary procedure, as it was already very sharp.

"I can't do better, can I?"

The bank clerk looked sharply round the room again, his eyes lighting on the desk, books, and various ornaments, with which the manager had surrounded himself.

"I don't know," he said at last.

"But I don't like keeping the money in the house, Mr Thickens. I always wake up about three, and fancy that thieves are breaking in."

"Give it to me, then, and I'll put it safely for you somewhere."

"In the bank, Mr Thickens?"

"I don't know yet," he said. "Give me the book. Thank you. I'll talk to you about the money another time;" and, placing the volume under his arm, he glanced once more sharply round the room, and then went off very thoughtful and strange of aspect—veritably looking, as Mrs Pinet said, as close as the safe up at Dixons' Bank.

Volume One—Chapter Six.

Sir Gordon is Troubled with Doubts.

First love is like furze; it is very beautiful and golden, but about and under that rich yellow there are thorns many and sharp. It catches fire, too, quickly, and burns up with a tremendous deal of crackling, and the heat is great but not always lasting.

Christie Bayle did not take this simile to heart, but a looker-on might have done so, especially such a looker-on as Robert Hallam, who visited at the doctor's just as of old—before the arrival of the new curate, whose many calls did not seem to trouble him in the least.

All the same, though, he was man of the world enough to see the bent of Christie Bayle's thoughts, and how quickly and strongly his love had caught and burned. For treating Gemp's statements as James Thickens suggested, and dividing them by five, the half-quotient was quite sufficiently heavy to show that if the curate did not marry Millicent Luttrell, it would be no fault of his.

He was, as his critics said, very young. Twenty-four numbered his years, and his educational capabilities were on a par therewith; but in matters worldly and of the heart twenty would better have represented his age.

He had come down here fresh from his studious life, to find the place full of difficulties, till that evening when he found in Millicent a coadjutor, and one who seemed to take delight in helping and advising him. Then the old Midland town had suddenly become to him a paradise, and a strange eagerness seemed to pervade him.

How was he to attack such and such an evil in one of the low quarters?

He would call in at the doctor's, and mention the matter to Miss Luttrell.

It was to find her enthusiastic, but at the same time full of shrewd common-sense, and clever suggestions which he followed out, and the way became smooth.

His means were good, for just before leaving college the death of an aunt had placed him in possession of a competency; hence he wished to be charitable, and Millicent advised him as to the best channels into which he could direct his molten gold.

Then there were the Sundays when, after getting easily and well through the service, he ascended the pulpit to commence his carefully elaborated sermon, the first sentences of which were hard, faltering, and dry, till his eyes fell upon one sweet, grave face in the middle of the aisle, watching him intently, and its effect was strange. For as their eyes met, Christie Bayle's spirit seemed to awaken: he ceased to read the sermon. Words, sentences, and whole paragraphs were crowding in his brain eager to be spoken, and as they were spoken it was with a fire and eloquence that deeply stirred his hearers; while when, perhaps, at the very last, his eyes fell once more upon Millicent's calm, sweet face, he would see that it was slightly flushed and her eyes were suffused.

He did not know it; but her influence stirred him in everything he did, and when he called, there was no mistaking the bright, eager look of pleasure, the friendly warmth, and the words that were almost reproachful if he had allowed three or four days to pass.

Work? No man could have worked harder or with a greater display of zeal. She would be pleased, he felt, to see how he had made changes in several matters that were foul with neglect. And it was no outer whitewashing of that which was unclean within. Christie Bayle was very young, and he had suddenly grown enthusiastic; so that when he commenced some work he never paused until it was either well in train or was done.

"You're just the man we wanted here," said Doctor Luttrell. "Why, Bayle, you have wakened me up. I tried all sorts of reformations years ago, but I had not your enthusiasm, and I soon wearied and jogged on in the old way. I shall have to begin now, old as I am, and see what I can do."

"But it is shameful, papa, what opposition Mr Bayle meets with in the town," cried Millicent warmly.

"Yes, my dear, it is. There's a great deal of opposition to everything that is for people's good."

Millicent was willing enough to help, for there was something delightfully fresh and pleasant in her association with Christie Bayle.

"He's working too hard, my dear," the doctor said. "He wants change. He's a good fellow. You and your mother must coax him here more, and get him out." Bayle wanted no coaxing, for he came willingly enough to work hard with the doctor in the garden; to inspect Mrs Luttrell's jams, and see how she soaked the paper in brandy before she tied them down; to go for walks with Millicent, or, on wet days, read German with her, or practise some instrumental or vocal duet.

How pleasantly, how happily those days glided by! Mr Hallam from the bank came just as often as of old, and once or twice seemed disposed to speak slightingly of the curate, but he saw so grave and appealing a look in

Millicent's eyes that he hastened, in his quiet, gentlemanly way, to efface the slight.

Sir Gordon Bourne, as was his custom, when not at the Hall or away with his yacht, came frequently to the doctor's evenings, heavy with the smartest of sayings and the newest of stories from town. Gravely civil to the bank manager, a little distant to the new curate, and then, by degrees, as the months rolled by, talking to him, inviting him to dinner, placing his purse at his disposal for deserving cases of poverty, and at last becoming his fast friend.

"An uncommonly good fellow, doctor, uncommonly. Very young—yes, very young. Egad, Sir, I envy him sometimes, that I do."

"I'm glad you like him, Sir Gordon," cried Millicent, one day.

"Are you, my dear, are you?" he said, half sadly. "Well, why shouldn't I? The man's sincere. He goes about his work without fuss or pretence. He does not consider it his duty to be always preaching at you and pulling a long face; but seems to me to be doing a wonderful deal of good in a quiet way. Do you know—"

He paused, and looked from the doctor to Mrs Luttrell, and then at Millicent, half laughingly.

"Do we know what?"

"Well, I'll confess. I've played chess with him, and we've had a rubber at whist here, and he never touched upon sacred subjects since I've known him, and it has had a curious effect upon me."

"A curious effect?" said Millicent wonderingly.

"Yes, egad, it's a fact; he makes me feel as if I ought to go and hear him preach, and if you'll take me next Sunday, Miss Millicent, I will."

Millicent laughingly agreed; and Sir Gordon kept his word, going to the doctor's on Sunday morning, and walking with the ladies to church.

It is worthy of remark though, that he talked a good deal to himself as he went home, weary and uncomfortable from wearing tight boots, and bracing up.

"It won't do," he said. "I'm old enough to know better, and if I can see into such matters more clearly than I could twenty years ago, Bayle's in love with her. Well, a good thing too, for I'm afraid Hallam is taken too, and—no, that would not do. I've nothing whatever against the fellow; a gentleman in his manners, the very perfection of a manager, but somehow I should not like to see her his wife."

"Why?" he said after a pause.

He shook his head.

"I can't answer that question," he muttered; and he was as far off from the answer when six months had passed.

Volume One—Chapter Seven.

A Terrible Mistake.

"Going out for a drive?"

"Yes, Mr Bayle; and it was of no use my speaking. No end of things to see to; but the doctor would have me come with him."

"I think the doctor was quite right, Mrs Luttrell."

"There you are. You see, my dear? What did I tell you? Plants must have air, mustn't they, Bayle?"

"Certainly."

"I wish you would not talk like that, my dear. I am not a plant."

"But you want air," cried the doctor, giving his whip a flick, and making his sturdy cob jump.

"Oh! do be careful, my dear," cried Mrs Luttrell nervously as she snatched at the whip.

"Oh, yes, I'll be careful. I say, Bayle, I wish you would look in as you go by; I forgot to open the cucumber-frame, and the sun's coming out strong. Just lift it about three inches."

"I will," said the curate; and the doctor drove on to see a patient half-a-dozen miles away.

"Well, you often tell me I'm a very foolish woman, my dear," said Mrs Luttrell, buttoning and unbuttoning the chaise-apron with uneasy fingers, "but I should not have done such a thing as that."

"Thing as what?" cried the doctor.

"As to send a gentleman on to our house where Milly's all alone. It doesn't seem prudent."

"What, not to ask a friend to look in and lift the cucumber-light?"

"But, with Milly all alone; and I never leave her without feeling that something is going to happen."

"Pish! fudge! stuff!" cried the doctor. "I never did see such a woman as you are. I declare you think of nothing but courting. You ought to be ashamed of yourself at your time of life."

"Now, you ought not to speak like that, my dear. It's very wrong of you, for it's not true. Of course I feel anxious about Millicent, as every prudent woman should."

"Anxious! What is there to be anxious about? Such nonsense! Do you think Bayle is a wolf in sheep's clothing?"

"No, of course I don't. Mr Bayle is a most amiable, likeable young man, and I feel quite surprised how I've taken to him. I thought it quite shocking at first when he came, he seemed so young; but I like him now very much indeed."

"And yet you would not trust him to go to the house when we were away. For shame, old lady! for shame!"

"I do wish you would not talk to me like that, my dear. I never know whether you are in earnest or joking."

"Now, if it had been Hallam, you might have spoken.—Ah! Betsy, what are you shying at?—Keep that apron fastened, will you? What are you going to do?"

"I was only unfastening it ready—in case I had to jump out," faltered Mrs Luttrell.

"Jump out! Why, mother! There, you are growing into quite a nervous old woman. You stop indoors too much."

"But is there any danger, my dear?"

"Danger! Why, look for yourself. The mare saw a wheelbarrow, and she was frightened. Don't be so silly."

"Well, I'll try not," said Mrs Luttrell, smoothing down the cloth fold over the leather apron, but looking rather flushed and excited as the cob trotted rapidly over the road. "You were saying, dear, something about Mr Hallam."

"Yes. What of him?"

"Of course we should not have sent him to the house when Milly was alone."

"Humph! I suppose not. I say, old lady, you're not planning match-making to hook that good-looking cash-box, are you?"

"What, Mr Hallam, dear? Oh, don't talk like that."

"Humph!" ejaculated the doctor, making the whiplash whistle about the cob's ears; "you are not very fond of him, then?"

"Well, no, dear, I can't say I am. He's very gentlemanly, and handsome, and particular, but somehow—"

"Ah!" said the doctor, with a dry chuckle, "that's it—'somehow.' That's the place where I stick. No, old lady, he won't do. I was a bit afraid at first; but he seems to keep just the same: makes no advances. He wouldn't do."

"Oh, dear me, no!" cried Mrs Luttrell, with quite a shudder.

"Why not?" said the doctor sharply; "don't you like him?"

"Perhaps it would not be just to say so," said Mrs Luttrell nervously, "but I'm glad Milly does not seem to take to him."

"So am I. Curate would be far better, eh?"

"And you charge me with match-making, my dear! It is too bad."

"Ah! well, perhaps it is; but don't you think—eh?"

"No," said Mrs Luttrell, "I do not. Millicent is very friendly to Mr Bayle, and looks upon him as a pleasant youth who has similar tastes to her own. And certainly he is very nice and natural."

"And yet you object to his going to see the girl when we are out! There, get along, Betsy; we shall never be there."

The whip whistled round the cob's head and the chaise turned down a pleasant woody lane, just as Christie Bayle lifted the latch and entered the doctor's garden.

It was very beautiful there in the bright morning sunshine; the velvet turf so green and smooth, and the beds vying one with the other in brightness. There was no one in the garden, and all seemed strangely still at the house, with its open windows and flower-decked porch.

Bayle had been requested to look in and execute a commission for the doctor, but all the same he felt guilty: and though he directed an eager glance or two at the open windows, he turned, with his heart throbbing heavily, to the end of the closely-clipped yew hedge, and passed round into the kitchen-garden, and then up one walk and down another, to the sunny-sheltered top, where the doctor grew his cucumbers, and broke down with his melons every year.

There was a delicious scent from the cuttings of the lawn, which were piled round the frame, fermenting and giving out heat: and as the curate reached the glass lights, there was the interior hung with great dewdrops, which began to coalesce and run off as he raised the ends of the lights and looked in.

Puff! quite a wave of heated air, fragrant with the young growth of the plants, all looking richly green and healthy, and with the golden, starry blossoms peeping here and there.

Quite at home, Christie Bayle thrust in his arm and took out a little block of wood cut like an old-fashioned gun-carriage or a set of steps, and with this he propped up one light, so that the heat might escape and the temperature fall.

This done he moved to the next, and thrust down the light, for he had seen from the other side a glistening, irregular, iridescent streak, which told of the track of an enemy, and this enemy had to be found.

That light uttered a loud plaintive squeak as it was thrust down, a sound peculiar to the lights of cucumber-frames; and, leaning over the edge, Bayle began to peer about among the broad prickly leaves.

Yes, there was the enemy's trail, and he must be found, for it would have been cruel to the doctor to have left such a devouring creature there.

In and out among the trailing stems, and over the soft black earth, through which the delicate roots were peeping, were the dry glistening marks, just as if someone had dipped a brush in a paint formed of pearl shells dissolved in oil, and tried to imitate the veins in a block of marble.

Yes; in and out—there it went, showing how busy the creature had been during the night, and the task was to find where it had gone to rest and sleep for the day, ready to come forth refreshed for another mischievous nocturnal prowl.

"Now where can that fellow have hidden himself?" said the follower of the trail, peering about and taking off his hat and standing it on the next light. "One of those great grey fellows, I'll be bound. Ah, to be sure! Come out, sir."

The tale-telling trail ended where a seed-pan stood containing some young Brussels sprouts which had attained a goodly size, and upon these the enemy had supped heartily, crawling down afterwards to sleep off the effects beneath the pan.

It was rather difficult to reach that pan, for the edge of the frame was waist-high; but it had to be done, and the slug raked out with a bit of stick.

That was it! No, it was not; the hunter could not quite reach, and had to wriggle himself a little more over and then try.

The search was earnest and successful, the depredator dying an ignominious death, crushed with a piece of potsherd against the seed-pan, and then being buried at once beneath the soil, but to a looker-on the effect was grotesque.

There was a looker-on here, advancing slowly along the path with a bunch of flowers in one hand, a pair of scissors in the other. In fact, that peculiar squeak given by the frame had attracted Millicent's attention, at a time when she believed every one to be away.

As she approached, she became conscious of the hind quarters of a man clothed in that dark mixture that used to be popularly known as "pepper-and-salt," standing up out of one of the cucumber-frames, and executing movements as if he were practising diving in a dry bath. Suddenly the legs subsided and sank down. Next they rose again, and kicked about, the rest of the man still remaining hidden in the frame, and then at last there was a rapid retrograde motion, and Christie Bayle emerged, hot, dishevelled, but triumphant for a moment, then scarlet with confusion and annoyance as he hastily caught up his hat, clapped it on, but hurriedly took it off and bowed.

"Miss Luttrell!" he exclaimed.

"Mr Bayle!" she cried, forbearing to smile as she saw his confusion. "I heard the noise and wondered what it could be."

"I—I met your father," he said, hastily adjusting the light; "he asked me to open the frames. A tiresome slug—"

"It was very kind of you," she said, holding out her hand and pressing his in her frank, warm grasp, and full of eagerness to set him at his ease. "Papa will be so pleased that you have caught one of his enemies."

"Thank you," he said uneasily; "it is very kind of you."—"I'm the most unlucky wretch under the sun, always making myself ridiculous before her," he added to himself.

"Kind of me? No, of you, to come and take all that trouble."—"Poor fellow!" she thought, "he fancies that I am going to laugh at him."—"I've been so busy, Mr Bayle: I've copied out the whole of that duet. When are you coming in to try it over?"

"Do you wish me to try it with you?" he said rather coldly.

"Why, of course. There are no end of pretty little passages solo for the flute. We must have a good long practice together before we play in public."

"You're very kind and patient with me," he said, as he gazed at the sweet calm face by his side.

"Nonsense," she cried. "I'm cutting a few flowers for Miss Heathery; she is the most grateful recipient of a present of this kind that I know."

They were walking back towards the house as she spoke, and from time to time Millicent stopped to snip off some flower, or to ask her companion to reach one that grew on high.

In a few minutes she had set him quite at his ease and they were talking quietly about their life, their neighbours, about his endeavours to improve the place; and yet all the time there seemed to him to be an undercurrent in his life, flowing beneath that surface talk. The garden was seen through a medium that tinted everything with joy; the air he breathed was perfumed and intoxicating; the few bird-notes that came from time to time sounded more sweetly than he had ever heard them before; and, hardly able to realise it himself, life—existence, seemed one sweetly calm, and yet paradoxically troubled delight.

His heart was beating fast, and there was a strange sense of oppression as he loosed the reins of his imagination for a moment; but the next, as he turned to gaze at the innocent, happy, unruffled face, so healthful and sweet, with the limpid grey eyes ready to meet his own so frankly, the calm came, and he felt that he could ask no greater joy than to live that peaceful life for ever at her side.

It would be hard to tell how it happened. They strolled about the garden till Millicent laughingly said that it would be like trespassing on her father's *carte blanche* to cut more flowers, and then they went through the open French window into the drawing-room, where he sat near her, as if intoxicated by the sweetness of her voice, while she talked to him in unrestrained freedom of her happy, contented life, and bade him not to think he need be ceremonious there.

Yes, it would be hard to tell how it happened. There was one grand stillness without, as if the ardent sunshine had drunk up all sound but the dull, heavy throb of his heart, and the music of that sweet voice which now lulled him to a sense of delicious repose, now made every nerve and vein tingle with a joy he had never before known.

It had been a mystery to him in his student life. Books had been his world, and ambition to win a scholarly fame his care. Now it had by degrees dawned upon him that there was another, a greater love than that, transcending it so that all that had gone before seemed pitiful and small. He had met her, her voice would be part of his life from henceforth, and at last—how it came about he could not have told—he was standing at her side, holding her hands firmly in his own, and saying in low and eager tones that trembled with emotion:

"Millicent, I love you—my love—my love!"

For a few moments Millicent Luttrell stood motionless, gazing wonderingly at her companion as he bent down over her hands and pressed his lips upon them.

Then, snatching them away, her soft creamy face turned to scarlet with indignation, but only for this to fade as she met his eyes, and read there the earnest look he gave her, and his act from that moment ceased to be the insult she thought at first.

"Miss Luttrell!" he said.

"Hush! don't speak to me," she cried.

He took a step forward, but she waved him back, and for a few moments sobbed passionately, struggling hard the while to master her emotion.

"Have I offended you?" he panted. "Dear Millicent, listen to me. What have I done?"

"Hush!" she cried. "It is all a terrible mistake. What have *I* done?"

There was a pause, and the deep silence seemed to be filled now with strange noises. There was a painful throbbing of the heart, a singing in the ears, and life was all changed as Millicent at last mastered her emotion, and her voice seemed to come to the listener softened and full of pity as if spoken by one upon some far-off shore, so calm, so grave and slow, so impassionately the words fell upon his ear.

Such simple words, and yet to him like the death-knell of all his hope in life.

Volume One—Chapter Eight.

Crossed in Love.

"Oh, Mr Bayle, I am so sorry!"

He looked piteously in the handsome pale young face before him, his heart sinking, and a feeling of misery, such as he had never before known, chilling him so that he strove in vain to speak.

The words were not cruel, they were not marked with scorn or contempt. There was no coquetry—no hope. They were spoken in a voice full of gentle sympathy, and there was tender pity in every tone, and yet they chilled him to the heart.

"Oh, Mr Bayle, I am so sorry!"

It needed no look to endorse those words, and yet it was there, beaming upon him from those sweet, frank eyes that had filled again with tears which she did not passionately dash aside, but which brimmed and softly dropped upon the hands she clasped across her breast.

He saw plainly enough that it had all been a dream, his dream of love and joy; that he had been too young to read a woman's heart aright, and that he had taken her little frank kindnesses as responses to his love; and he needed no explanations, for the tones in which she uttered those words crushed him, till as he stood before her in those painful moments, he realised that the deathblow to all his hopes had come.

He sank back in his chair as she stood before him, gazing up at her in so boyish and piteous a manner that she spoke again.

"Indeed, indeed, Mr Bayle, I thought our intimacy so pleasant, I was so happy with you."

"Then I may hope," he cried passionately. "Millicent, dear Millicent, all my life has been spent in study; I have read so little, I never thought of love till I saw you, but it has grown upon me till I can think only of you—your words, the tones of your voice, your face, all are with me always, with me now. Millicent, dear Millicent, it is a man's first true love, and you could give me hope."

"Oh, hush! hush!" she said gently, as she held out her hand to him, which he seized and covered with his kisses, till she withdrew it firmly, and shook her head. "I am more pained than I can say," she said softly. "I tell you I never thought of such a thing as this."

"But you will," he said, "Millicent, my love!"

"Mr Bayle," she said, with some attempt at firmness, "if I have ever by my thoughtlessness made you think I cared for you, otherwise than as a very great friend, forgive me."

"A friend!" he cried bitterly.

"Yes, as a friend. Is friendship so slight a thing that you speak of it like that?"

"Yes," he cried; "at a time like this, when I ask for bread and you give me a stone."

"Oh, hush!" she said again softly; and there was a sad smile through her tears. "I should be cruel if I did not speak to you plainly and firmly. Mr Bayle, what you ask is impossible."

"You despise me," he cried passionately, "because I am so boyish—so young."

"No," she said gently, as she laid her hand upon his shoulder. "Let me speak to you as an elder sister might."

"A sister!" he cried angrily.

"Yes, as a sister," replied Millicent gently. "Christie Bayle, it was those very things in you that attracted me first. I never had a brother; but you, with your frank and free-hearted youthfulness, your genuine freshness of nature, seemed so brotherly, that my life for the past few months has been brighter than ever. Our reading, our painting, our music—Oh, why did you dash all these happy times away?"

"Because I am not a boy," he cried angrily; "because I am a man—a man who loves you. Millicent, will you not give me hope?"

There was a pause, during which she stood gazing right over his head as he still sat there with outstretched hands, which he at last dropped with a gesture of despair.

"No," she said at last; "I cannot give you hope. It is impossible."

"Then you love some one else," he cried with boyish anger. "Oh, it is cruel. You led me on to love you, and now, in your coquettish triumph, you throw me aside for some other plaything of the hour."

Millicent's brow contracted, and a half-angry look came into her eyes.

"This talk to me of brotherly feeling and of being a sister, is it to mock me? It is as I thought," he cried passionately, "as I have heard, with you handsome women; you who delight in giving pain, in trifling with a weak, foolish fellow's heart, so that you may bring him to your feet."

"Christie—"

"No," he raged, as he started to his feet, "don't speak to me like that. I will not be led on again. Enjoy your triumph, but let it be made bitter by the knowledge that you have wrecked my life."

"Oh, hush! hush! hush!" she said softly. "You are not yourself, Christie Bayle, or you would not speak to me like this. You know that you are charging me with that which is not true. How can you be so cruel?"

"Cruel? It is you," he cried passionately. "But, there, it is all over. I shall leave here at once. I wish I had never seen the town."

"Christie," she said gently, "listen to me. Be yourself and go home, and think over all this. I cannot give you what you ask. Come, be wise and manly over this disappointment. Go away for a week, and then come back to me, and let our pleasant old friendship be resumed. You give me pain, indeed you do, by this outburst. It is so unlike you."

"Unlike me? Yes, you have nearly driven me mad."

"No, no. No, no," she said tenderly. "Be calm. Indeed and indeed, I have felt as warm and affectionate to you of late as a sister could feel for a brother. I have felt so pleased to see how you were winning your way here amongst the people; and when I have heard a light or contemptuous utterance about you, it has made me angry and ready to speak in your defence."

"Yes, I know," he cried; "and it is this that taught me that you must care for me—must love me."

"Cannot a woman esteem and be attached to a youth without loving him?"

"Youth! There! You treat me as if I were a boy," he cried angrily. "Can I help seeming so young?"

"No," she said, taking his hand, "But you are in heart and ways very, very young, Christie Bayle. Am I to tell you again that it was this brought about our intimacy, for I found you so fresh in your young manliness, so different to the gentlemen I have been accustomed to? Come: forget all this. Let us be friends."

"Friends? No, it is impossible," he cried bitterly. "I know I am boyish and weak, and that is why you hold me in such contempt."

"Contempt? Oh, no!"

"But, some day," he pleaded, "I'll wait—any time—"

"No, no, no," she said flushing, "it is impossible."

"Then," he raged as he started up, "I am right. You love some one else. Who is it? I will know."

"Mr Bayle!"

There was a calm queenly dignity in her look and words that checked his rage; and she saw it as he sank into the nearest chair, his face bent down upon his hands, and his shoulders heaving with the emotion that escaped now and then in a hoarse sob.

"Poor boy!" she said to herself as the indignation he had roused gave way to pity.

"Christie Bayle," she said aloud, as she approached him once more, and laid her hand upon his shoulder.

"Don't touch me," he cried hoarsely as he sprang up; and she started back, half frightened at his wild, haggard face. "I might have known," he panted. "Heaven forgive you! Good-bye—good-bye for ever!" Before Millicent could speak he had reached the door, and the next minute she heard his hurried steps as he went down the street.

Volume One—Chapter Nine.

The Scales Fall from Sir Gordon's Eyes.

Millicent stood listening till the steps had died away, and then sat down at the writing-table.

"Poor boy!" she said softly, as she passed her hand over her eyes, "I am so sorry."

She laid down the pen, and ran over her conduct—all that she had said and done since her first meeting with the curate; but ended by shaking her head, and declaring to herself that she could find nothing in her behaviour to call for blame.

"No," she said, rising from the table, after writing a few lines which she tore up, "I must not write to him; the wound must be left to time."

A double knock announced a visitor, and directly after Thisbe King, the maid, ushered in Sir Gordon, who, in addition to his customary dress, wore—what was very unusual for him—a flower in his button-hole, which, with a great show of ceremony, he detached, and presented to Millicent before taking his seat.

As a rule he was full of chatty conversation, but, to Millicent's surprise, he remained perfectly silent, gazing straight before him through the window.

"Is anything the matter, Sir Gordon?" said Millicent at last. "Papa is out, but he will not be long." These words roused him, and he smiled at her gravely.

"No, my dear Miss Luttrell," he said, "nothing is wrong; but at my time of life, when a man has anything particular to say, he weighs it well—he brings a good deal of thought to bear. I was trying to do this now."

"But mamma is out too," said Millicent.

"Yes, I know," he replied, "and therefore I came on to speak to you."

"Sir Gordon!"

"My dear Miss Luttrell—there, I have known you so long that I may call you my dear child—I think you believe in me?"

"Believe in you, Sir Gordon?"

"Yes, that I have the instincts, I hope, of a gentleman; that I am your father's very good friend; and that I reverence his child."

"Oh yes, Sir Gordon," said Millicent, placing her hand in his, as he extended it towards her.

"That is well, then," he said; and there was another pause, during which he gazed thoughtfully at the hand he held for a few moments, and then raised it to his lips and allowed it afterwards to glide away.

Millicent flushed slightly, for, in spite of herself, the thought of her visitor's object began to dawn upon her, though she refused to believe it at first.

"Let me see," he said at last, "time slides away so fast. You must be three-and-twenty now."

"I thought a lady's age was a secret, Sir Gordon," said Millicent smiling.

"To weak, vain women, yes, my child; but your mind is too clear and candid for such subterfuges as that. Twenty-three! Compared with that, I am quite an old man."

Millicent's colour began to deepen, but she made a brave effort to be calm, mastered her emotion, and sat listening to the strange wooing that had commenced.

"I am going to speak very plainly," her visitor said, gazing wistfully in her eyes, "and to tell you, Millicent, that for the past five years I have been your humble suitor."

"Sir Gordon!"

"Hush! hush! On the strength of our old friendship hear me out, my child. I will not say a word that shall wilfully give you pain; I only ask for a hearing."

Millicent sank back in her chair, clasped her hands, and let them rest in her lap, for she was too agitated to speak. The events of an hour or two before had unhinged her.

"For five years I have been nursing this idea in my breast," he continued, "one day determining to speak, and then telling myself that I was weak and foolish, that the thing was impossible; and then, as you know, I have gone away for months together in my yacht. I will tell you what I have said to myself: 'You are getting well on in life; she is young and beautiful. The match would not be right. Some day she will form an attachment for some man suited to her. Take your pleasure in seeing the woman you love happier than you could ever make her.'"

This was a revelation to Millicent, whose lips parted, and whose troubled eyes were fixed upon the speaker.

"The years went on, my child," continued Sir Gordon, "and I kept fancying that the man had come, and that the test of my love for you was to be tried. I was willing to suffer—for your sake—to see you happy; and though I was ready to offer you wealth, title, and the tender affection of an elderly man, I put it aside, striving to do my duty."

"Sir Gordon, I never knew of all this."

"Knew!" he said, with a smile, "no: I never let you know. Well, my child, not to distress you too much, I have waited; and, as you knew, I have seen your admirers flitting about you, one by one, all these years; and I confess it, with a sense of delight I dare not dwell upon, I have found that not one of these butterflies has succeeded in winning our little flower. She has always been heart-whole and—There, I dare not say all I would. At last, with a pang that I felt that I must suffer, I saw, as I believed, that the right man had come, in the person of our friend, Christie Bayle. It has been agony to me, though I have hidden it beneath a calm face, I hope, and I have fought on as I saw your intimacy increase. For, I said to myself, it is right. He is well-to-do; he is young and handsome; he is true and manly; he is all that her lover should be; and, with a sigh, I have sat down telling myself that I was content, and, to prove myself, I have made him my friend. Millicent Luttrell, he is a true-hearted, noble fellow, and he loves you."

Millicent half rose, but sank back in her chair, and her face grew calm once more.

"I am no spy upon your actions or upon those of Christie Bayle, my child; but I know that he has been to you this morning; that he has asked you to be his wife, and that you have refused him."

"Has Mr Bayle been so wanting in delicacy," said Millicent, with a flush of anger, "that he has told you this?"

"No, no. Pray do not think thus of him. He is too noble—too manly a fellow to be guilty of such a weakness. There are things, though, which a man cannot conceal from a jealous lover's eyes, and this was one."

"Jealous—lover!" faltered Millicent.

"Yes," he said; "old as I am, my child, I must declare myself as your lover. This last rejection has given me hopes that may be wild—hopes which prompted me to speak as I do now."

"Sir Gordon!" cried Millicent, rising from her seat; but he followed her example and took her hand.

"You will listen to me, my child, patiently," he said in low earnest tones; "I must speak now. I know the difference in our ages; no one better; but if the devotion of my life, the constant effort to make you happy can bring the reward I ask, you shall not repent it. I know that some women would be tempted by the title and by my wealth, but I will not even think it of you. I know, too, that some would, in their coquetry, rejoice in bringing such a one as I to their feet, and then laugh at him for his pains. I fear nothing of the kind from you, Millicent, for I know your sweet, candid nature. But tell me first, do you love Christie Bayle?"

"As a sister might love a younger brother, who seemed to need her guiding hand," said Millicent calmly. "Ah!"

It was a long sigh full of relief; and then taking her hand once more, Sir Gordon said softly:

"Millicent, my child, will you be my wife?"

The look of pain and sorrow in her eyes gave him his answer before her lips parted to speak, and he dropped the hand and stood there with the carefully-got-up look of youthfulness or early manhood seeming to fade from him. In a few minutes he appeared to have aged twenty years; his brow grew full of lines, his eyes seemed sunken, and there was a hollowness of cheek that had been absent before.

He stretched out his hand to the table, and slowly sat down, bending forward till his arms rested upon his knees and his hands hung down nerveless between.

"You need not speak, child," he said sadly. "It has all been one of my mistakes. I see! I see!"

"Sir Gordon, indeed, indeed I do feel honoured!"

"No, no! hush, hush!" he said gently. "It is only natural. It was very weak and foolish of me to ask you; but when this love blinds a man, he says and does foolish things that he repents when his eyes are open. Mine are open now— yes," he said, with a sad smile, "wide open; I can see it all. But," he added quickly as he rose, "you are not angry with me, my dear?"

"Angry? Sir Gordon!"

"No: you are not," he said, taking her hand and patting it softly. "Is it not strange that I could see you so clearly and well, and yet be so blind to myself? Ah, well, it is over now. I suppose no man is perfect, but in my conceit I did not think I could have been so weak. If I had not seen Bayle this morning and realised what had taken place, I should not have let my vanity get the better of me as I did."

"All this is very, very painful to me, Sir Gordon."

"Yes, yes, of course," he said quickly. "Come, then, this is our little secret, my child. You will keep it—the secret of my mistake? I do love you very much, but you have taught me what it is. I am getting old and not so keen of wits as I was once upon a time. I thought it was man's love for woman; but you are right, my dear, it is the love that a tender father might bear his child."

He took her unresistingly in his arms, and kissed her forehead reverently before turning away, to walk to the window and stand gazing out blindly, till a firm step with loudly creaking boots was heard approaching, when Sir Gordon slowly drew away back into the room.

Then the gate clanged, the bell rang, and a change came over Sir Gordon as Millicent ran to the drawing-room door.

"Not at home, Thisbe, to any one," she said hastily. "I am particularly engaged."

She closed the door quietly, and came back into the room to stand there, now flushed, now pale.

Sir Gordon took her hand softly, and raised it to his lips.

"Thank you, my child," he said tenderly. "It was very kind and thoughtful of you. I could not bear for any one else to see me in my weakness."

He was smiling sadly in her face, when he noticed her agitation, and at that moment the deep rich tones of Hallam's voice were heard speaking to Thisbe.

The words were inaudible, but there was no mistaking the tones, and at that moment it was as if the last scale of Sir Gordon's love blindness had fallen away, and he let fall Millicent's hand with a half-frightened look.

"Millicent, my child!" he cried in a sharp whisper. "No, no! Tell me it isn't that!"

She raised her eyes to his, looking pale, and shrinking from him as if guilty of some sin, and he flushed with anger as he caught her by the wrist.

"I give up—I have given up—every hope," he said, hoarsely, "but I cannot kill my love, even if it be an old man's, and your happiness would be mine. Tell me, then—I have a right to know—tell me, Millicent, my child, it is not that?"

Millicent's shrinking aspect passed away, and a warm flush flooded her cheeks as she drew herself up proudly and looked him bravely in the eyes.

"It is true, then?" he said huskily.

Millicent did not answer with her lips; but there was a proud assent in her clear eyes as she met her questioner's unflinchingly, while the deep-toned murmur ceased, the firm step was heard upon the gravel, and the door closed.

"Then it is so?" he said in a voice that was almost inaudible. "Hallam! Hallam! How true that they say love is blind! Oh, my child, my child!"

His last words were spoken beneath his breath, and he stood there, old and crushed by the fair woman in the full pride of her youth and beauty, both listening to the retiring step as Hallam went down the road.

No words could have told so plainly as her eyes the secret of Millicent Luttrell's heart.

Volume One—Chapter Ten.

Thisbe Gives Her Experience.

Thisbe King was huffy; and when Thisbe King was huffy, she was hard.

When Thisbe was huffy, and in consequence hard, it was because, as she expressed it, "Things is awkward;" and when things were like that, Thisbe went and made the beds.

Of course the beds did not always want making; but more than once after an encounter with Mrs Luttrell upon some domestic question, where it was all mild reproof on one side, acerbity on the other, Thisbe had been known to go up to the best bedroom, drag a couple of chairs forward, and relieve her mind by pulling the bed to pieces, snatching quilt and blankets and sheets off over the chairs, and engaging in a furious fight with pillows, bolster, and feather bed, hitting, punching, and turning, till she was hot; and then, having thoroughly conquered the soft, inanimate objects and her own temper at the same time, the bed was smoothly re-made, and Thisbe sighed.

"I shall have to part with Thisbe," Mrs Luttrell often used to say to husband and daughter; but matters went no farther: perhaps she knew in her heart that Thisbe would not go.

The beds had all been made, and there had been no encounter with Mrs Luttrell about any domestic matter relating to spreading a cloth in the drawing-room before the grate was blackleaded, or using up one loaf in the kitchen before a second was cut. In fact, Thisbe had been all smiles that morning, and had uttered a few croaks in the kitchen, which she did occasionally under the impression that she was singing; but all at once she had rushed upstairs like the wind in winter when the front door was opened, and to carry out the simile, she had dashed back a bedroom door, and closed it with a bang.

This done, she had made a bed furiously—so furiously that the feathers flew from a weak corner, and had to be picked up and tucked in again. After this, red-faced and somewhat refreshed, Thisbe pulled a housewife out of a tremendous pocket like a saddle-bag, threaded a needle, and sewed up the failing spot.

"It's dreadful, that's what it is!" she muttered at last, "and I'm going to speak my mind."

She did not speak her mind then, but went down to her work, and worked with her ears twitching like those of some animal on the *qui vive* for danger; and when Thisbe twitched her ears there was a corresponding action in the muscles about the corners of her mouth, which added to the animal look, for it suggested that she might be disposed to bite.

Some little time afterwards she walked into the drawing-room, looking at its occupant in a soured way.

"Letter for you, Miss Milly," she said.

"A note for me, Thisbe?" And Millicent took the missive which Thisbe held with her apron to keep it clean.

"Mr Bayle give it me hissen."

Millicent's face grew troubled, and Thisbe frowned, and left the room shaking her head.

The note was brief, and the tears stood in Millicent's eyes as she read it twice.

"Pity me. Forgive me. I was mad."

"Poor boy!" she said softly as she refolded it and placed it in her desk, to stand there, thoughtful and with her brow wrinkled.

She was in the bay-window, and after standing there a few minutes, her face changed; the troubled look passed away as a steady, regular step was heard on the gravel path beyond the hedge. There was the faint creaking noise, too, at every step of the hard tight boots, and as their wearer passed, Millicent looked up and returned the salute: for a glossy hat was raised, and he who bowed passed on, leaving her with her colour slightly heightened and an eager look in her eyes.

"Any answer, miss?"

Millicent turned quickly, to see that Thisbe had returned.

"Answer?"

"Yes, miss. The note."

"Is Mr Bayle waiting?"

"No, miss; but I thought you might want to send him one, and I'm going out and could leave it on the way."

"No, Thisbe, there is no answer."

"Are you sure, miss?"

"Sure, Thisbe? Of course."

Thisbe stood pulling the hem of her apron and making it snap.

"Oh! I would send him a line, miss. I like Mr Bayle. For such a young man, the way he can preach is wonderful. But, Miss Milly," she cried with a sudden, passionate outburst, "please, don't—don't do that!"

"What do you mean, Thisbe?"

"I can't abear it, miss. It frightens and worries me."

"Thisbe!"

"I can't help it, miss. I'm a woman too, and seven years older than you are. Don't, please don't, take any notice of me. There, don't look cross at me, miss. I must speak when I see things going wrong."

"What do you mean?" cried Millicent, crimsoning. "I mean I used to lead you about when you was a little thing and keep you out o' the puddles when the road was clatty, and though you never take hold o' my hand now, I must speak when you're going wrong."

"Thisbe, this is a liberty!"

"I can't help it, Miss Milly; I see him coming by in his creaking boots, and taking off his hat, and walking by here, when he has no business, and people talking about it all over the town."

"And in this house. Thisbe, you are forgetting your place."

"Oh, no, I'm not, miss. I'm thinking about you and Mr Hallam, miss. I know."

"Thisbe, mamma and I have treated you more as a friend than a servant; but—"

"That's it, miss; and I shouldn't be a friend if I was to stand by and see you walk raight into trouble without a word."

"Thisbe!"

"I don't care, Miss Milly, I will speak. Don't have nowt to do wi' him; he's too handsome; never you have nowt to do wi' a handsome man."

Millicent's ordinarily placid face assumed a look foreign to it—a look of anger and firmness combined; but she compressed her lips, as if to keep back words she would rather not utter, and then smiled once more.

"Ah, you may laugh, Miss Milly; but it's nothing to laugh at. And there's Mr Bayle, too. You're having letters from he."

Millicent's face changed again; but she mastered her annoyance, and, laying her hand upon Thisbe's shoulder, said with a smile:

"I don't want to be angry with you, Thisbe, but you have grown into a terribly prejudiced woman."

"Enough to make me, seeing what I do, Miss Milly."

"Come, come, you must not talk like this."

"Ah, now you're beginning to coax again, as you always did when you wanted your own way; but it's of no use, my dear, I don't like him, and I never shall. I'd rather you'd marry old Sir Gordon; he is nice, though he do dye his hair. I don't like him and there's an end of it."

"Nonsense, Thisbe!"

"No, it isn't nonsense. I don't like him, and I never shall."

"But why? Have you any good reason?"

"Yes," said Thisbe with a snort.

"What is it?"

"I told you before. He's so horrid handsome."

"Why, you dear, prejudiced, silly old thing!" cried Millicent, whose eyes were sparkling, and cheeks flushed.

"I don't care if I am. I don't like handsome men: they're good for nowt."

"Why, Thisbe!"

"I don't care, they arn't; my soldier fellow was that handsome it made you feel wicked, you were so puffed out with pride."

"And so you were in love once, Thisbe?"

"Why, of course I was. Think I'm made o' stone, miss? Enough to make any poor girl be in love when a handsome fellow like that, with moustache-i-ohs, and shiny eyes, and larnseer uniform making him look like a blue robin redbreast, came and talked as he did to a silly young goose such as I was then. I couldn't help it. Why, the way his clothes fitted him was enough to win any girl's heart—him with such a beautiful figure too! He looked as if he couldn't be got out of 'em wi'out unpicking."

"Think of our Thisbe falling in love with a soldier!" cried Millicent, laughing, for there was a wild feeling of joy in her heart that was intoxicating, and made her eyes flash with excitement.

"Ah, it's very funny, isn't it?" said Thisbe, with a vicious shake of her apron. "But it's true. Handsome as handsome he was, and talked so good that he set me thinking always about how nice I must be. Stuffed me out wi' pride, and what did he do then?"

"I'm sure I don't know, Thisbe."

"Borrered three pun seven and sixpence of my savings, and took my watch, as I bought at Horncastle fair, to be reggilated, and next time I see my gentleman he was walking out wi' Dixon's cook. Handsome is as handsome does, Miss Milly, so you take warning by me."

"There, I will not be cross with you, Thisbe," said Millicent, smiling. "I know you mean well."

"And you'll send an answer to Mr Bayle, miss?"

"There is no answer required, Thisbe," said Millicent gravely.

"And Mr Hallam, miss?"

"Thisbe," said Millicent gravely, "I want you always to be our old faithful friend as well as servant, but—"

She held up a warning finger, and was silent. Thisbe's lips parted to say a few angry words; but she flounced round, and made the door speak for her in a sharp bang, after which she rushed upstairs with the intent of having a furious encounter with a bed; but she changed her mind, and on reaching her own room, sat down, put her apron to her eyes, and had what she called "a good cry."

"Poor Miss Milly!" she sobbed at last; "she's just about as blind as I was, and she'll only find it out when it's too late."

Volume One—Chapter Eleven.

Another Evening at the Doctor's.

"But—but I don't like it, my dear," said Mrs Luttrell, wiping her eyes, and looking up at the doctor, as he stood rubbing his hands softly, to get rid of the harshness produced by freshly-dug earth used for potting.

"Neither do I," said the doctor calmly.

"But why should she choose him of all men?" sighed Mrs Luttrell. "I never thought Millicent the girl to be taken by a man only for his handsome face. I was not when I was young!"

"Which is saying that I was precious ugly, eh?"

"Indeed you were the handsomest man in Castor!" cried Mrs Luttrell proudly; "but you were the cleverest too, and—dear, dear!—what a little while ago it seems!"

"Gently, gently, old lady!" said the doctor, tenderly kissing the wrinkled forehead that was raised towards him. "Well, heaven's blessing be upon her, my dear, and may her love be as evergreen as ours."

Mrs Luttrell rose and laid her head upon his shoulder, and stood there, with a happy, peaceful look upon her pleasant face, although it was still wet with tears.

"That's what I'm afraid of," she sighed; "and it would be so sad."

"Ah, wife!" said the doctor, walking slowly up and down the room, with his arm about Mrs Luttrell's waist, "it's one of Nature's mysteries. We can't rule these things. Look at Milly. Some girls begin love-making at seventeen, ah, and before! and here she went calmly on to four-and-twenty untouched, and finding her pleasure in her books and music, and home-life."

"As good and affectionate a girl as ever breathed!" cried Mrs Luttrell.

"Yes, my dear; and then comes the man, and he has but to hold up his finger and say 'Come,' and it is done."

"But she might have had Sir Gordon, and he is rich, and then she would have been Lady Bourne!"

"He was too old, my dear, too old. She looked upon him like a child would look up to her father."

"Well, then, Mr Bayle, the best of men, I'm sure; and he is well off too."

"Too young, old lady, too young. I've watched them together hundreds of times. Milly always petted and patronised him, and treated him as if he were a younger brother, of whom she was very fond."

"Heigho! Oh dear me!" sighed Mrs Luttrell. "But I don't like him—this Mr Hallam. I never thought when Millicent was a baby that she would ever enter into an engagement like this. Can't we break it off?"

The doctor shook his head. "I don't like it, mother. Hallam is the last man I should have chosen for her; but we must make the best of it. He has won her; and she is not a child, but a calm, thoughtful woman."

"Yes, that's the worst of it," sighed Mrs Luttrell; "she is so thoughtful and calm and dignified, that I never can look upon her now as my little girl. I always seem to be talking to a superior woman, whose judgment I must respect. But this is very sad!"

"There, there! we must not treat it like that, old lady. Perhaps we have grown to be old and prejudiced. I own I have."

"Oh, no, no, my dear!"

"Yes, but I have. As soon as this seemed to be a certainty I began to try and find a hole in the fellow's coat."

"In Mr Hallam's coat, love? Oh, you wouldn't find that."

"No," said the doctor dryly, as he smiled down in the gentle old face, "not one. There, there! you must let it go! Now then, old lady, you must smile and look happy, here's Milly coming down."

Mrs Luttrell shook her head, and her wistful look seemed to say that she would never feel happy again; but as Millicent entered, in plain white satin, cut in the high-waisted, tight fashion of the period, and with a necklet of pearls for her only ornament, a look of pride and pleasure came into the mother's face, and she darted a glance at her husband, which he caught and interpreted, "I will think only of her."

"Oh, Milly!" she cried, "that necklace! what lovely pearls!"

"Robert's present, dear. I was to wear them to-night. Are they not lovely?"

"Almost as lovely as their setting," said the doctor to himself, as he kissed his child tenderly. "Why, Milly," he said aloud, "you look as happy as a bird!"

She laid her cheek upon his breast, and remained silent for a few moments, with half-closed eyes. Then, raising her head, she kissed him lovingly.

"I am, father dear," she said in a low voice, full of the calm and peaceful joy that filled her breast. "I am, father, I am, mother—so happy!" She paused, and then, laughing gently, added: "So happy I feel ready to cry."

It was to be a quiet evening, to which a few friends were invited; but it was understood as being an open acknowledgment of Millicent's engagement to Robert Hallam, and in this spirit the visitors came.

Miss Heathery generally arrived last at the social gatherings. It gave her entry more importance, and, at her time of life, she could not afford to dispense with adventitious aids. But there was the scent of matrimony in this little party, and she was dressed an hour too soon, and arrived first in the well-lit drawing-room.

"My darling!" she whispered, as she kissed Millicent.

That was all; but her voice and look were full of pity for the victim chosen for the next sacrifice, and she turned away towards the piano to get out her handkerchief, and drop a parting tear.

It was a big tear, one of so real and emotional a character that it brimmed over, fell on her cheekbone, and hopped into her reticule just as she was drawing open the top, and was lost in the depths within.

There was as much sorrow for herself as emotion on Millicent Luttrell's behalf. Had not Millicent robbed her of the chance of an offer? Mr Hallam might never have proposed: but still he might.

Suddenly her heart throbbed, for the next guest arrived also unusually early, and as Thisbe held open the door for him to pass, hope told again her flattering tale to the tune that Sir Gordon might have known that she, Miss Heathery, was coming early, and had followed.

The hopeful feeling did not die at once, but it received a shock as Sir Gordon entered, looking very bright and young, to shake hands warmly with the doctor and Mrs Luttrell, to bow to Miss Heathery, and then turn to Millicent, who, in spite of her natural firmness, was a good deal agitated. She had nerved herself for these meetings, and striven to keep down their importance; but now the night had arrived, she was fain to confess that hers was a difficult task, to meet two rejected lovers, and bear herself easily before them with the husband of her choice. First there was Sir Gordon, from whom she was prepared for reproachful looks, and perhaps others marked by disappointment; while from Christie Bayle—ah, how would he behave towards her? He was so young that she trembled lest he should make himself ridiculous in his loving despair.

And now here was the first shock to be sustained, so, forcing herself to be calm, she advanced with extended hand.

"Oh," whispered Sir Gordon, in tones that only reached Millicent's ear, "too bad—too bad. Supplanted twice. But there, I accept my fate." As he spoke he drew Millicent towards him, and kissed her forehead with tender reverence. "An old man's kiss, my dear, to the child of his very dear friends. God bless you! May you be very happy with the man of your choice. May I?" He dropped her hand to draw from his breast a string of large single pearls, so regular and perfect a match that they must have cost a goodly sum. For answer Millicent turned pale as she bent towards him and he clasped the string about her neck. "There," he said smiling, "I should have made a different choice if I had known."

Millicent would have spoken, but her voice failed, and to add to her agony at that moment, Bayle came in, looking, as she saw at a glance, pale and somehow changed.

"He will do or say something absurd," she said to herself as she bit her lip, and strove for composure. Then the blood seemed to rush to her heart and a pang shot through her as she realised more than if he had said a thousand things, how deeply her refusal had influenced his life.

Only four months since that day, when she had told him that they could be true friends, she speaking as an elder sister to one she looked upon as a boy. And now she felt ready to ask herself, who was this calm, grave man, who took her hand without hesitation, so perfectly at ease in his gentlemanly courtesy, and who had so thoroughly fallen into the place she had bidden him take?

"I see," he said with a smile, "I shall not be out of order, my dear Miss Luttrell. Will you accept this little offering too?"

He was holding a brilliant diamond ring in his hand.

For answer Millicent drew her long glove from her soft, white hand, and he took it gravely, and, in the presence of all, slipped on the ring, bending over it afterwards to kiss that hand, with the chivalrous delicacy of some courtier of a bygone school, then, raising his eyes to hers, he said softly, "Millicent Luttrell, our friendship must never fail."

Before she could say a word of thanks he had turned to speak to Mrs Luttrell, giving way to Sir Gordon Bourne, who began chatting to her pleasantly, while her eyes followed Christie Bayle's easy gestures, as she wondered the while at the change in his manner, unable to realise the agony of soul that he had suffered in this his first great battle with self before he had obtained the mastery, wounded and changed, stepping at once, as it were, from boyhood to the position of a thoughtful man.

Hallam soon arrived, smiling and agreeable, and it was piteous to see Mrs Luttrell's efforts to be very warm and friendly to him.

Millicent noticed it, and also that her father was quiet towards his son-in-law elect. She watched, too, the meeting between Hallam and Bayle, the former being as nearly offensive as his gentlemanly manner would allow; the latter warm, grave, and friendly.

"Has Bayle been unwell?" said Hallam the first time he was alone with Millicent.

"*I* have not heard," she replied, glancing at the curate, and wondering more and more, as the evening went on, at the change.

Among others, the Trampleasures arrived, and to Miss Heathery's grief, Mrs Trampleasure pretty well monopolised Bayle's remarks, or else made him listen to her own.

"And what do you think of this engagement, Mr Bayle?" she said, in so audible a voice that he was afraid it would be overheard.

"They make a very handsome couple," he replied.

"Ah, yes, handsome enough, I dare say; but good looks will not fill mouths. I wonder L. has allowed it. Mr Hallam is all very well, but he is, I may say, our servant, and if we, who are above him, find so much trouble to make both ends meet, I don't know what he'll do."

"But Mr Hallam has a very good salary, I presume?"

"I tell T. it is too much, and old Mr Dixon and Sir Gordon might have taken a hundred off, and let us draw it. I don't approve of the match at all."

"Indeed, Mrs Trampleasure," said Bayle, who felt hurt at hearing her speak like this.

"Yes; I'm Millicent's aunt, and I think I ought to have been consulted more— but there! it is of no use to speak to my brother; and as to Millicent—she always did just as she liked with her mother! Poor Kitty is very weak!"

"I always find Mrs Luttrell very sweet and motherly."

"Not so motherly as I am, Mr Bayle," said the lady bluntly. "Ah, it's a great stress on a woman—a large family—especially when the father takes things so coolly. I shouldn't speak to every one like this, you know, but one can talk to one's clergyman. Do you like Mr Hallam?"

"I find him very gentlemanly."

"Ah, yes, he's very gentlemanly. Well, I'm sure I hope they'll be happy; but there's always something in married life, and you do well to keep out of it; but, of course, you are so young yet."

"Yes," he said, with a grave, old-looking smile, "I am so young yet."

"You don't know what a family is, Mr Bayle. There's always something; when it isn't measles it's scarlatina, and when it isn't scarlatina it's boots and shoes."

"Oh, but children are a deal of comfort, Sophia," said the doctor, coming up after whispering to Mrs Luttrell that his sister looked grumpy.

"Some children may be, Joseph—mine are not," sighed Mrs Trampleasure, and the doctor went back to his wife. "Ah, Mr Bayle, if I were to tell you one-half of the troubles I've been through I should harass you."

"Kitty," said the doctor, "I want everything to go well to-night. Try and coax Sophia away, she's forcing her doldrums on Mr Bayle."

"But how am I to get her away, dear? You know what she is."

"Try to persuade her to taste the brandy cherries, or we shall be having her in tears. I'll come and help you." They walked back to where Mrs Trampleasure was still talking away hard in a querulous voice.

"Ah! you've come back, Joseph," she said, cutting short her remarks to the curate to return to her complaint to her brother. "I was saying that some children are a pleasure; but it did not seem as if you could listen to me."

"My dear Sophia, I'll listen to you all night, but Kitty wants you to give your opinion about some brandy cherries."

"My opinion?" said the lady loudly. "I have no opinion. I never taste such luxuries."

Millicent could not help hearing a portion of her aunt's querulous remarks, and, out of sheer pity for one of the recipients, she turned to her Uncle Trampleasure, who always kept on the other side of the room.

"Uncle, dear," she said, "aunt is murmuring so. Do try and stop it."

"Stop it, my dear?" he said smiling sadly. "Ah, if you knew your aunt as well as I do you would never check her murmurs; they carry off her ill-temper. No, no, my dear, it would be dangerous to stop it. I always let it go on."

There was no need to check Mrs Trampleasure after all. Mr Bayle threw himself into the breach, and made her forget her own troubles by consulting her about some changes that he proposed making in the parish.

That changed the course of her thoughts, and in the intervals of the music, and often during the progress of some song, she alluded to different matters that had given her annoyance ever since she had been a girl.

It was not an agreeable duty, that of keeping Mrs Trampleasure amused, but Millicent rewarded him with a grateful smile, and Bayle was content.

There was a pleasant little supper that was announced unpleasantly just as Miss Heathery had consented to sing again, and was telling the assembly in a bird-like voice how gaily the troubadour touched his guita-h-ah, as he was hastening home from the wah.

"Supper's ready," said a loud, harsh voice, which cut like an arrow right through Miss Heathery's best note.

"Now you shouldn't, Thisbe," said Mrs Luttrell in tones of mild reproach; but the reproof was not heard, for the door was sharply closed.

"It is only our Thisbe's way, Mr Bayle," whispered Mrs Luttrell; "please don't notice it. Excellent servant, but so soon put out."

She nodded confidentially, and then stole out on tiptoe, so as not to interrupt Miss Heathery, who went on—"singing from Palestine hither I come," to the end.

Then words of reproof and sharp retort could be heard outside; and after a while poor Mrs Luttrell came back looking very red, to lean over the curate from behind the sofa, brooding over him as if he were a favourite chicken.

"I don't like finding fault with the servants, Mr Bayle. Did you hear me?"

"I could not help hearing," he said smiling.

"She does provoke me so," continued Mrs Luttrell in a soft clucking way, that quite accorded with her brooding. "I know I shall have to discharge her."

"She does not like a little extra trouble, perhaps. Company."

"Oh, no; it's not that," said Mrs Luttrell. "She'll work night and day for one if she's in a good temper; but, the fact is, Mr Bayle, she does not like this engagement, and quite hates Mr Hallam."

Bayle drew his breath hard, but he turned a grave, smiling face to his hostess.

"That's the reason, I'm sure, why she is so awkward to-night, my dear—I beg pardon, I mean Mr Bayle," said the old lady colouring as ingenuously as a girl, "but she pretends it is about the potatoes."

"Potatoes?" said Bayle, who was eager to divert her thoughts.

"Yes. You see the doctor is so proud of his potatoes, and I was going to please him by having some roasted for supper and brought up in a napkin, but Thisbe took offence directly, and said that cold chicken and hot potatoes would be ridiculous, and she has been in a huff ever since."

Just then the door opened and the person in question entered, to come straight to Mrs Luttrell, who began to tremble and look at the curate for help.

"There's something gone wrong," she whispered.

"Can I speak to you, please, mum?" said Thisbe, glaring at her severely.

"Well, I don't know, Thisbe, I—"

"Let me go out and speak to Thisbe, mamma dear," said Millicent, who had crossed the room, divining what was wrong.

"Oh, if you would, my dear," said Mrs Luttrell eagerly; and Thisbe was compelled to retreat, her young mistress following her out of the room.

"That's very good of her, Mr Bayle," said Mrs Luttrell, with a satisfied sigh. "Millicent can always manage Thisbe. She has such a calm, dignified way with her. Do you know she is the only one who can manage her Aunt Trampleasure when she begins to murmur. Ah, I don't know what I shall do when she has gone."

"You will have the satisfaction of knowing that she is happy with the man she loves."

"I don't know, Mr Bayle, I—Oh dear me, I ought to be ashamed of myself for speaking like this. Hush! here she is."

In effect Millicent came back into the room to where her mother was sitting.

"Only a little domestic difficulty, Mr Bayle. Mamma, dear, it is all smoothed away, and Thisbe is very penitent."

"And she will bring up the roast potatoes in the napkin, my dear?"

"Yes," cried Millicent, laughing merrily, "she has retracted all her opposition, and we are to have two dishes of papa's best."

"In napkins, my dear?" cried Mrs Luttrell eagerly; "both in napkins?"

"Yes, mamma, in the whitest napkins she can find." She glanced at Christie Bayle's grave countenance, and felt her heart smite her for being so happy and joyous in his presence.

"Don't think us childish, Mr Bayle," she said gently. "It is to please my father."

He rose and stood by her side for a moment or two.

"Childish?" he said in a low voice, "as if I could think such a thing of you."

Millicent smiled her thanks, and crossed the room to where Hallam was watching her. The next minute supper was again announced—simple, old-fashioned supper—and Millicent went out on Hallam's arm.

"You are going to take me in, Mr Bayle? Well, I'm sure I'd rather," said Mrs Luttrell, "and I can then see, my dear, that you have a good supper. There, I'm saying 'my dear' to you again."

"It is because I seem so young, Mrs Luttrell," replied Bayle gravely.

"Oh no, my dear," said Mrs Luttrell innocently; "it was because you seemed to come among us so like a son, and took to the doctor's way with his garden, and were so nice with Millicent. I used to think that perhaps you two might— Oh, dear me," she cried, checking herself suddenly, "what a tongue I have got! Pray don't take any notice of what I say."

There was no change in Christie Bayle's countenance, for the smile hid the pang he suffered as he took in the pleasant garrulous old lady to supper; but that night he paced his room till daybreak, fighting a bitter fight, and asking for strength to bear the agony of his heart.

Volume One—Chapter Twelve.

James Thickens is Mysterious.

"I think, previous to taking this step, Sir Gordon, I may ask if you and Mr Dixon are quite satisfied? I believe the books show a state of prosperity."

"That does us credit, Mr Hallam," said Sir Gordon quietly. "Yes, Mr Dixon bids me say that he is perfectly satisfied—eh, Mr Trampleasure?"

"Quite, Sir Gordon—more than satisfied," replied Mr Trampleasure, who was standing with his hands beneath his coat-tails, balancing himself on toe and heel, and bowing as he spoke with an air that he believed to be very impressive.

"Then, before we close this little meeting, I suppose it only remains for me to ask you if you have any questions to ask of the firm, any demands to make?" Hallam rose from behind the table covered with books and balance-sheets in the manager's room of the bank, placed his hand in his breast, and in a quiet, dignified way, replied:

"Questions to ask, Sir Gordon—demands to make? No; only to repeat my former question. Are you satisfied?"

"*I* did reply to that," said Sir Gordon, who looked brown and sunburned, consequent upon six weeks' yachting in the Mediterranean; "but have you no other question or demand to make previous to your marriage?"

"Excuse me," said Mr Trampleasure, "excuse me. I want to say one word. Hem! hem!—I er—I er—"

"What is it, Trampleasure?" said Sir Gordon.

"It is in regard to a question I believe Mr Hallam is about to put to the firm. I may say that Mrs Trampleasure drew my attention to the matter, consequent upon a rumour in the town in connection with Mr Hallam's marriage."

Hallam raised his eyebrows and smiled.

"Have they settled the date?" he said pleasantly.

"No, sir, not that I am aware of; but Mrs Trampleasure has been given to understand that Mr Hallam, upon his marriage, will wish, and is about to send in a request for the apartments connected with this bank that I have always occupied. It would be a great inconvenience to Mrs Trampleasure with our family—I mean to me—to have to move."

"My dear Sir Gordon," said Hallam, interrupting, "allow me to set Mr Trampleasure at rest. I have taken the little Manor House, and have given orders for the furniture."

"There, Trampleasure," said Sir Gordon. "Don't take any notice of gossips for the future."

"Hem! I will not; but Mr Gemp is so well-informed generally."

"That he is naturally wrong sometimes," said Sir Gordon. "By-the-way, are they ever going to put that man under the pump? Now, Mr Hallam, have you anything more to ask?"

"Certainly not, Sir Gordon," replied the manager stiffly. "I understand your allusion, of course; but I have only to say that I look upon my engagement here as a commercial piece of business to be strictly adhered to, and that I know of nothing more degrading to a man than making every change in his life an excuse for asking an increase of salary."

"And you do not wish to take a holiday trip on the occasion of your wedding?"

"No, Sir Gordon."

"But the lady?"

"Miss Luttrell knows that she is about to marry a business man, Sir Gordon, and accepts her fate," said Hallam with a smile.

"Of course you can take a month. I'm sure Trampleasure and Thickens would manage everything in your absence."

"Excuse me, Sir Gordon, I have no doubt whatever that everything would run like a repeater-watch in my absence; but, with the responsibility of manager of this bank, I could not feel comfortable to run away just in our busiest time. Later on I may take a trip."

"Just as you like, Hallam, just as you like. Then that is all we have to do?"

"Everything, Sir Gordon. Yes, Mr Thickens, I will come;" for the clerk had tapped at the door and summoned him into the bank.

"Dig for you, Trampleasure, about the salary, eh?" said Sir Gordon, as soon as they were alone.

"And in very bad taste, too," said Trampleasure stiffly.

"Ah, well, he's a good manager," said Sir Gordon. "How I hate figures! They'll be buzzing in my head for a week."

He rose and walked to the glass to begin arranging his cravat and shirt-collar, buttoning the bottom of his coat, and pulling down his buff vest, so that it could be well seen. Then adjusting his hat at a correct gentlemanly angle, and tapping the tassels of his Hessian boots to make them swing free, he bade

Trampleasure good-morning and sauntered down the street, twirling his cane with all the grace of an old beau.

"I don't like that man," he said to himself, "and I never did; but his management of the bank is superb. Only one shaky loan this last six months, and he thinks we shall clear ourselves, if we wait before we sell. Bah! I'm afraid I'm as great a humbug as the rest of the world. If he had not won little Millicent, I should have thought him a very fine fellow, I dare say."

He strolled on towards the doctor's, thinking as he went.

"No, I don't think I should have liked him," he mused. "He's gentlemanly and polished; but too gentlemanly and polished. It is like a mask and suit that to my mind do not fit. Then, hang it! how did he manage to win that girl?"

"Cleverness. That calm air of superiority; that bold deference, and his good looks. I've seen it all; he has let her go on talking in her clever way—and she is clever; and then when he has thought she has gone on long enough, he has checked her with a touch of the tiller, and thrown all the wind out of her sails, leaving her swinging on the ocean of conjecture. Just what she would like; made to feel that, clever as she is, he could be her master when and where he pleased. Yes, that is it, and I suppose I hate him for it. No, no. It would not have been right, even if I could have won. I would not be prejudiced against him more than I can help; but I'm afraid we shall never be any closer than we are."

That afternoon Mr Hallam of the bank was exceedingly busy; so was James Thickens, at the counter, now giving, now receiving and cancelling and booking cheques or greasy notes, some of which were almost too much worn to be deciphered.

The time went on, and it was the hour for closing the doors. Thickens had had to go in and out of the manager's room several times, and Hallam was always busy writing letters. He looked up, and answered questions, or gave instructions, and then went on again, while each time, when James Thickens came out, he looked more uneasy. That is to say, to any one who thoroughly understood James Thickens, he would have looked uneasy. To a stranger he would only have seemed peculiar, for involuntarily at such times he had a habit of moving his scalp very slowly, drawing his hair down over his forehead, while his eyebrows rose up to meet it. Then, with mechanical regularity, they separated again; and all the while his eyes were fixed, and seemed to be gazing at something that was not there.

"You need not wait, Thickens," said Hallam, opening his door at length. "I want to finish a few letters."

The clerk rose and left the place after his customary walk round with keys, and the transferring of certain moneys to the safe; and, as soon as he was gone, Hallam locked his door communicating with the house, and began to busy himself in the safe, examining docketed securities, ticking them off, arranging and rearranging, hour after hour.

And during those hours James Thickens seemed to be prosecuting a love affair, for, instead of going home to his tea and gold-fish, he walked down the market place for some distance, turned sharp back, knocked at a door, and was admitted. Then old Gemp, who had been sweeping his narrow horizon, put on his hat, and walked across to Mrs Pinet, who was as usual watering her geraniums, and hunting for withered leaves that did not exist.

"Two weddings, Mrs P.!" he said with a leer.

"Lor', Mr Gemp, what do you mean?" she exclaimed.

"Two weddings, ma'am. Your Mr Hallam first, and Thickens directly after. No more bachelors at the bank, ma'am."

"Why, you don't mean to say that Mr Thickens—oh, dear me!"

"But I do mean to say it, ma'am. He's dropped in at Miss Heathery's as coolly as can be; and has hung his hat up behind the door."

"You don't say so!"

"Oh yes, I do. It's her doing. Going there four or five times a week to cash cheques, and he has grown reckless. Let's wait till he comes out."

"Perhaps, then," said Mrs Pinet primly, "people may begin saying things about me."

"There'll be no one to say it," said Gemp innocently. "Let's see how long he stops. I can't very well from my place."

"I couldn't think of such a thing," said Mrs Pinet, grandly. "Mr Hallam will be in directly, too. No, Mr Gemp, I'm no watcher of my neighbours' affairs;" and she went indoors.

"Very well, madam. *Ve-ry* well," said Gemp. "We shall see;" and he walked back home to stand in his doorway for three hours before he saw Thickens come from where he had ensconced himself behind Miss Heathery's curtain with his eyes fixed upon the bank.

At the end of those three hours Mr Hallam passed, looking very thoughtful, and five minutes later James Thickens went home to his gold-fish and tea.

"Took care Hallam didn't see him," chuckled Gemp, rubbing his hands. "Oh, the artfulness of these people! Thinks he has as good a right to marry as

Hallam himself. Well, why not? Make him more staid and solid, better able to take care of the deeds and securities, and pounds, shillings, and pence, and—hullo!—hello!—hello! What's the meaning of this!"

This was the appearance of a couple coming from the direction of the doctor's house, and the couple were Miss Heathery, who had been spending a few hours with Millicent—in other words, seeing her preparations for the wedding—and Sir Gordon Bourne, who was going in her direction and walked home with her.

"Why, Thickens didn't see her after all!"

No: James Thickens had not seen her, and Miss Heathery had not seen James Thickens.

"Who?" she cried, as soon as Sir Gordon had ceremoniously bidden her "Good-night," raising his curly brimmed hat, and putting it back.

"Mr Thickens, ma'am," cried the little maid eagerly; "and when I told him you was out, he said, might he wait, and I showed him in the parlour."

"And he's there now?" whispered Miss Heathery, who began tremblingly to take off the very old pair of gloves she kept for evening wear, the others being safe in her reticule.

"No, ma'am, please he has been gone these ten minutes."

"But what did he say?" cried Miss Heathery querulously.

"Said he wanted to see you particular, ma'am."

"Oh dear me; oh dear me!" sighed Miss Heathery. "Was ever anything so unfortunate? How could I tell that he would come when I was out?"

Volume One—Chapter Thirteen.

Mr Hallam has a Visitor.

Mysteries were painful to old Gemp. If any one had propounded a riddle, and gone away without supplying the answer, he would have been terribly aggrieved.

He was still frowning, and trying to get over the mystery of why James Thickens should be at Miss Heathery's when that lady was out, and his ideas were turning in the direction of the little maid, when a wholesome stimulus was given to his thoughts by the arrival of the London coach, the alighting of whose passengers he had hardly once missed seeing for years.

Hurrying up to the front of the "George," he was just in time to see a dashing-looking young fellow, who had just alighted from the box-seat, stretching his legs, and beating his boots with a cane. He had been giving orders for his little valise to be carried into the house, and was staring about him in the half-light, when he became aware of the fact that old Gemp was watching him curiously.

He involuntarily turned away; but seeming to master himself, he turned back, and said sharply, "Where does Mr Hallam live?"

"Mr Hallam!" cried Gemp eagerly; "bank's closed hours ago."

"I didn't ask for the bank. Where is Mr Hallam's private residence?"

"Well," said Gemp, rubbing his hands and laughing unpleasantly, "that's it—the 'Little Manor' as he calls it; but it's a big place, isn't it?"

"Oh, he lives there, does he?" said the visitor, glancing curiously at the ivy-covered house across the way.

"Not yet," said Gemp. "That's where he is going to live when—"

"He's married. I know. Now then, old Solomon, if you can answer a plain question, where does he live now?"

"Mrs Pinet's house, yonder on the left, where the porch stands out, and the flower-pots are in the window."

"Humph! hasn't moved, then. Let's see," muttered the visitor, "that's where I took the flower-pot to throw at the dog. No: that's the house."

"Can I—?" began Gemp insidiously.

"No, thankye. Good evening," said the visitor. "You can tell 'em I've come. Ta ta! Gossiping old fool!" he added to himself, as he walked quickly down the street; while, after staring after him for a few minutes, Gemp turned sharply on his heel, and made for Gorringe's—Mr Gorringe being the principal tailor.

Mr Gorringe's day's work was done, consequently his legs were uncrossed, and he was seated in a Christian-like manner—that is to say, in a chair just inside his door, smoking his evening pipe, but still in his shirtsleeves, and with an inch tape gracefully hanging over his neck and shoulders.

"I say, neighbour," cried Gemp eagerly, "you bank with Dixons'."

Mr Gorringe's pipe fell from his hand, and broke into a dozen pieces upon the floor.

"Is—is anything wrong?" he gasped; "and it's past banking hours."

"Yah! get out!" cried old Gemp, showing his yellow teeth. "You're always thinking about your few pence in the bank. Why, I bank there, and you don't see me going into fits. Yah! what a coward you are!"

"Then—then, there's nothing wrong?"

"Wrong? No."

"Hah!" ejaculated the tailor. "Mary, bring me another pipe."

"I only come in a friendly way," cried Gemp, "to put you on your guard."

"Then there is something wrong," cried the tailor, aghast.

"No, no, no. I want to give you a hint about Hallam."

"Hallam!"

"Ay! Has he ordered his wedding-suit of you?"

"No."

"Thought not," said Gemp, rubbing his hands. "I should be down upon him if I were you. Threaten to withdraw my account, man. Dandy chap down from London to-night to take his orders."

"No!"

"Yes. By the coach. Saw he was a tailor in a moment. Wouldn't stand it if I were you."

Mrs Pinet, who came to the door with a candle, in answer to a sharp rap with the visitor's cane, held up her candle above her head, and stared at him for a moment. Then a smile dimpled her pleasant, plump face.

"Why, bless me, sir! how you have changed!" she said.

"You know me again, then?" he said nodding familiarly.

"That I do, sir, and I am glad. You're the young gentleman Mr Hallam helped just about a year ago."

"Yes, that's me. Is he at home?"

"Yes, sir. Will you come this way?"

Mrs Pinet drew back to allow the visitor to enter, closed the door, set down her candle, and then tapped softly on the panel at her right.

"Here's that gentleman to see you, sir," she said, in response to the quick "Come in."

"Gentleman to see me? Oh, it's you," said Hallam, rising from his seat to stand very upright and stern-looking, with one hand in his breast.

"Yes, I've come down again," said the visitor slowly, so as to give Mrs Pinet time to get outside the door; and then, by mutual consent, they waited until her step had pattered over the carefully-reddened old bricks, and a door at the back closed.

Meanwhile Hallam's eyes ran rapidly over his visitor's garb, and he seemed satisfied, though he smiled a little at the extravagance of the attire.

"Why have you come down?" he said at last. "Because I didn't want to write. Because I thought you'd like to know how things were going. Because I wanted to see how you were getting on. Because I thought you'd be glad to see me."

"Because you wanted more money. Because you thought you could put on the screw. Because you thought you could frighten me. Pish! I could extend your list of reasons indefinitely, Stephen Crellock, my lad," said Hallam, in a quiet tone of voice that was the more telling from the anger it evidently concealed.

"What a one you are, Robby, old fellow! Just as you used to be when we were at—"

"Let the past rest," said Hallam in a whisper. "It will be better for both."

"Oh-h-h-h!" said his visitor, in a peculiar way. "Don't talk like that, Rob, old chap. It sounds like making plans, and a tall, handsome man in disguise waylaying a well-dressed gentleman from town, shooting him with pistols, carrying the body in the dead of the night to the bank, doubling it up in an iron chest, pouring in a lot of lime, and then shutting the lid, sealing it up, and locking it in the far corner of the bank cellar, as if it was somebody's plate. That's the game, eh?"

"I should like to," said Hallam coolly.

"Ha—ha—ha—ha!" laughed his visitor, sitting down; "but I'm not afraid, Rob, or I should not have put my head in the lion's den. That's not the sort of thing you would do, because you always were so gentlemanly, and had such a tender conscience. See how grieved you were when I got into trouble, and you escaped."

"Will you—"

"Will I what? Speak like that before any one else? Will I threaten you with telling tales, if you don't give me money to keep my mouth shut? Will I be a sneak?" cried Crellock, speaking quite as fiercely as Hallam, and rising to his feet, and looking, in spite of his ultra costume, a fine manly fellow.

"Well, yes, you cowardly cur; have you come down to do this now?" said Hallam menacingly.

"Pish!" said the other contemptuously as he let himself sink back slowly into his chair. "Don't try and bully, Rob. It did when I came down, weak and half-starved and miserable, after two years' imprisonment; but it won't do now. I don't look hard up, do I?"

"No; because you've spent my money on your wretched dress."

"I only spent your money when I couldn't make any for myself. I haven't had a penny of you lately; and as to being a coward and a cur, Rob, when I stood in the dock, and you were brought as a witness against me, and I could have got off half my punishment by speaking the truth, was I a sneak then, or did I stand, firm?"

There was a pause.

"Answer me; did I stand firm then?" cried Crellock.

"You did stand firm, and I have been grateful," said Hallam, in a milder tone. "Look here, Stephen, why should we quarrel?"

"Ah, that's better, man," said Crellock, laughing. "You were so terribly fierce with me last time, and I was brought down to a door-mat. Anybody might have wiped his shoes on me. I'm better now."

"And you've come down to try and bully me," said Hallam fiercely.

His visitor sat back, looking at him hard, without speaking for a few minutes, and then he said quietly:

"I give it up."

"Give what up—the attempt?"

"I couldn't give that up, because I was not going to attempt anything," said Crellock, smiling; "I mean give it up about you. What is it in you, Rob Hallam, that made so many fellows like you, and give way to you in everything? I don't know. But there, never mind that. Won't you shake hands?"

"Tell me first why you have come down here. Do you want money?"

"No."

"Then why did you come down?"

Crellock's face softened a little, and it was not an ill-looking countenance as he sat there, softly tapping the arm of the chair. At last he spoke.

"I never had many friends," he said huskily. "Father and mother went when I was a little one, and Uncle Richard gave me my education, telling me brutally that I was an encumbrance. I always had to stop at school through the holidays, and when I was old enough he put me, as you know, in the bank, and told me he had done his duty by me, and I must now look to myself."

"Yes, I know," said Hallam, coldly.

"Then I got to know you, Rob, and you seemed always to be everything a man ought to be—handsome, and clever at every game, the best writer, the best at figures. Then, after office hours, you could sing and play, and tell the best story. There, Rob, you know I always got to feel towards you as if I was your dog. There was nothing I wouldn't have done for you. Then came those—"

"Hush!"

"Well, I'm not going to say anything dangerous. You know how I behaved. I did think you would have made it a bit easier for me, when it was found out; but when you turned against me like the rest, I said to myself that it was all right, that it was no good for two to bear it when one could take the lot, and if you had turned against me it was only because it was what you called good policy, and it would be all right again when I came out I thought you'd stick to me, Rob."

"How could I, a man in a good position, know a—"

"Felon—a convicted thief? There, say it, old fellow, if you like. I don't mind; I got pretty well hardened down yonder. No: of course you couldn't, and I know I was a fool to come down as I did before, such a shack-bag as I was. Out of temper, too, and savage to see you looking so well; but I know it was foolish. It was enough to make you turn on me. But I'm different now: I've got on a bit."

"What are you doing?" said Hallam sharply.

"Oh, never mind," said the other, laughing. "I've opened an office, and I'm doing pretty well, and I thought I'd come down and see you again, Rob, old fellow, and—You'll shake hands?"

"Is this a bit of maudlin sentiment, Stephen Crellock, or are you playing some deep game?"

Hallam's visitor rose again and stood before him with his hand outstretched.

"Deep game!" he said softly. "Rob, old fellow, do you think a man can be all a blackguard, without one good spot in him? Ah, well, just as you like," he continued, dropping his hand heavily; "I was a fool to come; I always have been a fool. I was cat, Rob, and you were monkey, and I got my paws most preciously burned. But I didn't come down to grumble. There; good-night!"

"Where are you going?"

"Back to the 'George' and to-morrow I shall go up to the gold-paved streets. There, you need not be afraid, man. If I didn't tell tales when I was in the dock, I shan't now. I thought, after all, that you were my friend."

"And so I am, Steve!" cried Hallam, after a few moments' hesitation, and he held out his hand. "We'll be as good friends again as ever, and you shall not suffer this time."

Crellock stifled a sob as he caught the extended hand, to wring it with all his force; then, turning away, he laid his arms upon the chimney-piece, his head dropped upon them, and for a few minutes he cried like a child.

Hallam stood fuming and gazing down upon him, with an ugly look of contempt distorting his handsome features. Then taking a step forward, he laid his hand upon his visitor's shoulder.

"Come, come!" he said softly. "Don't go on like that." Crellock rose quickly, and dashed the tears from his eyes, with a piteous attempt at a laugh.

"That's me all over, Rob," he said. "Did you ever see such a weak fool? I was bad enough before I had that two years' low fever; I'm worse now, for it was spirit-breaking work."

"Soft wax, to mould to any shape," said Hallam to himself. Then aloud: "I don't see anything to be ashamed of in a little natural emotion. There, sit down, and let's have a chat."

Crellock caught his hand and gripped it hard. "Thank ye, Hallam," he said huskily, "thank ye; I shan't forget this. I told you I'd always felt as if I was your dog. I feel so more than ever now."

"They're sitting a long time," said Mrs Pinet, as she raked out the kitchen fire to the very last red-hot cinder. "Mr Hallam seemed quite pleased with him; he's altered so for the better. He said I needn't sit up, and so I will go to bed."

Mrs Pinet sought her room, and about twelve heard the door close on the stranger, between whom and Hallam a good deal of eager conversation had passed in a low tone.

"You see I'm trusting you," said Hallam as they parted.

"You know you can," was the reply. "And now, look here, if anything goes wrong—"

"I tell you, if you do as I have arranged, nothing can go wrong. I want an agent in London, whom I can implicitly trust, and I am going to trust you. Once more, your task is to do exactly what I tell you."

"But if anything goes wrong, I can't write to you."

"Nothing can go wrong, I tell you."

"Yes," said Crellock to himself, "you told me that once before." Then aloud:

"Well, we will say nothing can go wrong, for I shall do exactly what you have said; but if anything should, I shall come down, and if you see me—look out."

Volume One—Chapter Fourteen.

Like Gathering Clouds.

There is one very pleasant element in country-town life, and that is the breadth of the feeling known as neighbourly. It is often veined by scandal, disfigured by petty curiosity, but a genial feeling, like a solid stratum underlies it all, and makes it firm. Mrs White gets into difficulties, and her furniture is sold by auction; but the neighbours flock to the sale, and the love of bargains is so overridden that the old things often fetch as much as new. Mrs Black's family are ill, and every one around takes a real and helpful interest. Mrs Scarlet's husband dies, and a fancy fair is held on her behalf. Then how every one collects at the marriage: how all follow at the death! It must be something very bad indeed that has been committed if, after the customary unpleasant and censorious remarks about walking blindfold into such a slough, Green is not drawn out by helping hands—in fact, there is a kind of clannishness in a country-town, disfigured by the gossips, but very true and earnest all the same.

Consequently as soon as the day was fixed for Millicent Luttrell's wedding, presents came pouring in from old patients and young friends. A meeting was held at the Corn Exchange, at which Sir Gordon Bourne was to take the chair, but at which he did not put in an appearance, and the Reverend Christie Bayle took his place, while resolutions were moved and carried that a testimonial should be presented to our eminent fellow-townsman, Robert Hallam, Esq, on the occasion of his marriage with the daughter of our esteemed and talented neighbour, Dr Luttrell.

The service of plate was presented at a dinner, where speeches were made, to which Mr Hallam, of the bank, responded fluently, gracefully, and to the point.

Here, too, Christie Bayle took the chair, and had the task of presenting the silver, after reading the inscription aloud, amidst abundant cheers; and as he passed the glittering present to the recipient, their eyes met.

As their eyes met there was a pleasant smile upon Hallam's lip, and a thought in his heart that he alone could have interpreted, while Bayle's could have been read by any one skilled in the human countenance, as he breathed a hope that Millicent Luttrell might be made a happy wife.

The whole town was in a ferment—not a particular state of affairs for King's Castor—in fact, the people of that town in His Majesty's dominions were always waiting for a chance to effervesce and alter the prevailing stagnation for a time. Hence it was that the town band practised up a new tune; the grass was mowed in the churchyard, and some of the weeds cleared out from the gravel path. Miss Heathery went to the expense of a new bonnet and silk dress, and indulged in a passionate burst of weeping in the secrecy of her own room, because she was not asked to act as bridesmaid; and though Gorringe did not obtain any order from the bridegroom, he was favoured by Mr James Thickens to make him a blue dress-coat with triple-gilt buttons—a coat so blue, and whose buttons were such dazzling disks of metal, that it was not until it had been in the tailor's window, finished, and "on show" for three days, that James Thickens awakened to the fact that it was his, and paid a nocturnal visit to Gorringe to beg him to send it home.

"But you don't want it till the day, Mr Thickens," said the tailor, "and that coat's bringing me orders."

"But I shall never dare to wear it, Gorringe—everybody will know it."

"Of course they will, sir!" said the tailor proudly, and glancing towards his window with that half-smile an artist wears when his successful picture is on view, "that's a coat such as is not seen in Castor every day. Look at the collar! There's two days' hard stitching in that collar, sir!"

"I have looked at the collar," said Thickens hastily, "and I must have it home."

Gorringe gave way, and the coat went home; but he felt, as he said to his wife, as if he had been robbed, for that coat would have won the hearts of half the farmers round.

At the doctor's cottage Mrs Luttrell was in one constant whirl of excitement, with four clever seamstresses at work, for at King's Castor a bride's *trousseau* was called by a much simpler name, and provided throughout at home, along with the house-linen, which in those days meant linen of the finest and coolest, and it was absolutely necessary that every article that could be stitched should be stitched with rows of the finest stitches, carefully put in.

"You're about worrying yourself into a fever, my dear," said the doctor smiling, "and I can't afford such patients as you. Where can I have this bunch of radish-seed hung up to dry? Give it to Thisbe to hang in the kitchen."

"Now, my dear Joseph, how can you be so unreasonable!" cried Mrs Luttrell, half whimpering. "Radish-seed at a time like this! Thisbe is re-covering the pots of jam."

"What jam? What for?"

"For Millicent. You don't suppose I'm going to let her begin housekeeping without a pot of jam in the storeroom!"

"Thank goodness I've only one child!" said the doctor with a half-amused, half-vexed countenance.

"Why, papa, you always said you wished we had had a boy."

"Ah, I did not know that I should have to suffer all this when the wedding time came."

"Now, if you would only go into your garden, and see to your patients, my love, everything would go right!" cried Mrs Luttrell; "but you are so impatient! Look at Millicent, how quiet and calm she is!"

The doctor had looked at Millicent as she stole out to him in the garden—often now, as if moved by a desire to be as much with him as she could before the great step of her life was taken.

There was a quiet look of satisfaction in her eyes that told of her content, and the happy peace that reigned within her breast.

The doctor understood her, as she came to him when at work, questioning him about the blossoms of this rose, and the success of that creeper, and taking endless interest in all he did; and when she was summoned away to try something on, or to select some pattern, she smiled and said that she would soon be back.

"Ah!" he said with a sigh, "she is trying to break it off gently!" and his work ceased until he heard her step, when he became very busy and cheerful again, as they both played at hiding from one another the separation that was to come.

"Poor papa!" thought Millicent, "he will miss me when I am gone!"

"If that fellow does not behave well to her," said the doctor to himself, "and I do happen to be called in to him, I shall—well, I suppose it would not be right to do that." As for Mrs Luttrell, she was too busy to think much till she went to bed, and then the doctor complained.

"I must have some rest, my dear!" he said plaintively, "and I don't say that you will—but if you do have a bad face-ache from sleeping on a pillow soaked with tears, don't come to me to prescribe."

It was very near the time, and all was gliding on peacefully towards the wedding-day. Hallam came regularly every evening; and, after a good deal of struggling, Mrs Luttrell contrived to call him "my dear," while, by a similar effort of mind, the doctor habituated himself, from saying, "Mr Hallam" and "Hallam," to the familiar "Robert," though in secret both agreed that it did not seem natural, and did not come easily, and never would be Rob or Bob.

One soft, calm evening, as the moon was rising from behind the fine old church, and Millicent and Hallam lingered still in the garden among the shrubs, where they could see the shaded lamp shining down on Mrs Luttrell's white curls and pleasant, intent face, as she busily stitched away at a piece of linen for the new house, while the doctor was reading an account of some new plants brought home by Sir Joseph Banks, Millicent had become very silent.

Hallam was holding her tenderly to his side, and looking down at the sweet, calm face, lit by the rising moon, his own in shadow; and after watching her rapt aspect for a time, he said, in his deep, musical voice:

"How silent and absorbed! You are not regretting what is so soon to be?"

"Regretting!" she cried, starting; and, looking up in his face, she laid her hands upon his breast. "Don't speak to me like that, Robert dear. You know me better. As if I could regret!"

"Then you are quite happy?"

"Happy? Too happy; and yet so sad!" she murmured softly. "It seems as if life were too full of joy, as if I could not bear so much happiness, when it is at the cost of others, and I am giving them pain."

"Don't speak like that, my own!" he said tenderly. "It is natural that a woman should leave father and mother to cling unto her husband."

"Yes, yes: I know," she sighed; "but the pain is given. They will miss me so much. You are smiling, dear; but this is not conceit. I am their only child, and we have been all in all to each other."

"But you are not going far," he said tenderly.

"No, not far; and yet it is away from them," sighed Millicent, turning her head to gaze sadly at the pleasant picture seen through the open window. "Not far: but it is from home."

"But to home," he whispered—"to your home, our home, the home of the husband who loves you with all his heart. Ah, Millicent, I have been so poor a wooer, I have failed to say the winning, flattering things so pleasant to a woman's ear. I have felt half dumb before you, as if my pleasure was too great for words; and quick and strong as I am with my fellows, I have only been an awkward lover at the best."

She laid her soft white hand upon his lips, and gave him a half-reproachful look.

"And yet," she said, smiling, "how much stronger your silent wooing has been than any words that could have been said! Did I ever seem like one who wanted flattering words and admiration? Robert, you do not know me yet."

"No," he whispered passionately, "not yet, and never shall, for I find something more in you to love each time we meet, Millicent—my own—my wife!"

She yielded to his embrace, and they remained silent for a time.

At last he spoke.

"But you seemed sad and disappointed to-night. Have I grieved you in any way—have I given you pain?"

"Oh, no," she said, looking gravely in his face, "and you never could. Robert," she continued dreamily as she clung to him, "I can see our life mapped out in the future till it fades away. There are pains and sorrows, the thorns that strew the wayside of all; but I have always your strong, guiding arm to help and protect—always your brave, loving words, to sustain me when my spirit will be low, and together, hand in hand, we tread that path, patient, hopeful, loving to the end."

"My own!" he whispered.

"I have no fear," she continued; "my love was not given hastily, like that of some quickly dazzled girl; my love was slow to awaken; but when I felt that it was being sought by one whom I could reverence as well as love, I gave it freely—all I had."

"And you are content?"

"I should be truly happy, but for the pain I must give others."

"Only a pang, dear love; that will pass away in the feeling that their child is truly happy in her choice. There, there, the moonlight and the solemn look of the night have made you sad. Let us talk more cheerfully. Come, you must have something to ask of me?"

"No; you have told me everything," she said gravely. "I wish they could have been here to give their blessing on our love."

"Their blessing?" he said half-wonderingly.

"Your mother—your father, Robert," she whispered reverently as she bent her head.

"Hush!" he said, and for a few moments they were silent. "But come," he cried, as if trying to give their conversation a more cheerful turn, "you must have something more to ask of me. I mean for our house."

"No," she said; "it is everything I could wish."

"No," he said proudly, "it is too humble for my queen. If I were rich, you should have the fairest jewels, costly retinues—a palace."

"Give me your love, and I have all I need," she cried, laughing, as she clung to him.

"Then you must be very rich," he said. "But is there nothing? Come, you are a free agent now. In another week you will be my own—my property, my slave, bound to me by a ring. Come, use your liberty while you can."

"Well, then, yes," she said; "I will make a demand or two."

"That's right; I am the slave yet, and obey. What is the first wish?"

"I like Sir Gordon, dear; he has always been so good and kind to me. Ask him to come."

"Too late. He left the town by coach this evening. From a hint he dropped to Thickens about his letters, I think he has gone to Hull, and is going on to Spain."

"Oh!"

It was an ejaculation full of pain and sorrow.

"I am grieved," she said softly, and the news brought up that day when he had made her the offer of his hand.

Hallam watched her mobile face and its changes as she gazed straight before her, towards where the moon was beginning to flood the leaden roof of the old church, the crenulated wall, and the crockets on the tall spire standing out black and clear against the sky.

His face was still in the shadow.

"There is another request," she said at last, and her voice was very low as she spoke. "Robert, will you ask Mr Bayle to marry us? I would rather it was he."

"Bayle!" he exclaimed, starting, and the word jerked from his lips, as if he had suddenly lost control of himself. "No, it is impossible!"

"Impossible?" she said wonderingly.

"This man has caused me more suffering than I could tell you. If you knew the jealous misery—No, no, I don't mean that," he said quickly as he caught her to his breast.

"Oh, Robert!" she cried.

"No, no: don't notice me," he said hastily. "It was long ago. He loved you, and I was not sure of you then. Yes, darling, I will ask him, if you wish it. That folly is all dead now."

"Robert," she said, after a thoughtful pause, "do you wish me to give up that request?"

"Give up? No, I should be ready to insist upon it if you did. There, that is all past. It was the one boyish folly of my love, one of which I am heartily ashamed."

"I think he wants to be your friend as well as mine," she said, "and I should have liked it; but—"

"Your will is my law, Millicent! He shall marry us."

"But, Robert—"

"If you oppose me now in this, I shall think you have not forgiven the folly to which I have confessed. I can hardly forgive myself that meanness. You will not add to my pain."

"Add to your pain?" she said, laying her hand once more upon his breast. "Robert, you do not know me yet."

And so it was that Christie Bayle joined the hand of the woman he had loved to that of the man who had told her she would in future be his very own— his property, his slave.

Pretty well all Castor was present, and at the highest pitch of excitement, for a handsomer pair, they said, had never stood in the old chancel to be made one.

And they were made one. The register was signed, and then, in the midst of a murmuring buzz and rustle of garments that filled the great building like the gathering of a storm, Robert Hallam and his fair young wife moved down the aisle, towards where a man was waiting to give the signal to the ringers to begin; and the crowd had filled every corner near the door, and almost blocked the path. The sun shone out brilliantly, and the buzz and rustle grew more and more like the gathering of that storm, which burst at last as the young couple reached the porch, in a thundering cheer.

Millicent looked flushed, and there was a red spot in Hallam's cheeks as he walked out, proud and defiant, towards where the yellow chaise from the "George," with four post-horses, was waiting.

The coach had just come in, and the passengers were standing gazing at the novel scene.

Again the storm burst in a tremendous cheer as Hallam handed his young wife into the chaise, and then there seemed to be another nearing storm, sending its harbinger in a fashion which made firm, self-contained Robert Hallam turn pale, as a hand was laid upon his arm.

"He said that if anything did go wrong, he should come back," flashed through his brain.

Stephen Crellock was bending forward to whisper a few words in his ear.

Volume Two—Chapter One.

The Thorny Way—Millicent Hallam's Home.

"How dare you! Be off! Go to your mistress. Don't pester me, woman."

"Didn't know it were pestering you, sir, to ask for my rights. Two years doo, and it's time it was paid."

"Ask your mistress, I tell you. Here, Julia."

A dark-haired, thoughtful-looking child of about six years old loosened her grasp of Thisbe King's dress, and crossed the room slowly towards where Robert Hallam sat, newspaper in hand, by his half-finished breakfast.

"Here, Julia!" was uttered with no unkindly intent; but the call was like a command—an imperious command, such as would be given to a dog.

The child was nearly close to him when he gave the paper a sharp rustle, and she sprang back.

"Pish!" he exclaimed, laughing unpleasantly, "what a silly little girl you are! Did you think I was going to strike you?"

"N-no, papa," said the child nervously.

"Then why did you flinch away? Are you afraid of me?"

The child looked at him intently for a few moments, and then said softly:

"I don't know."

"Here, Thisbe," said Hallam, frowning, "I'll see to that. You can go now. Leave Miss Julia here."

"Mayn't I go with Thisbe, papa?" said the child eagerly.

"No; stay with me. I want to talk to you. Come here."

The child's countenance fell, and she sidled towards Hallam, looking wistfully the while at Thisbe, who left the room reluctantly and closed the door.

As soon as they were alone Hallam threw down the paper, and drew the child upon his knee, stroking her beautiful, long, dark hair, and held his face towards her.

"Well," he said sharply, "haven't you a kiss for papa?"

The child kissed him on both cheeks quickly, and then sat still and watched him.

"That's better," he said smiling. "Little girls always get rewards when they are good. Now I shall buy you a new doll for that."

The child's eyes brightened.

"Have you got plenty of money, papa?" she said quickly.

"Well, I don't know about plenty," he said with a curious laugh, as he glanced round the handsomely-furnished room, "but enough for that."

"Will you give me some?"

"Money is not good for little girls," said Hallam, smiling.

"But *I'm* not little now," said the child quietly. "Mamma says I'm quite a companion to her, and she doesn't know what she would do without me."

"Indeed!" said Hallam sarcastically. "Well, suppose I give you some money, what shall you buy—a doll?"

She shook her head. "I've got five dolls now," she said, counting on her little pink fingers, "mamma, papa, Thisbe, and me, and Mr Bayle."

Hallam ground out an ejaculation, making the child start from him in alarm.

"Sit still, little one," he said hastily. "Why, what's the matter? Here, what would you do with the money?"

"Give it to mamma to pay Thisbe. Mamma was crying about wanting some money yesterday for grand-mamma."

"Did your grandmother come and ask mamma for money yesterday?"

"Yes; she said grandpapa was so ill and worried that she did not know what to do."

Hallam rose from his seat, setting down the child, and began walking quickly about the room, while the girl, after watching him for a few moments in silence, began to edge her way slowly towards the door, as if to escape.

She had nearly reached it when Hallam noticed her, and, catching her by the wrist, led her back to his chair, and reseated himself.

"Look here, Julia," he said sharply, "I will not have you behave like this. Does your mother teach you to keep away from me because I seem so cross?" he added with a laugh that was not pleasant.

"No," said the child, shaking her head; "she said I was to be very fond of you, because you were my dear papa."

"Well, and are you?"

"Yes," said the child, nodding, "I think so;" and she looked wistfully in his face.

"That's right; and now be a good girl, and you shall have a pony to ride, and everything you like to ask for."

"And money to give to poor mamma?"

"Silence!" cried Hallam harshly, and the child shrank away, and covered her face with her hands. "Don't do that! Take down your hands. What have you to cry for now?"

The child dropped her hands in a frightened manner, and looked at him with her large dark eyes, that seemed to be watching for a blow, her face twitching slightly, but there were no tears.

"Any one would think I was a regular brute to the child," he muttered, scowling at her involuntarily, and then sitting very thoughtful and quiet, holding her on his knee, while he thrust back the breakfast things, and tapped the table. At last, turning to her with a smile, "Have a cup of coffee, Julie?" he said.

She shook her head. "I had my breakfast with mamma ever so long since."

He frowned again, looking uneasily at the child, and resuming the tapping upon the table with his thin, white fingers.

The window looking out on the market place was before them, quiet, sunny, and with only two people visible, Mrs Pinet, watering her row of flowers with a jug, and the half of old Gemp, as he leaned out of his doorway, and looked in turn up the street and down.

All at once a firm, quick step was heard, and the child leaped from her father's knee.

"Here's Mr Bayle! Here's Mr Bayle!" she cried, clapping her hands, and, bounding to the window, she sprang upon a chair, to press her face sidewise to the pane, to watch for him who came, and then to begin tapping on the glass, and kissing her hands as Christie Bayle, a firm, broad-shouldered man, nodded and smiled, and went by.

Julia leaped from the chair to run out of the room, leaving Robert Hallam clutching the edge of the table, with his brow wrinkled, and an angry frown upon his countenance, as he ground his teeth together, and listened to the opening of the front door, and the mingling of the curate's frank, deep voice with the silvery prattle of his child.

"Ha, little one!" And then there was the sound of kisses, as Hallam heard the rustle of what seemed, through the closed door, to be Christie Bayle taking the child by the waist and lifting her up to throw her arms about his neck.

"You're late!" she cried; and the very tone of her voice seemed changed, as she spoke eagerly.

"No, no, five minutes early; and I must go up the town first now."

"Oh!" cried the child.

"I shall not be long. How is mamma?"

"Mamma isn't well," said the child. "She has been crying so."

"Hush! hush! my darling!" said Bayle softly. "You should not whisper secrets."

"Is that a secret, Mr Bayle?"

"Yes; mamma's secret, and my Julia must be mamma's well-trusted little girl."

"Please, Mr Bayle, I'm so sorry, and I won't do so any more. Are you cross with me?"

"My darling!" he cried passionately, "as if any one could be cross with you! There, get your books ready, and I'll soon be back."

"No, no, not this morning, Mr Bayle; not books. Take me for a walk, and teach me about the flowers."

"After lessons, then. There, run away."

Hallam rose from his chair, with his lips drawn slightly from his teeth, as he heard Bayle's retiring steps. Then the front door was banged loudly; he heard his child clap her hands, and then the quick fall of her feet as she skipped across the hall, and bounded up the stairs.

He took a few strides up and down the room, but stopped short as the door opened again, and, handsomer than ever, but with a graver, more womanly beauty, heightened by a pensive, troubled look in her eyes and about the corners of her mouth, Millicent Hallam glided in.

Her face lit up with a smile as she crossed to Hallam, and laid her white hand upon his arm.

"Don't think me unkind for going away, dear," she said softly. "Have you quite done?"

"Yes," he said shortly. "There, don't stop me; I'm late."

"Are you going to the bank, dear?"

"Of course I am. Where do you suppose I'm going?"

"I only thought, dear, that—"

"Then don't *only think* for the sake of saying foolish things."

She laid her other hand upon his arm, and smiled in his face.

"Don't let these money matters trouble you so, Robert," she said. "What does it matter whether we are rich or poor?"

"Oh, not in the least!" he cried sarcastically. "You don't want any money, of course?"

"I do, dear, terribly," she said sadly. "I have been asked a great deal lately for payments of bills; and if you could let me have some this morning—"

"Then I cannot; it's impossible. There, wait a few days and the crisis will be over, and you can clear off."

"And you will not speculate again, dear?" she said eagerly.

"Oh, no, of course not," he rejoined, with the touch of sarcasm in his voice.

"We should be so much happier, dear, on your salary. I would make it plenty for us; and then, Robert, you would be so much more at peace."

"How can I be at peace?" he cried savagely, "when, just as I am harassed with monetary cares—which you cannot understand—I find my home, instead of a place of rest, a place of torment?"

"Robert!" she said, in a tone of tender reproach.

"People here I don't want to see; servants pestering me for money, when I have given you ample for our household expenses; and my own child set against me, ready to shrink from me, and look upon me as some domestic ogre!"

"Robert, dear, pray do not talk like this."

"I am driven to it," he cried fiercely; "the child detests me!"

"Oh no, no, no," she whispered, placing her arm round his neck.

"And rushes to that fellow Bayle as if she had been taught to look upon him as everybody."

"Nay, nay," she said softly; and there was a tender smile upon her lip, a look of loving pity in her eye. "Julie likes Mr Bayle, for he pets her, and plays with her as if he were her companion."

"And I am shunned."

"Oh, no, dear, you frighten poor Julie sometimes when you are in one of your stern, thoughtful moods."

"My stern, thoughtful moods! Pshaw!"

"Yes," she said tenderly; "your stern, thoughtful moods. The child cannot understand them as I do, dear husband. She thinks of sunshine and play. How can she read the depth of the father's love—of the man who is so foolishly ambitious to win fortune for his child? Robert—husband—my own, would it not be better to set all these strivings for wealth aside, and go back to the simple, peaceful days again?"

"You do not understand these things," he said harshly. "There, let me go. I ought to have been at the bank an hour ago, but I could not get a wink of sleep all the early part of the night."

"I know, dear. It was three o'clock when you went to sleep."

"How did you know?"

"The clock struck when you dropped off, dear. I did not speak for fear of waking you."

She did not add that she, too, had been kept awake about money matters, and wondering whether her husband would consent to live in a more simple style in a smaller house.

"There, good-bye," he said, kissing her. "It is all coming right. Don't talk to your father or mother about my affairs."

"Of course I should not, love," she replied; "such things are sacred."

"Yes, of course," he said hastily. "There, don't take any notice of what I have said. I am worried—very much worried just now, but all will come right soon." He kissed her hastily and hurried away, leaving Millicent standing thoughtful and troubled till she heard another step on the rough stones, when a calm expression seemed to come over her troubled face, but only to be chased away by one more anxious as the step halted at the door and the bell rang.

Meanwhile Julia had run upstairs to her own room, where, facing the door, five very battered dolls sat in a row upon the drawers, at which she dashed full of childish excitement, as if to continue some interrupted game.

She stopped short, looked round, and then gave her little foot a stamp.

"How tiresome!" she cried pettishly. "It's that nasty, tiresome, disagreeable old Thibs. I hate her, that I do, and—"

"Oh, you hate me, do you?" cried the object of her anger appearing in the doorway. "Very well, it don't matter. I don't mind. You don't care for anybody now but Mr Bayle."

The child rushed across the room to leap up and fling her arms round Thisbe's neck, as that oddity stood there, quite unchanged: the same obstinate, hard woman who had opposed Mrs Luttrell seven years before.

"Don't, don't, don't say such things, Thibs," cried the child, all eagerness and excitement now, the very opposite of the timid, shrinking girl in the breakfast-room a short time before; and as she spoke she covered the hard face before her with kisses. "You know, you dear, darling old Thibs, I love you. Oh, I do love you so very, very much."

"I know it's all shim-sham and pea-shucks," said Thisbe, grimly; but, without moving her face, rather bending down to meet the kisses.

"No, you don't think anything of the kind, Thibs, and I won't have you looking cross at me like papa."

"It's all sham, I tell you," said Thisbe again. "You never love me only when you want anything."

"Oh! Thibs!" cried the girl with the tears gathering in her eyes; "how can you say that?"

"Because I'm a nasty, hard, cankery, ugly, disagreeable old woman," said Thisbe, clasping the child to her breast; "and it isn't true, and you're my own precious sweet, that you are."

"And you took away my box out of the room, when I had to go down to papa."

"But you can't have a nasty, great, dirty candle-box in your bedroom, my dear."

"But I want it for a doll's house, and I'm going to line it with paper, and— do, Thibs, do, do let me have it, please?"

"Oh, very well, I shall have to be getting the moon for you next. I never see such a spoiled child."

"Make haste then, before Mr Bayle comes, to go on with my lessons. Quick! quick! where is it?"

"In the lumber-room, of course. Where do you suppose it is?"

Thisbe led the way along a broad passage and up three or four stairs to an old oak door, which creaked mournfully on its hinges as it was thrown back, showing a long, sloped, ceiled room, half filled with packing-cases and old fixtures that had been taken down when Hallam hired the house, and had it somewhat modernised for their use.

It was a roomy place with a large fireplace that had apparently been partially built up to allow of a small grate being set, while walls and ceiling were covered with a small patterned paper, a few odd rolls and pieces of which lay in a corner.

"I see it," cried Julia excitedly.

"No, no, no; let me get it," cried Thisbe. "Bless the bairn! why, she's like a young goat. There, now, just see what you've done!"

The child had darted at the hinged deal box, stood up on one end against the wall in the angle made by the great projecting fireplace, and in dragging it away torn down a large piece of the wall paper.

"Oh, I couldn't help it, Thibs," cried the child panting. "I am so sorry."

"So sorry, indeed!" cried Thisbe; "so sorry, indeed, won't mend walls. Why, how wet it is!" she continued, kneeling down and smoothing out the paper, and dabbing it back against the end of the great fireplace from which it had been torn. "There's one of them old gutters got stopped up and the rain soaks in through the roof, and wets this wall; it ought to be seen to at once."

All this while making a ball of her apron, Thisbe, who was the perfection of neatness, had been putting back the torn down corner of paper, moistening it here and there, and ending by making it stick so closely that the tear was only visible on a close inspection. This done she rose and carried the box out, and into the child's bedroom, when before the slightest advance had been made towards turning it into a doll's house, there was the ring at the door, and Thisbe descended to admit the curate, to whom Julia came bounding down.

Volume Two—Chapter Two.

Miss Heathery's Offering.

Nature, or rather the adaptation from Nature which we call civilisation, deals very hardly with unmarried ladies of twenty-five for the next ten or a dozen years. Then it seems to give them up, and we have arrived at what is politely known as the uncertain age. Very uncertain it is, for, from thirty-five to forty-five some ladies seem to stand still.

Miss Heathery was one of these, and the mid-life stage seemed to have made her evergreen, for seven years' lapse found her much the same, scarcely in any manner changed.

Poor Miss Heathery! For twenty years she had been longing with all the intensity of a true woman to become somebody's squaw. Her heart was an urn full of sweetness. Perhaps it was of rather a sickly cloying kind that many men would have turned from with disgust, but it was sweetness all the same, and for these long, long years she had been waiting to pour this honey of her nature like a blessing upon some one's head, while only one man had been ready to say, "Pour on," and held his head ready.

That one would-be suitor was old Gemp, and when he said it, poor Miss Heathery recoiled, clasping her hands tightly upon the mouth of the urn and closing it. She could not pour it there, and the love of Gemp had turned into a bitter hate.

If the curate in his disappointment would only have turned to her, she sighed to herself!

"Ah!"

And she went on thinking and working. What comforting fleecy undergarments she could have woven for him! What ornamental braces he should have worn; and, in the sanguine hopes of that swelling urn of sweets, she designed—she never began them—a set of slippers, a set of seven, all beautifully worked in wool and silks, and lined with velvet. Sunday: white with a gold sun; Monday: dominating with a pale lambent golden green, for it was moon's day; Tuesday puzzled her, for it took her into the Scandinavian mythology, and there she was lost hopelessly for a time, but she waded out with an idea that Tuisco was Mars, so the slippers should be red. The Wednesday slippers brought in Mercury, so they were silvery. Thursday was another puzzle till the happy idea came of crossing Thor's hammer, which would give the slippers quite a college look, black hammers on a red ground. Friday—Frèga, Venus—she would work a beauteous woman with golden hair on each. She felt rather doubtful about the woman's face; but love would find out the way. Then there was Saturday.

Just as she reached Saturday, she remembered having once heard that Sir Gordon had a set of razors for every day in the week, and the design halted.

Ah! if Sir Gordon would only have looked at her with that sad melancholy air of tenderness, how happy she could have been! How she would have prompted him to keep on that fight of his against time! But he never smiled upon her; and though she paid in all her little sums of money at the bank herself, and changed all her cheques, Mr James Thickens—as he was always called, to distinguish him from a Mr Thickens of whom some one had once heard somewhere—made no step in advance. The bank counter was always between them, and it was very broad.

"What could she do more to show her affection?" she asked herself. She had petitioned him to give her a "teeny weeny gold-fish, and a teeny weeny silver fish," and he had responded at once; but he was close in his ways: he was not generous. He did not purchase a glass globe of iridescent tints and goodly form; he borrowed a small milk tin at the dairy and sent them in that, with his compliments.

But there were the fish, and she purchased a beautiful globe herself, placed three Venus's ear-shells in the bottom, filled it with clear water from the river carefully strained through three thicknesses of flannel, and there the fish lived till they died.

Why they died so soon may have been from over-petting and too much food. For Miss Heathery secretly called the gold-fish James, and the silver fish Letitia, her own name, and she was never so happy as when feeding James and coaxing him to kiss the tips of her thin little fingers.

Perhaps it was from over-feeding, perhaps from too much salt, for as Miss Heathery, after long waiting, had to content herself with the chaste salutes of the gold-fish, dissolved pearls distilled from her sad eyes, and fell in the water like sporadic drops of rain.

Miss Heathery's spirit was low, and yet it kept leaping up strangely, for she had been at the bank one morning to change a cheque, and with the full intention of asking Mr James Thickens to present her with a couple more fish from the store of which she had heard so much, but which she had never seen.

That morning, as she noted how broad the pathway had grown from the forehead upwards, and had seen when he turned his back that it expanded into a circular walk round a bed of grizzle in the back of his crown, and was then continued to the nape, Mr James Thickens seemed to be extremely hard and cold. He looked certainly older too than he used; of that she was sure.

He seemed extremely abrupt and impatient with her when she wished him a sweet and pensive good-morning, which was as near a blessing upon his getting-bald head as the words would allow.

She said afterwards that it was a fine morning, a very fine morning, a fact that he did not deny, neither did he acknowledge, and so abstracted and strange did he seem that the gold-fish slipped out of her mind, and for a few moments she was agitated. She recovered though, and laying down a little bunch of violets beside her reticule, she went through her regular routine, received her change, and with a strange feeling of exultation at the artfulness of her procedure, she had reached the door after a most impressive "good-morning," for Miss Heathery always kept up the fiction of dining late, though she partook of her main meal at half-past one.

She had reached the door, when James Thickens spoke, his voice, the voice of her forlorn hope, thrilling her to the core. It was not a thrilling word, though it had that effect upon her, for it was only a summons—an arrest, a check, to her outward progress.

"Hi!"

That was all. "Hi!" but it did thrill her, and she stopped short with bounding pulses. It was abrupt, but still what of that! Gentlemen were not ladies; and if in their masterful, commanding way, they began their courtship by showing that they were the lords of women, why should she complain? He had only to order her to be his wife, and she was ready to become more—his very submissive slave.

She stopped, and, after a moment's hesitation, turned at that "Hi!" so full of hope to her thirsty soul. Her eyes were humid with pleasurable sensations, and but for that broad mahogany counter, she could have thrown herself at his feet. At that moment she was upon the dazzling pinnacle of joy; the next she was mentally sobbing despairingly in the vale of sorrow and despair into which she had fallen, for James Thickens said coldly:

"Here, you've left something behind."

Her violets! Her sweet offering that she had laid upon the altar behind which her idol always stood. That bunch was gathered by her own fingers, tied up with her own hands, incensed with kisses, made dewy with tears. It was the result of loving and painful thought followed by an inventive flash. It meant an easy confession of her love, and after laying it upon the mahogany altar, her sanguine imagination painted James Thickens lifting it, kissing it, holding it to his breast, searching among the leaves for the note which was not there; and, lastly, wearing it home in his button-hole, placing it in water for a time, and then keeping it dried yet fragrant in a book of poetry—the present of his love.

All that and more she had thought; and now James Thickens had called out, "Hi! you've left something behind."

She crept back to the counter, and said, "Thank you, Mr Thickens," in a piteous voice, her eyes beneath her veil too much blinded by the gathering tears to see Mr Trampleasure passing through the bank, though she heard his words, "Good-day, Miss Heathery," and bowed.

It was all over: James Thickens was not a man, he was a rhinoceros with an impenetrable hide; and, taking up her bunch of flowers, she was about to leave the bank when Thickens spoke again.

"Look here," he said, "I want to talk to you. Can't you ask me to tea?"

The place seemed to spin round, and the mahogany counter to heave and fall like a wave, as she tried to speak but could not for a few moments. Then she mastered her emotion, and in a hurried, trembling, half-hysterical voice, she chirped out:

"Yes; this evening, Mr Thickens, at six."

Volume Two—Chapter Three.

James Thickens Takes Tea.

"Rum little woman," said Thickens to himself as he hurried out of the bank. "Wonder whether she'd like another couple of fish."

Some men would have gone home to smarten up before visiting a lady to take tea, but James Thickens was not of that sort. His idea of smartness was always to look like a clean, dry, drab leaf, and he was invariably, whenever seen, at that point of perfection.

Punctually at six o'clock he rapped boldly at Miss Heathery's door, turning round to stare hard at Gemp, who came out eagerly to look and learn, before going in to have a fit—of temper, and then moving round to stare at Mrs Pinet's putty nose, rather a large one when flattened against the pane, as she strained to get a glimpse of such an unusual proceeding.

Several other neighbours had a look, and then the green door was opened. The visitor passed in and was ushered into the neat little parlour where the tea was spread, and Miss Heathery welcomed him, trembling with gentle emotion, and admiring the firmness, under such circumstances, of the animal man.

It was a delicious tea. There were Sally Lunns and toast biliously brimming in butter. Six spoonfuls of the best Bohea and Young Hyson were in the china pot. There was a new cottage loaf and a large pat of butter, with a raised cow grazing on a forest of parsley. There were thin slices of ham, and there were two glass dishes of preserve equal to that of which Mrs Luttrell was so proud; and then there was a cake from Frampton's at the corner, where they sold the Sally Lunns.

"I don't often get a tea like this, Miss Heathery," said Thickens, who was busy with his red and yellow bandanna handkerchief spread over his drab lap.

"I hope you are enjoying it," she said sweetly.

"Never enjoyed one more. Another cup, if you please, and I'll take a little more of that ham."

It was not a little that he took, and that qualifying adjective is of no value in describing the toast and Sally Lunns that he ate solidly and seriously, as if it were his duty to do justice to the meal.

And all the while poor Miss Heathery was only playing with her tea-cup and saucer. The only food of which she could partake was mental, and as she sat there dispensing her dainties and blushing with pleasure, she kept on thinking in a flutter of delight that all the neighbours would know Mr Thickens was taking tea with her, and be talking about this wicked, daring escapade on the part of a single lady.

He had not smiled, but he had seemed to be *so* contented, *so* happy, and he had asked her whether she worked that framed sampler on the wall, and the black cat with gold-thread eyes, and the embroidered cushion.

He had asked her if she liked poetry, and how long one of those rice-paper flowers took her to paint. He had admired, too, her poonah painting, and had at last sat back in his chair with one drab leg crossed over the other, and looking delightfully at home.

Still he didn't seem disposed to come to the point, and in the depth and subtlety of her cunning, Miss Heathery thought she would help him by leading the conversation towards matrimony.

"Dr and Mrs Luttrell seem to age very much," she said softly.

"Ah! they do," said Thickens tightening his lips and making a furrow across the lower part of his face. "Yes: trouble, ma'am, trouble."

"But they are a sweet couple, Mr Thickens."

"Models, madam, models," said the visitor, who became very thoughtful, and made a noise that sounded like "Soop!" as there was a pause, during which Mr Thickens took some tea.

"Have you seen Sir Gordon lately?" said Miss Heathery at last.

"No, madam. Back soon, though, I hope."

"Ah!" sighed Miss Heathery, "do you think he will ever—ahem! marry now?"

"Never, ma'am," said Thickens emphatically. "Too old."

"Oh, no, Mr Thickens."

"Oh, yes, Miss Heathery."

There was another pause.

"How beautiful Mrs Hallam grows! So pale, and sweet, and grave. She looks to me always, Mr Thickens, like some lovely lily. Dear Millicent, it seems only yesterday that she was married."

Thickens started and moved uneasily, sending a pang that must have had a jealous birth through Miss Heathery's breast.

"Seven years ago, Mr Thickens."

"Six years, eleven months, two weeks, ma'am."

"Ah, how exact you are, Mr Thickens!"

"Obliged to be, ma'am. Interest to calculate."

"But she looks thin, and not so happy as I could wish."

"Yes, ma'am. No, ma'am," said Thickens, paradoxically.

Again there was an uneasy change, for Mr Thickens's brow was puckered, and a couple of ridgy wrinkles ran across the top of his head.

"And they make such a handsome pair."

Thickens nodded and frowned, but became placid the next moment as his hostess said softly:

"That sweet child!"

"Hah! Yes! Bless her!—Hah! Yes! Bless her!—Hah! Yes! Bless her!"

Miss Heathery stared, for her guest fired these ejaculations and benedictions at intervals in a quick, eager way, smiling the while, and with his eyes brightening.

She stared more the next minute, and trembled as she heard her visitor's next utterance, and thought of a visit of his seven years ago when she was out, and which he had explained by saying that he had come to ask her if she would like a pair of gold-fish, that was all.

For all at once Mr Thickens exclaimed with his eyes glittering:

"If I had married I should have liked to have had a little girl like that."

There was a terrible pause here, terrible to only one though: and then, in a hesitating voice, Miss Heathery went on, with that word "marriage" buzzing in her ears, and making her feel giddy.

"Do you—do you think it's true, Mr Thickens?"

"What, that I never married?" he said sharply.

"No, no; oh, dear me, no!" cried Miss Heathery; "I mean that poor Mrs Hallam is terribly troubled about money matters, and that they are very much in debt?"

"Don't know, ma'am; can't say, ma'am; not my business, ma'am."

"But they say the doctor is terribly pinched for money too."

"Very likely, ma'am. Every one is sometimes."

"How dreadful!" exclaimed Miss Heathery.

"Very, ma'am. No: nothing more, thank you. Get these things taken away, I want to talk to you."

As the repast was cleared away, Miss Heathery felt that it was coming now, and as she grew more flushed, her head with its curls and great tortoise-shell comb trembled like a flower on its stalk. She got out her work, growing more and more agitated, but noticing that Thickens grew more cold and self-possessed.

"The way of a great man," she thought to herself as she felt that she had led up to what was coming, and that she had never before been so wicked and daring in the whole course of her life.

"It was the violets," she said to herself; and then she started, trembled more than ever, and felt quite faint, for James Thickens drew his chair a little nearer, spread his handkerchief carefully across his drab legs, and said suddenly:

"Now then, let's to business."

Business? Well yes, it was the great business of life, thought Miss Heathery, as she held her hands to her heart, ready to pour out the long pent-up sweetness with which it was charged.

"Look here, Miss Heathery," he went on, "I always liked you."

"Oh! Mr Thickens," she sighed, but she could not "look here" at the visitor, who was playing dumb tunes upon the red and lavender check table-cover, as if it were a harpsichord.

"I've always thought you were an extremely good little woman."

"At last," said Miss Heathery to herself.

"You've got a nice little bit of money in our bank, and also the deeds of this house."

"Don't—don't talk about money, Mr Thickens, please."

"Must," he said abruptly. "I'm a money man. Now look here, you live on your little income we have in the bank."

"Yes, Mr Thickens," sighed the lady.

"Ah! yes, of course. Then look here. Dinham's two houses are for sale next week."

"Yes; I saw the bill," she sighed.

"Let me buy them for you."

"Buy them? They would cost too much, Mr Thickens."

"Not they. You've got nearly enough, and the rest could stay on. They always let; dare say you could keep on the present tenants."

"But—"

That "but" meant that she would not have those excuses for going to the bank.

"You'll get good interest for your money then, ma'am, and you get little now."

"But, Mr Thickens—"

"I wish you to do it, ma'am, and I hope that you will."

"Oh! if you wish it, Mr Thickens, of course I will," she said eagerly.

"That's right; I do wish it. May I buy them for you?"

"Oh, certainly, Mr Thickens."

"All right, ma'am, then I will. Now I must get home and feed my fishes. Good evening."

He caught up his hat, shook hands, and was gone before his hostess had recovered from her surprise and chagrin.

"But never mind," she said, rubbing her hands and making two rings click.

The contact of those two rings made her gaze down and then take and fondle one particular finger, while, in spite of the abruptness of her visitor, she gazed down dreamily at that finger, and sighed as she sank into a reverie full of golden dreams.

"So odd and peculiar," she sighed; "but so different to any one else I ever knew; and, ah me! how shocking it all is: so many people must have seen him come."

Volume Two—Chapter Four.

Dr Luttrell's Troubles.

Dr Luttrell had taken a rake, and gone down the garden, according to his custom, and, as soon as he had left the house, Mrs Luttrell went to the window and watched him; after which, with a sorrowful face, she walked back into the drawing-room, to sit down and weep silently for a few minutes.

"It breaks my heart to see her poor sad face, and it's breaking his, though he's always laughing it off, and telling me it's all my nonsense. Oh, dear me! oh, dear me! How is it all to end?"

She sat rocking herself to and fro for a few minutes, and then jumped up hastily.

"It's dreadful, that it is!" she sighed; "but I can't stop here alone. Yes! I thought so!" she cried, as she went to the window, where she could catch sight of the doctor, rake in hand, but not using it, according to his wont, for he was resting upon it, and thinking deeply.

Mrs Luttrell snatched at a great grey ball of worsted and her needles, and went down the garden, making the doctor start as she reached his side.

"Eh? What is it?" he exclaimed. "Anything wrong at the Manor?"

"Wrong! what nonsense, dear!" said the old lady cheerily. "I'm sure, Joseph, you ought to take some medicine. You grow quite nervous!"

"What made you come, then?" he cried, beginning to use his rake busily.

"Why, I thought I'd come and chat while you worked, and—Joseph, my dear, don't—don't look like that!"

"It's of no use, old girl," said the doctor with a sigh; "we may just as well look it boldly in the face. I'm sick of all this make-believe."

"And so am I, dear. Let us be open."

"Ah, well! I will. Who is a man to be open to if not to his old wife?"

"There!" sobbed Mrs Luttrell, making a brave effort over herself, and speaking cheerfully. "I'm ready to face everything now."

"Even poverty, my dear?"

"Even poverty! What does it matter to us? Is it so very bad, dear?"

"It could not be worse. We must give up this house, and sell everything."

"But Hallam?"

"Is a scoundrel!—no, no! I won't say that of my child's husband. But I cannot get a shilling of him; and when I saw him yesterday, and threatened to go to Sir Gordon—"

"Well, dear?"

"He told me to go if I dared."

"And did you go?"

"Did I go, mother? Did I go?—with poor Milly's white face before my eyes, to denounce her husband as a cheat and a rogue! He has had every penny I possessed for his speculations, and they seem all to have failed."

"But you shouldn't have let him have it, dear!"

"Not let him have it, wife! How could I refuse my own son-in-law? Well, there, our savings are gone, and we must eat humble pie for the future. I have not much practice now, and I don't think my few patients will leave me because I live in a cottage."

"Do you think if I went and spoke to Robert it would do any good?"

"It would make our poor darling miserable. She would be sure to know. As it is, she believes her husband to be one of the best of men. Am I, her father, to be the one who destroys that faith? Hush, here is some one coming!"

For there was a quick, heavy step upon the gravel walk, and Christie Bayle appeared.

"I thought I should find you," he said, shaking hands warmly. "Well, doctor, how's the garden? Why, Mrs Luttrell, what black currants! There! you may call me exacting, but tithe, ma'am, tithe—I put in my claim at once for two pots of black currant jam. Those you gave me last year were invaluable."

Mrs Luttrell held his hand still, and laughed gently.

"Little bits of flattery for a very foolish old woman, my dear."

"Flattery! when I had such sore throats I could hardly speak, and yet had to preach! Not much flattery, eh, doctor?"

"Flattery! No, no," said the doctor, dreamily.

He glanced at Mrs Luttrell, then at Bayle, who went on chatting pleasantly about the garden, and then checked him suddenly.

"No one can hear us, Bayle. We want to talk to you—my wife and I."

"Certainly," said Bayle; and his tone and manner changed. "Is it anything I can do for you?"

"Wait a moment—let me think," said the doctor sadly. "Here, let's go and sit down under the yew hedge."

Bayle drew Mrs Luttrell's hand through his arm, and patted it gently, as she looked up tenderly in his face, a tenderness mingled with pride, as if she had part and parcel in the sturdy, manly Englishman who led her to the pleasant old rustic seat in a nook of the great, green, closely-clipped wall, with its glorious prospect away over the fair country side.

"I do love this old spot!" said Bayle, enthusiastically, for a glance at the doctor showed that he was nervous and hesitating, and he thought it well to give him time. "Mrs Luttrell, it is one of my sins that I cannot master envy. I always long for this old place and garden."

"Bayle!" cried the doctor, laying his hand upon the curate's knee, and with his former hesitancy chased away by an eager look, "are you in earnest?"

"In earnest, my dear sir? What about?"

"About—about the old place—the garden."

"Earnest!—yes. But I am going to fight it down," cried Bayle, laughing.

"Don't laugh, man. I am serious—things are serious with me."

"I was afraid so; but I dared not ask you. Come, come, Mrs Luttrell," he continued gently, "don't take it to heart. Troubles come to us all, and when they do there is their pleasant side, for then we learn the value of our friends, and I hope I am one."

"Friend, my dear!" said Mrs Luttrell, weeping gently, "I'm sure you have always seemed to me like a son. Do: pray do, Joseph, tell him all."

"Be patient, wife, and I will—all that I can."

The doctor paused and cleared his throat, while Mrs Luttrell sat with her hand in the curate's.

"You have set me thinking," said the doctor at last; "and what you said is like a ray of sunshine in my trouble."

"He's always saying things that are like rays of sunshine to us in our trouble, Joseph," said Mrs Luttrell, looking up through her tears at the earnest countenance at her side.

"Bayle, I shall have to lose the old place—the wife's old home, of which she is so proud—and my old garden. It's a bitter blow at my time of life, but it must come."

"I was afraid there was something very wrong," said Bayle; "but suppose we look the difficulties in the face. I'm a bit of a lawyer, you know, my dear doctor. Let's see what can be done. I want to be delicate in my offer, but I must be blunt. I am not a poor man, my wants are very simple, and I spend so little—let me clear this difficulty away. There, we will not bother Mrs Luttrell about money matters. Consider it settled."

"No," said the doctor firmly, "that will not do. I appreciate it all, my dear boy, truly; but there is only one way out of this difficulty—the old place must be sold."

"Oh, Joseph, Joseph!" sighed Mrs Luttrell, and the tears fell fast.

"It must be, wife," said the doctor firmly. "Bayle, after what you said, will you buy the old home? I could bear it better if it fell into your hands."

"Are you sure it must be sold?"

"There is no other way out of the difficulty, Bayle. Will you buy it?"

"If you tell me that there is certainly no other way out of the difficulty, and that it is your wish and Mrs Luttrell's, I will buy the place."

"Just as it stands—furniture—everything?"

"Just as it stands—furniture—everything."

"Ah!" ejaculated the doctor with a sigh of relief. "Thank God, Bayle!" he cried, shaking the curate's hand energetically. "I have not felt so much at rest for months. Now I want, you to tell me a little about the town—about the people. What do they say?"

"Say?"

"Yes: say about us—about Hallam—about Millicent, about our darling?"

"My dear doctor, I shall have to go and fetch old Gemp. He will point at game, and tell you more in half-an-hour than I shall be able to tell you in a year. Had we not better change the conversation?—here is Mrs Hallam with Julia."

As he spoke the garden gate clicked, and Millicent came into sight, with her child, the one grave and sad, the other all bright-eyed eagerness and excitement.

"There they are, mamma—in the yew seat!" And the child raced across the lawn, bounded over a flowerbed, and leaped upon the doctor's knee.

"Dear old grandpa!" she cried, throwing her arms round his neck and kissing him effusively, but only to leap down and climb on Mrs Luttrell's lap, clasping her neck, and laying her charming little face against the old lady's cheek. "Dear, sweet old grandma!" she cried.

Then, in all the excitement of her young life, she was down again to seize Bayle's hand.

"Come and get some fruit and flowers. We may, mayn't we, grandpa?"

"I'm sure we may," said Bayle, laughing, "only I must go."

"Oh!" cried the child pouting, "don't go, Mr Bayle! I do like being in the garden with you so very, very much!"

Mrs Hallam turned her sweet, grave face to him.

"Can you give her a few minutes? Julie will be so disappointed."

"There," cried Bayle merrily, "you see, doctor, what a little tyrant she grows! She makes every one her slave!"

"I don't!" said the child, pouting. "Mamma always says a run in the garden does me so much good, and it will do Mr Bayle good too. Thibs says he works too hard."

"Come along, then," he cried laughing; and the man seemed transformed, running off with the child to get a basket, while Millicent gazed after them, her countenance looking brighter, and the old people seemed to have forgotten their troubles, as they gazed smilingly after the pair.

"Bless her!" said Mrs Luttrell, swaying herself softly to and fro, and passing her hands along her knees.

"Yes, that's the way, Milly. Give her plenty of fresh air, and laugh at me and my tribe."

Then quite an eager conversation ensued, Mrs Hallam brightening up; and on both sides every allusion to trouble was, by a pious kind of deception, kept out of sight, Millicent Hallam being in the fond belief that her parents did not even suspect that she was not thoroughly happy, while they were right in thinking that their child was ignorant of the straits to which they had been brought.

"Why, we are quite gay this morning!" cried Mrs Luttrell; "or, no: perhaps he comes as a patient, he looks so serious. Ah, Sir Gordon, it is quite an age since you were here?"

"Yes, madam; I'm growing old and gouty, and—your servant, Mrs Hallam," he said, raising his hat. "Doctor, I wish I had your health. Ah, how peaceful and pleasant this garden looks! They told me—old Gemp told me—that I should find Bayle here. I called at his lodgings—bless my soul! how can a man with his income live in such a simple way! The woman said he was out visiting, and that old scoundrel said he was here. Egad! I believe the fellow lies in wait to hear everything. Eh? Ah, I'm right, I see!"

Just then there was a silvery burst of childish laughter, followed by a deep voice shouting, "Stop thief! stop thief!" Then there was a scampering of feet, and Julia came racing along, with her dark curls flying, and Christie Bayle in full pursuit, right up to the group by the yew hedge.

"She ran off with the basket!" cried Bayle. "Did you ever see—Ah, Sir Gordon!" he cried, holding out a currant-stained hand.

"Humph!" cried Sir Gordon grimly, raising his glass to his eye, and looking at the big, brown, fruit-stained fingers; "mighty clerical, 'pon my honour, sir! Who do you think is coming to listen to a parson on Sundays who spends his weeks racing about gardens after little girls? No, I'm not going to spoil my gloves; they're new."

"I—I don't think you ought to speak to—to Mr Bayle like that, Sir Gordon!" cried Mrs Luttrell, flushing and ruffling up like a hen. "If you only knew him as we do—"

"Oh, hush, mamma dear!" said Mrs Hallam, smiling tenderly, and laying her hand upon her mother's arm.

"Yes, my dear; but I cannot sit still and—"

"Know him, ma'am!" said Sir Gordon sharply. "Oh, I know him by heart; read him through and through! He was never meant for a parson; he's too rough!"

"Really, Sir Gordon, I—"

"Don't defend me, Mrs Luttrell," said Bayle merrily. "Sir Gordon doesn't like me, and he makes this excuse for not coming to hear me preach."

"Well, little dark eyes!" cried Sir Gordon, taking Julia's hand, and leading her to the seat. "Ah, that's better! I do get tired so soon, doctor. Well, little dark eyes!" he continued, after seating himself, and drawing the child between his knees, after which he drew a clean, highly-scented, cambric handkerchief from his breast pocket, and leaned forward. "Open your mouth, little one," he said.

Julia obeyed, parting her scarlet lips.

"Now put out your tongue."

"Is grandpa teaching you to be a doctor?" said the child innocently.

"No; but I wish he would, my dear," said Sir Gordon, "so that I could doctor one patient—myself. Out with your tongue."

The child obeyed, and the baronet gravely moistened his handkerchief thereon, and, taking the soft little chin in one gloved hand, carefully removed a tiny purple fruit-stain.

"That's better. Now you are fit to kiss." He bent down, and kissed the child slowly. "Don't like me much, do you, Julia?"

"I don't know," said the child, looking up at him with her large serious eyes. "Sometimes I do, when you don't talk crossly to me; but sometimes I don't. I don't like you half so well as I do Mr Bayle."

"But he's always setting you hard lessons, and puzzling your brains, isn't he?"

"No," said the child, shaking her head. "Oh, no! we have such fun over my lessons every morning! But I do like you too—a little."

"Come, that's a comfort!" said Sir Gordon, rising again. "There, I must go. I want to carry off Mr Bayle—on business."

Mrs Hallam glanced sharply from one to the other, and then, to conceal her agitation, bent down over her child, and began to smooth her tangled curls.

Volume Two—Chapter Five.

Sir Gordon Bourne Asks Questions.

"I want a few words with you, Bayle," said Sir Gordon, as the pair walked back towards the town.

"Shall we talk here, or will you come to my rooms?" and he indicated Mrs Pinet's house, to which he had moved when Hallam married.

"Your rooms! No, man; I never feel as if I can breathe in your stuffy lodgings. How can you exist in them?"

"I do, and very happily," said Bayle, laughing. "Shall we go to your private room at the bank?"

"Bless my soul! no, man!" cried Sir Gordon hastily. "The very last place. Let's get out in the fields, and talk there. More room, and no tattling, inquisitive people about. No Gemps."

"Very good," said Bayle, wondering, and very anxious at heart, for he knew the baronet's proclivities.

They turned off on to one of the footpaths, chatting upon indifferent matters, till all at once Sir Gordon exclaimed:

"'Pon my honour, I don't think I like you, Bayle."

"I'm very sorry, Sir Gordon, because I really do like you. I've always found you a true gentleman at heart, and—"

"Stuff, sir! Silence, sir! Egad, sir, will you hold your tongue? Talking such nonsense to a confirmed valetudinarian with a soured life, and—pish! I don't want to talk about myself. I was going to say that I did not like you."

"You did say so," replied the curate, smiling.

"Ah! well, it's the truth. Why do you stop here?"

"To annoy you, perhaps," said Bayle laughing. "Well, no: I like my people, and I'm vain enough to think I am able to do a little good."

"You do, Bayle, you do," said Sir Gordon, taking his arm and leaning upon him in a confidential way. "You're a good fellow, Bayle; and Castor here would miss you horribly, if you left."

"Oh, nonsense!"

"It is not nonsense, sir. Why, you do more good among the people in one year than I have done in all my life."

"Well, I think I have amerced you pretty well lately for my poor, Sir Gordon."

"Yes, man, but it was your doing. I shouldn't have given a shilling. But look here, I was going to say, why is it that I come to you, and make such a confidant of you?"

"Do you wish to confide something to me now?"

"Yes, of course; one can't go to one's solicitor, and I've no friends. Plenty of club acquaintances: but no friends. There, don't shake your head like that, man. Well, only a few. By-the-way, charming little girl that."

"What, little Julie?" cried Bayle, with his cheeks flushing with pleasure.

"Yes; and your prime favourite, I see. I don't like her, though. Too much of her father."

"She has his eyes and hair," said Bayle thoughtfully; "but there is the sweet grave look in her face that her mother used to wear when I first came to Castor."

"Hush! Silence! Hold your tongue!" cried Sir Gordon impatiently. "Look here—her father—I want to talk about him."

"About Mr Hallam?"

"Yes. What do you think of him now?"

Bayle laid his hand upon Sir Gordon's.

"We are old friends, Sir Gordon; I know your little secret; you know mine. Don't ask me that question."

"As a very old trusty friend I do ask you. Bayle, it is a duty. Look here, man; I hold an important trust in connection with that bank. I'm afraid I have not done my duty. It is irksome to me, a wealthy man, and I am so much away yachting. Let me see; you never have had dealings with us."

"No, Sir Gordon, never."

"Well, as I was saying, I am so much away. You are always feeling the pulses of the people. Now, as you are a great deal at Hallam's, tell me as a friend in a peculiar position, what do you think of Hallam?"

"Do you mean as a friend?"

"I mean as a business man, as our manager. What do the people say?"

"I cannot retail to you all their little tattle, Sir Gordon. Look here, sir, what do you mean? Speak out."

Sir Gordon grew red and was silent for a few minutes.

"I will be plain, Bayle," he said at last. "The fact is I am very uneasy."

"About Hallam?"

"Yes. He occupies a position of great trust."

"But surely Mr Trampleasure shares it."

"Trampleasure shares nothing. He's a mere dummy: a bank ornament. There, I don't say I suspect Hallam, but I cannot help seeing that he is living far beyond his means."

"But you have the books—the statements?"

"Yes; and everything is perfectly correct. I do know something about figures, and at our last audit there was not a penny wrong."

Bayle drew a breath full of relief.

"Every security, every deed was in its place, and the bank was never in a more prosperous state."

"Then of what do you complain?"

"That is what I do not know. All I know, Bayle, is that I am uneasy, and dissatisfied about him. Can you help me?"

"How can I help you?"

"Can you tell me something to set my mind at rest, and make me think that Hallam is a strictly honourable man, so that I can go off again yachting. I cannot exist away from the sea."

"I am afraid I can tell you nothing, Sir Gordon."

"Not from friend to friend?"

"I am the trusted friend of the Hallams'. I am free of their house. They have entrusted a great deal of the education of their child to me!"

"Well, tell me this. You know the people. What do they say of Hallam in the town?"

"I have never heard an unkind word respecting him unless from disappointed people, to whom, I suppose from want of confidence in their securities, he has refused loans."

"That's praising him," said Sir Gordon. "Do the people seem to trust him?"

"Oh! certainly."

"More praise. But do they approve of his way of living? Hasn't he a lot of debts in the town?"

Bayle was silent.

"Ah! that pinches. Well, now does not that seem strange?"

"I know nothing whatever of Mr Hallam's private affairs. He may perhaps have lost his own money, and his indebtedness be due to his endeavours to recoup himself."

"Yes," said Sir Gordon, dryly. "What a lovely day!"

"It is delightful," said the curate, with a sigh of relief, as they turned back.

"I was going to start to-morrow for a run up the Norway fiords."

"Indeed; so soon?"

"Yes," said Sir Gordon, dryly; "but I am not going now."

They parted at the entrance of the town, and directly after the curate became aware of the fact that old Gemp was looking at him very intently.

He forgot it the next moment as he entered his room, to be followed directly after by his landlady, who drew his attention to a note upon the chimney-piece in Thickens's formal, clerkly hand.

"One of the school children brought this, sir; and, begging your pardon," cried the woman, colouring indignantly, "if it isn't making too bold to ask such a thing of you, sir, don't you think you might say a few words next Sunday about Poll-prying, and asking questions?"

"Really," said Bayle, smiling; "I'm afraid it would be very much out of place, Mrs Pinet."

"Well, I'm sorry you say so, sir, for the way that Gemp goes on gets to be beyond bearing. He actually stopped that child, took the letter from him, read the direction, and then asked the boy who it was from, and whether he was to wait for an answer."

"Never mind, Mrs Pinet; it is very complimentary of Mr Gemp to take so much interest in my affairs."

"It made me feel quite popped, sir," cried the woman; "but of course it be no business of mine."

Bayle read the letter, and changed colour, as he connected it with Sir Gordon's questions, for it was a request that the curate would come up and see Thickens that evening on very particular business.

Volume Two—Chapter Six.

James Thickens Makes a Communication.

"Master's in the garden feeding his fish," said the girl, as she admitted Bayle. "I'll go and tell him you're here, sir."

"No; let me go to him," said Bayle quietly.

The girl led the way down a red-bricked floored passage, and opened a door, through which the visitor passed, and then stood looking at the scene before him.

There was not much garden, but James Thickens was proud of it, because it was his own. It was only a strip, divided into two beds by a narrow walk of red bricks—so many laid flat with others set on edge to keep the earth from falling over, and sullying the well-scrubbed path, which was so arranged by its master that the spigot of the rain-water butt could be turned on now and then and a birch broom brought into requisition to keep all clean.

Each bed was a mass of roses—dwarf roses that crept along the ground by the path, and then others that grew taller till the red brick wall on either side was reached, and this was clambered, surmounted, and almost completely hidden by clusters of small blossoms. No other flower grew in this patch of a garden; but, save in the very inclement weather, there were always buds and blossoms to be picked, and James Thickens was content.

From where Bayle stood he could just see Thickens at the hither side of the great bricked and cemented tank that extended across the bottom of his and the two adjoining gardens, while beyond was the steam-mill, where Mawson the miller had introduced that great power to work his machinery. He it was who had contrived the tank for some scheme in connection with the mill, and had then made some other plan after leading into it through a pipe the clear water of the dam on the other side of the mill, and arranging a proper exit when it should be too full. Then he had given it up as unnecessary, merely turning into it a steam-pipe, to get rid of the waste, and finally had let it to Thickens for his whim.

There was a certain prettiness about the place seen from the bank clerk's rose garden. Facing you was the quaintly-built mill, one mass of ivy from that point of view, while numberless strands ran riot along the stone edge of the tank, and hung down to kiss the water with their tips. To the left there was the great elder clump, that was a mass of creamy bloom in summer, and of clustering black berries in autumn, till the birds had cleared all off.

As Bayle stood looking down, he could see the bank clerk upon his knees, bending over the edge of the pool, and holding his fingers in the water.

Every now and then he took a few crumbs of broken well-boiled rice from a basin at his side, and scattered them over the pool, while, when he had done this, he held the tips of his fingers in the water.

He was so intent upon his task, that he did not hear the visitor's approach, so that when Bayle was close up, he could see the limpid water glowing with the bright scales of the golden-orange fish that were feeding eagerly in the soft evening light. Now quite a score of the brilliant metallic creatures would be making at the crumbs of rice. Then there would be as many—quite a little shoal—that were of a soft pearly silver, while mingled with them were others that seemed laced with sable velvet or purple bands.

The secret of the hand-dipping was plain too, for, as Thickens softly placed his fingers to the surface, first one and then another would swim up and seem to kiss the ends, taking therefrom some snack of rice, to dart away directly with a flourish of the tail which set the water all a ripple, and made it flash in the evening light.

Thickens was talking to his pets, calling them by many an endearing name as they swam up, kissed his finger tips, and darted away, till, becoming conscious of the presence of some one in the garden, he started to his feet, but stooped quickly again to pick up the basin, dip a little water, rinse out the vessel, and throw its contents far and wide.

"I did not hear you come, Mr Bayle," he said hastily.

"I ought to have spoken," replied the curate gravely. "How tame your fishes are!"

"Yes, sir, yes. They've got to know people from being petted so. Dip your fingers in the water and they'll come."

The visitor bent down and followed the example he had seen, with the result that fish after fish swam up, touched a white finger tip with its soft wet mouth, and then darted off.

"Strange pets, Mr Thickens, are they not?"

"Yes, sir, yes. But I like them," said Thickens with a droll sidewise look at his visitor. "You see the water's always gently warmed from the mill there, and that makes them thrive. They put one in mind of gold and silver, sir, and the bank. And they're nice companions: they don't talk."

He seemed then to have remembered something. A curious rigidity came over him, and though his visitor was disposed to linger by the pool where, in the evening light, the brightly-coloured fish glowed like dropped flakes of the sunset, Thickens drew back for him to pass, and then almost backed him into the house.

"Sit down, please, Mr Bayle," he said, rather huskily; and he placed a chair for his visitor. "You got my note, then?"

"Yes, and I came on. You want my—"

"Help and advice, sir; that's it. I'm in a cleft stick, sir—fast."

"I am sorry," said Bayle earnestly, for Thickens paused. "Is it anything serious?"

Thickens nodded, sat down astride a Windsor chair, holding tightly by the curved back, and rested his upper teeth on the top, tapping the wood gently.

Bayle waited a few moments for him to go on; but he only began rubbing at the top of the chair back, and stared at his visitor.

"You say it is serious, Mr Thickens."

"Terribly, sir."

"Is it—is it a monetary question?"

Thickens raised his head, nodded, and lowered it again till his teeth touched the chair back. "Some one in difficulties?"

Thickens nodded.

"Not you, Mr Thickens? You are too careful a man."

"No: not me, sir."

"Some friend?"

Thickens shook his head, and there was silence for a few moments, only broken by the dull sound of the clerk's teeth upon the chair.

"Do you want me to advance some money to a person in distress?"

Thickens raised his head quickly, and looked sharply in his visitor's eye; but only to lower his head again.

"No. No," he said.

"Then will you explain yourself?" said the curate gravely.

"Yes. Give me time. It's hard work. You don't know."

Bayle looked at him curiously, and waited for some minutes before Thickens spoke again.

"Yes," he said suddenly and as if his words were the result of deep thought; "yes, I'll tell you. I did think I wouldn't speak after all; but it's right, and I will. I can trust you, Mr Bayle?"

"I hope so, Mr Thickens."

"Yes, I can trust you. I used to think you were too young and boyish, but you're older much, and I didn't understand you then as I do now."

"I was very young when I first came, Mr Thickens," said Bayle smiling. "It was almost presumption for me to undertake such a duty. Well, what is your trouble?"

"Give me time, man; give me time," said Thickens fiercely. "You don't know what it is to be in my place. I am a confidential clerk, and it is like being torn up by the roots to have to speak as I want to speak."

"If it is a matter of confidence ought you to speak to me, Mr Thickens?" said Bayle gravely. "Do I understand you to say it is a bank matter?"

"That's it, sir."

"Then why not go to Mr Dixon?"

Thickens shook his head.

"Mr Trampleasure? or Sir Gordon Bourne?"

"They'll know soon enough," said Thickens grimly. A curious feeling of horror came over Bayle, as he heard these words, the cold, damp dew gathered on his brow, his hands felt moist, and his heart began to beat heavily.

He could not have told why this was, only that a vague sense of some terrible horror oppressed him. He felt that he was about to receive some blow, and that he was weak, unnerved, and unprepared for the shock, just when he required all his faculties to be at their strongest and best.

And yet the clerk had said so little—nothing that could be considered as leading up to the horror the hearer foresaw. All the same though, Bayle's imagination seized upon the few scant words—those few dry bones of utterance, clothed them with flesh, and made of them giants of terror before whose presence he shook and felt cowed.

"Tell me," he said at last, and his voice sounded strange to him, "tell me all."

There was another pause, and then Thickens, who looked singularly troubled and grey, sat up.

"Yes," he said, "I'll tell you all. I can trust you, Mr Bayle. I don't come to you because you are a priest, but because you are a man—a gentleman who will help me, and I want to do what's right."

"I know—I believe you do, Thickens," said the curate huskily, and he looked at him almost reproachfully, as if blaming him for the pain that he was about to give.

He felt all this. He could not have explained why, but as plainly as if he had been forewarned, he knew that some terrible blow was about to fall.

Thickens sat staring straight before him now, gnawing hard at one of his nails, and looking like a man having a hard struggle with himself.

It was a very plainly-furnished but pleasant little room, whose wide, low window had a broad sill upon which some half-dozen flowers bloomed, and just then, as the two men sat facing each other, the last glow of evening lit up the curate's troubled face, and left that of Thickens more and more in the shade.

"That's better," he said with a half laugh. "I wish I had left it till it was dark. Look here, Mr Bayle, I've been in trouble these five years past."

"You?"

"Yes, sir. I say it again: I've been in trouble these six or seven years past, and it's been a trouble that began like a little cloud as you'd say—no bigger than a man's hand; and it grew slowly bigger and bigger, till it's got to be a great, thick, black darkness, covering everything before the storm bursts."

"Don't talk riddles, man; speak out."

"Parables, Mr Bayle, sir, parables. Give me time, sir, give me time. You don't know what it is to a man who has trained himself from a boy to be close and keep secrets, to have to bring them out of himself and lay them all bare."

"I'll be patient; but you are torturing me. Go on."

"I felt it would, and that's one of the things that's kept me back, sir; but I'm going to speak now."

"Go on."

"Well, sir, a bank clerk is trained to be suspicious. Every new customer who comes to the place is an object of suspicion to a man like me. He may want to cheat us. Every cheque that's drawn is an object of suspicion because it may be a forgery, or the drawer may not have a balance to meet it. Then money—the number of bad coins I've detected, sir, would fill a big chest full of sham gold and silver, so that one grows to doubt and suspect every sovereign one handles. Then, sir, there's men in general, and even your own people. It's a bad life, sir, a bad life, a bank clerk's, for you grow at last so that you even begin to doubt yourself."

"Ah! but that is a morbid feeling, Thickens."

"No, sir, it's a true one. I've had such a fight as you couldn't believe, doubting myself and whether I was right: but I think I am."

"Well," said the curate, smiling a faint, dejected smile; "but you are still keeping me in the dark."

"It will be light directly," said Thickens fiercely, "light that is blinding. I dread almost to speak and let you hear."

"Go on, man; go on."

"I will, sir. Well, for years past I've been in doubt about our bank."

"Dixons', that every one trusts?"

"Yes, sir, that's it. Dixons' has been trusted by everybody. Dixons', after a hundred years' trial, has grown to be looked upon as the truth in commerce. It has been like a sort of money mill set going a hundred years ago, and once set going it has gone on of itself, always grinding coin."

"But you don't mean to tell me that the bank is unsafe? Man, man, it means ruin to hundreds of our friends!"

He spoke in an impassioned way, but at the same time he felt more himself; the vague horror had grown less.

"Hear me out, sir; hear me out," said Thickens slowly. "Years ago, sir, I began to doubt, and then I doubted myself, and then I doubted again, but even then I couldn't believe. Doubts are no use to a man like me, sir; he must have figures, and figures I couldn't get to prove it, sir. I must be able to balance a couple of pages, and then if the balance is on the wrong side there's something to go upon. It has taken years to get these figures, but I've got them now."

"Thickens, you are torturing me with this slow preamble."

"For a few minutes, sir," said the clerk pathetically, "for an hour. It has tortured me for years. Listen, sir. I began to doubt—not Dixons' stability, but something else."

The vague horror began to increase again, and Christie Bayle's hands grew more damp.

"I have saved a little money, and that and my writings were in the bank. I withdrew everything. Cowardly? Dishonest? Perhaps it was; but I doubted, sir, and it was my little all. Then you'll say, if I had these doubts I ought to have spoken. If I had been sure perhaps I might; but I tell you, sir, they were doubts. I couldn't be false to my friends though, and where here and there they've consulted me about their little bits of money I've found out investments for them, or advised them to buy house property. A clergyman for whom I changed a cheque one day, said it would be convenient for him to have a little banking account with Dixons', and I said if I had an account with a good bank in London I wouldn't change it. Never change your banker, I said."

"Yes, Thickens, you did," said the curate eagerly, "and I have followed your advice. But you are keeping me in suspense. Tell me, is there risk of Dixons' having to close their doors?"

"No, no, sir; it's not so bad as that. Old Mr Dixon is very rich, and he'd give his last penny to put things straight. Sir Gordon Bourne is an honourable gentleman—one who would sacrifice his fortune so that he might hold up his head. But things are bad, sir, bad; how bad I don't know."

"But, good heavens, man! your half-yearly balance-sheets—your books?"

"All kept right, sir, and wonderfully correct. Everything looks well in the books."

"Then how is it?"

"The securities, sir," said Thickens, with his lip quivering. "I've done a scoundrelly thing."

"You, Thickens? You? I thought you were as honest a man as ever trod this earth!"

"Me, sir?" said the clerk grimly. "Oh, no! oh, no! *I'm* a gambler, I am."

The vague horror was dissolving fast into thin mist. "You astound me!" cried Bayle, as he thought of Sir Gordon's doubts of Hallam. "You, in your position of trust! What are you going to do?"

The grim smile on James Thickens's lips grew more saturnine as he said:

"Make a clean breast of it, sir. That's why I sent for you."

"But, my good man!—oh, for heaven's sake! go with me at once to Sir Gordon and Mr Hallam. I ought not to listen to this alone."

"You're going to hear it all alone," said James Thickens, growing still more grim of aspect; "and when I've done you're going to give me your advice."

Bayle gazed at him sternly, but with the strange oppression gone, and the shadow of the vague horror fading into nothingness.

"I'm confessing to you, sir, just as if I were a Roman Catholic, and you were a priest."

"But I decline to receive your confession on such terms, James Thickens," cried Bayle sternly. "I warn you that, if you make me the recipient of your confidence, I must be free to lay the case before your employers."

"Yes, of course," said Thickens with the same grim smile. "Hear me out, Mr Bayle, sir. You'd never think it of me, who came regularly to church, and never missed—you'd never think I had false keys made to our safe; but I did. Two months ago, in London."

Bayle involuntarily drew back his chair, and Thickens laughed—a little hard, dry laugh.

"Don't be hard on the man, Mr Bayle, who advised you not to put your money and securities in at Dixons'."

"Go on, sir," said the curate sternly.

"Yes: I will go on!" cried Thickens, speaking now excitedly, in a low, harsh voice. "I can't carry on that nonsense. Look here, sir," he continued, shuffling his chair closer to his visitor, and getting hold of his sleeve, "you don't know our habits at the bank. Everything is locked up in our strong-room, and Hallam keeps the key of that, and carefully too! I go in and out there often, but it's always when he's in the room, and when he is not there he always locks it, so that, though I tried for years to get in there, I never had a chance."

"Wretched man!" cried Bayle, trying to shake off his grip, but Thickens's fingers closed upon his arm like a claw.

"Yes, I was wretched, and that's why I had the keys made, and altered again and again till I could get them to fit. Then one day I had my chance. Hallam went over to Lincoln, and I had a good examination of the different securities, shares, deeds—scrip of all kinds—that I had down on a paper, an abstract from my books."

"Well, sir?"

"Well, sir? Half of them are not there. They're dummies tied up and docketed."

"But the real deeds?"

"Pledged for advances in all sorts of quarters. Money raised upon them at a dozen banks, perhaps, in town."

"But—I don't understand you, Thickens; you do not mean that you—"

"That I, Mr Bayle!" cried the clerk passionately. "Shame upon you!—do you think I could be such a scoundrel—such a thief?"

"But these deeds, and this scrip, what are they all?"

"Valuable securities placed in Dixons' hands for safety."

"And they are gone?"

"To an enormous amount."

"But, tell me," panted Bayle, with the horror vague no longer, but seeming to have assumed form and substance, and to be crushing him down, "who has done this thing?"

"Who had the care of them, sir?"

"Thickens," cried Bayle, starting from his chair, and catching at the mantelpiece, for the room seemed to swim round, and he swept an ornament from the shelf, which fell with a crash, "Thickens, for heaven's sake, don't say that."

"I must say it, sir. What am I to do? I've doubted him for years."

"But the money—he has lived extravagantly; but, oh! it is impossible. It can't be much."

"Much, sir? It's fifty thousand pounds if it's a penny!"

"But, Thickens, it means felony, criminal prosecution, a trial."

He spoke hoarsely, and his hands were trembling. "It means transportation for one-and-twenty years, sir—perhaps for life."

Bayle's face was ashy, and with lips apart he stood gazing at the grim, quiet clerk.

"Man, man!" he cried at last; "it can't be true."

"Do you doubt too, sir? Well, it's natural. I used to, and I tried to doubt it; a hundred times over when I was going to be sure that he was a villain, I used to say to myself as I went and fed my fish, it's impossible, a man with a wife and child like—"

"Hush! for God's sake, hush!" cried Bayle passionately, and then with a burst of fury, he caught the clerk by the throat. "It is a lie; Robert Hallam could not be such a wretch as that!"

"Mr Bayle, sir," said Thickens calmly, and in an appealing tone; "can't you see now, sir, why I sent to you? Do you think I don't know how you loved that lady, and how much she and her bright little fairy of a child are to you? Why, sir, if it hadn't been for them I should have gone straight to Sir Gordon, and before now that scoundrel would have been in Lincoln jail."

"But you are mistaken, Thickens. Man, man, think what you are saying. Such a charge would break her heart, would brand that poor innocent child as the daughter of a felon. Oh, it cannot be!" he cried excitedly. "Heaven would not suffer such a wrong."

"I've been years proving it, sir; years," said Thickens slowly; "and until I was sure, I've been as silent as the dead. Fifty thousand pounds' worth of securities at least have been taken from that safe, and dummies filled up the spaces. Why, sir, a score of times people wanted these deeds, and he has put them off for a few days till he could go up to London, raise money on others, and get those wanted from the banker's hands."

"But you knew something of this, then?"

"Yes, I knew it, sir—that is, I suspected it. Until I got the keys made, I was not sure."

"Does—does any one else know of this?"

"Yes, sir."

"Ah!" ejaculated Bayle, with quite a moan.

"Robert Hallam, sir."

"Ah!" ejaculated Bayle, drawing a breath full of relief. "You have not told a soul?"

"No, sir. I said to myself there's that sweet lady and her little child; and that stopped me. I said to myself, I must go to the trustiest friend they have, sir, and that was you. Now, sir, I have told you all. The simple truth. What am I to do?"

Christie Bayle dropped into a chair, his eyes staring, his blanched face drawn, and his lips apart, as he conjured up the scene that must take place—the arrest, the wreck of Mrs Hallam's life, the suffering that would be her lot. And at last, half maddened, he started up, and stood with clenched hands gazing fiercely at the man who had fired this train.

"Well, sir," said Thickens coldly, "will you get them and the old people away before the exposure comes?"

"No," cried Bayle fiercely, "this must not—shall not be. It must be some mistake. Mr Hallam could not do such a wrong. Man, man, do you not see that such a charge would break his wife's heart?"

"It was in the hope that you would do something for them, sir, that I told you all this first."

"But we must see Mr Dixon and Sir Gordon at once."

"And they will—you know what."

"Hah! the matter must be hushed up. It would kill her!" cried Bayle incoherently. "Mr Thickens, you stand there like this man's judge; have you not made one mistake?"

Thickens shook his head and tightened his lips to a thin line.

"Do you not see what it would do? Have you no mercy?"

"Mr Bayle, sir," said Thickens slowly, "this has served you as it served me. It's so stunning that it takes you off your head. Am I, the servant of my good masters, knowing what I do, to hide this from them till the crash comes first—the crash that is only a matter of time? Do you advise—do you wish me to do this?"

Christie Bayle sat with his hands clasping his forehead, for the pain he suffered seemed greater than he could bear. He had known for long enough that Hallam was a harsh husband and a bad father; but it had never even entered his dreams that he was other than an honest man. And now he was asked to decide upon this momentous matter, when his decision must bring ruin, perhaps even death, to the woman he esteemed, and misery to the sweet, helpless child he had grown to love.

It was to him as if he were being exposed to some temptation, for even though his love for Millicent had long been dead, to live again in another form for her child, Christie Bayle would have gone through any suffering for her sake. As he bent down there the struggle was almost greater than he could bear.

And there for long he sat, crushed and stunned by the terrible stroke that had fallen upon him, and was about to fall upon the helpless wife and child. His mind seemed chaotic. His reasoning powers failed, and as he kept clinging to little scraps of hope, they seemed to be snatched away.

It was with a heart full of grief mingled with rage that he started to his feet at last, and faced Thickens, for the clerk had again spoken in measured tones. "Mr Bayle, what am I to do?"

The curate gazed at him piteously, as he essayed to speak; but the words seemed smothered as they struggled in his breast.

Then, by a supreme effort, he mastered his emotion, and drew himself up.

"Once more, sir, what am I to do?"

"Your duty," said Christie Bayle, and with throbbing brain he turned and left the house.

Volume Two—Chapter Seven.

Christie Bayle Changes his Mind.

"God help me! What shall I do?" groaned Christie Bayle, as he paced his room hour after hour into the night. A dozen times over he had been on the point of going to Thickens, awakening him and forcing him to declare that he would keep the fearful discovery a secret until something could be done.

"It is too horrible," he said. "Poor Millicent! The disgrace! It would kill her."

He went to the desk and began to examine his papers and his bank-book.

Then he relocked his desk and paced the room again. "Julie, my poor little child, too. The horror and disgrace to rest upon her little innocent head. Oh, it is too dreadful! Will morning never come?"

The hours glided slowly by, and that weary exclamation rose to his lips again and again:

"Will morning never come?"

It seemed as if it never would be day, but long before the first faint rays had streaked the east he had made his plans.

"It is for her sake; for her child's sake. At whatever cost, I must try and save them."

His first ideas were to go straight to Hallam's house; but such a course would have excited notice. He felt that Millicent would think it strange if he went there early. Time was of the greatest importance, but he felt that he must not be too hasty, so seated himself to try and calm the throbbings of his brain, and to make himself cool and judicial for the task he had in hand.

Soon after seven he walked quietly downstairs, and took his hat. It would excite no surprise, he thought, for him to be going for a morning walk, and, drawing in a long breath of the sweet refreshing air, he began to stride up the street.

"How bright and beautiful is thy earth, O God!" he murmured, as the delicious morning sunshine bathed his face, "and how we mar and destroy its beauties with our wretched scheming and plans! Ah! I must not feel like this," he muttered, as a restful hopefulness born of the early day seemed to be infusing itself throughout his being.

He had no occasion to check the feeling of content and rest, for he had not gone a dozen yards before the whole force of his position flashed upon him. He felt that he was a plotter against the prosperity of the town—that scores of the people whose homes he was passing were beginning the day in happy ignorance that perhaps the savings of a life were in jeopardy. Ought he not to warn them at once, and bid them save what they could out of the fire?

For his conscience smote him, asking him, how he, a clergyman, the preacher of truth and justice and innocence, could be going to temporise, almost to join in the fraud by what he was about to do?

"How can I meet my people after this?" he asked himself; and his face grew careworn and lined. The old reproach against him had passed away. No one could have called him young and boyish-looking now.

"Morning, sir," cried a harsh voice.

Bayle started, and flushed like some guilty creature, for he had come suddenly upon old Gemp as he supposed, though the reverse was really the case.

"Going for a walk, sir?" said Gemp, pointing at him, and scanning his face searchingly.

"Yes, Mr Gemp. Fine morning, is it not?"

Gemp stood shaving himself with one finger, as the curate passed on, and made a curious rasping noise as the rough finger passed over the stubble. Then he shook his head and began to follow slowly and at a long distance.

"I felt as if that man could read my very thoughts," said Bayle, as he went along the street, past the bank, and out into the north road that led towards the mill.

He shuddered as he passed Dixons', and pictured to himself what would happen if the doors were closed and an excited crowd of depositors were hungering for their money.

"It must be stopped at any cost," he muttered; and once more the sweet sad face of Millicent seemed to be looking into his for help.

"I ought to have suspected him before," he continued; "but how could I, when even Sir Gordon could see no wrong? Ha! Yes. Perhaps Thickens is mistaken after all. It may be, as he said, only suspicion."

His heart seemed like lead, though, the next moment, as he neared the clerk's house. Thickens was too just, too careful a man to have been wrong.

He stopped, and rapped with his knuckles at the door directly after, to find it opened by Thickens himself, and, as the clerk drew back, he passed in, ignorant of the fact that Gemp was shaving himself with his rough forefinger a hundred yards away, and saying to himself, "Which is it? Thickens going to marry skinny Heathery on the sly; or something wrong? I shan't be long before I know."

The brightness of the morning seemed to be shut out as the clerk closed the door, and followed his visitor into the sitting-room.

"Well, Mr Bayle," he said, for the curate was silent. "You've come to say something particular."

"Yes," said Bayle firmly. "Thickens, this exposure would be too horrible. It must not take place."

"Ah," said Thickens in his quiet, grave way, "you're the Hallams' friend."

"I hope I am the friend of every one in this town."

"And you advise me to keep this quiet and let your friends be robbed?"

"Silence, man! How dare you speak to me like that?" cried Bayle furiously, and he took a step in advance. "No, no," he said, checking himself, and holding out his hand; "we must be calm and sensible over this, Thickens. There must be no temper. Now listen. You remember what I said you must do last night."

"Yes; and *I'm* going directly after breakfast to Sir Gordon."

"No; I retract my words. You must not go."

"And the people who have been robbed?"

"Wait a few moments, Thickens," cried Bayle, flushing, as he saw that his hand was not taken. "Hear me out. You—yes, surely, you have some respect for Mrs Hallam—some love for her sweet child."

Thickens nodded.

"Think, then, man, of the horrible disgrace—the ruin that would follow your disclosures."

"Yes; it is very horrid, sir; but I must do my duty. You owned to it last night."

"Yes, man, yes; but surely there are times when we may try and avert some of the horrors that would fall upon the heads of the innocent and true."

"That don't sound like what a parson ought to say," said Thickens dryly.

Bayle flushed angrily again, but he kept down his wrath.

"James Thickens," he said coldly, "you mistake me."

"No," said Thickens, "you spoke out like a man last night. This morning, sir, you speak like Robert Hallam's friend."

"Yes; as his friend—as the friend of his wife; as one who loves his child. Now listen, Thickens. To what amount do you suppose Hallam is a defaulter?"

"How can I tell, sir? It is impossible to say. It can't be hushed up."

"It must, it shall be hushed up," said Bayle sternly. "Now, look here; I insist upon your keeping what you know quiet for the present."

Thickens shook his head.

"I did not tell you, but Sir Gordon suspects something to be wrong."

"Sir Gordon does, sir?"

"Yes; he consulted me about the matter."

"Then my course is easy," said Thickens brightening.

"Not so easy, perhaps, as you think," said Bayle coldly. "You must be silent till I have seen Hallam."

"Seen him, sir? Why, it's giving him warning to escape."

"Seen him and Sir Gordon, James Thickens. It would be a terrible scandal for Dixons' Bank if it were known, and utter ruin and disgrace for Hallam."

"Yes," said Thickens, "and he deserves it."

"We must not talk about our deserts, Thickens," said Bayle gravely. "Now listen to me. I find I can realise in a very few days the sum of twenty-four thousand pounds."

Thickens's eyes dilated.

"Whatever amount of that is needed, even to the whole, I am going to place in Robert Hallam's hands, to clear himself and redeem these securities, and then he must leave the town quietly, and in good repute."

"In good repute?"

"For his wife's sake, sir. Do you understand?"

"No," said Thickens quietly. "No man could understand such a sacrifice as that. You mean to say that you are going to give up your fortune—all you have—to save that gambling scoundrel from what he deserves?"

"Yes."

"But, Mr Bayle—"

"Silence! I have made my plans, sir. Now, Mr Thickens, you see that I am not going to defraud the customers of the bank, but to replace their deeds."

"God bless you, sir! I beg your pardon humbly. I'm a poor ignorant brute, with no head for anything but figures and—my fish. And just now I wouldn't take your hand. Mr Bayle, sir, will you forgive me?"

"Forgive! I honour you, Thickens, as a sterling, honest man—shake hands. There, now you know my plans."

"Oh yes, sir, I understand you!" cried Thickens; "but you must not do that, sir. You must not indeed!"

"I can do as I please with my own, Thickens. Save for my charities, money is of little use to me. There, now I must go. I shall see Hallam as soon as he is at the bank. I will not go to his house, for nothing must be done to excite suspicion. You will help me?"

Thickens hesitated.

"I ask it for Mrs Hallam's sake—for the sake of Doctor and Mrs Luttrell. Come, you will help me in this. You came to me for my advice last night. I have changed it during the past few hours. There, I have you on my side?"

"Yes, sir; but you must hold me free with Sir Gordon. Bah! no; I'll take my chance, sir. Yes: I'll help you as you wish."

"I trust you will, Thickens," said Bayle quietly.

"And you are determined, sir?—your fortune—all you have?"

"I am determined. I shall see you at the bank about ten."

Volume Two—Chapter Eight.

Brought to Book.

"He—he—he—he—he! how cunning they do think themselves! What jolly owd orstridges they are!" chuckled old Gemp, as he saw Bayle leave the clerk's house, and return home to his breakfast. "Dear me! dear me! to think of James Thickens marrying that old maid! Ah well! Of course, he didn't go to her house for nothing!"

He was in the street, again, about ten, when the curate came out, and, as soon as he saw him, Gemp doubled down one of the side lanes to get round to the church, and secure a good place.

"They won't know in the town till it's over," he chuckled. "Sly trick! He—he—he!"

The old fellow hurried round into the churchyard, getting before Bayle, as he thought, and posting himself where he could meet the curate coming in at the gate, and give him a look which should mean, "Ah! you can't get over me!"

An observer would have found old Gemp's countenance a study, as he stood there, waiting for Bayle to come, and meaning afterwards to stay and see Thickens and Miss Heathery come in. But from where he stood he could see the bank, and, to his surprise, he saw James Thickens come out on the step, and directly after the curate went up to him, and they entered the place together.

Gemp's countenance lengthened, and he began shaving himself directly, his eyes falling upon one of the mouldering old tombstones, upon which he involuntarily read:

"Lay not up for yourselves treasure—" The rest had mouldered away.

"Where thieves break through and steal," cried Gemp, whose jaw dropped. "They're a consulting—parson and Sir Gordon—parson and Thickens twiced—parson at the bank—Hallam up to his eyes in debt!"

He reeled, so strong was his emotion, but he recovered himself directly.

"My deeds! my money!" he gasped, "my—"

He could utter no more, for a strange giddiness assailed him, and after clutching for a moment in the air, he fell down in a fit.

"Yes, he's in his room, sir," said Thickens, meeting Bayle at the bank door. "I'll tell him you are here."

Hallam required no telling. He had seen Bayle come up, and he appeared at the door of his room so calm and cool that his visitor felt a moment's hesitation.

"Want to see me, Bayle? Business? Come in."

The door closed behind the curate, and James Thickens screwed his face into wrinkles, and buttoned his coat up to the last button, as he seated himself upon his stool.

"Well, what can I do for you, Bayle?" said Hallam, seating himself at his table, after placing a chair for his visitor, which was not taken.

Bayle did not answer, but stood gazing down at the smooth, handsome-looking man, with his artificial smile and easy manner; and it seemed as if the events of the past few years—since he came, so young and inexperienced, to the town— —were flitting by him.

"A little money?—a little accommodation?" said Hallam, as his visitor did not speak.

Could Thickens be wrong? No: impossible. Too many little things, that had seemed unimportant before, now grew to a vast significance, and Bayle cast aside his hesitancy, and, taking a step forward, laid his hand upon the table.

"Robert Hallam!" he said, in a low, deep voice, full of emotion, "are you aware of your position—how you stand?"

The manager started slightly, but the spasm passed in a moment, and he said calmly, with a smile:

"My position? How I stand? I do not comprehend you! My dear Bayle, what do you mean?" The curate gazed in his eyes, a calm, firm, judicial look in his countenance; but Hallam did not flinch. And again the idea flashed across the visitor's mind, "Suppose Thickens should be wrong!"

Again, though, he cast off his hesitation, and spoke out firmly.

"Let me be plain with you, Robert Hallam, and show you the precipice upon whose edge you stand."

"Good heavens, Mr Bayle, are you ill?" said Hallam in the coolest manner.

"Yes; sick at heart, to find of what treachery to employers, to wife and child, a man like you can be guilty. Hallam, your great sin is discovered! What have you to say?"

"Say!" cried Hallam, laughing scornfully, "say, in words that you use so often, 'Who made you a ruler and a judge?' What do you mean?"

"I came neither as ruler nor judge, but as the friend of your wife and child. There—as your friend. Man, it is of no use to dissimulate!"

"Dissimulate, sir!"

"Am I to be plainer?" cried Bayle angrily, "and tell you that but for my interposition James Thickens would at this moment be with Sir Gordon and Mr Dixon, exposing your rascality."

"My rascality! How dare—"

"Dare!" cried Bayle sternly. "Cast off this contemptible mask, and be frank. Do I not tell you I come as a friend?"

"Then explain yourself."

"I will," said Bayle; and for a few minutes there was a silence almost appalling. The clock upon the mantelpiece ticked loudly; the stool upon which James Thickens sat in the outer office gave a loud scroop; and a large bluebottle fly shut in the room beat itself heavily against the panes in its efforts to escape.

Bayle was alternately flushed and pale. Hallam, perfectly calm, paler than usual, but beyond seeming hurt and annoyed, there was nothing to indicate the truth of the terrible charge being brought against him.

"Well, sir," he said at last, "why do you not speak?"

Bayle gazed at him wonderingly, for all thought of his innocence had passed away.

"I will speak, Hallam," he said. "Tell me the amount for which the deeds you have abstracted from that safe are pledged."

"The deeds I have abstracted from that safe?" said Hallam, rising slowly, and standing at his full height, with his head thrown back.

"Yes; and in whose place you have installed forgeries, dummies—imitations, if you will."

That blow was too straight—too heavy to be resisted. Hallam dropped back in his chair; while James Thickens, at his desk behind the bank counter, heard the shock, and then fidgeted in his seat, and rubbed his right ear, as he heard Hallam speak of him in a low voice, and say hoarsely:

"Thickens, then, has told you this?"

"Yes," said Bayle in a lower tone. "He came to me for advice, and I bade him do his duty."

"Hah!" said Hallam, and his eyes wandered about the room.

"This morning I begged him to wait."

"Hah!" ejaculated Hallam again, and now there was a sharp twitching about his closely-shaven lips. "And you said that you came as our friend?"

"I did."

"What do you mean?"

Bayle waited for a few moments, and then said slowly: "If you will redeem those deeds with which you have been entrusted, and go from here, and commence a new career of honesty, I will, for your wife and child's sake, find the necessary money."

"You will? You will do this, Bayle?" cried Hallam, extending his hands, which were not taken.

"I have told you I will," said Bayle coldly. "But—the amount?"

"How many thousands are they pledged for?—to some bank, of course?"

"It was to cover an unfortunate speculation. I—"

"I do not ask you for explanations," said Bayle coldly. "What amount will clear your defalcations?"

"Twenty to twenty-one thousand," said Hallam, watching the effect of his words.

"I will find the money within a week," said Bayle.

"Then all will be kept quiet?"

"Sir Gordon must be told."

"No, no; there is no need of that. The affairs will be put straight, and matters can go on as before. It was an accident; I could not help it. Stop, man, what are you going to do?"

"Call in Mr Thickens," said Bayle.

"To expose and degrade me in his eyes!"

Bayle turned upon him a withering contemptuous look.

"I expose you? Why, man, but for me you would have been in the hands of the officers by now. Mr Thickens!"

Thickens got slowly down from his stool and entered the manager's room, where Hallam met his eye with a look that made the clerk think of what would have been his chances of life had opportunity served for him to be silenced for ever.

"I have promised Mr Hallam to find twenty-one thousand pounds within a week—to enable him to redeem the securities he has pledged."

"And under these circumstances, Mr Thickens, there is no need for this trouble to be exposed."

"Not to the public perhaps," said Thickens slowly, "but Sir Gordon and Mr Dixon ought to know."

"No, no," cried Hallam, "there is no need. Don't you see, man, that the money will be made right?"

"No, sir, I only see one thing," said Thickens sturdily, "and that is that I have my duty to do."

"But you will ruin me, Thickens."

"You've ruined yourself, Mr Hallam; I've waited too long."

"Stop, Mr Thickens," said Bayle. "I pay this heavy sum of money to save Mr Hallam from utter ruin. The bank will be the gainer by twenty thousand pounds."

"Twenty-one thousand you offered, sir," said Thickens.

"Exactly. More if it is needed. If you expose this terrible affair to Sir Gordon and Mr Dixon they may feel it their duty to hand Mr Hallam over to the hands of justice. He must be saved from that."

"What can I do, sir? There, then," said Thickens, "since you put it so I will keep to it, but only on one condition."

"And what is that?"

"Mr Hallam must go away from the bank and leave all keys with me and Mr Trampleasure."

"But what excuse am I to make?" said Hallam huskily.

"I don't think you want teaching how to stop at home for a few days, Mr Hallam," said Thickens sternly; "you can be ill for a little while. It will not be the first time."

"I will agree to anything," said Hallam excitedly, "only save me from that other horror. Bayle, for our old friendship's sake, for the sake of my poor wife and child, save me from that."

"Am I not fighting to save you for their sake?" said Bayle bitterly. "Do you suppose that I am as conscienceless as yourself, and that I do not feel how despicable, how dishonest a part I am playing in hindering James Thickens from exposing your rascality? There, enough of this: let us bring this terribly painful meeting, with its miserable subterfuges, to an end. Thickens is right; you must leave this building at once and not enter it again. He must take all in charge until your successor is found."

"As you will," said Hallam, humbly. "There are the keys, Thickens, and I am really ill. When Mr Bayle brings the money I will help in every way I can. There."

Bayle hesitated a moment, and then mastered his dislike. "Come," he said to Hallam, "there must be no whisper of this trouble in the town. I will walk down with you to your house."

"As my gaoler?" said Hallam with a sneer.

"As another proof of what I am ready to sacrifice to save you," said Bayle. He walked with him as far as his door.

"Stop a moment," said Hallam in a whisper. "You will do this for me, Bayle?"

"I have told you I would," replied the curate coldly. "And at once?"

"At once."

"You will have to bring me the money. No, you must go up to town with me, and we can redeem the papers. It will be better so."

"As you will," said Bayle. "I have told you that I will help you, will put myself at your service. I will let you know when I can be ready. Rest assured I shall waste no time in removing as much of this shadow as I can from above their heads."

He met Hallam's eyes as he spoke, just as the latter had been furtively Measuring, as it were, his height and strength, and then they parted.

End of Volume One.

Volume Two—Chapter Nine.

A Few Words on Love.

"What has papa been doing in the lumber-room, mamma?" asked Julia that same evening.

"Examining some of the old furniture there, my dear," said Millicent, looking up with a smile. "I think he is going to have it turned into a play-room for you."

"Oh!" said Julia indifferently; and she turned her thoughtful little face away, while her mother rose with the careworn look that so often sat there, giving place to the happy, maternal smile that came whenever she was alone with her child.

"Why, Julie darling, you seem so quiet and dull to-night. Your little head is hot. You are not unwell, dear?"

She knelt down beside the child, and drew the soft little head to her shoulder, and laid her cheek to the burning forehead.

"That is nice," said the child, with a sigh of content. "Oh! mamma, it does do me so much good. My head doesn't ache now."

"And did it ache before?"

"Yes, a little," said the child thoughtfully, and turning up her face, she kissed the sweet countenance that was by her side again and again. "I do love you so, mamma."

"Why of course you do, my dear."

"I don't think I love papa."

"Julie!" cried Millicent, starting from her as if she had been stung. "Oh I my child, my child," she continued, with passionate energy, "if you only knew how that hurts me. My darling, you do—you do love him more than you love me."

Julia shook her head and gazed back full in her mother's eyes, as Millicent held her back at arm's length, and then caught her to her breast, sobbing wildly.

"*I* do try to love him, mamma," said the child, speaking quickly, in a half-frightened tone; "but when I put my arms round his neck and kiss him he pushes me away. I don't think he loves me; he seems so cross with me. But if it makes you cry, I'm going to try and love him ever so much. There."

She kissed her mother with all a child's effusion, and nestled close to her.

"He does love you, my darling," said Millicent, holding the child tightly to her, "as dearly as he loves me, and *I'm* going to tell you why papa looks so serious sometimes. It is because he has so many business cares and troubles."

"But why does papa have so many business cares and troubles?" said the child, throwing back her head, and beginning to toy with her mother's hair.

"Because he has to think about making money, and saving, so as to render us independent, my darling. It is because he loves us both that he works so hard and is so serious."

"I wish he would not," said the child. "I wish he would love me ever so instead, like Mr Bayle does. Mamma, why has not Mr Bayle been here to-day?"

"I don't know, my child; he has been away perhaps."

"But he did walk to the door with papa, and then did not come in."

"Maybe he is busy, my dear."

"Oh! I do wish people would not be busy," said the child pettishly, "it makes them so disagreeable. Thibs is always being busy, and then oh! she is so cross."

"Why, Julie, you want people always to be laughing and playing with you."

"No, no, mamma, I like to work sometimes—with Mr Bayle and learn, and so I do like the lessons I learn with you. You never look cross at me, and Mr Bayle never does."

"But, my darling, the world could not go on if people were never serious. Why, the sun does not always shine: there are clouds over it sometimes."

"But it's always shining behind the clouds, Mr Bayle says."

"And so is papa's love for his darling shining behind the clouds—the serious looks that come upon his face," cried Millicent. "There, you must remember that."

"Yes," said the child, nodding, and drawing two clusters of curls away from her mother's face to look up at it laughingly and then kiss her again and again. "Oh! how pretty you are, mamma! I never saw any one with a face like yours."

"Silence, little nonsense talker," cried Millicent, with her face all happy smiles and the old look of her unmarried life coming back as she returned the child's caresses.

"I never did," continued Julia, tracing the outlines of the countenance that bent over her, with one rosy finger. "Grandma's is very, very nice, and I like grandpa's face, but it is very rough. Mamma!"

"Well, my darling."

"Does papa love you very, very much?"

"Very, very much, my darling," said her mother proudly.

"And do you love him very, very much?"

"Heaven only knows how dearly," said Millicent in a deep, low voice that came from her heart.

"But does papa know too?"

"Why, of course, my darling."

"I wish he would not say such cross things to you sometimes."

"Yes, we both wish he had not so much trouble. Why, what a little babbler it is to-night! Have you any more questions to ask before we go up and fetch papa down and play to him?"

"Don't go yet," cried the child. "I like to talk to you this way, it's so nice. I say, mamma, do people get married because they love one another?"

"Hush, hush! what next?" said Millicent smiling, as she laid her hand upon the child's lips. "Of course, of course."

Julie caught the hand in hers, kissed it, and held it fast.

"Why does not Mr Bayle love some one?"

A curious, fixed look came over Millicent's face, and she gazed down at her babbling child in a half-frightened way.

"He will some day," she said at last.

"No, he won't," said the child, shaking her head and looking very wise.

"Why, what nonsense is this, Julie?"

"I asked him one day when we were sitting out in the woods, and he looked at me almost like papa does, and then he jumped up and laughed, and called me a little chatterer, and made me run till I was out of breath. But I asked him, though."

"You asked him?"

"Yes; I asked him if he would marry a beautiful lady some day, as beautiful as you are, and he took me in his arms and kissed me, and said that he never should, because he had got a little girl to love—he meant me. And oh! here's papa: let's tell him. No, I don't think I will. I don't think he likes Mr Bayle."

Millicent rose from her knees as Hallam entered the room, looking haggard and frowning. He glanced from one to the other, and then caught sight of himself in the glass, and saw that there was a patch as of lime or mortar upon his coat.

He brushed it off quickly, being always scrupulously particular about his clothes, and then came towards them.

"Send that child away," he said harshly. "I want to be quiet."

Millicent bent down smiling over the child and kissed her.

"Go to Thisbe now, my darling," she whispered; "but say good-night first to papa, and then you will not have to come to him again. Perhaps he may be out."

The child's face became grave with a gravity beyond its years. It was the mother's young face repeated, with Hallam's dark hair and eyes.

She advanced to him, timidly putting out her hand, and bending forward with that sweetly innocent look of a child ready so trustingly to give itself into your arms as it asks for a caress.

"Good-night, papa dear," she cried in her little silvery voice.

"Good-night, Julie, good-night," he said abruptly; and he just patted her head, and was turning away, when he caught sight of the disappointed, troubled look coming over her countenance, paused half wonderingly, and then bent down and extended his hands to her.

There was a quick hysteric cry, a passionate sob or two, and the child bounded into his arms, flung her arms round his neck, and kissed him, his lips, his cheeks, his eyes again and again, in a quick, excited manner.

Hallam's countenance wore a look of half-contemptuous doubt for a moment, as he glanced at his wife, and then the good that was in him mastered the ill. His face flushed, a spasm twitched it, and clasping his child to his breast, he held her there for a few moments, then kissed her tenderly, and set her down, her hair tumbled, her eyes wet, but her sweet countenance irradiated with joy, as, clasping her hands, she cried out:

"Papa loves—he loves me, he loves me! I am so happy now."

Then half mad with childish joy, she turned, kissed her hands to both, and bounded out of the room.

Volume Two—Chapter Ten.

Husband and Wife.

There was a momentary silence, and then as the door closed, Millicent laid her hands upon her husband's shoulders, and gazed tenderly in his face.

"Robert, my own!" she whispered.

No more; her eyes bespoke the mother's joy at this breaking down of the ice between father and daughter. Then a look of surprise and pain came into those loving eyes, for Hallam repulsed her rudely.

"It is your doing, yours, and that cursed parson's work. The child has been taught to hate me. Curse him! He has been my enemy from the very first."

"Robert—husband! Oh, take back those words!" cried Millicent, throwing herself upon his breast. "You cannot mean it. You know I love you too well for that. How could you say it!"

She clung to him for a few moments, gazing wildly in his face, and then she seemed to read it plainly.

"No, no, don't speak," she cried tenderly. "I can see it all. You are in some great trouble, dear, or you would not have spoken like that. Robert, husband, I am your own wife; I have never pressed you for your confidence in all these money troubles you have borne; but now that something very grave has happened, let me share the load."

She pressed him back gently to a chair, and, overcome by her earnest love, he yielded and sank back slowly into the seat. The next instant she was at his knees, holding his hands to her throbbing breast.

"No, I don't mean what I said," he muttered, with some show of tenderness; and a loving smile dawned upon Millicent's careworn face.

"Don't speak of that," she said. "It was only born of the trouble you are in. Let me help you, dear; let me share your sorrow with you. If only with my sympathy there may be some comfort."

He did not answer, but sat gazing straight before him.

"Tell me, dear. Is it some money trouble? Some speculation has failed?"

He nodded.

"Then why not set all those ambitious thoughts aside, dear husband?" she said, nestling to him. "Give up everything, and let us begin again. With the love of my husband and my child, what have I to wish for? Robert, we love you so dearly. You, and not the money you can make, are all the world to us."

He looked at her suspiciously, for there was not room in his narrow mind for full faith in so much devotion. It was more than he could understand, but his manner was softer than it had been of late, as he said:

"You do not understand such things."

"Then teach me," she said smiling. "I will be so apt a pupil. I shall be working to free my husband from the toils and troubles in which he is ensnared."

He shook his head.

"What, still keeping me out of your heart, Rob!" she whispered, with her eyes beaming love and devotion. Then, half-playfully and with a tremor in her voice, "Robert, my own brave lion amongst men, refuse the aid of the weak mouse who would gnaw the net?"

"Pish, you talk like a child," he cried contemptuously. "Net, indeed!" and in his insensate rage, he piled his hatred upon the man who had stepped in to save him. "But for that cursed fellow, Bayle, this would not have happened."

"Robert, darling, you mistake him. You do not know his heart. How true he is! If he has gone against you in some business matter, it is because he is conscientious and believes you wrong."

"And you side with him, and believe too?"

"I?" she cried proudly. "You are my husband, and whatever may be your trouble, I stand with you against the world."

"Brave girl!" he cried warmly; "now you speak like a true woman. I will trust you, and you shall help me. I did not think you had it in you, Milly. That's better."

"Then you will trust me?"

"Yes," he said, raising one hand to his face, and beginning nervously to bite his nails. "I will trust you; perhaps you can help me out of this cursed trap."

"Yes, I will," she cried. "I feel that I can. Oh, Robert, let it be always thus in the future. Treat me as your partner, your inferior in brain and power, but still your helpmate. I will toil so hard to make myself worthy of my husband. Now tell me everything. Stop! I know," she cried; "it is something connected with the visits of that Mr Crellock, that man you helped in his difficulties years ago."

"I helped? Who told you that?"

She smiled.

"Ah! these things are so talked of. Mrs Pinet told Miss Heathery, and she came and told me. I felt so proud of you, dear, for your unselfish behaviour towards this man. Do you suppose I forget his coming on our wedding-day, and how troubled you were till you had sent him away by the coach?"

"You said nothing?"

"Said nothing? Was I ever one to pry into my husband's business matters? I said to myself that I would wait till he thought me old enough in years, clever enough in wisdom, to be trusted. And now, after this long probation, you will trust me, love?"

He nodded.

"And your troubles shall grow less by being shared. Now tell me I am right about it. Your worry is due to this Mr Crellock?"

"Yes," he said in a low voice.

"I knew it," she cried. "You have always been troubled when he came down, and when you went up to town. I knew as well as if you had told me that you had seen him when you went up. There was always the same harassed, careworn look in your eyes; and Robert, darling, if you had known how it has made me suffer, you would have come to me for consolation, if not for help."

"Ah! yes, perhaps."

"Now go on," she said firmly, and rising from her place by his knees, she took a chair and drew it near him.

"There," she said smiling; "you shall see how business-like I will be."

He sat with his brow knit for a few minutes, and then drew a long breath.

"You are right," he said. "Stephen Crellock is mixed up with it. You shall know all. And mind this, whatever people may say—"

"Whatever people may say!" she exclaimed contemptuously.

"I am innocent; my hands are clean."

"As if I needed telling that," she said with a proud smile. "Now I am waiting, tell me all."

"Oh, there is little to tell," he said quickly. "That fellow Crellock, by his plausible baits, has led me into all kinds of speculations."

"I thought so," she said to herself.

"I failed in one, and then he tempted me to try another to cover my loss; and so it went on and on, till—"

"Till what?" she said with her eyes dilating; and a chill feeling of horror which startled her began to creep to her heart.

"Till the losses were so great that large sums of money were necessary, and—"

"Robert!"

"Don't look at me in that way, Milly," he said, with a half-laugh, "you are not going to begin by distrusting me?"

"No, no," she panted.

"Well, till large sums were necessary, and the scoundrel literally forced me to raise money from the bank."

She felt the evil increasing; but she forced it away with the warm glow of her love.

"I've been worried to death," he continued, "to put these things straight, and it is this that has kept me so poor."

"Yes, I see," she cried. "Oh, Robert, how you must have suffered!"

"Ah! Yes! I have," he said; "but never mind that. Well, I was getting things straight as fast as I could; and all would now have been right again had not Bayle and his miserable jackal, Thickens, scented out the trouble, and they have seized me by the throat."

"But, Robert, why not clear yourself? Why not go to Sir Gordon? He would help you."

"Sir Gordon does not like me. But there, I have a few days to turn myself round in, and then all will come right; but if—"

He stopped, and looked rather curiously.

"Yes?" she said, laying her hand in his.

"If my enemies should triumph. If Bayle—"

"If Mr Bayle—"

"Silence!" he said. "I have told you that this man is my cruel enemy. He has never forgiven me for robbing him of you."

"You did not rob him," she said tenderly. "But are you not mistaken in Mr Bayle?"

"You are, in your sweet womanly innocency and trustfulness. I tell you he is my enemy, and trying to hound me down."

"Let me speak to him."

"I forbid it," he cried fiercely. "Choose your part. Are you with me or the men whom I know to be my enemies? Will you stand by me whatever happens?"

"You know," she said, with a trustful smile in her eyes.

"That's my brave wife," he said. "This is better. If my enemies do get the better of me—if, for Crellock's faults, charges are brought against me—if I am by necessity forced to yield, and think it better to go right away from here for a time—suddenly—will you come?"

"And leave my mother and father?"

"Are not a husband's claims stronger? Tell me, will you go with me?"

"To the world's end, Robert," she cried, rising and throwing her arms about his neck. "I am glad that this trouble has come."

"Glad?"

"Yes, for it has taught you at last the strength of your wife's love."

He drew her to his heart, and kissed her, and there she clung for a time.

"Now listen," he said, putting her from him. "We must be business-like."

"Yes," she said firmly.

"The old people must not have the least suspicion that we have any idea of leaving."

"Might I not bid them good-bye?"

"No. That is, if we left. We may not have to go. If we do, it must be suddenly."

"And in the meantime?"

"You must wait."

Just then the door opened, and Thisbe appeared.

"There's a gentleman to see you, sir—that Mr Crellock."

"Show him in my study, and I'll come."

Thisbe disappeared, and Millicent laid her hand upon her husband's arm.

"Don't be afraid," he said quietly. "I know how to deal with him now. Only trust me, and all shall be well."

"I do trust you," said Millicent, and she sat there with a face like marble, listening to her husband's step across the hall, and then sat patiently for hours, during which time the bell had been rung for the spirit stand and hot water, while the fumes of tobacco stole into the room.

At last there were voices and steps in the hall; the front door was opened and closed, and as Millicent Hallam awoke to the fact that she had not been up to see her child since she went to bed, and that it was nearly midnight, Hallam entered the room, looking more cheerful, and crossing to her he took her in his arms.

"Things are looking brighter," he said. "We have only to wait. Now, mind this—don't ask questions—it is better that I should not go to the bank for a few days. I am unwell."

Millicent looked at him hard. Certainly his eyes were sunken, and for answer, as she told herself that he must have suffered much, she bowed her head.

Volume Two—Chapter Eleven.

Getting Near the Edge.

"Quite out of the question," said James Thickens.

"But what is there to fear?"

"I don't know that there is anything to fear," said Thickens dryly. "What I know is this, and I've thought it over. You are not going up to town with him, but by yourself, to get this money—if you still mean it."

"I still mean it! There, go on."

"Well, you will go up, and sign what you have to sign, get this money in notes, and bring it down yourself."

"But Hallam will think it so strange—that I mistrust him."

"Of course he will. So you do; so do I. And after thinking this matter over, I am going to have that money deposited here, and I'm going to redeem the bonds and deeds myself, getting all information from Hallam."

"But this will be a hard and rather public proceeding."

"I don't know about hard, and as to public, no one will know about it but we three, for old Gemp will not smell it out. He is down with the effects of a bad seizure, and not likely to leave his bed for days."

"But, Thickens—"

"Mr Bayle, I am more of a business man than you, so trust me. You are making sacrifice enough, and are not called upon to study the feelings of one of the greatest scoundrels—"

"Oh! hush! hush!"

"I say it again, sir—one of the greatest scoundrels that ever drew breath."

Bayle frowned, and drew his own hard.

"I don't know," he said, "that I shall care to carry this money—so large a sum."

"Nonsense, sir, a packet of notes in a pocket-book. These things are comparative. When I was a boy I can remember thinking ninepence a large amount; now I stand on a market day shovelling out gold and fingering over greasy notes and cheques, till I don't seem to know what a large sum is. You take my advice, go and get it without saying a word to Hallam; and I tell you what it is, sir, if it wasn't for poor Mrs Hallam and that poor child, I should be off my bargain, and go to Sir Gordon at once."

"I will go and get the money without Hallam, Thickens; but as I undertook to go with him, I shall write and tell him I have gone."

"Very well, sir, very well. As you please," said Thickens; "I should not: but you are a clergyman, and more particular about such things than I am."

Bayle smiled, and shook hands, leaving Thickens looking after him intently as he walked down the street.

"He wouldn't dare!" said Thickens to himself thoughtfully. "He would not dare. I wish he had not been going to tell him, though. Humph! dropping in to see poor old Gemp because he has had a fit."

He paused till he had seen Bayle enter the old man's house, and then went on muttering to himself.

"I never could understand why Gemp was made; he never seems to have been of the least use in the world, though, for the matter of that, idlers don't seem much good. Hah! If Gemp knew what I know, there'd be a crowd round the bank in half-an-hour, and they'd have Hallam's house turned inside out in another quarter. I don't like his telling Hallam about his going," he mused. "It's a large sum of money, though I made light of it, and the mail's safe enough. We've about got by the old highwayman days, but I wish he hadn't told him, all the same."

Meanwhile the curate had turned in at Gemp's to see how the old fellow was getting on.

"Nicedly, sir, very nicedly," said the woman in charge; "he've had a beautiful sleep, and Doctor Luttrell says he be coming round to his senses fast."

Poor old Gemp did not look as if he had been progressing nicely, but he seemed to recognise his visitor, and appeared to understand a few of his words.

But not many, for the old man kept putting his hand to his head and looking at the door, gazing wistfully through the window, and then heaving a heavy sigh.

"Oh, don't you take no notice o' that, sir," said the woman; "that be only his way. He's been used to trotting about so much that he feels it a deal when he is laid up, poor old gentleman; he keeps talking about his money, too, sir. Ah, sir, it be strange how old folks do talk about their bit o' money when they're getting anigh the time when they won't want any of it more."

And so on till the curate rose and left the cottage.

That night he was on his way to London, after sending a line to Hallam to say that upon second thoughts he had considered it better to go up to town alone.

Three days passed with nothing more exciting than a few inquiries after Hallam's health, the most assiduous inquirer being Miss Heathery, who called again on the third evening.

"I know you think me a very silly little woman, Millicent, my dear, and I'm afraid that perhaps I am, but I do like you, and I should like to help you now you are in trouble."

"I always did, and always shall, think you one of my best and kindest friends, Miss Heathery," replied Millicent, kissing her.

"Now, that's very kind of you, my dear. It's touching," said Miss Heathery, wiping her eyes. "You do think me then a very dear friend?" she said, clinging to Mrs Hallam, and gazing plaintively in her face.

"Indeed I do."

"Then may I make a confidant like of you, dear?"

"Yes, certainly," said Millicent.

"But first of all, can I help you nurse Mr Hallam, or take care of Julie?"

"Oh, no, thank you. Mr Hallam is much better, and Julie is happiest with Thisbe."

"Or Mr Bayle," said Miss Heathery; "but I have not seen her with him lately. Oh, I forgot, he has gone to London."

"Indeed!" said Millicent, starting, for she connected his absence with her husband's trouble.

"Yes; gone two, three days; but, Millicent dear, may I speak to you plainly?"

"Of course. Tell me," said Millicent smiling, and feeling amused as she anticipated some confidence respecting an engagement.

"And you are sure you will not feel hurt?"

"Trust me, I shall not," said Millicent, with her old grave smile.

"Well then, my dear," whispered the visitor, "it is about money matters. You know I have none in the bank now, because I bought a couple of houses, but I have been asking, and I find that I can borrow some money on the security, and I thought—there! I knew you would feel hurt."

For Millicent's eyes had begun to dilate, and she drew back from her visitor.

"I only meant to say that I could not help knowing you—that Mr Hallam kept you—oh! I don't know how to say it, Millicent dear, but—but if you would borrow some money of me, dear, it would make me so very happy."

The tears sprang to Millicent's eyes as she rose and kissed her visitor.

"Thank you, dear Miss Heathery," she cried. "I shall never forget this unassuming kindness, but it is impossible that I can take your help."

"Oh, dear me! I was afraid you would say so, and yet it is so sad to run short. Couldn't you really let me help you, my dear?"

"No, it is impossible," said Millicent, smiling gently. "Is it quite impossible?" said Miss Heathery.

"Yes, dear; but believe me, if I were really in great need I would come to you for help."

"You promise me that, dear?" cried the little woman, rising.

"I promise you that," said Millicent, and her visitor went away overjoyed.

Volume Two—Chapter Twelve.

Robert Hallam Wants Fresh Air.

"That woman seemed as if she would never go," said Hallam, entering the room hastily, and glancing at the clock.

"She does like to stop and chat," replied Millicent, wondering at his manner. "What are you going to do?"

"I am off for a short run. I cannot bear this confinement any longer. It is dark, and no one will see me if I go out for a change."

"Shall I go with you?"

"Go with me! No, not now," he said hastily. "I want a little fresh air. Don't stop me. I shall be back soon."

His manner seemed very strange, but Millicent said nothing, only followed him into the hall.

"No, no," he said hastily; "don't do that. It is as if you were watching me."

She drew back in a pained way, and he followed her.

"I'm pettish and impatient, that's all," he said smiling; and, closing the door after her, he hurriedly put on a cloak and travelling cap, muffling his face well; and then going softly out, and turning from the main street, he was soon after in the lane that led down by Thickens's house and the mill.

"At last!" said a voice from the hedge-side, just beyond where the last oil lamp shed a few dim rays across the road. "I thought you were never coming."

"Don't talk. Have you everything ready?"

"Yes, everything. It is only a cart, but it will take you easily."

"And are you sure of the road?"

"Certain. I've done it twice so as to be sure."

"Good horse?"

"Capital. We can get over the twenty miles in three hours, and catch the York coach easily by twelve. It does not pass before then."

"Mind, Stephen, I'm trusting you in this. If you fail me—"

"If I fail you! Bah! Did I ever fail you?"

"No, never."

"Then don't talk like that. You've failed me pretty often, all the same. Going?"

"Yes; I must get back."

"What's that—the Castor coach?"

"Yes," said Hallam, starting. "It's early."

"Don't be longer than you can help; but, I say, have you plenty of money for the journey? I've only a guinea or two left."

"I have enough," said Hallam grimly; and bidding his companion wait three hours, and if he did not come then to go back and return the next night, Hallam turned to hurry back to the town.

It was intensely dark as he approached the mill, where the stream was gurgling and plashing over the waste-water shoot. In the distance there was the oil lamp glimmering, and a light or two shone in the scattered cottages, but there was none at Thickens's as Hallam passed.

There was a space of about a hundred yards between Thickens's house and the next cottage, and Hallam had about half traversed this when he heard a step that seemed familiar coming, and his doubt was put an end to by a voice exclaiming, "Mind! Take care!"

Was it fate that had put this in his way?

He asked himself this as, like lightning, the thought struck him that Bayle had just come off the coach—he the sharer in the knowledge of his iniquity.

A sharp struggle, and close at hand there was the bridge and the flowing river. It might have been an accident. But even then there was Thickens. What if he closed with him, and—disguised as he was, Bayle could never know—Bayle—the bearer of that heavy sum of money! He intended flight that night; was it fate, he asked himself again, that had thrown this in his way? And as the thoughts flashed through his brain, they encountered roughly upon the path, and Hallam's hand touched the thick pocket-book in Bayle's breast.

It was a matter of moments. Even to Hallam it was like an encounter in a dream. A blind desire to possess himself of the money he had touched had come over him; and reckless now, half mad, he seized the curate by the throat. There was a furious struggle, a few inarticulate cries, a heavy fall, and he was kneeling upon him, and dragging the pocket-book from his breast.

All, as it were, in a dream!

Millicent Hallam stood listening at the window to her husband's steps, and then pressed her hands to her burning forehead to try and think more clearly about her position. It was so hard to think ill of Bayle; she could not do it;

and yet her husband had said he was his enemy, and fighting against him to destroy him. Besides, Bayle had not been near them for days. It was so strange that he should go away without telling her!

And so, as she stood there, the two currents of thought met—that which ran love and trust in her husband, and that which was full of gentle sisterly feeling for Bayle; and as they met there was tumult and confusion in her brain, till the first current proved the stronger, and swept the latter aside, running strongly on towards the future.

"He is my husband, and he trusts me now as I trust him," she said proudly. "It is impossible. He could do no wrong."

She went up to the bed-room where Julie lay asleep, and stood watching the sweet, happy little face for some time, ending by kneeling down, taking one of the little hands in hers, and praying fervently for help, for guidance, and for protection in the troubled future, that appeared to be surrounding her with clouds.

How dense they seemed! How was it all to end? Would she be called upon by her husband to leave their home and friends, and go far away? Well, and if that were her fate, husband and child were all in all to her, and it was her duty.

"He trusts me now," she said smiling; and feeling happier and more at rest than she had for months with their petty cares and poverty and shame, she bent over and kissed Julie, when the child's arms were clasped about her neck and clung there for a moment, before dropping listlessly back upon the bed.

Passing her hand over the child's forehead to be sure that she was cool and that no lurking fever was there, Millicent went down to the dining-room again, to sit and listen for the coming step.

She had heard the coach come and go, but instead of the place settling down again into its normal quiet, there seemed to be a great many people about, and hurrying footsteps were heard, such as would be at times when there was an alarm of fire in the town.

And yet it was not like that. More, perhaps, as if there were some meeting, and the steps died away.

For a moment or two Millicent had been disposed to summon Thisbe, and send her to see what was wrong; but on drawing aside the curtains and looking out, the street seemed deserted, and though there were a few figures in the market-place, they did not excite her surprise.

"I am overwrought and excited," she said to herself. "Ah! at last."

There was no mistaking that step, and starting up, she ran into the hall to admit Hallam, who staggered in, closed the door quickly, and catching her hand, half dragged her into the dining-room.

She clung to him in affright, for she could see that the cloak he wore was torn and muddied, that his face was ghastly pale, and that as he threw off his travelling cap, there was a terrible swelling across his forehead, as if he had received some tremendous blow.

"Robert," she exclaimed, "what is the matter?"

"Hush," he said quickly; "be quiet and calm. Has Thisbe gone to bed?"

"Yes. Yes, I think so."

"Quick, then; a basin and water, sponge and towel. I must bathe this place."

"Did you fall?" she cried, as she hastily helped him off with the cloak.

"No. But quick; the water."

She hurried away, shivering with the dread of some new trouble to come, but soon returned with the sponge, and busied herself in bathing the hurt.

"I was attacked—by some ruffian," said Hallam hoarsely, as the water trickled and plashed back in the basin. "He struck me with a bludgeon and left me senseless. When I came to he was gone."

"Robert, you horrify me!" cried Millicent. "This is dreadful."

"Might have been worse," he said coolly. "There, now dry it, and listen to me the while."

"Yes, Robert," she said, forcing herself to be firm, and to listen to the words in spite of the curious doubting trouble that would oppress her.

"As soon as I go upstairs to put a few things together and get some papers, you will put on your bonnet and cloak, and dress Julie."

"Dress Julie!"

"Yes," he said harshly, "without you wish me to leave you behind."

"You are going away, then?"

"Yes, I am going away," he said bitterly, "after hesitating, with a fool's hesitation, all these days. I ought to have gone before."

"How strangely you speak!" she said.

"Don't waste time. Now go."

"One word, love," she whispered imploringly; "do we go for long?"

"No; not for long," he said. And then, with an impatient gesture: "Bah!" he exclaimed; "yes, for ever."

She shrank from him in alarm.

"Well," he said harshly, as he glanced at his injury in the mirror, "you are hesitating. I do not force you. I am your husband, and I have a right to command; but I leave you free. Do you wish to stay?"

A feeling of despair so terrible that it seemed crushing came over Millicent. To go from the home of her childhood—to flee like this with her husband, probably in disgrace, even if only through suspicion—was for the moment more than she could bear; and as he saw her momentary hesitation, an ugly sneering laugh came upon his face. It faded, though, as she calmly laid her hand upon his arm.

"Am I to take any luggage?" she said.

"Nothing but your few ornaments of value. Be quick."

She raised her lips and kissed him, and then seemed to glide out of the room.

"Yes," he said, "I have been a fool and an idiot not to have gone before. Curse the fellow: who could it be?" he cried, as he pressed his hand to his injured forehead.

He took out his keys and opened a drawer in a cabinet, taking from it a hammer and cold chisel, and then stood thinking for a few moments before hurrying out, and into a little lobby behind the hall, from which he brought a small carpet-bag.

"That will just hold it," he said, "and a few of the things that she is sure to have."

He turned into the dining-room, going softly, as if he were engaged in some nefarious act. Then he picked up the hammer and chisel, and was about to return into the hall, when he heard a low murmur, which seemed to be increasing, and with it the trampling of feet, and shouts of excited men.

"What's that?" he cried, with his countenance growing ghastly pale; and the cold chisel fell to the floor with a clang.

Volume Two—Chapter Thirteen.

A Human Storm.

The woman who had been acting the part of nurse to old Gemp was seated by the table, busily knitting a pair of blue worsted stockings by the light of a tallow candle, and every few minutes the snuff had so increased, and began to show so fungus-like a head, that the needles had to be left, a pair of snuffers taken out of their home in a niche that ran through the stem of the tin candlestick, and used to cut off the light-destroying snuff, with the effect that the snuffers were not sufficiently pinched to, and a thread of pale blue smoke rose from the incandescence within, and certainly with no good effect as far as fragrance was concerned.

Old Gemp had become a great deal better. He had been up and dressed, and sat by the fireside for a couple of hours that afternoon, and had then expressed his determination not to go to bed.

But his opposition was very slight, and he was got to bed, where he seemed to be lying thinking, and trying to recall something which evidently puzzled him. In fact all at once he called his nurse.

"Mrs Preddle! Mrs Preddle!"

"Yes," said that lady with a weary air.

"What was I thinking about when I was took badly?"

"I don't know," said the woman sourly. "About somebody else's business, I suppose."

Old Gemp grunted, and shook his head. Then he was silent, and lay staring about the room, passing his hand across his forehead every now and then, or shaving himself with one finger, with which all at once he would point at his nurse.

"I say!" he cried sharply.

"Bless the man! how you made me jump!" cried Mrs Preddle. "And, for goodness' sake, don't point at me like that! Easy to see you're getting better, and won't want me long."

"No, no! don't go away!" he exclaimed. "I can't think about it."

"Well, and no wonder neither! Why, bless the man! people don't have bad fits o' 'plexy and not feel nothing after! There, lie still, and go to sleep, there's a good soul! It'll do you good."

Mrs Preddle snuffed the candle again, and made another unpleasant smell of burning, but paid no heed to it, fifty years of practice having accustomed her to that odour—an extremely common one in those days, when in every little town there was a tallow-melter, the fumes of whose works at certain times made themselves pretty well-known for some distance round.

The question was repeated by old Gemp at intervals all through the evening—"What was I thinking about when I was took badly?" and Mrs Preddle became irritated by his persistence.

But this made no difference whatever to the old man, who scraped his stubbly chin with his finger, and then pointed, to ask again. For the trouble that had been upon his mind when he was stricken hung over him like a dark cloud, and he was always fighting mentally to learn what it all meant.

"What was it?—what was it? What was I thinking about?" Over and over and over, and no answer would come. Mrs Preddle went on with her knitting, and ejaculated "Bless the man!" and dropped stitches, and picked them up again, and at last grew so angry, that, upon old Gemp asking her, for about the hundredth time that night, that same wearisome question, she cried out:

"Drat the man! how should I know? Look ye here, if you—Oh! I won't stand no more of this nonsense?" She rose and went into the kitchen. "Doctor Luttrell said if he got more restless he was to have it," she grumbled to herself, "and he's quite unbearable to-night!"

She poured out a double dose from a bottle left in her charge, and chuckled as she said to herself, "That'll quiet him for the night."

Old Gemp was sitting up in bed when she returned to the bed-room; and once more his pointing finger rose, and he was about to speak, when Mrs Preddle interfered.

"There, that'll do, my dear! and now you've got to take this here physic directly, to do you good."

The old man looked at her in a vacant, helpless way for a few moments, and then his countenance grew angry, and he motioned the medicine aside.

"Oh, come now, it's of no use! You've got to take it, so now then!"

She pressed the cup towards his lips; but the old man struck at it angrily, and it flew across the room, splashing the bed with the opium-impregnated liquid, and then shattering on the cemented floor.

"Well, of all the owd rips as ever I did see!" cried the woman. "Oh, you are better, then!"

"What was I thinking about when I was took badly?" cried Gemp, pointing as if nothing had happened.

"Oh, about your money in the bank for aught I know!" cried the woman.

"Ha!"

The old man clapped his hands to his forehead, and held them there for a few minutes, staring straight before him at the bed-room wall.

He had uttered that ejaculation so sharply that the woman started, and recoiled from him, in ignorance of the fact that she had touched the key-note that had set the fibres of his memory athrill.

"Why, what's come to you?" she said. "Sakes, man, you're not worse?"

Old Gemp did not reply for a few moments. Then, stretching out one hand, and pointing at his nurse:

"Go and fetch doctor. Go at once! Quick, I say, quick!"

The woman stared in alarm for a few moments, and then, catching her bonnet and shawl from a nail, she hurriedly put them on and went out.

"And I've been a-lying here," panted Gemp, sliding his legs out of bed, and dressing himself quickly. "I remember now. I know. And perhaps all gone— deeds, writings—all gone. I knew there was something wrong—I knew there was something wrong!"

In five minutes he was out in the street, and had reached his friend the tailor, who stared aghast at him at first, but as soon as he heard his words blazed up as if fire had been applied to tow, and then subsided with a cunning look.

"Let's keep it quiet, neighbour," he said; "and go to-morrow morning, and see what we can do with Hallam. Ah!" he cried, as a thought flashed across his mind, "he has not been at the bank these three or four days. You're right, neighbour, there is something wrong."

Just at that moment, seeing the door open, another neighbour stepped in, heard the last words, and saw Gemp's wild, miserly face agitated by the horror of his loss.

"What's wrong?" he cried.

"Wrong? That scoundrel Hallam! that thief! that—"

The new-comer started.

"Don't say there's owt wrong wi' Dixons'!" he panted.

"Yes, yes!" cried Gemp. "My deeds! my writings! I saw parson and Thickens busy together. They were tackling Hallam when I was took badly. Hallam's a rogue! I warned you all—a rogue! a rogue! See how he has been going on!"

"Neighbour," groaned the new-comer, "they've got all I have in the world up yonder in the bank."

"Oh, but it can't be true," said the tailor, with a struggle to catch at a straw of hope.

"*Ay*, but it is true," said the last comer, whose face was ghastly; "and I'm a ruined man."

"Nay, nay, wait a bit. P'r'aps Hallam has only been ill."

"Ill? It was he, then, I'll swear, I saw to-night, walk by me in a cloak and cap. He were going off. Neighbours, are we to sit still and bear a thing like this?"

"I'll hev my writings! I'll hev my writings!" cried Gemp hoarsely, as he clawed at the air with his trembling hands.

"Is owt wrong?" said a fresh voice, and another of the Castor tradesmen sauntered in, pipe in mouth.

In another minute he knew all they had to tell and the light was indeed now applied to the tow. Reason and common-sense were thrown to the winds, and a wild, selfish madness took their place.

Dixons', the stable, the most substantial house in the county, the stronghold where the essence of all the property for miles round was kept, was now a bank of straw; and the flame ran from house to house like the wildfire that it was. Had an enemy invaded the place, or the fire that burns, there could not have been greater consternation. The stability of the bank touched so many; while, as the news flew from mouth to mouth, hundreds who had not a shilling in the bank, never had, nor ever would have, took up the matter with the greatest indignation, and joined in the excitement, and seemed the most aggrieved.

There was nothing to go upon but the old man's suspicion; but that spark had been enough to light the fire of popular indignation, and before long, in the midst of a score of different proposals, old Gemp started for the bank, supported by his two nearest neighbours, and across the dim market-place the increasing crowd made its way.

Mr Trampleasure was smoking his evening cigar on the step of the private door. The cigar, a present from Sir Gordon: the permission to smoke it there a present from Mrs Trampleasure.

He heard wonderingly the noise of tumult, saw the crowd approaching, and prudently went in and shut and bolted the doors, going up to a window to parley with the crowd, as the bell was rung furiously, and some one beat at the door of the bank with a stick.

"What is it?" he said.

"My deeds! my writings!" cried Gemp. "I want my deeds!"

"Who's that? Mr Gemp? My dear sir, the bank's closed, as you know. Come to-morrow morning."

"No, no! Give the man his deeds. Here, break down the door!" cried a dozen voices; and the rough element that was to be found in King's Castor, as well as elsewhere, uttered a shout, and began to kick at the panels.

"Come away, Gemp. We shall get nothing if these fellows break in."

"Look here!" cried a shrill voice at the window; and there was a cessation of the noise, as Mrs Trampleasure leaned out. "We've got pistols and blunderbusses here, as you all know, and if you don't be off, we shall fire."

"Open the doors then," cried a rough voice.

"We haven't got the keys. Mr Thickens keeps them."

There was a shout at this, for the crowd, like all crowds, was ready to snatch at a change, and away they ran towards the mill.

In five minutes though, they were tearing back, failing to find Thickens; and a cry had been raised by the man with the rough voice, and one of the poorest idlers of the town, the keenest redresser of wrong now.

"Hallam's! To Hallam's!" he yelled. "Hev him out, lads. We'll hev him out. Hurray, lads, come on!"

The tradesmen and depositors at Dixons' Bank looked aghast now at the mischief done. They saw how they had opened a crack in the dam, and that the crack had widened, the dam had given way, and the turbulent waters were about to carry all before them.

It was in vain to speak, for the indignant poor were in the front, and the tailor, Gemp, and others who had been the leaders in the movement found themselves in a pitiful minority, and were ready to retreat.

But that was impossible. They were in the crowd, and were carried with them across the market-place and down the street, to Hallam's house, where they beat and thumped at the door.

There was no answer for a few minutes, and they beat and roared. Then some one threw a stone and smashed a pane of glass. This earned a cheer, and a shower of stones followed, the panes shivering and tinkling down inside and out of the house.

Millicent was wrong when she said that Thisbe had gone to bed, for that worthy was having what she called a quiet read in her room, and now as the windows were breaking, and Millicent was shielding Julie whom, half-awake, she had just dressed, there was an increase in the roar, for Thisbe had gone down, more indignant than alarmed, and thrown open the door.

Then there was a dead silence, the silence of surprise, as Thisbe stood in the doorway, and as a great hulking lad strove to push by her, struck him a sounding slap on the face.

There was a yell of laughter at this, and silence again, as the woman spoke.

"What do you want?" she cried boldly.

"Hallam! Hallam! In with you, lads: fetch him out."

"No, no; stop! stop! My deeds, my writings!" shrieked Gemp; but his voice was drowned in the yelling of the mob, who now forced their way in, filling the hall, the dining and drawing-rooms, and then making for the old-fashioned staircase.

"He's oop-stairs, lads; hev him down!" cried the leader, and the men pressed forward, with a yell, their faces looking wild and strange by the light of the lamp and the candle Thisbe had placed upon a bracket by the stairs.

But here their progress was stopped by Millicent, who, pale with dread, but with a spot as of fire in either cheek, stood at the foot of the staircase, holding the frightened child to her side, while Thisbe forced her way before her.

"What do you want?" she cried firmly.

"Thy master, missus. Stand aside, we won't hurt thee. We want Hallam."

"What do you want with him?" cried Millicent again.

"We want him to give oop the money he's stole, and the keys o' bank. Stand aside wi' you. Hev him down."

There was a rush, a struggle, and Millicent and her shrieking child were dragged down roughly, but good-humouredly, by the crowd that filled the hall, while others kept forcing their way in. As for Thisbe, as she fought and struck out bravely, her hands were pinioned behind her, and the group were held in a corner of the hall, while with a shout the mob rushed upstairs.

"Here, let go," panted Thisbe to the men who held her. "I won't do so any more. Let me take the bairn."

The men loosed her at once, and they formed a ring about their prisoners.

"Let me have her, Miss Milly," she whispered, and she took Julie in her arms, while Millicent, freed from this charge, made an effort to get to the stairs.

"Nay, nay, missus. Thou'rt better down here," said one of her gaolers roughly; and the trembling woman was forced to stay, but only to keep imploring the men to let her pass.

Meanwhile the mob were running from room to room without success; and at each shout of disappointment a throb of hope and joy made Millicent's heart leap.

She exchanged glances with Thisbe.

"He has escaped," she whispered.

"More shame for him then," cried Thisbe. "Why arn't he here to protect his wife and bairn?"

At that moment a fierce yelling and cheering was heard upstairs, where the mob had reached the attic door and detected that it was locked on the inside.

The door was strong, but double the strength would not have held it against the fierce onslaught made, and in another minute, amidst fierce yelling, the tide began to set back, as the word was passed down, "They've got him."

Millicent's brain reeled, and for a few moments she seemed to lose consciousness; but as she saw Hallam, pale, bleeding, his hair torn and dishevelled, dragged down the stairs by the infuriated mob, her love gave her strength. Wresting herself from those who would have restrained her, she forced her way to her husband's side, flung her arms about him as he was driven back against the wall, and, turning her defiant face to the mob, made of her own body a shield.

There was a moment's pause, then a yell, and the leader's voice cried:

"Never mind her. Hev him out, lads, and then clear the house."

There was a fresh roar at this, and then blows were struck right and left in the dim light; the lamp was dashed over; while the curtains by the window, where it stood, blazed up, and cast a lurid light over the scene. For a moment the crowd recoiled as they saw the flushed and bleeding face of Christie Bayle, as he struck out right and left till he had fought his way to where he could plant himself before Millicent and her husband, and try to keep the assailants back.

The surprise was only of a few minutes' duration.

"You lads, he's only one. Come on! Hallam: Let's judge and jury him."

"You scoundrels!" roared Bayle, "a man must be judged by his country, and not by such ruffians as you."

"Hev him out, lads, 'fore the place is burnt over your heads."

"Back! stand back, cowards!" cried Bayle; "do you not see the woman and the child? Back! Out of the place, you dogs!"

"Dogs as can bite, too, parson," cried the leader. "Come on."

He made a dash at Hallam, getting him by the collar, but only to collapse with a groan, so fierce was the blow that struck him on the ear.

Again there was a pause—a murmur of rage, and the wooden support of the valance of the curtains began to crackle, while the hall was filling fast with stifling smoke.

One leader down, another sprang in his place, for the crowd was roused.

"Hev him out, lads! Quick, we have him now."

There was a rush, and Hallam was torn from Millicent's grasp—from Christie Bayle's protecting arms, and with a yell the crowd rushed out into the street, lit now by the glow from the smashed hall windows and the fire that burned within.

"My husband! Christie—dear friend—help, oh, help!" wailed Millicent, as she tottered out to the front, in time to see Bayle literally leap to Hallam's side and again strike the leader down.

It was the last effort of his strength; and now a score of hands were tearing and striking at the wretched victim, when there was the clattering of horses' hoofs and a mounted man rode right into the crowd with half-a-dozen followers at his side.

"Stop!" he roared. "I am a magistrate. Constables: your duty."

The mob fell back, and as five men, with whom was Thickens, seized upon Hallam, Millicent tottered into the circle and sank at her husband's knees.

"Saved!" she sobbed, "saved!"

For the first time Hallam found his voice, and cried, as he tried to shake himself free:

"This—this is a mistake—constables. Loose me. These men—"

"It is no mistake, Mr Hallam, you are arrested for embezzlement," said the mounted man sternly.

"Three cheers for Sir Gordon Bourne and Dixons'," shouted one in the crowd.

Christie Bayle had just time to catch Millicent Hallam in his arms as her senses left her, and with a piteous moan she sank back utterly stunned.

Volume Two—Chapter Fourteen.

Writing in her Agony.

"Mother!—father! Oh, in heaven's name, speak to me! I cannot bear it. My heart is broken. What shall I do?"

"My poor darling!" sobbed Mrs Luttrell, holding her child to her breast and rocking to and fro, while the doctor sat with wrinkled face nursing and caressing Julia, who clung to him in a scared fashion, not having yet got over the terrors of the past night.

She had her arms about her grandfather, and nestled in his breast, but every now and then she started up to gaze piteously in his face.

"Would my dolls all be burnt, grandpa?"

"Oh, I hope not, my pet," he said soothingly; "but never mind if they are: grandpa will buy you some better ones."

"But I liked those, grandpa, and—and is my little bed burnt too?"

"No, my pet; I think not. I hope not. They put the fire out before it did a great deal of harm."

The child laid her head down again for a few moments, and then looked up anxiously.

"Thibs says the bad men tore the place all to pieces last night and broke all the furniture and looking-glasses. Oh! grandpa, I—I—I—"

Suffering still from the nervous shock of the nocturnal alarm, the poor child's breast heaved, and she burst into a pitiful fit of sobbing, which was some time before it subsided.

"Don't think about it all, my pet," said the doctor, tenderly stroking the soft little head. "Never mind about the old house, you shall come and live here with grandpa, and we'll have such games in the old garden again."

"Yes, and I may smell the flowers, and—and—but I want our own house too."

"Ah, well, we shall see. There, you are not to think any more about that now."

"Why doesn't Mr Bayle come, grandpa? Did the bad people hurt him very much?"

"Oh no, my darling: he's all right, and he punished some of them."

"And when will papa come?"

"Hush, child," cried Millicent in a harsh, strange voice, "I cannot hear to hear you."

The child looked at her in a scared manner and clung to her grandfather, but struggled from his embrace directly after, and ran to her mother, throwing her arms about her, and kissing her and sobbing.

"Oh, my own dear, dear mamma!"

"My darling, my darling!" cried Millicent, passionately clasping her to her breast; and Mrs Luttrell drew away to leave them together, creeping quietly to the doctor's side, and laying her hand upon his shoulder, looking a while in his eyes as if asking whether she were doing wisely.

The doctor nodded, and for a few minutes there was no sound heard but Millicent's sobs.

"I wish Mr Bayle would come," said Julia all at once in her silvery childish treble.

"Silence, child!" cried Millicent fiercely. "Father dear, speak to me; can you not help me in this trouble? You know the charge is all false?"

"My darling, I will do everything I can."

"Yes, yes, I know, but every one seems to have turned against us—Sir Gordon, Mr Bayle, the whole town. It is some terrible mistake: all some fearful error. How dare they charge my husband with a crime?"

She gazed fiercely at her father as she spoke, and the old man stood with his arms about Mrs Luttrell and his lips compressed.

"You do not speak," cried Millicent; "surely you are not going to turn against us, father?"

"Oh! Milly, my own child," sobbed Mrs Luttrell, running to her to take her head to her breast, "don't speak to us like that; as if your father would do anything but help you."

"Of course, of course," cried Millicent excitedly; "but there, I must put off all this pitiful wailing."

She rose in a quiet, determined way, and wiped her eyes hastily, arranged her hair, and began to walk up and down the room. Then, stopping, she forced a smile, and bent down and kissed Julia, sending a flash of joy through her countenance.

"Go and look round the garden, darling. Pick mamma a nice bunch of flowers."

"Will you come too, grandpa?" cried the child eagerly.

"I'll come to you presently, darling," said the doctor nodding; and the child bounded to the open window with a sigh of relief, but ran back to kiss each in turn.

"Now we can speak," cried Millicent, panting, as she forced herself to be calm. "There is no time for girlish sobbing when such a call as this is made upon me. The whole town is against poor Robert; they have wrecked and burnt our house, and they have cast him into prison."

"My darling, be calm, be calm," said the doctor soothingly.

"Yes, I am calm," she said, "and I am going to work—and help my husband. Now tell me, What is to be done first? He is in that dreadful place."

"Yes, my child, but leave this now. I will do all I can, and will tell you everything. You have had no sleep all night; go and lie down now for a few hours."

"Sleep! and at a time like this!" cried Millicent. "Now tell me. He will be brought up before the magistrates to-day?"

"Yes, my child."

"And he must have legal advice to counteract all this cruel charge that has been brought against him. Poor fellow! so troubled as he has been of late."

The doctor looked at her with the lines in his forehead deepening.

"If they had given him time he would have proved to them how false all these attacks are. But we are wasting time. The lawyer, father, and he will have to be paid. You will help me, dear; we must have some money."

The doctor exchanged glances with his wife.

"You have some, of course?" he said, turning to Millicent.

"I? No. Robert has been so pressed lately. But you will lend us all we want. You have plenty, father."

The doctor was silent, and half turned away.

"Father!" cried Millicent, catching his hand, "don't you turn from me in my distress. I tell you Robert is innocent, and only wants time to prove it to all the world. You will let me have the money for his defence?"

The doctor remained silent.

"Father!" cried Millicent in a tone of command.

"Hush! my darling; your poor father has no money," sobbed Mrs Luttrell, "and sometimes lately we have not known which way to turn for a few shillings."

"Oh, father!" cried Millicent reproachfully. "But there's the house. You must borrow money on its security, enough to pay for the best counsel in London. Robert will repay you a hundredfold."

The doctor turned away and walked to the window.

"Father!" cried Millicent, "am I your child?"

"My child! my darling!" he groaned, coming quickly back, "how can you speak to me in such a tone?"

"How can you turn from me at such a time, when the honour of my dear husband is at stake? What are a few paltry hundred pounds to that? You cannot, you shall not refuse. There, I know enough of business for that. The lawyers will lend you money on the security of this house. Go at once, and get what is necessary. Why do you hesitate?"

"My poor darling!" cried Mrs Luttrell piteously, "don't, pray don't speak to your father like that."

"I must help my husband," said Millicent hoarsely. "Yes, yes, and you shall, my dear; but be calm, be calm. There, there, there."

"Mother, I must hear my father speak," said Millicent sternly. "I come to him in sore distress and poverty. My home has been wrecked by last night's mob, my poor husband half killed, and torn from me to be cast into prison. I come to my father for help—a few pitiful pounds, and he seems to side with my husband's enemies."

"Milly, my darling, I'll do everything I can," cried the doctor; "but you ask impossibilities. The house is not mine."

"Not yours, father?"

"Hush! hush, my dear!" sobbed Mrs Luttrell. "I can't explain to you now, but poor papa was obliged to sell it a little while ago."

"Where is the money?" said Millicent fiercely.

"It was all gone before—the mortgages," said Mrs Luttrell.

"And who bought it?" cried Millicent.

"Mr Bayle."

There was a pause of a few moments' duration, and then the suffering woman seemed to flash out into a fit of passion.

"Mr Bayle again!" she cried.

"Yes, Mr Bayle, our friend."

At that moment there came a burst of merry laughter from the garden, the sounds floating in through the open window with the sweet scents of the flowers, and directly after Julia, looking flushed and happy, appeared, holding Christie Bayle's hand.

Bayle paused as he saw the group within, and then slowly entered.

"Mamma, I knew Mr Bayle would come!" cried Julia excitedly. "But, oh, look at him, he has hurt himself so! He is so—so—oh, I can't bear it, I can't bear it!"

The memories of the past night came back in a flash—the hurried awaking from sleep, the dressing, the sounds of the mob, the breaking windows, the fire, and the wild struggle; and the poor child sobbed hysterically and trembled, as Bayle sank upon his knees and took her to his breast.

There she clung, while he caressed her and whispered comforting words, Millicent the while standing back, erect and stern, and Mrs Luttrell and the doctor with troubled countenances looking on.

In a few minutes the child grew calm again, and then, without a word, Millicent crossed to the fireplace and rang the bell. It was answered directly by the doctor's maid.

"Send Thisbe here," said Millicent sternly.

In another minute Thisbe, who looked very white and troubled, appeared at the door, gazing sharply from one to the other.

"Julie, go to Thisbe," said Millicent in a cold, harsh voice.

The child looked up quickly, and clung to Bayle, as she gazed at her mother with the same shrinking, half-scared look she had so often directed at her father.

"Julie!"

The child ran across to Thisbe, and Bayle bit his lip, and his brow contracted, for he caught the sound of a low wail as the door was closed.

Then, advancing to her, with his face full of the pity he felt, Bayle held out his hand to Millicent, and then let it fall, as she stood motionless, gazing fiercely in his face, till he lowered his eyes, and his head sank slowly, while he heaved a sigh.

"You have come, then," she said, "come to look upon your work. You have come to enjoy your triumph. False friend! Coward! Treacherous villain! You have cast my husband into prison, and now you dare to meet me face to face!"

"Mrs Hallam! Millicent!" he cried, looking up, his face flushing as he met her eyes, "what are you saying?"

"The truth!" she cried fiercely. "He knew you better than I. He warned me against you. His dislike had cause. I, poor, weak, trusting woman, believed you to be our friend, and let you crawl and enlace yourself about our innocent child's heart, while all the time you were forming your plans, and waiting for your chance to strike!"

"Mrs Hallam," said Bayle calmly, and with a voice full of pity, "you do not know what you are saying."

"Not know! when my poor husband told me all!—how you waited until he was in difficulties, and then plotted with that wretched menial Thickens to overthrow him! I know you now: cowardly, cruel man! Unworthy of a thought! But let me tell you that you win no triumph. You thought to separate us—to make the whole world turn from him whom you have cast into prison. You have succeeded in tightening the bonds between us. The trouble will pass as soon as my husband's innocency is shown, while your conduct will cling to you, and show itself like some stain!"

A look as angry as her own came over his countenance, but it passed in a moment, and he said gravely: "I came to offer you my sympathy and help in this time of need."

"Your help, your sympathy!" cried Millicent scornfully. "You, who planned, here, in my presence, with Sir Gordon, my husband's ruin! Leave this house, sir! Stay! I forgot. By your machinations you are master here. Mother, father, let us go. The world is wide, and heaven will not let such villainy triumph in the end."

"Oh, hush! hush!" exclaimed Bayle sternly. "Mrs Hallam, you know not what you say. Doctor, come on to me, I wish to see you. Dear Mrs Luttrell, let me assist you all I can. Good-bye! God help you in your trouble. Good-bye!"

He bent down and kissed the old lady; and as he pressed her hand she clung to his, and kissed it in return.

"Good-bye, Mrs Hallam," he said, holding out his hand once more.

She turned from him with a look of disgust and loathing, and he went slowly out, as he had come, with his head bent, along the road, and on to the market-place.

Volume Two—Chapter Fifteen.

A Critical Time.

There was only one bit of business going on in King's Castor that morning among the mechanics, and that was where two carpenters were busy nailing boards across the gaping windows and broken door of Hallam's house.

The ivy about the hall window was all scorched, and the frames of that and two windows above were charred, but only the hall, staircase, and one room had been burned before the fire was extinguished. The greater part of the place, though, was a wreck, the mob having wreaked their vengeance upon the furniture when Hallam was snatched from their hands by the law; and for about an hour the self-constituted avengers of the customers at Dixons' Bank had behaved like Goths.

It was impossible for work to go on with such a night to canvass. One group, as Bayle approached, was watching the little fire-engine, and the drying of its hose which was hauled up by one end over the branch of an oak-tree at Poppin's Corner.

There was nothing to see but the little, contemptible, old-fashioned pump on wheels; still fifty people, who had seen it in the belfry every Sunday as they went to church, stopped to stare at it now.

But the great group was round about the manager's house, many of them being the idlers and scamps of the place, who had been foremost in the destruction.

The public-houses had their contingents; and then there were the farmers from all round, who had driven in, red-hot with excitement; and, as soon as they had left their gigs or carts in the inn-yard, were making their way up to the bank.

Some did not stop to go to the inn, but were there in their conveyances, waiting for the bank to open, long before the time, and quite a murmur of menace arose, when, to the very moment, James Thickens, calm and cool and drab as usual, threw open the door, to be driven back by a party of those gathered together.

Fortunately the news had spread slowly, so that the crowd was not large; but it was augmented by a couple of score of the blackguards of the place, hungry-eyed, moist of lip, and ready for any excuse to leap over the bank counter and begin the work of plunder.

For the first time in his life James Thickens performed that feat—leaping over the counter to place it between himself and the clamorous mob, who saw Mr Trampleasure there and Sir Gordon Bourne in the manager's room, with the door open, and something on the table.

"Here—Here"—"Here—Me"—"No, me."

"I was first."

"No, me, Thickens."

"My money."

"My cheque."

"Change these notes."

The time was many years ago, and there were no dozen or two of county constabulary to draft into the place for its protection. Hence it was that as Thickens stood, cool and silent, before the excited crowd, Sir Gordon, calm and stern, appeared in the doorway with a couple of pistols in his left hand, one held by the butt, the other by the barrel passed under his thumb.

"Silence!" he cried in a quick, commanding tone.

"I am prepared—"

"Yah! No speeches. Our money! Our—"

"Silence!" roared Sir Gordon. "We are waiting to pay all demands."

"Hear, hear! Hooray!" shouted one of the farmers, who had come in hot haste, and his mottled face grew calm.

"But we can't—"

"Yah—yah!" came in a menacing yell.

"Over with you, lads!" cried a great ruffian, clapping his hands on the counter and making a spring, which the pressure behind checked and hindered, so that he only got one leg on the counter.

"Back, you ruffian!" cried Sir Gordon, taking a step forward, and, quick as lightning, presenting a pistol at the fellow's head. "You, Dick Warren, I gave you six months for stealing corn. Move an inch forward, and as I am a man I'll fire."

There was a fierce murmur, and then a pause.

The great ruffian half crouched upon the counter, crossing his eyes in his fear, and squinting crookedly down the pistol barrel, which was within a foot of his head.

"I say, gentlemen and customers, that Mr Thickens here is waiting to pay over all demands on Dixons' Bank."

"Hear, hear!" cried the farmer who had before spoken.

"But there are twenty or thirty dirty ruffians among you, and people who do not bank with us, and I must ask you to turn them out."

There was a fierce murmur here, and Sir Gordon's voice rose again high and clear.

"Mr Trampleasure, you will find the loaded firearms ready in the upper room. Go up, sir, and without hesitation shoot down the first scoundrel who dares to throw a stone at the bank."

"Yes, Sir Gordon," said Trampleasure, who dared not have fired a piece to save his life, but who gladly beat a retreat to the first-floor window, where he stood with one short blunderbuss in his hand, and Mrs Trampleasure with the other.

"Now, gentlemen," cried Sir Gordon, "I am waiting for you to clear the bank."

There was another fierce growl at this; but the mottled-faced farmer, who had ridden in on his stout cob, and who carried a hunting crop with an old-fashioned iron hammer head, spat in his fist, and turned the handle—

"Now, neighbours and friends as is customers!" he roared in a stentorian voice, "I'm ready when you are." As he spoke he caught the man half on the counter by the collar, and dragged him off.

"Here, keep your hands off me!"

"Yow want to fight, yow'd—"

"Yah! hah!"

Then a scuffling and confused growl, and one or two appeals to sticks and fists; but in five minutes every man not known as a customer of the bank was outside, and the farmers gave a cheer, which was answered by a yell from the increasing mob, a couple of dozen of whom had stooped for stones and began to flourish sticks.

But the stout farmer, who was on the steps between the two pillars that flanked the entrance, put his hand to his mouth, as if about to give a view halloo!

"Look out for the bloonder-boosh, my lads." And then, turning his head up to the window where Mr Trampleasure stood, weapon in hand, "Tak' a good aim on the front, and gie it 'em—whang! Mr Trampleasure, sir. Thee'll scatter the sloogs fine."

Not a stone was thrown, and by this time James Thickens was busy at work cancelling with his quill pen, and counting and weighing out gold. He never offered one of Dixons' notes: silver and gold, current coin of the realm, was all he passed over the counter, and though the customers pressed and hurried to get their cheques or notes changed, Thickens retained his coolness and went on.

At the end of a quarter of an hour the excitement was subsiding, but the bank was still full of farmers and tradespeople, the big burly man with the hunting crop being still by the counter unpaid.

All at once, after watching the paying over of the money for some time, he began hammering the mahogany counter heavily with the iron handle of his whip.

"Here, howd hard!" he roared.

Sir Gordon, who had put the pistols on the table, and was sitting on the manager's chair, coolly reading his newspaper in full view, laid it down, and rose to come to the open glass door.

"Ay, that's right, Sir Gordon. I want a word wi' thee. I'm not a man to go on wi' fullishness; but brass is brass, and a hard thing to get howd on. Now, look ye here. Howd hard, neighbours, I hevn't got much to saya."

"What is it, Mr Anderson?" said Sir Gordon calmly.

"Why, this much, Sir Gordon and neighbours. Friend o' mine comes out o' the town this morning and says, 'If thou'st got any brass i' Dixons' Bank, run and get it, lad, for Maester Hallam's bo'ted, and bank's boosted oop.' Now, Sir Gordon, it don't look as if bank hev boosted oop."

"Oh, no," said Sir Gordon, smiling.

"Hev Maester Hallam bo'ted, then, or is that a lie too?"

"I am sorry to say that Mr Hallam has been arrested on a charge of fraud."

"That be true, then?" said the farmer. "Well, now, look here, Sir Gordon; I've banked wi' you over twanty year, and I can't afford to lose my brass. Tween man and man, is my money safe?"

"Perfectly, Mr Anderson."

"That'll do, Sir Gordon," said the farmer, tearing up the cheque he held in his hand, and scattering it over his head. "I'll tak' Sir Gordon's word or Dixons' if they say it's all right. I don't want my brass."

"Gentlemen," said Sir Gordon, flashing slightly, "if you will trust me and my dear old friend Mr Dixon, you shall be paid all demands to the last penny we

- 181 -

have. I am sorry to say that I have discovered a very heavy defalcation on the part of our late manager, and the loss will be large, but that loss will fall upon us, gentlemen, not upon you."

"But I want my deeds, my writings," cried a voice. "I'm not a-going to be cheated out o' my rights."

"Who is that?" said Sir Gordon.

"Mr Gemp, Sir Gordon," said Thickens quickly. "Deposit of deeds of row of houses in Rochester Close; and shares."

"Mr Gemp," said Sir Gordon, "I am afraid your deeds are amongst others that are missing."

"Ay! Ay! Robbers! Robbers!" shouted Gemp excitedly.

"No, Mr Gemp, we are not robbers," said Sir Gordon. "If you will employ your valuer, I will employ ours; and as soon as they have decided the amount, Mr James Thickens will pay you—to-day if you can get the business done, and the houses and shares are Dixons'."

"Hear, hear, hear," shouted Anderson. "There, neighbour, he can't say fairer than that."

"Nay, I want my writings, and I don't want to sell. I want my writings. I'll hev 'em too."

"Shame on you, Gemp," said a voice behind him. "Three days ago you were at death's door. Your life was spared, and this is the thank-offering you make to your neighbours in their trouble."

"Nay, don't you talk like that, parson, thou doesn't know what it is to lose thy all," piped Gemp.

"Lose?" cried Bayle, who had entered the bank quietly to see Sir Gordon. "Man, I have lost heavily too."

Thickens was making signs to him now with his quill pen.

"Ay, but I want my writings. I'll hev my writings," cried Gemp. "Neighbours, you have your money. Don't you believe 'em. They're robbers."

"If I weer close to thee, owd Gemp, I'd tak' thee by the scruff and the band o' thy owd breeches and pitch thee out o' window. Sir Gordon's ready to do the handsome thing."

"Touch me if you dare," cried old Gemp. "I want my writings. It was bank getting unsafe made me badly. You neighbours have all thy money out, for they haven't got enough to last long."

There was a fresh murmur here, and Sir Gordon looked anxious. Mr Anderson stood fast; but it was evident that a strong party were waiting for their money, and more than one began to twitch Thickens by the sleeve, and present cheques and notes.

Thickens paid no heed, but made his way to where Christie Bayle was standing, and handed him a pocket-book.

"Here," he said. "I couldn't come to you. I had to watch the bank."

"My pocket-book, Thickens?"

"Yes, sir. I was just in time to knock that scoundrel over as he was throttling you. I'd come to meet the coach."

"Why, Thickens!" cried Bayle, flushing—"Ah, you grasping old miser! What! turn thief?"

The latter was to old Gemp, who saw the pocket-book passed, and made a hawk-like clutch at it, but his wrist was pinned by Bayle, who took the pocket-book and slipped it into his breast.

"It's my papers—it's writings—it's—"

His voice was drowned in a clamour that arose, as about twenty more people came hurrying in at the bank-door, eager to make demands for their deposits.

Sir Gordon grew pale, for there was not enough cash in the house to meet the constant demand, and he had hoped that the ready payment of a great deal would quiet the run.

The clamour increased, and it soon became evident that the dam had given way, and that nothing remained but to go on paying to the last penny in the bank, while there was every possibility of wreck and destruction following.

"Howd hard, neighbours," cried Anderson; "Sir Gordon says it's all right. Dixons' 'll pay."

"Dixons' can't pay," shouted a voice. "Hallam's got everything, and the bank's ruined."

There was a roar here, and the fire seemed to have been again applied to the tow. Thickens looked in despair at Bayle, and then with a quick movement locked the cash drawer, and clapped the key in his pocket. The action was seen. There was a yell of fury from the crowd in front, and a dozen hands seized the clerk.

Sir Gordon darted forward, this time without pistols, and hands and sticks were raised, when in a voice of thunder Christie Bayle roared:

"Stop!"

There was instant silence, for he had leaped upon the bank counter.

"Stand back!" he said, "and act like Christian men, and not like wild beasts. Dixons' Bank is sound. Look here!"

"It's failed! it's failed!" cried a dozen voices.

"It has not failed," shouted Bayle. "Look here: I have been to London."

"Yes, we know."

"To fetch twenty-one thousand pounds—my own property!"

There was dead silence here.

"Look! that is the money, all in new Bank of England notes."

He tore them out of the large pocket-book.

"To show you my confidence in Dixons' Bank and in Sir Gordon Bourne's word, I deposit this sum with them, and open an account. Mr Thickens, have the goodness to enter this to my credit; I'll take a chequebook when you are at liberty."

He passed the sheaf of rustling, fluttering, new, crisp notes to the cashier, and then, taking Sir Gordon's offered hand, leaped down inside the counter of the bank.

"There, Sir Gordon," he said, with a smile, "I hope the plague is stayed."

"Christie Bayle," whispered Sir Gordon huskily, "Heaven bless you! I shall never forget this day!" Half-an-hour later the bank business was going on as usual, but the business of the past night and morning was more talked of than before.

Volume Two—Chapter Sixteen.

In misery's depths.

One of many visits to the gloomy, stone-built, county gaol where Hallam was waiting his trial—for all applications for the granting of bail had been set aside—Millicent had insisted upon going alone, but without avail.

"No, Miss Milly, you may insist as long as you like; but until I'm berried, I'm going to keep by you in trouble, and I shall go with you."

"But Thibs, my dear, dear old Thibs," cried Millicent, flinging her arms about her neck, "don't you see that you will be helping me by staying with Julie?"

"No, my dear, I don't; and, God bless her! she'll be as happy as can be with her grandpa killing slugs, as I wish all wicked people were the same, and could be killed out of the way."

"But, Thibs, I order you to stay!"

"And you may order, my dear," said Thisbe stubbornly. "You might order, and you might cut off my legs, and then I'd come crawling like the serpent in the Scripters—only I hope it would be to do good."

"Oh, you make me angry with you, Thisbe. Haven't I told you that Miss Heathery has been pressing to come this morning, and I refused her?"

"Why, of course you did, my dear," replied Thisbe contemptuously. "Nice one she'd be to go with you, and strengthen and comfort you! Send her to your pa's greenhouse to turn herself into a pot, and water the plants with warm water, and crying all over, and perhaps she'd do some good; but to go over to Lindum! The idea! Poor little weak thing!"

"But, Thisbe, can you not see that this is a visit that I ought to pay alone?"

"No, miss."

"But it is: for my husband's sake."

"Every good husband who had left his wife in such trouble as you're in would be much obliged to an old servant for going with you all that long journey. There, miss, once for all—you may go alone, if you like, but I shall follow you and keep close to you all the time, and sit down at the prison gate."

"Oh, hush, Thibs!" cried Millicent, with a spasm of pain convulsing her features.

"Yes, miss, I understand. And now I'm going. I shan't speak a word to you; I shan't even look at you, but be just as if I was a nothing, and all the same I'm there ready for you to hear, and be a comfort in my poor way, so that you may lean on me as much as you like; and, please God, bring us all well out of our troubles. Amen."

Poor Thisbe's words were inconsequent, but they were sincere, and she followed her mistress to the coach, and then through the hilly streets of the old city, and finally, as she had suggested, seated herself upon a stone at the prison gates while her mistress went in.

The sound of lock and bolt chilled Millicent; the aspect of the gloomy, high-walled enclosure, with the loose bricks piled on the top to show where the wall had been tampered with, and to hinder escape, the very aspect, too, of the governor's house, with its barred windows to keep prisoners out, as the walls were to keep them in—a cage within a cage—made her heart sink, and when after traversing stone passages, and hearing doors locked and unlocked, she found herself in the presence of her husband, her brain reeled, a mist came before her eyes, and for a while her tongue refused to utter the words she longed to speak.

"Humph!" said Hallam roughly. "You don't seem very glad to see me."

Her reproachful eyes gave him the lie; and, looking pale, anxious, and terribly careworn, he began to pace the floor.

The careful arrangement of the hair, the gentlemanly look, seemed to have given place to a sullen, half-shrinking mien, and it was plain to see how confinement and mental anxiety had told upon him.

In a few minutes, though, he had thrown off a great deal of this, and spoke eagerly to his wife, who, while tender and sympathetic in word and look, seemed ever ready to spur him on to some effort to free himself from the clinging stain.

This had been her task from the very first. Cast down with a feeling of degradation and sorrow, when the arrest had been made, she had, as we know, recoiled.

She had made every effort possible; had gone to her husband for advice and counsel, and had ended at his wish by taking the money Miss Heathery offered, to pay a good attorney to conduct his case; but on the first hearing, she was informed by the lawyer that a gentleman was down from town, a barrister of some eminence, who said that he had been instructed to defend Mr Hallam, and he declined to give any further information.

The despair that came over Millicent was terrible to witness; but she mastered these fits of despondency by force of will and the feverish energy with which she set to work. She visited Hallam, questioning, asking advice, instruction, and bidding him try to see his way out of the difficulty, till he grew morose and sullen, and seemed to find special pleasure in telling her that it was "all the work of that parson."

In her feverish state, in the despair with which she had bidden herself do her duty to her wronged, her injured husband, she took all this as fact, and shutting herself up at Miss Heathery's, refused to read the letters Bayle sent to her, or to give him an interview.

It was as if a savage spirit of hate and revenge had taken possession of her, and with blind determination she went on her way, praying for strength to make her worthy of the task of defending her injured husband, and for the overthrow of the cruel enemies who were fighting to work his ruin.

And now she was having the last interview with Hallam, for the authorities had interfered, she had had so much latitude, and he had given her certain instructions which made her start.

"Go to him?" she said, looking up wonderingly.

"Yes, of course," he said sharply; "do you wish me to lose the slightest chance of getting off?"

"But, Robert, dear," she said innocently, but with the energy that pervaded her speaking, "why not go bravely to your trial? The truth must prevail."

"Oh, yes," he said cynically; "it is a way it has in courts of law."

"Don't speak like that, love. I want you to hold up your head bravely in the face of your detractors, to show how you have been tricked and injured, that this man Crellock, whom you have helped, has proved a villain—deceiving, robbing, and shamefully treating you."

"Yes," he said; "I should like to show all that."

"Then don't send me to Sir Gordon. I feel that there is no mercy to be expected from either him or Mr Bayle. They both hate you."

"Most cordially, dear. By all that's wearisome, I wish they would let me have a cigar here."

"No, no; think of what you are telling me to do," she cried eagerly, as she saw him wandering from the purpose in hand. "You say I must go to Sir Gordon?"

"Yes. Don't say it outright, but give him to understand that if he will throw up this prosecution of his, it will be better for the bank. That I can give such information as will pay them."

"You know so much about Stephen Crellock?" she said quickly.

"Yes; I can recover a great deal, I am sure."

"And I am to show him how cruelly he has wronged you?"

"Yes, of course."

"You desire me to do this; you will not trust to your innocence, and the efforts of the counsel?"

"Do you want to drive me mad with your questions?" he cried savagely. "If you decline to go, my lawyer shall see Sir Gordon."

"Robert!" she said reproachfully, but with the sweet gentleness of her pitying love for the husband irritated, and beyond control of self in his trouble, apparent in her words.

"Well, why do you talk so and hesitate?" he cried petulantly.

"I will go, dear," she said cheerfully, "and I will plead your cause to the uttermost."

"Yes, of course. It will be better that you should go. He likes you, Millicent; he always did like you, and I dare say he will listen to you. I don't know but what it might be wise to knock under to Bayle. But no: I hate that fellow. I always did from the first. Well, leave that now. See Sir Gordon; tell him what I say, that it will be best for the bank. You'll win. Hang it, Millicent, I could not bear this trial: it would kill me."

"Robert!"

"Ah, well, I'm not going to die yet, and it would be very sad for my handsome little wife to be left a widow if they hang me, or to exist with a live husband serving one-and-twenty years in the bush."

"Robert, you will break my heart if you speak like that," panted Millicent.

"Ah, well, we must not do that," he cried laughingly. "Look here, though; this barrister who is to defend me, I know him—Granton, Q.C. Did your father instruct him?"

"No: he could not. Robert, we are frightfully poor."

"Ah! it is a nuisance," he said, "thanks to my enemies; but we'll get through. Now then, who has instructed this man?"

"I cannot tell, dear."

"I see it all," he said; "it's a plan of the enemy. They employ their own man, and he will sell me, bound hand and foot, to the Philistines."

"Oh! Robert, surely no one would be so base."

"I don't know," he said. "They want to win. It's Sir Gordon's doing. No, it's Christie Bayle. I'd lay a thousand pounds he has paid the fellow's fees."

"Then, Robert, you will not trust him; you will refuse to let him defend you. Husband, my brave, true, innocent husband," she cried, with her pale face flushing, "defend yourself!"

"Hush! Go to Sir Gordon at once. Say everything. I must be had out of this, Milly. I cannot stand my trial." She could only nod her acquiescence, for a gaoler had entered to announce that the visit was at an end.

Then, as if in a dream, confused, troubled in spirit, and hardly seeing her way for the mist before her eyes, Millicent Hallam followed the gaoler back along the white stone passages and through the clanging gates, to be shut out of the prison and remain in a dream of misery and troubled thought, conscious of only one thing, and that one that a gentle hand had taken her by the arm and led her back to where they waited for the conveyance to take them home.

"These handsome men; these handsome men!" sighed Thibs, as she sat by Julia's bed that night, tired with her journey, but reluctant to go to her own resting-place—a mattress upon the floor. "Oh! how I wish sometimes we were back at the old house, and me scolding and stubborn with poor old missus, and in my tantrums from morning to night. Ah! those were happy days."

Thisbe shook her head, and rocked herself to and fro, and sighed and sighed again.

"My old kitchen, and my old back door, and the big dust-hole! What a house it was, and how happy we used to be! Ah! if we could only change right back and be there once more, and Miss Milly not married to no handsome scamp. Ah! and he is; Miss Milly may say what she likes, and try to believe he isn't. He is a scamp, and I wish she had never seen his handsome face, and we were all back again, and then—Oh!—Oh! Oh!—Oh!—Oh!" cried hard, stubborn Thisbe as she sank upon her knees by the child's bedside, sobbing gently and with the tears running down her cheeks, "and then there wouldn't be no you. Bless you! bless you! bless you!"

She kissed the child as a butterfly might settle on a flower, so tender was her love, so great her fear of disturbing the little one's rest.

"Oh! dear me, dear me!" she said, rising and wiping the tears from her hard face and eyes, "well, there's whites and blacks, and ups and downs, and pleasures and pains, and I don't know what to say—except my prayers; and the Lord knows what's best for us after all."

Ten minutes after, poor Thisbe was sleeping peacefully, while, with burning brow, Millicent was pacing her bed-room, thinking of the morrow's interview with Sir Gordon Bourne.

Volume Two—Chapter Seventeen.

Mr Gemp is Curious.

"I know'd—I know'd it all along," said Old Gemp to his friends, for the excitement of his loss seemed now to have acted in an opposite direction and to be giving him strength. "I know'd he couldn't be living at that rate unless things was going wrong. What did the magistrates say?"

"Said it was a black case, and committed him for trial," replied Gorringe the tailor. "Ah, I don't say that clothes is everything, Mr Gemp; but a well-made suit makes a gentleman of a man, and you never heard of Mr Thickens doing aught amiss."

"Nor me neither, eh, Gorringe? and you've made my clothes ever since you've been in business."

The tailor looked with disgust at his neighbour's shabby, well-worn garments, and remained silent.

"I'd have been in the court mysen, Gorringe, on'y old Luttrell said he wouldn't be answerable for my life if I got excited again, and I don't want to die yet, neighbour; there's a deal for me to see to in this world."

"Got your money, haven't you?"

"Ye-es, I've got my money, and it's put away safe; but I wanted my deeds— my writings. I've lost by that scoundrel, horribly."

"Ah, well, it might have been worse," said Gorringe, giving a snip with his scissors that made Gemp start as if it were his own well-frayed thread of life being cut through.

"Oh, of course it might have been worse; but a lot of us have lost, eh, neighbour?"

"Dixons' and Sir Gordon have come down very handsome over it," said Gorringe, who was designing a garment, as he called it, with a piece of French chalk.

"And the parson," said Gemp; "only to think of it—a parson, a curate, with one-and-twenty thousand pound in his pocket."

"Ay, it come in handy," said Gorringe.

"Now, where did he get that money, eh? It's a wonderful sight for a man like him," said Gemp, with a suspicious look.

"London. I heerd tell that he said he had been to London to get it."

"Ay, he said so," cried Gemp, shaking his head, "but it looks suspicious, mun. Here was he hand and glove with the Hallams, always at their house and mixed up like. I want to know where he got that money. I say, sir, that a curate with twenty thousand pound of his own is a sort o' monster as ought to be levelled down."

The tailor pushed up his glasses to the roots of his hair, and left off his work to hold up his shears menacingly at his crony.

"Gemp, old man," he said, "I would not be such a cantankerous, suspicious old magpie as you for a hundred pounds; and look here, if you're going to pull buttons off the back o' parson's coat, go and do it somewhere else, and not in my shop."

"Oh! you needn't be so up," said Gemp. "Look here," he cried, pointing straight at his friend, "what did Thickens say about the writings?"

"Spoke fair as a man could speak," said Gorringe, resuming his architectural designs in chalk and cloth, "said he felt uncomfortable about the matter first when he saw Hallam give a package to a man named Crellock—chap who often come down to see him; that he was suspicious like that for two years, but never had an opportunity of doing more than be doubtful till just lately."

"Why didn't he speak out to a friend—say to a man like me?"

"Because, I'm telling you, it was only suspicion. Hallam managed the thing very artfully, and threw dust in Thickens's eyes; but last of all he see his way clear, and went and told parson. And just then Sir Gordon were suspicious, too, and had got something to go upon, and they nabbed my gentleman just as he was going away."

"And do you believe all this?" cried Gemp.

"To be sure I do. Don't you?"

"Tchah! I'm afraid they're all in it."

"Ah! well, I'm not; and, as we've nothing to lose, I don't care."

"How did Hallam look?"

"Very white; and, my word! he did give parson a look when he was called up to give his evidence. He looked black at Thickens and at Sir Gordon, but he seemed regularly savage with parson."

"Ah, to be sure!" cried Gemp. "What did I say about being thick with parson? It's my belief that if all had their deserts parson would be standing in the dock alongside o' Hallam."

"And it's my belief, Gemp, that you're about the silliest owd maulkin that ever stepped! There, I won't quarrel with thee. Parson? Pshaw!"

"Well, thou'lt see, mun, thou'lt see! Committed for trial, eh? And how about the other fellow!"

"What, Crellock? Oh, they've got him too. He came smelling after Hallam, who was like a decoy bird to him. Wanted to see him in the cage; and they let him see Hallam, and—"

"Ah, I heard that Hallam told the constable Crellock was worse than he, and they took him too. Yes, I heard that. Hallo! here comes Hallam's maid—doctor's owd lass, Thisbe. Let's get a word wi' her."

Gemp shuffled out of the tailor's shop, and made for Thisbe, who was coming down the street, with her head up and her nose in the air.

"Mornin', good mornin'," he said, with one of his most amiable grins.

"I didn't say it wasn't," said Thisbe sharply; and she went straight on to Miss Heathery's, knocked sharply, and waited, gazing defiantly about the place the while.

"Well, she's a stinger, she is!" muttered Gemp, standing scraping away at his face with his forefinger. "Do her good to be married, and hev some one with the rule over her. Humph! she's gone. Now what does she want there?"

The answer was very simple, though it was full of mystery to Gemp. Thisbe wanted her mistress and the child, who had gone to Miss Heathery's after dark, Millicent's soul revolting against the idea of staying at the old home now that it was in the possession of Christie Bayle, her husband's bitterest foe.

The gossips were quite correct. Hallam had been examined thrice before the county magistrates, and enough had been traced to prove that for a long time he had been speculating largely, losing, and making up his losses by pledging, at one particular bank, the valuable securities with which Dixons' strong-room was charged. When one of these was wanted he pledged another and redeemed it, while altogether the losses were so heavy that, had not the old bank proprietors been very wealthy men, Dixons' must have gone.

"Now, where's she a-going, neighbour?" said Gemp, scraping away at his stubbly face. "I don't feel up to it like I did, but I shall have to see."

Gorringe peered through his glasses and the window at the figure in black that had just left Miss Heathery's, leaning on Thisbe's arm for a few moments, and then, as if by an effort, drawing herself up and walking alone.

The day was lovely, the sky of the deepest blue; the sun seemed to be brightening every corner of the whole town, and making the flowers blink and brighten, and the sparrows that haunted the eaves to be in a state of the greatest excitement. King's Castor had never looked more quaintly picturesque and homelike, more the beau-ideal of an old English country town, from the coaching inn with yellow post-chaise outside, and the blue-jacketed postboy with his unnecessarily knotted whip, down to the vegetable stall at the corner of the market, where old Mrs Dims sat on an ancient rush-bottomed chair, with her feet in a brown earthenware bread-pancheon to keep them dry.

Mrs Pinet's flower-pots were so red that they seemed like the blossoms of her plants growing unnaturally beneath the leaves, and her window, and every one else's panes, shone and glittered with the true country brilliancy in the morning sun. Even the grass looked green growing between the cobble-stones—those pebbles that gave the town the aspect that, being essentially pastoral, the inhabitants had decided, out of compliment to their farm neighbours, to pave it with sheep's kidneys.

But there was one blot upon it—one ugly scar, where the yellow deal boards had been newly nailed up, and the walls and window-frames were blackened with smoke; and it was when passing these ruins of her home that Millicent Hallam first shuddered, and then drew herself up to walk firmly by.

"Ah!" said Gorringe, making his shears click, "you wouldn't feel happy if you didn't know what was going on, would you, neighbour?"

"Eh? Know? Of course not. If it hadn't been for me looking after the bank, where would you have all been, eh?"

Gemp spoke savagely, and pointed at the tailor as if he were going to bore a hole in his chest.

"Well, p'r'aps you did some good there, Master Gemp; but if you'd take my advice, you'd go home and keep yoursen quiet. I wouldn't get excited about nothing, if I was you."

"Humph! No, you wouldn't, Master Gorringe; but some folk is different to others," said Gemp, talking away from the doorway, with his head outside, as he peered down the street.

"Hey! look at 'em now!—the curiosity of these women folk! Here's owd Mother Pinet with her neck stretched out o' window, and Barton at the shop, and Cross at the 'Chequers,' and Dawson the carrier, all got their heads out, staring after that woman. Now, where's she going, I wonder?"

Old Gemp stumped back into the shop, shaving away at his cheek.

"She can't be going over to Lindum to see Hallam, because she went yesterday."

The tailor's shears clicked as a corner was taken out of a piece of cloth.

"She ain't going up to the doctor's, because he drove by half-an-hour ago with the owd lady."

Another click.

"Can't be going for a walk. Wouldn't go for a walk at a time like this. I've often wondered why folk do go for walks, Master Gorringe. I never did."

Click!

"Nay, Master Gemp, you could always find enough to see and do in the town, eh?"

"Plenty! plenty, mun, plenty!—I've got it!"

"Eh?"

"She's going—Hallam's wife, yonder—to see owd Sir Gordon, and beg Hallam off; and, look here, I wean't hev it!"

Gemp banged his stick down upon the counter in a way that made the cloth spread thereon rise in waves, and became very broad of speech here, though it was a matter of pride amongst the Castor people that they spoke the purest English in the county, and were not broad of utterance, like the people on the wolds, and "down in the marsh."

Volume Two—Chapter Eighteen.

A Painful Meeting.

Whether Gemp would have it or no, Millicent Hallam was on her way to Sir Gordon's quiet, old-fashioned house on the North Road—a house that was a bit of a mystery to the Castor children, whose young brains were full of conjecture as to what could be inside a place whose windows were blanks, and with nothing but a door to the road, and a high wall right and left to complete the blankness of the frontage.

It ought to have been called the backage; for Sir Gordon Bourne's house was very pleasant on the other side, with a compact garden and flowers blooming to brighten it—a garden in which he never walked.

Millicent Hallam pulled at the swinging handle of the bell at Sir Gordon's door with the determination of one who has called to demand a right.

The door was opened by a quiet-looking, middle-aged man in drab livery, whose brown hair and cocoa-nut fibry whiskers, joined to a swinging, easy gait, suggested that he would not have been out of place on the deck of a vessel, an idea strengthened by an appearance, on one side of his face, as if he were putting his tongue in his cheek.

He drew back respectfully before Millicent could say, "Is Sir Gordon at home?" allowed her to pass, and then, as Thisbe followed her mistress, he gave her a very solemn wink, but without the vestige of a smile.

Thisbe gave her shawl a violent snatch, as if it were armour that she was drawing over a weak spot; but Tom Porter, Sir Gordon's factotum, did not see it, for he was closing the door and thinking about how to hide the fact that his hands were marked with rouge with which he had been polishing the plate when the bell rang.

He led the way across the hall, which was so full of curiosities from all parts of the globe that it resembled a museum, and, opening a door at the end, ushered Millicent into Sir Gordon's library, a neatly kept little room with a good deal of the air of a captain's cabin in its furnishing; telescopes, compasses, and charts hung here and there, in company with books of a maritime character, while one side of the place was taken up by a large glass case containing a model of "The *Sea Dream* schooner yacht, the property of Gordon Bourne." So read an inscription at the foot, engraved upon a brass plate.

Millicent remained standing with her veil down, while Tom Porter retired, closed the door, and, after giving notice of the arrival, went back into the hall, where Thisbe was standing in a very stern, uncompromising fashion.

Sir Gordon's man wanted to arrange his white cravat, but his fingers were red, and for the same reason he was debarred from pushing the Brutus on his head a little higher, so that, unable to rearrange his plumage, he had to let it go.

He walked straight up to Thisbe, stared very hard at her, breathing to match, and then there was a low deep growl heard which bore some resemblance to "How are you?"

Thisbe was "Nicely, thank you," but she did not say it nicely; it was snappish and short.

Mr Tom Porter did not seem to object to snappish shortness, for he growled forth:

"Come below?" and added, "my pantry?"

"No, thank you," was Thisbe's reply, full of asperity.

"Won't you take anything—biscuit?"

"No, I—thank—you," replied Thisbe, dividing her words very carefully; and Tom Porter stood with his legs wide apart and stared.

"I would ha' been at sea, if it hadn't ha' been for the trouble yonder," he said, after a pause.

"Ho!"

Tom Porter raised his hand to scratch his head, but remembered in time, and turned it under his drab coat tail.

"Very sorry," he said at last, without moving a muscle.

"Thank you," said Thisbe sharply and then. "You needn't wait."

"Needn't wait it is," said Tom Porter in a gruff growl, and giving one hand a sort of throw up towards his forehead, and one leg a kick out behind, he went off through a door, perfectly unconscious of the fact that Thisbe's countenance had unconsciously softened, as she stood admiring the breadth of Tom Porter's shoulders and the general solidity of his build.

Meanwhile Millicent stood waiting until a well-known cough announced the coming of Sir Gordon, who entered the room and with grave courtesy placed a chair for his visitor.

"I expected you, Mrs Hallam," he said with a voice full of sympathy; and, as he spoke, he remained standing.

Millicent raised her veil, looked at him with her handsome face contracted by mental pain and with an angry, almost fierce glow in her eyes.

"You expected me?" she said, repeating his words with no particular emphasis or intonation.

"Yes; I thought you would come to an old friend for help and counsel at a time like this."

A passionate outburst was ready to rush forth, but Millicent restrained it, and said coldly:

"My old friend—my father's old friend."

"Yes," he replied; "I hope a very sincere old friend."

"Then why is my poor injured husband in prison?" There was a fierce emphasis in the words that made Sir Gordon raise his brows. He looked at her wonderingly, as if he had not expected his visitor to take this line of argument.

Then he pointed again to a chair.

"Will you not take a seat, Mrs Hallam?" he said gently. "You have come to me then for help?"

"No," she cried, ignoring his request. "I have come for justice to my poor husband, who for the faults of others, by the scheming of his enemies, is now lying in prison awaiting his trial."

Sir Gordon leaned his elbow on the chimney-piece, and with his finger nails tapped the top of the black marble clock that ticked so steadily there.

"You went over to Lindum yesterday to see Hallam?"

"I did."

"He requested you to come and see me?"

"Yes; it was his wish, or—"

"You would not have come," he said with a sad smile upon his lips.

"No. I would have stood in the place where the injustice of men had placed me, and trusted to my own integrity and innocence for my acquittal."

Sir Gordon drew a long breath like a sigh of relief. He had been watching Millicent closely, as if he were suspicious either that she was playing a part, or had been biassed by her husband. But the true loving trust and belief of the woman shone out in her countenance and rang in her words. True woman—true wife! Let the world say what it would, her place was by her husband, and in his defence she was ready to lay down her life.

Sir Gordon sighed then with relief, for even now his old love for Millicent burned brightly. She had been his idol of womanly perfection, and he had felt, as it were, a contraction about his heart as the suspicion crept in for a moment that she was altered for the worse—changed by becoming the wife of Robert Hallam.

"Mrs Hallam—Millicent, my child, what am I to say to you?" he cried at length. "How am I to speak without wounding you? I would not give you pain to add to that which you already suffer."

She looked at him angrily. His words seemed to her, in her overstrained anxiety, hypocritical and evasive.

"I asked you why my husband is cast into prison for the crimes of others?"

Sir Gordon gazed at her pityingly.

"You do not answer," she said. "Then tell me this: Are you satisfied with the degradation he has already suffered? Is he not to be set free?"

"Can you not spare me, Mrs Hallam? Will you not spare yourself?"

"No. I cannot spare you. I cannot spare myself. My husband is helpless: the fight against his enemies must be carried on by me."

"His enemies, Mrs Hallam? Who are they? Himself and his companions."

"You, and that despicable creature who has professed to be our friend, the companion of my child. I saw you planning it together with your wretched menial, Thickens."

Sir Gordon shook his head sadly.

"My dear Mrs Hallam," he said, "you do us all an injustice. Let us change this conversation. Believe me, I want to help you, your child, and your ruined parents."

Millicent started at the last words—ruined parents. There her ideas were obscured and wanting in the clearness with which she believed she saw the truth. But even the explanation of this seemed come at last, and there was a scornful look in her eyes as she exclaimed:

"I want no help. I want justice."

"Then what do you ask of me?" he said coldly, as he felt the impossibility of argument at such a time.

"My husband's freedom, your apology, and declaration to the whole world that he has been falsely charged. You can do no more. It is impossible to wipe out this disgrace."

He made a couple of steps towards her, and took her cold hands in his, raised them to his lips with tender reverence, and kissed them.

"Millicent, my child," he said, with his voice sounding very deep and soft, "do not blame me. My position was forced upon me, and you do not know the sacrifice it has cost me as I thought of you—the sacrifice it will be to Mr Dixon and myself to repair the losses we have sustained."

She snatched her hands from his, and her eyes flashed with anger.

Her rage was but of a few moments' duration. Then she had flung herself upon her knees at his feet, and, with clasped hands and streaming eyes, sobbed forth:

"I am mad! I am mad! I don't know what I say. Sir Gordon—dear Sir Gordon, help us. It is not true. He is innocent. My noble husband could not have descended to such baseness. Sir Gordon, save him! save him!—my poor child's father—my husband, whom I love so well. You do not answer. You do not heed my words. Is man so cruel, then, to the unfortunate? Can you so treat the girl who reverenced you as a child—the woman you said you loved? Man—man!" she cried passionately, "can you not see that my heart is breaking? and yet you, who by a word could save him, now look on and coldly turn a deaf ear to my prayers. Oh, fool! fool! fool! that I was to think that help could come from man. God, help me now, or else in Thy mercy let me die!"

As she spoke these last words, she threw her head back and raised her clasped hands in passionate appeal, while Sir Gordon's lips moved as he repeated the first portion of her prayer, and then stayed and stood gazing down upon the agonised face.

"Millicent," he said at last, as he raised her from where she knelt, and almost placed her in an easy-chair, where she subsided, weak and helpless almost as a child, "listen to me."

He paused to clear his voice, which sounded very husky. Then continuing:

"For your sake—for the sake of your innocent child, I promise that on the part of Mr Dixon and myself there shall be no harsh treatment, no persecution. Your husband shall have justice."

"That is all I ask," cried Millicent, starting forward. "Justice, only justice; for he is innocent."

"My poor girl!" said Sir Gordon warmly; "there," he cried, with a pitying smile, "you see I speak to you as if the past six or seven years had not glided away."

"Yes, yes," she said, clinging to his hand, "forget them, and speak as my dear old friend."

"I will," he said firmly. "And believe me, Millicent, if it were a question merely of the money—my money that I have lost—I would forgive your husband."

"Forgive—"

"I would ignore his defalcation for your sake; but I am not a free agent in a case like this. You do not understand."

"No, no," she said piteously, "everything is contained in one thought to me. They have taken my poor husband and treated him as if a thief."

"Listen, my child," continued Sir Gordon, "I found that the valuable documents of scores of the customers of an old bank had been taken away. They were in your husband's charge."

"Yes, but he says it can all be explained."

Sir Gordon paused, tightening his lips, and a few indignant words trembled on the balance, but he spared the suffering woman's bleeding heart, and continued gravely:

"I was bound in honour to consult with my partner at once, and the result you know."

"Yes; he was arrested. You, you, Sir Gordon, gave the order."

"Yes," he said gravely; "had I not, he would have been beaten and trampled to death by the maddened crowd. Millicent Hallam, be just in your anger. I saved his life."

"Better death than dishonour," she cried passionately.

"Amen!" he responded; and in imagination he saw before him the convict's cell, and went on picturing a horror from which he turned shuddering away.

"Come," he said, "be sure of justice, my child. And now what can I do to help you? Money you must want."

"No," she said drearily.

"Well; means to procure good counsel for your husband's defence."

"He said that you must have procured the counsel he already has."

"I? No, my child; no, I did not even think of such a thing. How could I?"

"Who then has paid fees to this man who has been to my husband?"

"I do not know. I cannot say."

Millicent rose heavily, her eyes wandering, her face deadly white.

"I can do no more here," she said, wringing her hands and passing one over the other in a weak, helpless way; and as Sir Gordon watched her, he saw a faint smile come over her pinched features. She was gazing down at her wedding ring, which seemed during the past few weeks to have begun to hang loosely on her finger. She raised it reverently to her lips, and kissed it in a rapt, absent way, gazing round at last as if wondering why she was there.

"Justice! You have promised justice," she cried suddenly, with a mental light irradiating her face. "I know I may trust you."

"You may," he said reverently, for this woman's love seemed to inspire him with awe.

"And you will forgive me—all I have said?" she whispered.

"Forgive you?" he said, taking her hand and speaking gravely. "Millicent Hallam has no truer servant and friend than Gordon Bourne."

"No truer servant and friend than Gordon Bourne," he repeated, as he returned to his room, after seeing the suffering wife to the door. "Ah! how Heaven's gifts are cast away here and there! What would my life have been if blessed by the love of this man's wife?"

Volume Two—Chapter Nineteen.

The Verdict.

"How is she now, dear Mrs Luttrell—how is she now?" Miss Heathery looked up from out of the handkerchief in which her face was being constantly buried, and it would have been hard to say which was the redder, eyes or nose.

Poor Mrs Luttrell, who had come trembling down from the bed-room, caught at her friend's arm, and seemed to stay herself by it, as she said piteously:

"I can't bear it, my dear; I can't bear it. I was obliged to come down for a few minutes."

"My poor dear," whispered little Miss Heathery, who, excluded from the bed-room, passed her time in hot water that she shed, and that she used to make the universal panacea for woe—a cup of tea—one she administered to all in turn.

"You seem so overcome, you poor dear," she whispered; and, helping Mrs Luttrell to the couch, she poured out a cup of tea for her with kindliest intent, but the trembling mother waved it aside.

"She begged me so, my dear, I was obliged to come out of the room. The doctor says it would be madness; and it is all Thisbe and he can do to keep her lying down. What am I to say to you for giving you all this trouble?"

The tears were running fast down Miss Heathery's yellow cheeks, as she took Mrs Luttrell's grey head to her bony breast.

"Don't! don't! don't!" she sobbed. "What have I ever done that you should only think me a fine-weather friend? If I could only tell you how glad I am to be able to help dear Millicent, but I can't."

"Heaven bless you!" whispered Mrs Luttrell, clinging to her—glad to cling to some one in her distress; "you have been a good friend indeed!"

Just then the stairs creaked slightly, and Thisbe, looking very hard and grim, came into the room.

"How is she, Thisbe?" cried Miss Heathery in a quick whisper.

Thisbe shook her head.

"Seems to be dozing a little now, miss; but she keeps asking for the news."

"Poor dear! poor dear!" sobbed Miss Heathery, with more tears running slowly down her face, to such an extent that if there had been any one to notice, he or she would have wondered where they all came from, and have then set it down to the tea.

"Sit down, Thisbe," sighed Mrs Luttrell, "you must be worn out."

"Poor soul! yes," said Miss Heathery, and pouring out a fresh cup, she took it to where Thisbe—who had not been to bed for a week, watching, as she had been, by Millicent's couch—was sitting on the edge of a chair.

"There, drink that, Thisbe," said Miss Heathery. "You're a good, good soul!"

As she bent forward and kissed the hard-looking woman's face, Thisbe stared half wonderingly at her, and took the cup. Then her hard face began to work, she tried to sip a little tea, choked, set down the cup, and hurried sobbing from the room.

For Millicent Hallam, strong in her determination to help her husband, had had to lean on Thisbe's arm as they returned from Sir Gordon's house that day. When she reached Miss Heathery's house she was compelled to lie down on the couch. An hour later she began to talk wildly, and when her father was hastily summoned she was in a high state of fever.

This, with intervals of delirium and calmness, had gone on ever since, up to the day of Robert Hallam's trial.

On the previous night, as Millicent lay holding her child to her breast—the little thing having been brought at her wish, to bound to the bedside and bury her flushed, half-frightened face in her mother's bosom—a soft tap had come to the door below.

Millicent's hearing, during the intervals of the fever and delirium, was preternaturally keen, and she turned to her mother.

"It is Mr Bayle!" she said, in a hoarse whisper. "I know now. I understand all. It is to-morrow. I want to know. Ask him."

"Ask him what, my darling? But pray be calm. Remember what your father said."

"Yes, yes, I remember; but ask him. No; of course he must be there. Tell Christie Bayle to come to me directly it is over—and bring my husband. Directly, mind. You will tell him?"

"Yes, yes, my darling," said Mrs Luttrell, with her face working as she moved towards the door.

"Stop, mother!" cried Millicent. "Hush! lie still, Julie; mamma is not cross with you. Mother, tell Christie Bayle to bring me the news of the trial the moment it is over. I can trust him. He will," she said to herself with a smile, as her mother left the room, and delivered the message to him who was below.

He left soon after, sick at heart, to join Sir Gordon, and together they took their places in the coach, the only words that passed being:

"How is she, Bayle?"

"In the Great Physician's hands," was the reply. "Man's skill is nothing here."

And she of whom they spoke lay listening to the cheery notes of the guard's horn, the trampling of the horses, and the rattle of the wheels, as the coach rolled away, with James Thickens outside, thinking of the horrors of passing the night in a strange bed, in a strange town, and wishing the troubles of this case of Hallam's at an end.

The next morning Millicent Hallam insisted upon rising and dressing, to go over to Lindum and be present at the trial.

All opposition only irritated her, and at last Thisbe was summoned to the room.

"I shall be just outside," whispered the doctor. "It is better than fighting against her."

In less than five minutes he was once more by his child's side, trying to bring her back from the fainting fit in which she had fallen back upon the bed, for she had learned her weakness, and her utter impotence to take such a journey upon an errand like that.

And then the weary day had crept on, with the delirium sometimes seizing upon the tottering brain, and then a time of comparative coolness supervening.

Dr Luttrell looked serious, and told himself that he was in doubt.

"The bad news will kill her," he said to himself, as he went outside to walk up and down Miss Heathery's garden, which was fifteen feet long and twelve feet wide, "but very secluded," as its owner often said.

There, with bare head and wrinkled brow, the doctor walked up and down, stopping, from habit, now and then to pinch off a dead leaf, or give a twist to one of the scarlet runners that had slipped from its string.

The night at last; and the doctor was sitting by the bedside, having sent Mrs Luttrell down, and then Thisbe, both utterly worn out and unhinged.

Millicent was, as Thisbe had said, dozing; but the fever was high, and Dr Luttrell shook his grey head.

"Who'd have thought, my poor flower," he said, "that your young life would be blighted like this!"

He could hardly bear his suffering, and, rising from his chair, he stole softly into the back room, where Julia was sleeping calmly, the terrible trouble affecting her young heart only for the minute, and then passing away.

The old man bent down and kissed the sleeping face, and, as her custom was, Julia's little arms went softly up and clasped the neck of him who pressed her soft cheek, and fell away again, heavy with sleep.

"He will come and tell me the truth."

The words fell clearly on the doctor's ear as he was re-entering the sick-room, but Millicent lay apparently sound asleep in the little white dimity-hung bed of Miss Heathery's best room, while the soft murmur of voices came from below.

Millicent's words were those of truth, for the moment the trial was over Christie Bayle had rushed out, and sprung into the post-chaise he had had in waiting, and for which changes of horses were harnessed at the three towns they would have to pass through to reach King's Castor, over thirty miles away, and as fast as horses urged by man could go over the rough cross-road, that post-chaise was being hurried along.

The night was settling down dark as the first pair of steaming horses were taken out, and a couple of country candles were lit in the battered lamps. Then on and on, uphill slowly, down the far slope at a good gallop, with the chaise dancing and swaying about on its C-springs, and time after time the whole affair nearly being thrown over upon its side.

"It's too dark to go so fast, sir," remonstrated the wheeler postboy, as Bayle leaned his head out of the window to urge him on.

"Ten shillings a-piece, man. It's for life or death," cried Bayle; and the whips cracked, and the horses plunged into their collars, as the hedges on either side seemed to fly by like a couple of blurred lines.

"I must get up now, father," said Millicent suddenly.

"My child, no, it is impossible. You remember this morning?"

"My dressing-gown," she said in a low, decided voice. "Thisbe will carry me down."

"No, no," said Dr Luttrell decidedly. "You must obey me, child."

"Dear father," she whispered, "if I lie here in the agony of suspense I shall die. I must go down."

"But why, my child?"

"Why," she said. "Do you think I could bear any one else to hear his news but me?"

It was in vain to object, and in the belief that he was doing more wisely by giving way, Dr Luttrell summoned Thisbe, and, with Mrs Luttrell's help, the suffering woman was partially dressed and borne down to the sitting-room. She bore the change wonderfully, and lay there very still and patient, waiting for the next two hours. The fever had greatly abated, and she listened, her eyes half-closed, as if in the full confidence that the news for which she hungered would not be long.

Thisbe and Miss Heathery had stolen out into the kitchen to sit and talk in whispers as, one by one, the last sounds in the town died out. The shutters here and there had long been rattled up. The letter-carriers from the villages round had all come in, and only a footfall now and then broke the silence of the little town.

Ten o'clock had struck, and Doctor and Mrs Luttrell exchanged glances, the former encouraging his wife with a nod, for Millicent seemed to be asleep. A quarter-past ten was chimed by the rickety clock in the old stone tower, and the only place now where there was any sign of business was up at the "George," where lamps burned inside and out, and the ostlers brought out two pairs of well-clothed horses ready for the coach that would soon be through. By-and-by there was the rattle of wheels and the cheery notes of a horn, but they did not wake Millicent, who still seemed to sleep, while there was a little noise of trampling hoofs, the banging of coach doors, a few shouts, a cheery "All right!" and then the horses went off at a trot, the wheels rattled, and the lamps of the mail shone through the drawn-down blind. Then the sounds died away; all was still, and the clock chimed half-past. As the last tones throbbed and hummed in the still night air, Millicent suddenly stirred, sat up quickly, and pressed back her hair from her face.

"Help me! The chair!" she said hoarsely.

"Yes," said the doctor, in answer to Mrs Luttrell's look; and with very little aid Millicent left the couch, gathered her dressing-gown round her, and sat back listening.

"He will soon be here," she said softly, and she bowed her head upon her breast.

She was right, for the horses were tearing over the ground in the last mile of the last stage, with Christie Bayle almost as breathless, as he sat back pale with excitement, and trembling for the news he had to impart. At the end of the trial and in his desire to keep his word, all had seemed strange and confused. He could feel nothing but that he had to get back to King's Castor and tell her all. It was her command. But now that he was rapidly nearing home, the horror of his position began to weigh him down, and he felt ready to shrink from his duty, but all the time there was a sensation as if something was urging him on, fast as the horses seemed to fly.

The miles had seemed leagues before. This last seemed not a quarter its length; for there was the mill, there Thickens's cottage, there the great draper's, the market-place, the "George," before which the horses were checked covered with foam.

With the feeling still upon him that he could not bear this news, and that it should have been brought by Sir Gordon, who had refused to come, he ran across to Miss Heathery's house, and when he reached the door, it was opened. He stepped in and it was closed by Mrs Luttrell, who was trembling like a leaf.

"Come here! quick!"

Bayle knew and yet did not recognise the voice, it was so changed; but, as in a dream, he went past the little candlestick on the passage bracket, and in at the open parlour-door, where the light of the shaded globe lamp fell upon Millicent's pale face.

"Father! mother!" she said quickly. "Leave us. I must hear the news alone!"

The doctor's eyes sought Bayle's, but his face was contracted as he stood there, hat and cloak in hand, pale as if from a sick-bed and his eyes closed.

Then he and Millicent were alone, and, as if stung by some agonising mental pang, he said wildly:

"No, no! Your father—mother! Let me tell them." Millicent rose slowly, and laid her hand upon his arm.

"You bear me news of my husband," she said, in an unnaturally calm voice. "I know: it is the worst!" He made no reply, but looked at her beseechingly. "I can bear it now," she said, shivering like one whom pain had ended by numbing against further agony. "I see it is the worst; he is condemned!" There was a faint smile upon her lips as he caught her hands in his.

"You forced me to this," he said hoarsely, "and you will hate me more for giving you this pain."

"No," she said, speaking in the same unnaturally calm, strained manner. "No: for I have misjudged you, Christie Bayle. Boy and man, you were always true to me. And—and—he is condemned?"

His eyes alone spoke, and then she tottered as if she would have fallen, but he caught her, and placed her in a chair.

"Yes: I know—I knew it must be," she said with her eyes half-closed. "Every one will know now!"

"Let me call your father in?" he whispered.

"No: not yet. I have something to say," she murmured almost in a whisper. "If—I die—my little child—Christie Bayle? She—she loves you!"

Millicent Hallam's eyes filled up the gaps in her feeble speech, and Christie Bayle read her wish as if it had been sounded trumpet-tongued in his ears.

"Yes; I understand. I will," he said in a voice that was more convincing than if he had spoken on oath.

By that time the news which the postboys had caught as it ran from lip to lip, before Christie Bayle could force his way through the crowd at Lindum assize court, was flashing, as such news can flash through a little inquisitive town like Castor, and, almost at the same moment as Christie Bayle made his promise, old Gemp stumbled into Gorringe's shop to point at him and pant out:

"Transportation for life!"

Volume Three—Chapter One.

After Twelve Years—Back from a Voyage.

"Why, my dear Sir Gordon, I am glad to see you back again. You look brown and hearty, and not a day older."

"Don't—don't shake quite so hard, my dear Bayle. I like it, but it hurts. Little gouty in that hand, you see."

"Well, I'll be careful. I am glad you came."

"That's right, that's right. Come down to my club and dine, and we'll have a long talk; and—er—don't take any notice of the jokes if you hear any."

"Jokes?"

"Ye-es. The men have a way there—the old fellows—of calling me 'Laurel,' and 'Yew,' and the 'Evergreen.' You see, I look well and robust for my age."

"Not a bit, Sir Gordon. You certainly seem younger, though, than ever."

"So do you, Bayle; so do you. Why, you must be—"

"Forty-two, Sir Gordon. Getting an old man, you see."

"Forty! Pooh! what's that, Mr Bayle? Why, sir, I'm—Never mind. I'm not so young as I used to be. And so you think I look well, eh, Bayle?"

"Indeed you do, Sir Gordon; remarkably well."

"Hah! That confounded Scott! Colonel Scott at the club set it about that I'd been away for two years so as to get myself cut down and have time to sprout up again, I looked so young. Bah, what does it matter? It's the sea life, Bayle, keeps a man healthy and strong. I wish I could persuade you to come with me on one of my trips."

"No, no! Keep away with your temptations. Too busy."

"Nonsense, man! Fellow with your income grinding day after day as you do. But how young you do look! How is Mrs Hallam?"

"Remarkably well. I saw her yesterday."

"And little Julie?"

"Little!" said Christie Bayle laughing frankly, and justifying Sir Gordon's remarks about his youthful looks. "Really, I should like to be there when you call. You will be astonished."

"What, has the child grown?"

"Child? Grown? Why, my dear sir, you will have to be presented to a beautiful young lady of eighteen, wonderfully like her mother in the old days."

"Indeed! Hah! yes. Old days, Bayle. Yes, old days, indeed. The thought of them makes me feel how time has gone. Look young, eh? Bah! I'm an old fool, Bayle. Deal better if I had been born poor. You should see me when Tom Porter takes me to pieces, and puts me to bed of a night. Why, Bayle, I don't mind telling you. Always were a good lad, and I liked you. I'm one of the most frightful impositions of my time. Wig, sir; confound it! sham teeth, sir, and they are horribly uncomfortable. Whiskers dyed, sir. The rest all tailor's work. Feel ashamed of myself sometimes. At others I say to myself that it's showing a bold front to the enemy. No, sir, not a bit of truth in me anywhere."

"Except your heart," said Bayle, smiling.

"'Tchut! man, hold your tongue. Now about yourself. Why don't you get a comfortable rectory somewhere, instead of plodding on in this hole?"

"Because I am more useful here."

"Nonsense! Get a good West-end lectureship."

"I prefer the North here."

"My dear Christie Bayle, you are throwing yourself away. There, I can't keep it back. Old Doctor Thomson is dead, and if you will come I have sufficient interest with the bishop, providing I bring forward a good man, to get him the living at King's Castor."

Christie Bayle shook his head sadly.

"No, Sir Gordon," he said, with a curious, wistful look coming into his eyes. "That would be too painful—too full of sad memories."

"Pooh! nonsense, man! You can't be a curate all your life."

"Why not? I do not want the payment of a better post in the Church."

"Of course not; but come, say 'Yes.' As to memories, fudge! man, you have your memories everywhere. If you were out in Australia you'd have them, same as I dare say a friend of ours has. Let the past go."

Bayle shook his head.

"I'm thinking of settling down yonder myself. Getting too old for sea-trips. If you'd come down, that would decide me."

"No, no. It would never do. I could not leave town."

"Ah, so you pretend, sir. I'll be bound that, if you had a good motive, you'd be off anywhere, in spite of what you say."

"Perhaps. Your motive is not strong enough."

"What, not your own interest, man?"

"My dear Sir Gordon, no. What interest have I in myself? Why, I have been blessed by Providence with a good income and few wants, and for the past eighteen years I've been so busy thinking about other people, that I should feel guilty of a crime if I began to be selfish now."

"You're a queer fellow, Bayle, but you may alter your mind. I've made up mine that you shall have the old living at King's Castor. I shan't marry now, so I don't want you for that; but, please God I don't go down in some squall, I should like you to say 'Ashes to ashes, dust to dust' over the remains of a very selfish old man, for I sometimes think that it can't be long first now."

"My dear old friend," said Bayle, shaking his hand warmly, "I pray that the day may be very far distant. When it does come, as it comes to us all, I shall be able to think that the selfishness of which you speak was mere outside show. Gordon Bourne, I seem to be a simple kind of man, but I think I have learned to read men's hearts."

The old man's lip quivered a little, and he tried vainly to speak. Then, giving his stout ebony cane a stamp on the floor, he raised it, and shook it threateningly.

"Confound you, Bayle! I wish you were as poor as Job."

"Why?"

"So that I might leave you all I've got. Perhaps I shall."

"No, no, don't do that," said Bayle seriously, and his frank, handsome face looked troubled; "I have more than I want. But, come, tell me; you have been down to Castor, then?"

"Yes, I was there a week."

"And how are they all?"

"Older, of course, but things seem about the same. Place like that does not change much."

"But the people do."

"Not they. By George! sir, one of the first men I saw as I limped down the street in a pair of confoundedly tight Hessians Hoby made for me—punish my poor corns horribly. What with them and the stiff cravats a gentleman is forced to wear, life is unendurable. Ah! you don't study appearances at sea. Wish I could wear boots like those, Bayle."

"You were saying that you saw somebody."

"Ah, yes; to be sure, I trailed off about my boots. Why, I am getting into—lose leeway, sir. But I remember now. First man I saw was old Gemp, sitting like a figure-head outside his cottage. Regular old mummy; but he seemed to come to life as soon as he heard a step, and turned his eyes towards me, looking as inquisitive as a monkey. Poor old boy—almost paralysed, and has to be lifted in and out. I often wonder what was the use of such men as he."

Christie Bayle's broad shoulders gave a twitch, and he looked up in an amused manner.

"Ah, well, what was the use of me, if you like? Doctor looked well; so does the old lady. Said they were up here three months ago, and enjoyed their visit I say, Bayle, you'd better have the living. Mrs Hallam might be disposed to go down to the old home again, eh?"

A quiet, stern look, that made Christie Bayle appear ten years older, and changed him in aspect from one of thirty-five to nearer fifty, came over his face.

"No," he said, "I am sure Mrs Hallam would never go back to Castor to live."

"Humph! Well, you know best. I say, Bayle, does she want help? It is such a delicate matter to offer it to her, especially in our relative positions."

"No, I am sure she does not," said Bayle quickly; "you would hurt her feelings by the offer."

Sir Gordon nodded, and sat gazing at one particular flower in the carpet of his host's simply-furnished room, which he poked and scraped with his stick.

"How was Thickens?"

"Just the same; not altered a bit, unless it is to look more drab. Mrs Thickens—that woman's an impostor, sir. She has grown younger since she married."

"Yes, she astonished me," said Bayle, smiling with satisfaction that his visitor had gone off dangerously painful ground, "plump, pleasant little body."

"With fat filling up her creases and covering up her holes and corners!" cried Sir Gordon, interrupting. "Confound it all, sir, I could never get the fat to come and fill up my creases and furrows. I saw her standing there, feeding Thickens's fish, smiling at them, and as happy as the day was long. Deal happier than when she was Miss Heathery. Everybody seems to be happy but me. I never am."

"See the Trampleasures?" said Bayle.

"Oh, yes, saw them, and heard them, too. Regular ornament to the bank, Trampleasure. People believe in him, though. Talks to them, and asks the farmers in to lunch. If he were not there, they'd think Dixons' was going. Poor old Dixon, how cut up he was over that Hallam business! It killed him, Bayle."

"Think so?" said Bayle, with his brow wrinkling.

"Sure of it, sir. It was not the money he cared for; it was the principle of the thing. Dixons' name had stood so high in the town and neighbourhood. There was a mystery, too, about the matter that was never cleared up."

"Hadn't we better change the subject, Sir Gordon?"

"No, sir," said Bayle's visitor curtly. "Garrulity is one of the privileges of old age. We old men don't get many privileges; let me enjoy that. I like to gossip about old times to some one who understands them as you do. If you don't like to hear me, say so, and I will go."

"No, no, pray stay, and I'll go down with you to the club."

"Hah! That's right. Well, as I was saying, there was a bit of mystery about that which worried poor old Dixon terribly. We never could make out what the scoundrel had done with the money. He and that other fellow, Crellock, could easily get rid of a good deal; but there was a large sum unaccounted for, I'm sure."

There was a pause here, and Sir Gordon seemed to be hesitating about saying something that was on his mind.

"You wanted to tell me something," said Bayle at last.

"Well, yes, I was going to say you see a deal of the widow, don't you?"

"Widow? What widow? Oh, Mrs Richardson. Poor thing, yes; but how did you know I took an interest in her? Hah! there: you may give me ten pounds for her."

"Mrs Richardson! Pooh! I mean Mrs Hallam."

"Widow?"

"Well, yes; what else is she? Husband transported for life. The man is socially dead."

"You do not know Mrs Hallam," said Bayle gravely.

"Do you think she believes in him still?"

"With her whole heart. He is to her the injured man, a victim to a legal error, and she lives in the belief which she has taught her child, that some day her martyr's reputation will be cleared, and that he will take his place among his fellow-men once more."

"I wish I could think so too, for her sake," said Sir Gordon, after a pause.

"Amen!"

"But, Bayle, you—you don't ever think there was any mistake?"

"It is always painful to me to speak of a man whom I never could esteem."

"But to me, man—to me."

"For twelve years, Sir Gordon, I have had the face of that loving, trusting woman before me, steadfast in her faith in the husband she loves."

"Loves?"

"As truly as on the day she took him first to her heart."

"But do you think that she really still believes him innocent?"

"In her heart of hearts; and so does her child. And I say that this is the one painful part of our intimacy. It has been the cause of coldness and even distant treatment at times."

"But she seemed to have exonerated you from all credit in his arrest."

"Oh, yes, long ago. She attributes it to the accident of chance and the treachery of the scoundrel Crellock."

"Who was only Hallam's tool."

"Exactly. But she forgives me, believing me her truest friend."

"And rightly. The man who fought for her at the time of the—er—well, accident, Bayle, eh?"

"Shall we change the subject?" said Bayle coldly.

"No; I like to talk about poor Mrs Hallam, and I will call and see her soon."

"But you will be careful," said Bayle earnestly. "Of course your presence will bring back sad memories. Do not pain her by any allusion to Hallam."

"I will take care. But look here, Bayle; you did come up here to be near them?"

"Certainly I did. Why, Sir Gordon, that child seemed to be part of my life, and when Mrs Hallam had that long illness the little thing came to me as if I were her father. She had always liked me, and that liking has grown."

"You educated her?"

"Oh, I don't know; I suppose so," said Bayle, looking up with a frank, ingenuous smile. "We have always read together, and painted, and then there was the music of an evening. You must hear her sing!"

"Hah! I should like to, Bayle. Perhaps I shall. Don't think me impertinent, but you see I am so much away in my yacht. Selfish old fellow, you know; want to live as long as I can, and I think I shall live longer if I go to sea than if I stroll idling about Castor or in London at my club. I've asked you a lot of questions. I suppose you have done all the teaching?"

"Oh, dear, no; her mother has had a large share in the child's education."

"Humph! when I called her child, I was snubbed." Bayle laughed. "Well, I've grown to think of her as my child, and she looks upon me almost as she might upon her father."

"Humph!" said Sir Gordon rather gruffly. "I half expected, every time I came back, to find you married, Bayle."

"Find me married?" said Bayle, laughing. "My dear sir, I am less likely to marry than you. Confirmed old bachelor, and I am very happy—happier than I deserve to be."

"Don't cant, Bayle," cried Sir Gordon peevishly. "I've always liked you because you never threw sentiments of that kind at me. Don't begin now. Well, there, I must trot. You are going to dine with me?"

"Yes; I've promised."

"Ah," said Sir Gordon, looking at Bayle almost enviously, "you always were quite a boy. What a physique you have! Why, man, you don't look thirty-five."

"I'm very sorry."

"Sorry, man?"

"Well, then, I'm very glad."

"Bah! There, put on your hat, and come down at once. I hate this part of London."

"And I have grown to love it. 'The mind is its own place.' You know the rest."

"Oh, yes, I know the rest," said Sir Gordon gruffly. "Come along. Where can we get a coach?"

"I'll show you," said Bayle, taking his arm and leading him through two or three streets, to stop at last in a quiet, new-looking square close by St. John's Street.

"Well, what's the matter?" said Sir Gordon testily. "Nothing, I hope; only I must make a call here before I go down with you."

"For goodness' sake, make haste, then, man! My boots are torturing me!"

"Come in, then, and sit down," said Bayle, smiling, as a stern-looking woman opened the door, and curtsied familiarly.

"I must either do that or sit upon the step," said the old gentleman peevishly; and he followed Bayle into the passage, and then into the parlour, for he seemed quite at home.

Then a change came over Sir Gordon's face, for Bayle said quietly:

"My dear Mrs Hallam, I have brought an old friend."

Volume Three—Chapter Two.

A Peep behind the Clouds.

The meeting was painful, for Millicent Hallam and Sir Gordon had never stood face to face since that day when he had himself opened the door for her on the occasion of her appeal to him on her husband's behalf.

"Bless my soul!" exclaimed Sir Gordon. "I did not know this."

"It is a surprise, too, for me," said Mrs Hallam, as she coloured slightly, and then turned pale; but in a moment or two she was calm and composed—a handsome, grave-looking lady, with unlined face, but with silvery streaks running through her abundant hair.

"You—you should have told me, Bayle," said Sir Gordon testily.

"And spoilt my surprise," said Bayle.

"I am very, very glad to see you, Sir Gordon," said Mrs Hallam in a grave, sweet way, once more thoroughly mistress of her emotions. "Julie, my dear, you hardly recollect our visitor?"

"Yes, oh yes!" said a tall, graceful girl, coming forward to place her hand in Sir Gordon's. "I seem to see you back as if through a mist; but—oh, yes, I remember!" She hesitated, and blushed, and laughed. "You one day—you brought me a great doll."

Sir Gordon had taken both her hands, letting fall hat and stick. He tried to speak, but the words would not come. His lip quivered, his face twitched, and Julia felt his hands tremble, as she looked at him with naïve wonder, unable to comprehend his emotion.

He raised her hand as if to press it to his lips, but let it fall, and, drawing her towards him, kissed her tenderly on the brow, ending by retaining her hand in both of his.

"An old man's kiss, my child," he said, gazing at her wistfully. "You remind me so of one I loved—twenty years ago, my dear, and before you were born." He looked round from one to the other, as if apologising for his emotion. "My dear Bayle," he said at last, recovering himself, and speaking with chivalrous courtesy, "I am in your debt for introducing me to our young friend. Mrs Hallam, you will let me come and see you?"

Millicent hesitated, and there was a curious, haughty, defiant look in her eyes as she gazed at her visitor, as if at bay.

"I am sure Mrs Hallam will be glad to see a very dear old friend of mine," said Bayle quietly; and as he spoke Mrs Hallam glanced at him. Her eyes softened, and she held out her hand to her visitor.

"Always glad to see you," she said.

Sir Gordon smiled and looked pleased, as he glanced round the pretty, simply-furnished room, with tokens of the busy hands that adorned it on every side. Here was Julia's drawing, there her embroidery; they were her flowers in the window; the bird that twittered so sweetly from its cage hung on the shutter, and the piano, were hers too. There was only one jarring note in the whole interior, and that was the portrait in oils of the handsome man, in the most prominent place in the room—a picture that at one corner was a little blistered, as if by fire, and whose eyes seemed to be watching the visitor wherever he turned.

There were many painful memories revived during that visit, but on the whole it was pleasant, and with the agony of the past softened by time, Millicent Hallam found herself speaking half reproachfully to Sir Gordon for not visiting her during all these years.

"Don't blame me," he said in reply; "I have always felt that there was a wish implied on your part that our acquaintance should cease, as being too painful for both."

"Perhaps it was," she said, with a sigh; "and I am to blame."

"Let us share it, if there be any blame," said Sir Gordon, smiling, "and amend our ways. You must remember, though, that I have always kept up my friendship with the doctor whenever I have been at home, and I have always heard of your well-beings or—"

"Oh, yes!" said Mrs Hallam hastily, as if to check any allusion to assistance. "When I recovered from my serious illness I was anxious to leave Castor. I thought perhaps that my child's education—in London—and Mr Bayle was very kind in helping me."

"He is a good friend," said Sir Gordon gravely.

"Friend!" cried Mrs Hallam, with her face full of animation, "he has been to me a brother. When I was in utter distress at that terrible time, he extricated my poor husband's money affairs from the miserable tangle in which they were left, and by a wise management of the little remainder so invested it that there was a sufficiency for Julia and me to live on in this simple manner."

"He did all this for you," said Sir Gordon dryly.

"Yes, and would have placed his purse at my disposal, but that he saw how painful such an offer would have been."

"Of course," said Sir Gordon, "most painful."

"I often fear that I did wrong in allowing him to leave Castor; but he has done so much good here that I tell myself all was for the best."

And so the conversation rippled on, Julia sometimes being drawn in, and now and then Bayle throwing in a word; but on the whole simply looking on, an interested spectator, who was appealed to now and then as if he had been the brother of one, the uncle of the other.

At last Sir Gordon rose to go, taking quite a lingering farewell of Julia, at whom he gazed again in the same wistful manner.

"Good-bye," he said, smiling tenderly at her, while holding her little hand in his. "I shall come again—soon—yes, soon; but not to bring you a doll."

There was a jingle of a tiny bell as they closed the door, and the hard-faced woman had to squeeze by the visitors to get to the door, the passage was so small.

Sir Gordon stared hard, and then placed his large square glass to his eye.

"To be sure—yes. It's you," he said. "The old maid, Thisbe—"

"Some people can't help being old maids," said that lady tartly, "and some wants to be, sir."

"I beg your pardon," said Sir Gordon with grave politeness. "You mistake me. I meant the maid who used to be with Doctor and Mrs Luttrell in the old times. To be sure, yes, and with Mrs Hallam afterwards."

"Yes, Sir Gordon."

"So you've kept to your mistress all through—I mean you have stayed."

"Yes, sir, of course I have."

"And been one of the truest and best of friends," said Bayle, smiling.

Thisbe gave herself a jerk and glanced over her shoulder, as though to see if the way was clear for her escape—should she have to run and avoid this praise.

"Ah, yes," said Sir Gordon, looking at her still very thoughtfully. "To be sure," he continued, in quite dreamy tones, "I had almost forgotten. Tom Porter wants to marry you."

"Then Tom Porter must—"

"Tchut! tchut! tchut! woman; don't talk like that. Make your hay while the sun shines. Good fellow, Tom. Obstinate, but solid, and careful. Come, Bayle."

"Ah," he sighed, as they walked slowly down the street.

> "Gather your rosebuds while you may,
> Old Time is still a-flying.

"You and I have never been rosebud gatherers, Christie Bayle. It will give us the better opportunity for watching those who are. Bayle, old friend, we must look out: there must be no handsome, plausible scoundrel to come and cull that fragrant little bloom—we must not have another sweet young life wrecked—like hers." He made a backward motion with his head towards the house they had left.

"Heaven forbid!" cried Bayle anxiously; and his countenance was full of wonder and dismay.

"You must look out, sir, look out," said Sir Gordon, thumping his cane.

"But she is a mere girl yet."

"Pish! man; tush! man. It is your mere girls who form these fancies. What have you been about?"

"About?" said Bayle. "About? I don't know. I have thought of such a thing as my little pupil forming an attachment, but it seemed to be a thing of the far-distant future."

Sir Gordon shook his head.

"There is nothing then now?"

"Oh, absurd! Why, she is only eighteen!"

"Eighteen!" said Gordon sharply; "and at eighteen girls are only cutting their teeth and wearing pinafores, eh? Go to: blind mole of a parson! Why, millions of them lose their hearts long before that. Come, come, man, wake up! A pretty watchman of that fair sweet tower you are, to have never so much as thought of the enemy, when already he may be making his approach." Bayle turned to him, looking half-bewildered, but the look passed off.

"No," he said firmly; "the enemy is not in sight yet, and you shall not have cause to speak to me again like, that."

"That's right, Bayle; that's right. Dear, dear," he sighed as they walked slowly towards the city, "how time does gallop on! It seems just one step from

Millicent Luttrell's girlhood to that of her child. Yes, yes, yes: these young people increase, and grow so rapidly that they fill up the world and shoulder us old folk over the edge."

"Unless they have yachts," said Bayle, smiling. "Plenty of room at sea."

"Ah, to be sure; that reminds me. I have been at sea. Man, man, what an impostor you are."

"I!" exclaimed Bayle, looking round at his companion in a startled manner.

"To be sure. Poor lady! She has been confiding to me while you were chatting with little Julia about the piano."

Bayle gave an angry stamp.

"And your careful management of the remains of her husband's property."

Bayle knit his brow and increased his pace.

"No, no," cried Sir Gordon, snatching at and taking his arm. "No running away from unpleasant truths, Christie Bayle. You paid the counsel for Hallam's defence, did you not?"

Bayle nodded shortly, and uttered an angry ejaculation.

"And there was not a shilling left when Hallam was gone?"

No answer.

"Come, come, speak. I am going to have the truth, my friend: priesthood and deception must not go hand in hand. Now then, did Hallam have any money?"

"If he had it would have been handed over to Dixons' Bank," said Bayle sharply. "I should have seen it done."

"Hah! I thought so. Then look here, sir, you have been investing your money for the benefit of that poor woman and her child."

No answer.

"Christie Bayle: do you love that woman still?"

"Sir Gordon! No; I will not be angry. Yes; as a man might love a dear sister smitten by affliction; and her child as if she were my own."

"Hah! and you have had invested so much money—your own, for their benefit. Why have you done this?"

"I thought it was my duty towards the widow and fatherless in their affliction," said Bayle simply; and Sir Gordon turned and peered round in the brave, honest face at his side to find it slightly flushed, but ready to meet his gaze with fearless frankness.

"Ah," sighed Sir Gordon at last, "it was not fair."

"Not fair?" said Bayle wonderingly.

"No, sir. You might have let me do half."

Volume Three—Chapter Three.

By the Fire's Glow.

"Won't you have the lamp lit, Miss Millicent?"

"No, Thisbe, not yet," said Mrs Hallam, in a low, dreamy voice, and without a word the faithful follower of her mistress in trouble went softly out, closing the door, and leaving mother and daughter alone.

"She's got one of her fits on," mused Thisbe. "Ah, how it does come over me sometimes like a temptation—just about once a month ever since—to have one good go at her and tell her I told her so; that it was all what might be expected of wedding a handsome man. 'Didn't I warn you?' I could say. 'Didn't I tell you how it would be?' But no: I couldn't say a word to the poor dear, and her going on believing in the bad scamp as she does all these years. She's different to me. It's just for all the world like a temptation that comes over me, driving me like to speak, but I've kept my mouth shut all these years and I'm going to do it still."

Thisbe had reached her little brightly-kept kitchen, where she stood thoughtfully gazing at the fire, with one hand upon her hip, for some minutes.

Then a peculiar change came upon Thisbe's hard face. It seemed as if it had been washed over with something sweet, which softened it; then it suggested the idea that she was about to sneeze, and ended by a violent spasmodic twitch, quite a convulsion. Thisbe's body remained motionless, though her face was altered, and by degrees her eyes, after brightening and sparkling, grew suffused and dreamy, as she gazed straight before her and seemed to be thinking very deeply. Her countenance was free from the spasm now, and as the candle shone upon it, it brought prominently into notice the fact that in her love of cleanliness Thisbe was not so particular as she might have been in the process of rinsing; for the fact was patent that she rubbed herself profusely with soap, and left enough upon her face after her ablutions to produce the effect of an elastic varnish or glaze.

Everything was very still, the only sounds being the dull wooden tick of the Dutch clock, and the drowsy chirp of an asthmatic cricket, which seemed to have wedded itself somewhere in a crack behind the grate, and to be bemoaning its inability to get out; while the clock ticked hoarsely, as if its life were a burden, and it were heartily sick of having that existence renewed by a nightly pulling up of the two black iron sausages that hung some distance below its sallow face.

Suddenly Thisbe walked sharply to the fire, seized the poker, and cleared the bottom bar. This done she replaced the poker, and planted one foot upon the fender to warm, and one hand upon the mantel-piece with so much inadvertence that she knocked down the tinder-box, and had to pick the flint and steel from out of the ashes with the brightly polished tongs.

"I don't know what's come to me," she said sharply, as soon as the tinder-box was replaced. "Think of her holding fast to him all these years, and training up my bairn to believe in him as if he was a noble martyr! My word, it's a curious thing for a woman to be taken like that with a man, and no matter what he does, to be always believing him!"

Thisbe pursed up her lips, and twitched her toes up and down as they rested upon the fender, while she directed her conversation at the golden caverns of the fire.

"They say Gorringe the tailor used to beat his wife, but that woman always looked happy, and I've seen her smile on him as if there wasn't such another man in the world."

Just then the clock gave such a wheeze that Thisbe started and stared at it.

"Quite makes me nervous," she said, turning back to the fire. "What with the thinking and worry, and her keeping always in the same mind—oh, my!"

She took her hand from the mantel-piece to clap it upon its fellow as a sudden thought struck her, which made her look aghast.

"If he did!" she said after a pause. "And yet she expects it some day. Oh, dear me! oh, dear me! what weak, foolish, trusting things women are! They take a fancy to a man, and then because you don't believe in him, too, it's hoity-toity and never forgive me. Well, poor soul! perhaps it's all for the best. It may comfort her in her troubles. I wonder what Tom Porter looks like now," she said suddenly, and then looked sharply and guiltily round to see if her words had been heard. "I declare I ought to be ashamed of myself," she said, and rushing at some work, she plumped herself down and began to stitch with all her might.

In the little parlour all was very quiet, save the occasional footstep in the street. The blind was not drawn down, and the faint light from outside mingled with the glow from the fire, which threw up the face of Julia Hallam, where she sat dreamily gazing at the embers, against the dark transparency, giving her the look of a painting by one of the Italian masters of the past.

At the old-fashioned square piano her mother was seated with her hands resting upon the keys which were silent. Farther distant from the fire her figure, graceful still, seemed melting into a darker transparency, one which grew deeper and deeper, till in the corner of the room and right and left of the fireplace the shadows seemed to be almost solid. Then the accustomed eye detected the various objects that furnished the room, melting, as it were, away.

Only on one spot did there seem a discordant note in the general harmony of the softly glowing scene, and that was where the rays from a newly-lighted street lamp shone straight upon the wall and across the picture of Robert Hallam, cutting it strangely asunder, and giving to the upper portion of the face a weird and almost ghastly look.

Thisbe's steps had died out and her kitchen door had closed, but the musings of the two women had been interrupted and did not go back to their former current.

All at once, soft as a memory of the bygone, the notes of the piano began to sound, and Julia changed her position, resting one arm upon the chair by her side and listening intently to a dreamy old melody that brought back to her the drawing-room in the old house at Castor—a handsomely-furnished, low-ceiled room with deep window-seat, on whose cushion she had often knelt to watch the passing vehicles while her mother played that very tune in the half light.

So dreamy, so softened, as if mingled there with a strange sadness. Now just as it was then, one of the vivid memories of childhood, Weber's "Last Waltz," an air so sweet, so full of melancholy, that it seems wondrous that our parents could have danced to its strains, till we recall the doleful minor music of minuet, coranto, and saraband. Dancing must have been a serious matter in those days.

Soft and sweet, chord after chord, each laden with its memory to Julia Hallam.

Her mother was playing that when her father came in hastily one night, and was so angry because there were no lights; that night when she stole away to Thisbe.

She was playing it too that afternoon when Grandmamma Luttrell came and was in such low spirits, and would not tell the reason why. Again, that night when she shrank away from her father, and he flung her hands from him, and said that angry word.

Memory after memory came back from the past as Millicent Hallam played softly on, making her child's face lustrous, eyes grow more dreamy, the curved neck bend lower, and the tears begin to gather, till, with quite a start, the young girl raised her head and saw the rays from the gas-lamp shining across the picture beyond her mother's dimly-seen profile.

Julia rose to cross to her mother's side, and knelt down to pass her arms round the shapely waist and there rest.

"Go on playing," she said softly. "Now tell me about poor papa."

The notes of the old melody seemed to have an additional strain of melancholy as they floated softly through the room, sometimes almost dying away, while after waiting a few minutes they formed the accompaniment to the sad story of Millicent Hallam's love and faith, told for the hundredth time to her daughter.

For Millicent talked on without a tremor in her voice, every word distinct and firm, and yet softly sweet and full of tenderness, as it seemed to her that she was telling the story of a martyr's sufferings to his child.

"And all these years, and we have heard so little," sighed Julia. "Poor papa! Poor father!"

The music ceased as she spoke, but went on again as she paused.

"Waiting, my child; waiting as I wait, and as my child waits, for the time when he will be declared free, and will take his place again among honourable men."

"But, mother," said Julia, "could not Mr Bayle or Sir Gordon have done more; petitioned the king, and pointed out this grievous wrong?"

"I could not ask Sir Gordon, my child. There were reasons why he could not act; but I did all that was possible year after year till, in my despair, I found that I must wait."

"How glad he must be of your letters!" said Julia suddenly.

Millicent Hallam sighed.

"I suppose he cannot write to us. Perhaps he feels that it would pain us. Mother, darling, was I an ill-conditioned, perverse child?"

"My Julia," said Mrs Hallam, turning to her and drawing her closely to her breast, "what a question! No. Why do you ask?"

"Because I seem just to recollect myself shrinking away from papa as if I were sulky or obstinate. It was as if I was afraid of him."

"Oh, no, no!" cried Mrs Hallam anxiously, "you were very young then, and your poor father was constrained, and troubled with many anxieties, which made him seem cold and distant. It was his great love for us, my child."

"Yes, dear mother, his great love for us—his misfortune."

"His misfortune," sighed Mrs Hallam.

"But some day—when he returns—oh, mother! how we will love him, and make him happy! How we will force him to forget the troubles of the past!"

"My darling!" whispered Mrs Hallam, pressing her fondly to her heart.

"Do you think papa had many enemies, then?"

"I used to think so, my child, but that feeling has passed away. I seem to see more clearly now that those who caused his condemnation were but the creatures of circumstances. It was the villain who seemed to be your father's evil genius caused all our woe. He made me shiver on the morning of our wedding, coming suddenly upon us as he did, as if he were angry with your father for being so happy."

"But could we not do something?" said Julia earnestly. "It seems to be so sad—year after year goes by, and we sit idle."

"Yes," said Mrs Hallam with a sob; "but that is all we can do, my child—sit and wait, sit and wait, but keeping the home ready for our darling when he comes—the home here—and in our hearts."

"He is always there, mother," said Julia in a low, sweet voice, "always. How I remember him, with his soft dark hair, and his dark eyes! I think I used to be a little afraid of him."

"Because he seemed stern, my child, that was all. You loved him very dearly."

"He shall see how I will love him when he returns, mother," she added after a pause. "Do you think he gives much thought to us?"

"Think, my darling? I know he prays day by day for the time when he may return. Ah!" she sighed to herself, "he reproached me once with teaching his child not to love him. He could not say so now."

"I wonder how long it will be?" said Julia thoughtfully. "Do you think he will be much changed?"

She glanced up at the picture.

"Changed, Julia?" said her mother, taking the sweet, earnest face between her hands, to shower down kisses upon it, kisses mingled with tears, "no, not in the least. It is twelve long years since, now; heaven only knows how long to me! Years when, but for you, my darling, I should have sunk beneath my burden. I think I should have gone mad. In all those years you have been the link to bind me to life—to make me hope and strive and wait, and now I feel sometimes as if the reward were coming, as if this long penance were at an end. My love! my husband! come to me! oh, come!"

She uttered these last words with so wild and hysterical a cry that Julia was alarmed.

"Mother," she whispered, "you are ill!"

"No, no, my child; it is only sometimes that I feel so deeply stirred. Your words about his being changed seemed to move me to the quick. He will not be changed; his hair will be grey, his face lined with the furrows of increasing age and care; but he himself—my dear husband, your loving father—will be at heart the same, and we shall welcome him back to a life of rest and peace."

"Yes, yes!" cried Julia, catching the infection of her mother's enthusiasm; "and it will be soon, will it not, mother—it will be soon?"

"Let us pray that it may, my child."

"But, mother, why do we not go to him?" Mrs Hallam shivered slightly. "We should have been near him all these years, and we might have seen him. Oh, mother! if it had been only once! Why did you not go?" She rose from her knees, as if moved by her excitement. "Why, I would have gone a hundred times as far!" she said excitedly. "No distance should have kept me from the husband that I loved."

"Julie! Julie! are you reproaching me?"

"Mother!" cried the girl, flinging herself upon her neck, "as if I could reproach you!"

"It would not be just, my child," said Mrs Hallam, caressing the soft dark head, "for I have tried so hard."

"Yes, yes, I know, dear; and I have known ever since I have been old enough to think."

"In every letter I have sent I have prayed for his leave to come out and join him—that I might be near him, for I dared not take the responsibility upon myself with you."

"Mother!"

"If I had been alone in the world, Julia, I should have gone years upon years ago; but I felt that I should be committing a breach of trust to take his young, tender child all those thousands of miles across the sea, to a land whose society is wild, and often lawless."

"And so you asked papa to give his consent?"

"Every time I wrote to him, Julia—letters full of trust in the future, letters filled with the hope I did not feel. I begged him to give me his consent that I might come."

"And he has not replied, mother?"

"Not yet, my child. Innocent and guilty alike have a long probation to pass through."

"But he might have written, dear."

"How do we know that, Julia?" said Mrs Hallam, with a shade of sternness in her voice. "I have studied the matter deeply from the reports and dispatches, and often the poor prisoners are sent far up the country as servants—almost slaves—to the settlers. In places sometimes where there are no fellow-creatures save the blacks for miles upon miles. No roads, Julia; no post; no means of communication."

"My poor father!" sighed Julia, sinking upon the carpet, half sitting, half kneeling, with her hands clasped upon her knees, and her gaze directed up at the dimly-seen picture on the wall.

"Yes, my child, I know all," said Mrs Hallam. "I know him and his pride. Think of a man like him, innocent, and yet condemned; dragged from his home like a common felon, and forced to herd with criminals of the lowest class. Is it not natural that his heart should rebel against society, and that he should proudly make his stand upon his innocency, and wait in silent suffering for the day when the law shall say: 'Innocent and injured man, come back from the desert. You have been deeply wronged!'"

"Yes, dear mother. Poor father! But not one letter in all these years!"

"Julia, my child, you pain me," cried Mrs Hallam excitedly. "When you speak like that, your words seem to imply that he has had the power to send letter or message. He is your father—my husband. Child, you must learn to think of him with the same faith as I."

"Indeed I will, dear," cried Julia passionately; and then she started to her feet, for there was a quick, decided knock at the front door.

Mrs Hallam hurriedly tried to compose her features; and as Thisbe's step was heard in the passage she drew in her breath, gazed wildly at the picture, just as Julia drew down the blind and blotted it from her sight. Then the door was opened, and their visitor came in the centre of the glow shed by the passage light.

"Aha! In the dark!" cried Bayle in his cheery voice, as Thisbe opened the door. "How I wish I had been born a lady! I always envy you that pleasant hour you spend in the half light, gazing into the fire."

Julia echoed his laugh in a pleasant silvery trill, as she hastily lit the lamp, Bayle watching her as the argand wick gradually burned round, and she put on the glass chimney, the light throwing up her handsome young face against the gloom till she lifted the great dome-shaped globe, which emitted a musical sound before being placed over the lamp, and throwing Julia's countenance once more into the shade.

"What are you laughing at?" said Bayle.

"At the idea of our Mr Bayle being idle for an hour, sitting and thinking over the fire," said Julia playfully, to draw his attention from her mother's disturbed countenance.

The attempt was a failure, for Bayle saw clearly that something was wrong; that pain and suffering had been there before him; and he sighed as he asked himself what he could do more, in his unselfish way, to chase earthly cares from that quiet home.

Volume Three—Chapter Four.

The Dreaded Message.

There was quite a change in the little house in the Clerkenwell Square. Life had been very calm and peaceful there for Julia, though she made no friends. Any advances made by neighbours were gravely and coldly repelled by Mrs Hallam.

Once, when she had felt injured by her mother's refusal of an invitation for her to some young people's party, and had raised her eyes reproachfully to her face, Mrs Hallam had taken her in her arms, kissing her tenderly.

"Not yet, my child; not yet," she whispered. "We must wait."

Julia coloured, and then turned pale, for she understood her mother's meaning. They stood aloof from ordinary society, and they possessed a secret.

But now, since Sir Gordon had been brought to the house by Christie Bayle, their life appeared to Julia to be changed. Her mother seemed less oppressed and sad during the evenings when Sir Gordon came, as he did now frequently. There was so much to listen to in the animated discussions between the banker and the clergyman; and as they discussed some political question with great animation, Julia leaned forward smiling and slightly flushed, as Bayle, with all the force of a powerful orator, delivered his opinions, that were, as a rule, more sentimental than sound, more full of heart than logic.

He would always end with a fine peroration, from the force of habit; and Julia would clap her hands while Mrs Hallam smiled.

"Wait a bit, my dear," Sir Gordon would say, nodding his head, "one story is good till the other is told."

Then, in the coolest and most matter-of-fact way, he would proceed to demolish Bayle's arguments one by one, battering them down till the structure crumbled into nothingness.

All this, too, was without effort. He simply drew logical conclusions, pointed out errors, showed what would be the consequences of following the clergyman's line of argument, and ended by giving Julia a little nod.

At the beginning the latter would feel annoyed, for her sympathies had all been with Bayle's plans; then some clever point would take her attention; her young reason would yield to the ingenuity of the highly-cultivated old man's attack; and finally she would mentally range herself upon his side, and reward him with plaudits from her little white hands, darting a triumphant look now at Bayle, as if saying, "There we have won!"

Highly good-tempered were all these encounters; and they were always followed by another harmony, that of music, Bayle playing, as of old, to Millicent's accompaniment; more often to that of her child.

It was a calm and peaceful little English home, that every day grew more attractive to the old club-lounger and lover of the sea.

He coloured slightly the first time Bayle came and found him there. The next time he nodded, as much as to say, "I thought I would run up." The next it seemed a matter of course that an easy-chair should be ready for him in one corner, where he took his place after pressing Mrs Hallam's hand warmly, and drawing Julia to him to kiss her as if she were his child.

There was a delicacy, a display of tender reverence, that disarmed all suspicion of there being an undercurrent at work. "He is one of my oldest friends," Mrs Hallam had said to herself; "he feels sympathy for me in my trouble, and he seems to love Julie with a father's love. Why should I estrange him? Why keep Julie from his society?"

It never entered into her mind that, by the sentence of the law, she was, as it were, a woman in the position of a widow, for her husband was socially dead. The seed of such an idea would have fallen upon utterly barren ground, and never have put forth germinating shoots.

No; there was the one thought ever present in her heart, that sooner or later her husband's innocence would be proclaimed, and then this terrible present would glide away, to be forgotten in the happiness to come.

Sir Gordon, with all his frank openness of manner, saw everything. The slightest word was weighed; each action was watched; and when he returned to his chambers in St. James's—a tiny suite of very close and dark rooms, which Tom Porter treated as if they were the cabins of a yacht—he would cast up the observations he had made.

"Bayle means the widow," he said to himself, as he sat alone; "yes, he means the widow. She is a widow. Well, he is a young man, and I am—well, an old fool."

Another night he was off upon the other tack.

"It's an insult to her," he said indignantly. "Bless her grand, true, sweet, innocent heart! She never thinks of him but as the good friend he is. She will never think of any one but that rascal. Good heavens! what a fate for her! What a woman to have won!"

The thought so moved him that he paced his little bed-room for some time uneasily.

"As for that fellow Bayle," he cried, "I see through him. He means to marry my sweet little flower Julie. Hah!"

He sat down smiling, as if there was a pleasant fragrance in the very thought of the fair young girl that refreshed him, and sent him into a dreamy state full of visions of youth and innocence.

"I don't blame him," he said, after a pause. "I should do the same if I were his age. Yes," he said firmly, and as if to crush down some offered opposition, "even if she be a convict's daughter. It is not her fault. We do not mark out our own paths."

Again, another night, and Sir Gordon arrested himself several times over in the act of spoiling his carefully-trimmed nails by nibbling them—a somewhat painful operation—with his false teeth.

"It's time I died; I honestly believe it's time I died," he said testily. "When a man has grown to an age in which he spends his days suspecting the motives of his fellow-creatures—hah! of his best friends—it's time he died, for every year he lives makes him worse—gives him more to answer for."

"Poor Bayle!" he continued, shaking hands with himself, "he looks upon each of those two women as something holy."

"No," he mused, "that does not express it; there's something too fatherly, too brotherly. No, that's not it. Too friendly; I suppose that's it; but friendship seems such a weak, pitiful word to express his feelings towards them."

"Christie Bayle, my dear friend," he said aloud, as he rose and gazed straight before him, "I ask your pardon; and—heaven helping me—I'll never suspect you again."

The old man seemed to feel better after this; and throwing himself into an easy-chair, he smiled and looked wrinkled—as he had a way of looking in his dressing-room—and happy.

At first Sir Gordon had gone to the little house at Clerkenwell feeling out of his element, and with an uncomfortable sensation upon him that the neighbours—poor souls who were too much occupied with the solution of the problem of how to get a sufficiency of bread and meat to preserve life—were watching him.

After a second and third visit, this uneasiness wore off, and he found himself walking proudly up to the house, smiling at Thisbe, who only gave him a hard look in return, consequent upon his remark concerning Tom Porter.

Sometimes Christie Bayle would be there. As often not. But the chair was always ready for him, and Julia took his hat and stick.

It was generally after his dinner at the club that he found his way up there; and on these occasions Thisbe asked no questions. The moment she had closed the door and shown the visitor into the little parlour, she went downstairs and put on the kettle.

As a rule, precisely at nine, Thisbe took up the supper-tray with its simple contents; but on these evenings the supper-tray gave place to the tea-tray, and Sir Gordon sat for quite an hour sipping his tea and talking, Julia crossing now and then to fetch his cup.

One pleasant evening, when the chill of winter had passed away, and the few ragged trees in the square garden, washed less sooty than usual by the cold rains, were asserting that there was truth in the genial, soft breaths of air that came floating from the west, and that it really was spring, Mrs Hallam, Julia, and Sir Gordon were seated at tea in the little parlour with the window open, and the sound of the footsteps without coming in regular beats. From time to time Julia walked to the window to look out, turning her head aside to lay her cheek against the pane and gaze as far up the side of the square as she could, giving Sir Gordon a picture to watch of which he seemed never to tire, as he sat with half-closed eyes. Then the girl returned to seat herself at the piano and softly play a few notes.

"That must be he," she said, suddenly, and Sir Gordon's face twitched.

"No, my dear," said Mrs Hallam, quietly; "that is not his step."

Sir Gordon's hair seemed to move suddenly down towards his eyebrows, and his lips tightened, so did his eyelids, as he gave a sharp glance at mother and daughter. Then his conscience gave him a twinge, and he made a brave effort to master his unpleasant thoughts.

"Bayle is uncommonly late to-night, is he not?" he said.

"He is late like this sometimes," said Mrs Hallam. "He works very hard amongst the people, and attends parish meetings, where there may be long discussions."

"Humph, yes, so I suppose. I hope he does some good."

"Some good?" cried Julia excitedly. "Oh, you don't know how much!"

"And you do, I suppose," said Sir Gordon in rather a constrained tone of voice.

"Oh, not a hundredth part!" cried Julia naïvely, "Oh, Sir Gordon, I wish you were half so good a man!"

"Julia!" exclaimed Mrs Hallam.

"Upon my word, young—bless my soul! I!—tut, tut!—hush! hush! Mrs Hallam."

Sir Gordon began angrily, but his testiness was of a few moments' duration, and he laughed at first in a forced, half-irritable manner, then more heartily, and ended by becoming quite overcome with mirth, and wiping the tears from his eyes while mother and daughter exchanged glances.

"And here have I been deferential, and treating you, Miss Julie, like a grown-up young lady, while all the time you are only one of those innocent little maidens who say unpleasant truths before elderly people."

"Oh, Sir Gordon," cried Julia, colouring deeply, "I am so sorry!"

"Oh, sorrow is no good after such a charge as that!" said Sir Gordon with mock severity. "So you and your mamma have determined that I am a very wicked old man, eh?"

"Sir Gordon!" cried Julia, taking his hand. "Indeed, indeed, I only meant that Mr Bayle was the best and kindest of friends."

"While I was the most testy, exacting, and—"

"Indeed, no," cried Julia, with spirit; "and I will not have you condemn yourself. Next to Mr Bayle, mamma and I like you better than any one we know."

"Ah! well, here is Bayle," said Sir Gordon, as a knock was heard; and the curate appeared next minute in the doorway.

The lamp had been lit, and his face looked so serious and pale that Sir Gordon noticed the fact on the instant.

"Why, Bayle," he cried warmly, "how bad you look! Not ill?"

"Ill? No; oh, no!" he said quietly. "I have been detained by business."

Mrs Hallam looked at him anxiously, for beneath the calm there was ever a strange state of excitement waiting to break forth. For years she had been living in the expectation that the next day some important news would come from her husband. Letters she had very few, but the postman's knock made her turn pale and place her hand to her heart, to check its wild beatings, while the coming of a stranger to the house had before now completely unnerved her. It was but natural, then, that she should become agitated by Bayle's manner. A thousand—ten thousand things might have happened to disturb her old friend, but in her half-hysterical state she could find but one cause—her own troubles; and, starting up with her hand on her breast, she exclaimed:

"You have news for me!"

Christie Bayle had no more diplomatic power than a child, perhaps less than some; and he sank back in his chair, with his hand half-raised to his lips, gazing at her in a pained, appealing manner that excited her further.

"Yes," she cried, "you are keeping something back. You think I cannot bear it, but I can. Yes, I am strong. Have I not borne all this pain these twelve years? And do you think me a child that you treat me so? Speak, I say—speak!"

"My dear Mrs Hallam," began Sir Gordon soothingly.

"Hush, sir!" cried the trembling woman. "Let him speak. Mr Bayle, why do you torture me—you, my best friend? What have I done that you—ah! I see now. I—Julie—my child—he is dead!—he is dead!"

Julia had started to her side and caught her in her arms as she burst into a passionate wail, the first display of the wild despair in her heart that Bayle had seen for many years.

"No, no!" he cried, starting up and speaking with energy. "Mrs Hallam, you are wrong. He is alive and well."

Millicent Hallam threw up her hands, clasped them together, reeled, and would have fallen but for her child's sustaining arms. It was as if a sudden vertigo had seized her, but it passed as quickly as it came. Years of suffering had strengthened as well as weakened, and the woman's power of will was tremendous.

"I am better," she said in a hoarse, strangely altered voice. "Hush, Julie—I *can* bear it," she cried imperiously. "Tell me all. You have heard of my husband?"

"Yes, Mrs Hallam, yes; but be calm and you shall know all."

"I am calm."

Christie Bayle felt the cold dew stand upon his brow as he faced the pale, stern face before him. It did not seem the Millicent Hallam he knew, but one at enmity with him for holding back from her that which was her very life.

"Why do you not speak?" she said angrily; and she took a step forward.

In a flash, as it were, Christie Bayle seemed to see into the future, and in that future he saw, as it were, the simple happy little home he had made for the woman he had once loved crumbling away into nothingness, the years of peace gone for ever, and a dark future of pain and misery usurping their place. The dew upon his brow grew heavier, and as Sir Gordon's eyes ranged from one to the other he could read that the anguish in the countenance of the man he had made his friend was as great as that suffered by the woman to whom, in the happy past, they had talked of love. He started as Bayle spoke; his voice sounded so calm and emotionless; at times it was slightly husky, but it gained strength as he went on, its effect being, as he took Mrs Hallam's hands to make her sink upon her knees at his feet her anger gone, and the calm of his spirit seeming to influence her own.

"I hesitated to speak," he said, "until I had prepared you for what I had to say."

"Prepared?" she cried. "What have all these terrible years been but my probation?"

"Yes, I know," said Bayle; "but still I hesitated. Yes," he said quickly, "I have heard from Mr Hallam. He has written to me—enclosing a letter for his wife." As he spoke he took the letter from his breast, and Mrs Hallam caught it, reading the direction with swimming eyes.

"Julie!" she panted, starting to her feet, "read—read it—quickly—whisper, my child!"

She turned her back to the men, and held the unopened letter beneath the lamp.

Julia stretched out her hand to take the letter, but her mother drew it quickly back, with an alarmed look at her child, holding it tightly with both hands the next moment to the light; and Julia read through her tears in a low quick voice:

"Private and confidential.

"To Mrs Robert Hallam, formerly Miss Millicent Luttrell, of King's Castor, in the county of Lincoln.

"N.B.—If the lady to whom this letter is addressed be dead, it is to be returned unopened to—

"Robert Hallam,—

"9749,—

"Nulla Nulla Prison,—

"Port Jackson."

"Mrs Hallam," said Bayle in his calm, clear voice, "Sir Gordon and I are going. You would like to be alone. Could you bear to see us again—say to-night—in an hour or two?"

"Yes, yes," she cried, catching his hand; "you will come back. There! you see I am calm now. Dear friends, make some excuse for me if I seem half mad." Sir Gordon took the hand that Bayle dropped, and kissed it respectfully.

Bayle was holding Julia's.

"God protect you both, and give you counsel," he whispered, half speaking to himself. "Julie, you will help her now."

"Help her!" panted Julia. "Why, it is a time of joy, Mr Bayle; and you don't seem glad."

"Glad!" he said in a low voice, looking at her wistfully. "Heaven knows how I should rejoice if there were good news for both."

The next minute he and Sir Gordon were arm-in-arm walking about the square; for though Bayle had left the place intending to go to his own rooms, Mrs Hallam's house seemed to possess an attraction for them both, and they stayed within sight of the quiet little home.

Volume Three—Chapter Five.

The Wife Speaks.

Sir Gordon was the first to break the silence, and his voice trembled with passion and excitement.

"The villain!" he said in an angry whisper. "How dare he write to her! She suffered, but it was a calm and patient suffering, softened by time. Now he has torn open the wound to make it bleed afresh, and it will never heal again."

"I have lived in an agonising dread of this night for the past ten years," said Bayle hoarsely.

"You?"

"Yes: I. Does it seem strange? I have seen her gradually growing more restful and happy in the love of her child. I have gone on loving that child as if she were my own. Was it not reasonable that I should dread the hour when that man might come and claim them once again?"

"But they are not his now," cried Sir Gordon. "The man is socially dead."

"To us and to the law," said Bayle; "but is the husband of her young love dead to the heart of such a woman as Millicent Hallam?"

"Luttrell, man; Luttrell," cried Sir Gordon excitedly; "don't utter his accursed name!"

"As Millicent Hallam," said Bayle gravely. "She is his wife. She will never change."

"She must be made to change," cried Sir Gordon, whose excitement and anger were in strong contrast to the calm, patient suffering of the man upon whose arm he hung heavily as they tramped on round and round the circular railings within the square. "It is monstrous that he should be allowed to disturb her peace, Bayle. Look here! Did you say that letter came enclosed to you?"

"Yes."

"Then—then you were a fool, man—a fool! You call yourself her friend—the friend of that sweet girl?"

"Their truest, best friend, I hope."

"You call yourself my friend," continued Sir Gordon, in the same angry, unreasoning way, "and yet you give them that letter? You should have sent it back to the scoundrel, marked dead. They are dead to him. Bayle, you were a fool."

"Do you think so?" he said smiling, and looking round at his companion. "My dear sir, is your Christianity at so low an ebb that you speak those words?"

"Now you are beginning to preach, sir, to excuse yourself."

"No," replied Bayle quietly. "I was only about to say, suppose these long years of suffering for his crime have changed the man; are we to say there is to be no ray of hope in his darkened life?"

"I can't argue with you, Bayle," cried Sir Gordon. "Forgive me. I grow old and easily excited. I called you a fool: I was the fool. It was misplaced. You are not very angry with me?"

"My dear old friend!"

"My dear boy!"

Sir Gordon's voice sounded strange, and something wonderfully like a sob was heard. Then, for some time they paced on round and round the square, glancing at the illumined window-blind, both longing to be back in the pleasant little room.

And now the same feeling that had troubled Bayle seemed to have made its way into Sir Gordon's breast. The little home, with its tokens of feminine taste and traces of mother and daughter everywhere, had grown to be so delightful an oasis in his desert life that he looked with dismay at the chance of losing it for ever.

He knew nothing yet, but that home seemed to be gliding away. He had not heard the letter read, but a strange horror of what it might contain made him shudder for what he knew; and as the future began to paint terrors without end, he suddenly nipped the arm of his silent, thoughtful companion.

"There! there!" he said, "we are thinking about ourselves, man."

"No," said Bayle, in a deep, sad voice, "I was thinking about them."

"It's my belief," said Sir Gordon, half angrily, "that you have gone on all these years past thinking about them. But come! We must act. Tell me about the letter. Do you say he wrote to you?"

"Yes."

"But why to you? He must have hated you with all his heart."

"I believe he did," replied Bayle. "Even my love for his child was a grievance to him."

"And yet he wrote to you, enclosing the letter to his wife."

"I suppose he felt that I should not forsake them in their distress; and that whatever changes might have taken place my whereabouts would be known—a clergyman being easily traced. See!"

He took another letter from his pocket, and stopped beneath a gas-lamp.

"No, no, I cannot read it by this light; tell me what he says," exclaimed Sir Gordon.

"The letter is directed to me at King's Castor, and above the direction Hallam has written, 'If Rev. Christie Bayle has left King's Castor, the postal authorities are requested to find his address from the Clerical Directory.' The people at Castor of course knew my address, and sent it on."

"Yes, I see. Well, well, what does he say?"

Bayle read, in a calm, clear voice, the following letter:

> "Prison, Nulla Nulla,—
>
> "Port Jackson, Australia,—
>
> "December 9th, 18—.
>
> "Sir,—
>
> "You and I were never friends, and in my trouble perhaps you were harder on me than you need have been. But I always believed you to be a true gentleman, and that you liked my wife and child. I can trust no one else but a clergyman, being a convict; but your profession must make you ready, like our chaplain here, to hear all our troubles, so I write to ask you to help me by placing the letter enclosed in my wife's hands, and in none other's. It is for her sight alone.
>
> "I cannot offer to reward you for doing me this service, but I ask you to do a good turn to a suffering man, who has gone through a deal since you saw him.
>
> "Please mark: the letter is to be given to my wife alone, or to my child. If they are both dead, the letter is to be sent back to me unopened, as I tell you it contains private matters, only relating to my wife and me.
>
> "I am, Reverend Sir,—
>
> "Your obedient, humble servant,—
>
> "Robert Hallam, 9749.

"To the Rev. Christie Bayle,—

"Curate of King's Castor."

"Why, the fellow seems to have grown vulgarised and coarse in style. That is not the sort of letter our old manager would have written."

"The handwriting is greatly changed too."

"Of course it is his?"

"Oh, yes; there is no doubt about it. The change is natural, if the life the poor wretches lead out there be as bad as I have heard."

"Hah! I don't suppose they find them feather beds, Bayle."

"If half I know be true," said Bayle indignantly, "the place is a horror. It is a scandal to our country and our boasted Christianity!"

"What, Botany Bay?"

"The whole region of the penal settlement."

"There, there, Bayle! you are too easy, man! You infect me. I shall begin to repent of my share in sending that fellow out of the country. Let's get back. We must have been out here an hour."

"An hour and a half," said Bayle, looking at his watch. "Yes; we will ask if they can see us to-night. We will not press it if they prefer to be alone."

Thisbe must have been in the passage, the door was opened so quickly. Her face was harder than ever, and her moustache, by the light of the candle upon the bracket, looked like a dark line drawn by a smutty finger. There was a defiant look, too, in her eyes; but it was evident that she had been crying, as she ushered the friends into the room where Mrs Hallam was sittings with Julia kneeling at her feet and resting her arms upon her mother's knees.

Both rose as Bayle and Sir Gordon entered.

"We only wish to say good-night," said the latter apologetically.

"I have been expecting you both for some time," said Mrs Hallam calmly; but it was plain to her friends that she was fighting hard to master her emotion.

Sir Gordon signed to Bayle to speak, but the latter remained closed of lip, and the silence became most painful.

Julia looked wistfully at her mother, whose face was transfigured by the joy that illumined it once more, though it had no reflection in her child's face, which was rendered sad by the traces of the tears that she had lately shed.

"Your husband is well?" said Bayle at last, for Mrs Hallam was looking at him reproachfully.

"Yes, oh yes, he is quite well," she said proudly; and something of her old feeling seemed to come back, for the eyes that looked from Sir Gordon to Bayle gave a defiant flash.

"Well?" she said impatiently, as if weary of waiting to be questioned.

"Do you wish your friends to know the contents of your husband's letter?"

"Yes!" she cried; "all that is not of a private nature."

Bayle paused again. Then his lips parted, but no words came; and Sir Gordon saw that there was a tender, yearning look in his eyes, a pitying expression in his face.

Then he seemed to recover himself. He moistened his feverish lips, and said in a low, pained voice:

"Then the term of his imprisonment is over? He is coming back?"

"My poor husband was sentenced to exile for life," said Mrs Hallam, with her head erect, as if she were defending the reputation of a patriot.

"But he has received pardon?"

"No. The world is still unjust."

Sir Gordon met her eyes full of reproach; but as she gazed at him her features softened, and she took a step forward and caught his hand.

"Forgive my bitterness," she said quickly. "It was all a grievous error. Only, now that this message has come from beyond the seas,"—she unconsciously adopted the language used a short time before—"the old wound seems to be opened and to bleed afresh."

Bayle had uttered a sigh of relief at her words respecting the injustice of the world, and he waited till Mrs Hallam turned to him again.

"I wish to be plain—to speak as I should at another time, but I am too agitated, too much overcome with the great joy that has fallen to me at last—the joy for which I have prayed so long. At times it seems a dream—as if I were mocked by one of the visions that have haunted my nights; but I know it is true. I have his words here—here!"

She snatched the letter from her breast, her eyes sparkling and a feverish flush coming into her face, while, as she stood there in the softened light shed by the lamp, her lips apart, and a glint of her white teeth just seen, it seemed to both Bayle and Sir Gordon that the Millicent Luttrell of the old days was before them. Even the tones of her voice had lost their harshness, and sounded mellow and round.

They stood wondering and rapt, noticing the transformation, the animated way; the eager excitement, as of one longing to take action, after an enforced sealing up of every energy; and as they stood before her half-stunned in thought, she seemed to gather the force they lost, and mentally towered above them in her words.

"You ask me of his letter," she said at last, half bitterly, but again fighting this bitterness down. "I will tell you what he says to me and to his child."

"Yes," said Bayle, almost mechanically; and in the same half-stunned way he looked from her to Julia, who stood with her hands clasped and hanging before her, wistful, troubled, and evidently in pain.

"Yes, Mrs Hallam," said Sir Gordon, for she had sought his eyes as she released those of Bayle, "tell me what he says."

She paused with the letter in her hands, holding it pressed against her bosom. Then raising it slowly, she placed it against her lips, and remained silent for what seemed an interminable time.

At last she spoke, and there was a strange solemnity in her words as she said in less deep tones:

"It is the voice of the husband and father away beyond, the wild seas—there on the other side of the wide world, speaking to the wife and child he loves, and its essence is, 'I am weary of waiting—wife—child—I bid you come.'"

As she spoke, Bayle felt his legs tremble, and he involuntarily caught at a chair, tilting it forward and resting upon its back till, as she said the last words, he spasmodically snatched his hands from the chair, which fell with a heavy crash into the grate.

It was not noticed by any there, only by Thisbe, who ran to the door in alarm, as Bayle was speaking excitedly.

"No, no. It is impossible. You could not go!"

"My husband tells me," continued Mrs Hallam, gazing now at Sir Gordon, who seemed to shrink and grow older of aspect than before—"that after such a long probation as his the Government have some compassion towards the poor exiles in their charge; that they extend certain privileges to them, and ameliorate their sufferings; that his wife and child would be allowed to see him, and that under certain restrictions he would be free so long as he did not attempt to leave the colony."

"It is too horrible!" groaned Sir Gordon to himself, as in imagination he saw the horrors of the penal settlement, and this gently-nurtured woman and her child landed there.

"I say it is impossible," said Bayle again; and there were firmness and anger combined in his tones. "Mrs Hallam, you must not think of it."

"Not think of it?" she said sternly.

"For your own sake: no."

"You say this to me, Christie Bayle?"

"Yes, to you; and if I must bring forward a stronger argument—for your child's sake you must not go."

A look that was half joy, half grief, flashed from Julia's eyes; and Mrs Hallam looked to her, and took her hand firmly in her own.

"Will you tell me why, Mr Bayle?" she said sternly.

"I could not. I dare not," he said firmly. "Believe me, though, when I tell you this. As your friend—as Julia's protector, almost foster-father—knowing what I do, I have mastered everything possible, from the Government minutes and despatches, respecting the penal settlement out there. It is no place for two tender women. Mrs Hallam, it is impossible for you to go."

"Again I ask you why?" said Mrs Hallam sternly.

"I cannot—I dare not paint to you what you would have to go through," said Bayle almost fiercely.

"Mrs Hallam," said Sir Gordon, coming to his aid; "what he says is right. Believe me too. You cannot: you must not go."

There was a pause for a few moments, and then Mrs Hallam drew her child more closely to her side.

"You dare not paint the horrors that await us there, Christie Bayle," she then said in a softened tone. "There is no need. The recital would fall on barren ground. The horrors suffered by the husband and father, his wife and child will gladly dare."

"You cannot. You shall not. For God's sake pause!"

"When my husband bids me come? Christie Bayle, you do not know me yet," she said softly.

"But, Mrs Hallam—Millicent, my child!" cried Sir Gordon imploringly.

"I cannot listen to your appeals," she said in a piteous tone, and with the tears at last gushing from her aching eyes.

"Ah," cried Bayle excitedly, "she is giving way. Millicent Luttrell, for your own, for your child's sake, you will stay."

She rose up proudly once more.

"Millicent *Hallam* and her child will go."

Sir Gordon made an imploring movement.

"It is to obtain his release, Julie, my child!" said Mrs Hallam in a tender voice, "the release of our long-suffering martyr. What say you? He calls to us from beyond the seas to come and help him, what must we do?"

Again there was a painful silence in that room, every breath seemed to be held till Julia said, in a low, dreamy voice:

"Mother, we must go."

As she ended, a faint sigh escaped her lips, and she sank as if insensible upon her mother's breast.

"Yes," cried Millicent Hallam, gazing straight before her, "were the world a hundred times as wide."

Volume Three—Chapter Six.

In Her Service.

No, not even to Julia—his own child—for that part of the letter was a commission for her alone to execute. After all these long years of absence he sent her his orders—he, the dear husband of her first love.

And, oh! the joy, the intense delight of being able at last to execute his wishes, to work and strive for him, following out his most minute commands.

It was a long letter, containing few words of affection, but those she found studded through the ill-written pages, that seemed to have been the work of one who had not touched pen for years, a word that bore a loving guise, shining brightly here and there, as Millicent kissed it with all the fervour of a girl.

He said that he had not heard from her all these years, and that she might have written; that he had had to suffer fearful hardships, which he would not inflict upon her, though he was explicit enough to draw agonised tears from the loving woman's eyes; that he had had much to endure, mentally and bodily; that his health had been often bad, and so on, right through the greater portion of the letter.

It never struck the patient wife that Hallam barely alluded to her, or suggested that she must have suffered terribly during his long absence. He had left her absolutely penniless, after ruining her father and mother; but here was his first letter, and there was not an allusion to how she had managed to struggle on for all this time—how had she lived? what had she done? how had she managed to keep her child?

Not a word of this kind; but it did not trouble the woman who knew all his pains and sufferings by heart, for she was hungering for news of him to whom she had blindly given herself, and the letter was full of that.

She did not wish to bathe her sorrowing face in the fount of her own tears, but in the fount of his, and she greedily drank in every word and allusion, making each the text which she mentally expanded in the silence of the night, till she seemed to be reading the complete history of her husband's life for the past twelve years.

Certainly he hoped she was quite well, and that little Julie was the same. He supposed she would be so grown that he should hardly know her again, but he hoped she would not have forgotten him.

He made but little allusion to his sentence. And here perhaps Millicent Hallam felt a little disappointed, for he dealt in no severe strictures against those who had caused his punishment, neither did he reiterate his innocency.

He merely said that he supposed Australia would always be his home now; and that she was to part with everything she possessed, take passage in the first ship with Julie, and come and join him at once—he would explain their future when she came.

No word about the old people either; or the repugnance wife and child might feel to leaving home to go to a strange land to join a convict father—not a word of this, for they were his wife and child. He wanted them, and he bade them come.

Millicent Hallam knew that the letter was selfish in the extreme, but it was the kind of selfishness that elated her, and filled her with joy.

He was innocent; he had suffered in silence a very martyrdom, all these years; but she was still the one woman in the world to him, and he had turned to her to bid her come and chase away his cares.

Blindly infatuated, strong, and yet weak as a girl; foolish in her trust in an utterly heartless and selfish, scoundrel; but how loving! Her young heart had opened like a flower at the breath of his love. He had been the sun that had warmed it with that wondrous new life, and it wanted something far stronger than occasional harshness, neglect, or the charges of man against man, to tear out the belief that had fast rooted itself in Millicent Hallam's nature.

Blame—pity—what you will, and then thank God that in spite of modern society ways, follies of fashion, errors of education, weakness, vanity, and the hundred biassing influences, the world abounds with such loving, trusting women, always has done so, and always will to the very end.

One great joy that seemed to take ten years from her life as she read and re-read that letter to herself, and to Julie, who became infected by her mother's enthusiasm, and at last believed that she was gladdened by the news, and sobbed in secret, she knew not why, as she thought of the time of parting.

But there was that one portion of the letter separated by two broad lines, ruled evidently with the pen drawn along the side of an old book, the rough edges showing where the point of a spluttering quill pen dipped in coarse ink had followed each irregularity.

Here are the lines that Robert Hallam emphasised by a few warning words at the beginning, telling her that they were of vital importance.

"And mind this, by carefully and secretly following out my instructions, you will free your husband from this wretched, degraded life."

Could she want a greater impulse than that last to make her dwell upon his words, and prepare herself to execute the instructions which followed to the letter?

"He may trust me," she said with a smile, as she carefully cut these instructions out of the letter, gummed them upon a piece of paper, and doubling this, carefully hid it in her purse.

There was a poignant feeling of pity and remorse in Millicent Hallam's breast the next morning when, in spite of the way in which her heart was filled with the thoughts of their coming journey, the recollection of Christie Bayle's tender care for them both pierced its way in like some keen point.

"I cannot help it," she cried passionately. "It is my duty, and he will soon forget us."

But when he of whom she thought came that morning, looking grave and pale, her heart reproached her more and more, for she knew that he was not of the kind to forget. This knowledge influenced her words and the tone of her voice, as she laid her hand in his, and then passed her arm round Julie.

"Once more," she said, with a sad smile, "you are going in your unselfishness to help me, Christie Bayle."

"Are you still determined?" he said, with a slight tremor in his voice, which grew firm directly, even stern.

"Yes!"

"Have you thought of the peril of the voyage for yourself and for Julie?"

"Yes; of everything."

"The wild, strange life out yonder; your future—have you thought of this?"

"Yes, yes!" said Millicent Hallam calmly. "Can you ask me these questions, and at such a time?"

Christie Bayle remained silent, looking stern and cold; but it was a mere mask. He could not trust himself to speak, lest he should grow by turns piteous of appeal, angry and denunciatory of manner, so fully did he realise the horrors of the fate to which this man's wife in her blind faith was hurrying.

"Do not think me ungrateful, dear friend," she continued. "I cannot tell you how in my heart of hearts the truest gratitude dwells for all that you have done. Christie! brother! I am again in terrible distress. This once more you will be my help and stay?"

She approached and took his hand, raising it to her lips, feeling startled it was so icily cold.

But the next moment a change came over him, his sternness seemed to melt, his old manner to come back, as he said gently:

"You know that you have only to speak and I shall do all you wish; but let us sit down, and talk calmly and dispassionately about this letter. There, I will be only the true, candid friend. I do not attempt to fight against your present feeling; I only ask you to wait, to give the matter quiet consideration for a few days. It seems impertinent of me to speak of rashness; but before you decide to give up your little home—"

"Hush!" said Mrs Hallam firmly; and the bright light in her daughter's eyes died out. "Do not speak to me like this. No consideration, no time could change me. Christie Bayle, think for a moment. For twelve long years I have been praying for this letter. From my heart I felt it hopeless to expect my husband's pardon. Now the letter has come, you ask me to wait—to consider—to give up this plan—to refuse to obey these commands. Of what kind do you think my love for my husband?"

Bayle drew a long breath, and remained silent for quite a minute, while Julia watched him with a strange wrinkling of her broad, fair brow. The silence was painful, but at last he broke it, speaking as if the question had been that moment put.

"As of the love of a true wife. Yes, I will help you to the end. Tell me what you wish me to do?"

Julia turned away her face, for the tears were falling softly down her cheeks, but they were not seen by the other occupants of the room.

"I knew I could count upon you," said Mrs Hallam eagerly, and as if in hot haste. "I know it will be a bitter pang to part from where I have spent these— yes, happy years; but it is our duty, and I will not waste an hour. I am only a helpless woman, Mr Bayle, so I must look to you."

He nodded quickly.

"My husband bids me part with everything that remains of my little property."

"Did he say that?" said Bayle dryly.

"He said, part with everything, take passage in the first ship, and come and join me."

Bayle nodded.

"Then we shall pack up just sufficient necessaries for our voyage, Julie and I; and everything else must be sold. I shall realise enough to pay our passage from my furniture."

"Oh, yes, certainly," said Bayle quickly; "and you will have to spare."

"And the ship; what am I to do? Oh! here is Sir Gordon, he will know."

There was the tap of the ebony cane upon the pavement, a well-known knock, and, looking very wrinkled and careworn, Sir Gordon came in, glancing suspiciously from one to the other.

"Not the time to call, perhaps. I'm not Bayle here; but I've not had a wink of sleep all night, thinking of that outrageous letter, and so I came up at once to tell you, my dears, that it's all outrageous madness. He—he must be out of his mind to propose it. I'll—I'll do anything! I'll see the Secretary of State! I'll try for a remission—a pardon! but you two girls—you children—you cannot, you shall not go out there!"

Mrs Hallam's eyes flashed at this renewed opposition; but she crossed to the old man, took his hand, and led him to a chair by the window, where she began talking to him earnestly, while Bayle turned to Julie.

"And so you are going?" he said tenderly.

She gave him one quick look and then said:

"Yes. It is my father's wish."

Bayle gazed down at her sweet face, then wildly about the room, as memories of hundreds of happy lessons and conversations flowed back. Then his lips tightened, his brow smoothed, and he said in a cold, hard way: "The path of duty seems difficult at times, Julie, but we must tramp it without hesitating."

"And you, too, will help me?" Mrs Hallam said aloud. "Any way, in anything," said Sir Gordon sadly. "I would sail you both over in my yacht, but it would be madness to expose you to the risk. Yes; I'll do the best I can to get you a passage in a good ship. Yes—yes—yes! I'll do my best."

He looked at Bayle in a troubled way, but found no sympathy in the cold, stern face that seemed to be unchanged when they left together an hour later, each pledged to do his best to expatriate two tender women, and so send them to what was then a wilderness of misery—and worse.

"It must be, I suppose, Bayle, my dear boy?" said Sir Gordon.

"Yes; it must be," was the reply.

"I'm glad she says she will go down to Castor first, and stay a few days with the old people."

"Did she say that?"

"Yes. It made me wonder whether she could be persuaded to leave Julie with them."

"No," said Bayle firmly; "they would never part, because he has ordered her to bring their child."

"Yes; I saw that. Ah, Bayle, it's a bad business; but we must make the best of it. Confound it all! why am I worrying myself about other people's troubles? Here am I, an old man, with plenty of money and nothing to do but take care of myself and make myself happy, and live as long as I can. I say, why am I pestered with other people's troubles?"

Bayle smiled sadly, and laid one hand upon that which rested upon his arm.

"Simply because you are a true man, that is all." They parted soon afterwards, Sir Gordon to visit a friend in Whitehall, Bayle to speak to an auctioneer about the furniture and effects at the little house, giving orders to sell his own property to supply the funds for the voyage, and then to make a supposed further sale of Consols to realise the capital which Millicent Hallam honestly believed to be her own.

Volume Three—Chapter Seven.

The Old Home.

Millicent Hallam was closely veiled as she descended from the coach at the inn-door, while Julia's handsome young face was free for the knot of gossips of the little town to notice, as they clustered about as of old to see who came in the coach and who were going on.

A quiet, drab-looking man had just handed a basket to the guard and was turning away, when he caught sight of Julia's face and stopped suddenly.

"Bless my soul, Mrs Hallam! Oh! I beg your pardon," he stammered; "I thought—why, it must be Miss—and Mr Bayle, I—I really—I—"

He could not speak. The tears stood in his eyes, and he stood there shaking away at both of Christie Bayle's hands for some moments before he became aware of Millicent Hallam's presence.

"Only to think," he cried; "but come along."

"We are going up to the doctor's," said Bayle.

"Yes, yes, you shall; but pray come into my place—only for a minute. My wife will be so—so very pleased to see—Ah, my dear, how you have grown!"

James Thickens had become aware that his eccentric behaviour was exciting attention, so he hurried the visitors up to his house.

"Your people are quite well, Mrs Hallam," he said, hardly noticing that there was a curious distance in her manner towards him. "They're not expecting you, for the doctor was in the bank this morning, and he would have been sure to tell me."

Mrs Hallam could not speak. She had felt so strengthened by tribulation, so hardened by trouble, that she had told herself that she could visit King's Castor and her old home without emotion; but as she alighted from the coach, the sight of the place and their house brought back so vividly the troubles of the past, and her misery as Robert Hallam's wife, that her knees trembled, and, but for Julia's arm, she could hardly have gone on.

"Be brave," whispered a voice at her ear as Thickens prattled on. "This is not like you."

She darted a grateful look through her veil at Christie Bayle, almost wondering at the same time that he should have noticed her emotion. Once she glanced back towards their old house; and her heart gave a throb as she saw there was a painted board upon the front, which could only mean one thing—that it was to let.

All feeling of distance and coldness was chased away as Thickens opened the door and let them in to where a plump, pleasant-looking, little, elderly lady was sitting busily knitting, and so changed from the Miss Heathery they had all known that Bayle gazed at her wonderingly.

The plump little body started up excitedly and then dropped back in her chair, turning white and then red. She gasped and pressed her hands upon her sides, and then looked up helplessly.

"Why, don't you know who it is?" cried Thickens with boisterous hospitality in his tones.

"Know? Yes, James, I know; but what a turn it has given me! My dear—my darling!—oh, I—I—I—I am so glad to see you again."

The little woman had recovered herself and had caught Mrs Hallam to her breast, rocking her to and fro and clinging to her so affectionately that Millicent's tears began to flow.

Bayle turned aside, moved by the warmth of the faithful little woman's affection, when he felt a dig in his side from an elbow.

"Come and have a look at my gold fish, Mr Bayle," said a husky voice; and with true delicacy Thickens hurried him out, and along his rose-path to where the gold and silver fish were basking in the spring afternoon sun. "Let them have their cry out together," he whispered. "My little woman quite worships Mrs Hallam. There isn't a day but she talks about her, and I'd promised to bring her up to town this summer to see her again."

Meantime little Mrs Thickens had left Mrs Hallam, to make wet spots all over Julia's cheeks as she kissed and fondled her.

"My beautiful darling," she sobbed; "and grown so like—oh, so like—and—and—oh! if I had only known."

The reception was so strange, the little lady's ways so droll, that, in spite of the weariness of her journey and the trouble hanging over her young life, Julia had felt amused; but the next moment she was clinging to little Mrs Thickens, warmly returning her embrace and feeling a girlish delight in the affectionate caresses showered upon her by her mother's simple old friend.

The stay was but short, for Millicent Hallam was trembling to see her old home and those she loved once more.

How little changed all seemed! A dozen years had worked no alterations. The old shops, the old houses, just the same.

Yes, there was one change; Mr Gemp sitting at his door, not standing, and with movement left apparently in one part only—his head, which turned towards them, with a fixed look, as they went down the street, and turned and followed them till they were out of sight.

"How I recollect it all!" whispered Julia, as she held her mother's arm. "That old man who used to make Thisbe so cross. Walk more quickly, mamma, he is calling out our name to some one."

It was true; and, as the words seemed to pursue them, Julia uttered an angry ejaculation, as she heard a sob escape from her mother's breast.

"Hi! Gorringe, here's that shack Hallam's wife come down. Quick! dost ta hear?"

Bayle had stayed back with Thickens to allow his travelling companions to go to the cottage alone, or these words might not have been uttered.

And as they appeared to come hissing through the air, Millicent Hallam seemed to realise more and more how Bayle had been their protector, and how she had done wisely in fleeing from the little town, where every flaw in a man's life was noted and remembered to the end.

"How dare he?" cried Julia indignantly; and her young eyes flashed. "Mother, we ought not to have come down here."

"Hush, my child!" said Mrs Hallam softly; "who are we that we cannot bear patiently a few revolting words? If we were guilty, there would be a sting."

The episode was forgotten as they passed out of the town, and along the pleasant road, nearer and nearer to the sweet old home. For Millicent Hallam's breath came more quickly. She threw back her veil; her eyes brightened, and her pale cheeks flushed.

There it all was, unchanged. The great hedges, the yews, the shrubs, and the pleasant rose and creeper-covered cottage, with its glittering windows, and door beneath the rustic porch, open as if to give them welcome.

"Yes, yes, yes!" cried Julia eagerly, and her voice sounding full of excitement; "I am beginning to remember it all again so well. I know, yes—the gate fastening inside. I'll undo it. Up this path, and grandpapa used to be there busy by his frames—round past the big green hedge, where grandmamma's seat used to be, so that she could watch him while he was at work. And I used to run—and, oh! yes, yes, there! Grandpa! grandpa! here we are."

Had the past twelve years dropped away? Millicent Hallam asked herself, as, seeing all dimly through a veil of tears, she heard Julia's words, excited, broken, with all a child's surging excitement and delight, as she ran from her side, across the smooth lawn to where that grey little old lady sat beneath the yew hedge, to swoop down upon her, folding her in one quick caress, and then, before she had recovered from her surprise, darting away, and off the path, over the newly-dug ground, to where that grey old gentleman dropped the hoe with which he was drawing a furrow for his summer marrowfats.

The twelve years had dropped from Julia's mind for the time, and, a child once more, she was clinging to and kissing the old man, with whom she returned to where her mother was kneeling, locked in Mrs Luttrell's arms.

"The dear, dear, dear old place!" cried Julia, with childlike ecstasy. "Grandpa, grandma, we're come down to stay, and we must never leave you again."

She stopped, trembling, her beautiful eyes dilated, and a feeling of chilling despair clutching at her heart, as her mother turned her ghastly face towards her, and her name seemed to float to her ears and away into the distance, in a cry that was like the wail of a stricken, desolate heart.

"Julia!"

"Mother, dearest mother, forgive me!" she cried, as she threw herself upon her breast, sobbing as if her heart would break. "I did not think: I had forgotten all."

Volume Three—Chapter Eight.

Julia Seems Strange.

It was as if that forlorn cry uttered by Millicent Hallam pervaded their visit to the old home. It was a happy reunion, but how full of pain! Joy and sorrow were hand in hand. It was life in its greatest truth.

The sweet, peaceful old home, with its garden in the early livery of spring; the fragrance of the opening leaves; the delicious odour of the earth after the soft rain that had fallen in the night; the early flowers, all so bright in the clear country air, to those who had been pent up in town; while clear ringing, and each tuned to that wondrous pitch that thrills the heart in early spring, there were the notes of the birds.

Millicent Hallam's eyes closed as she stood in that garden, clasping her child's hand in hers, and listening to each love-tuned call. The thrush, that; now soft, mellow, and so sweet that the tears came, there was the blackbird's pipe; then again, from overhead, that pleasant little sharp "pink, pink," of the chaffinch, followed by its musical treble, as of liquid gems falling quickly into glass; while far above in the clear blue sky, softened by the distance, came the lark's song—a song she had not listened to for a dozen years.

"For the last time—for the last time, good-bye, dear home, good-bye!"

"Mother!"

"Did I speak?" said Millicent, starting.

"Speak?" cried Julia excitedly. "Oh, mother, dear mother, your words seemed so strange; they almost break my heart."

"Hearts do not break, Julie," said Mrs Hallam softly; "they can bear so much, my darling, so much."

"But you spoke as if you never thought to see this dear old place again."

"Did I, my child?" said Mrs Hallam, dreamily, as she gazed wistfully round. "Well, who knows? who knows? Life cannot be all joy, and we must be prepared for change."

"And we must go, mother, away—to that place?"

"Yes," said Mrs Hallam sternly, and she drew herself up, and seemed as if she were trying to harden her heart against the weakness of her child.

It had been a painful meeting, over which Mrs Luttrell had broken down, while the old doctor had stood with quivering lip.

"I can't say a word, my child. I could only beg of you to stay."

"And tear and wring my heart anew, dear father," Millicent had said in return with many a tender caress.

Then the old people had pleaded that Julia might remain; and there had been another painful scene, and the night of their coming had been indeed a mingling of joy and sorrow.

Bayle had been up to sit with them for a short time in the evening; but with kindly delicacy he had left soon, and at last sleep had given some relief to the sorrow-stricken hearts in the old home.

Then had come the glorious spring morning, and, stealing through the garden, mother and child had felt their hearts lifted by the mysterious influence of the budding year, till over all, like a cloud, came Millicent's farewell to the home she would never see again.

Prophetic and true—or the false imaginings of a sorrow-charged brain? Who could say?

The stay was to be but short, for they returned that night by the coach which passed through, as it had gone on passing since that night when the agonised wife had sat watching for the news from the assize town.

"It will be better so," Millicent Hallam had said. "It will be less painful to my dear ones in the old home, and Julie. Christie Bayle, I could not bear this strain for long. We must finish and away. He is waiting for us now."

About midday Bayle came up to the cottage, quiet and grave as ever, but with a smile for Julia, as she hurried to meet him, Millicent coming more slowly behind.

"I have brought the keys," he said. "I found they were in Mr Thickens's charge. May I give you a word of advice?"

"Always," said Mrs Hallam smiling; but he noticed that she was deadly pale.

"I would not stay there long. I understand the feeling that prompts you to visit the old home again. See it and come away, for it must be full of painful memories; and now you must be firm and strong."

"Yes, yes," she said quickly. "You will stay here?"

"Certainly," he replied.

"You are going out?" cried Julia.

"I must see our old home again, before I go," said Mrs Hallam, in a sharp, nervous manner.

"And I may go with you, dear?" pleaded Julia.

"No; I must go alone," said her mother in a strained, imperious manner. "Stay here."

For answer, Julia shrank back, but only for a moment. Then her arms were round her mother's neck, and she kissed her, saying:

"Remember Mr Bayle's advice, dear. Come back soon."

Mrs Hallam kissed her tenderly, nodded, and hurried into the house.

Ten minutes later, as Julia was seated in the little drawing-room at the tinkling old square piano, and Bayle was leaning forward watching her hands, with his arms resting upon his knees, thinking—thinking of the boyish curate who, in that very place, had told of his first passion, and then gone heart-broken away, there was a quick step on the gravel, and he turned to see the dark, graceful figure of the woman he had loved, her face closely veiled, and her travelling satchel upon her arm, pass through the gate, which closed with a sharp click.

"To stand face to face with the ghosts of her early married life," he said, in a low voice. "Heaven be merciful, and soften Thou her fate."

He started, for as but a short time since Julia had heard her mother's audible thoughts, she had now heard his; and she was standing before him, pale, and with her hands clasped, as she looked in his care-lined face.

"Julia—my child!" he said wonderingly.

"I cannot bear it—I cannot bear it," she cried, bursting into a passionate fit of sobbing; and she fled from the room.

Volume Three—Chapter Nine.

The Strange Quest.

"She be going to look over the owd house again, Gorringe," shouted Gemp, as he watched the dark veiled figure. "You mark my words; they're a coming back, and he'll be keeping bank; and the sooner thou teks out thy money the better."

There was a strange echo in the place that made a shudder run through Millicent Hallam's frame as she turned the key; but she had nerved herself to her task, and though hands and brow were damp, she did not hesitate, but went in.

A quick glance told her that a couple of score pairs of eyes were watching her movements, but for that she was prepared, and, taking out the key, she inserted it in the inside of the lock, closed the door, and slipped one of the rusty bolts.

"I must be firm," she muttered as she glanced round the empty hall, shuddering as she recalled the scene on that night, and seeming to see once more the crowd—the fire—her husband struggling for his life.

"I will not think," she cried, stamping her foot, and placing her hands to her eyes, as if to shut out the terrible recollections; and an echo ran through the place, and seemed to go from room to room and die away in the great attic where Julia used to play.

No; she had not come to stand face to face with the ghosts of past memories: she had driven them away. She did not go into the old panelled dining-room, where she had watched for such long hours for her husband's return, neither did she turn the handle to enter the melancholy cobweb-hung drawing-room, or note that the papers in the chambers were soiled and faded and different, and that the damp made some hang in festoons from the corners, and other pieces fold right over and peel down from the wall.

No; she paused for none of these, but, as if moved by some strong impulse, ran right up to the top of the house, and stood in the great attic lumber-room, brightly lit by a skylight, and a dormer at the farther end.

Then, with her heart beating quickly, she took from her bosom the portion she had cut from Hallam's letter, and read it in a low, hoarse voice.

> "Go to Castor if you have left there, and get possession of the old house for a day if it is empty. If not, you must get there by some excuse that your woman's wit may find. As a last resource, take it, and buy the tenant out at any cost, but get there. Go alone, and take with you a hammer and screw-

driver. Shut yourself up securely in the place, and then go upstairs to the attic where we kept the old lumber. There, on the right-hand side of the fireplace, in the built-up wall, just one foot from the floor, and right in the centre, drive in the screw-driver with the hammer, and chip away the plaster. Do not fail. You will find there a little recess carefully plastered, and papered over. In that recess is a small locked tin box. Take it out, and bring it to me unopened. That box contains papers of vital importance to me, for they will set me free.

"Read above again. Strike in the screw-driver boldly, for the box is there, and I charge you, my wife, to bring it safely and untouched to me.

"Once more, this must be secretly done. No one must know but you. If it were known, I might not succeed in getting my liberty."

Millicent Hallam thrust the paper back in her bosom and stood there in that unoccupied room with a strange buzzing in her ears, and films floating before her eyes.

"I am choking," she gasped; "water—air."

She reeled, and seemed about to fall, but by a supreme effort she forced her tottering way to the dormer window, opened it, and the fresh air recovered her.

"Oh, for strength—strength!" she gasped as she clung to the sill. "It is for his freedom—to save him I am come."

Her words gave her the force, and, looking down, she saw that her act had been observed by those who watched the house.

That gave her additional strength, and, with a look of contempt, she closed the window and was calm. Quickly opening her bag, she took from it a stout short hammer and a screw-driver.

"I must risk the noise," she said, as she drew off her gloves; and then noting the spot described in the directions, she found the paper ready to peel off on being touched, and placing the screw-driver just where she had been told, she struck the end sharply and stopped, trembling, for the blow resounded throughout the house.

The cold sweat gathered on her face, and she began to tremble; but, smiling at her fears, she doubled her gloves, held them on the top of the screw-driver, and struck again and again, driving the chisel end right into the plaster, through which, after a blow or two, it passed, and her heart throbbed, for there was the hollow place behind, just as the letter said.

At that moment there was a loud sound without, as of a blow upon the front door, and she stopped, trembling, to listen.

No; it was the jolt of a heavy-laden springiest cart, and as it rattled over the cobble-stones she struck again and again with quick haste at the plaster, and then, wrenching, tore out piece after piece, till she could thrust in her hand to utter a cry of joy, for she touched a tin box.

The rest was the work of a few minutes. She had only to enlarge the hole a little, and then she could draw out that of which she was in search—a black, dust-covered tin box about the width and depth of an ordinary brick, but a couple or three inches longer.

Her hands were scratched and bleeding, and covered with lime, but she did not heed that in her excitement. Raising the box to her lips she kissed it, and taking out her kerchief wiped from it the dust. Then she asked herself the question, what should she do next, now that the treasure, the sacred papers that should prove her husband's innocence, were found? It was easy enough. The box was light, as one containing papers would be, and would just pass into her travelling satchel. That, was soon done and the strings drawn. Then there were the hammer and screw-driver.

She looked around. There was a loose board close by, easily lifted, and down beneath this she thrust the hammer, while a rat-hole at the base of the wall invited occupation for the screw-driver.

The plaster? The wall? She could do nothing there. It was impossible to hide that, and she stood trembling again. But who would suspect her, if any one came? She glanced at herself, brushed off a few scraps of plaster, and put on her gloves over her bleeding hands. A thought struck her: she might lock the door of the attic.

Again she started, for there was a sound below, a loud rat-tat at the front door, and she stood with her heart beating horribly till she heard the sound of racing footsteps and a burst of children's laughter. Some mischievous urchins had knocked at the door of the empty house.

Forcing herself to be calm, Millicent Hallam felt the box in her bag, and asked herself whether she had fully obeyed her husband's command and succeeded. Was this the box? She repeated the directions with her eyes fixed upon the spot from whence she had extracted it. Yes; there could be no mistake, she must be right, and, lowering her veil, she passed out of the attic with its littered floor, closed and locked the door, took out the key, and descended as if in a dream to the hall, where she paused to satisfy herself that her dress showed no traces of her work, and that the box was safely hidden.

All was right, and she drew a long breath.

And now once more came the tremor and faintness; the memories of the old place seemed to be crowding round her; and in the agony of her spirit she felt that she would faint, and perhaps all would be discovered. She fought this down and another horror assailed her. She had come there like a thief; she had broken open part of the house and stolen this case which she was bearing away, and she trembled like a leaf. But once more her womanhood and faith asserted themselves.

"His papers, his own hiding, in our own house," she said proudly. "Robert, husband, I have them safe. I will bear them to you over the sea."

Opening the door with firm hand she passed out, the soft pure air reviving her, and she started, for a well-known voice said:

"I will close the door for you, Mrs Hallam. Forgive me for coming. You have been so long, I had grown uneasy."

"Long?" she said, looking at Bayle wildly.

"Yes; time passes quickly when we are deep in thought. It is two hours since you left me at the cottage."

It had seemed to her but a few minutes' wild, exciting search.

Volume Three—Chapter Ten.

Kindly Acts.

Tom Porter had a way of his own when he was puzzled as to his course, and that was to go to the door and keep a bright look-out; in other words, follow old Gemp's example, and stare up and down the street until he had attained a correct idea as to which way he had better steer.

He had been looking thoughtfully out for about an hour on this particular night before he came to the conclusion that he knew the right way. But once determined, he entered, and, closing the door softly, he stopped for a minute to pull himself together, rearranging his necktie, pulling down his vest, and carefully fastening the top and bottom buttons, which had a rollicking habit of working themselves clear of their respective holes. His hair, too, required a little attention, being carefully smoothed with his fingers. This done, he moistened his hands, as if about to haul a rope, before going straight up to where his master was seated in front of the fire which the cool spring night made comfortable, who, as he sat there gazing very thoughtfully in between the bars, said:

"Well, Tom, what is it?"

"Been a-thinking, Sir Gordon—hard."

"Well, what about?"

"'Bout you, Sir Gordon. It's these here east winds getting into your bones again; as if I might be so bold—"

"There, there, man, don't stand hammering and stammering like that! You want to say something. Say it."

"'Bout the east wind, Sir Gordon, and whether you wouldn't think it as well to take a trip."

"Yes, yes, man, I'm going on one—Mediterranean—in a few days," said the old man dreamily.

"Glad to hear it, Sir Gordon; but, if I might make so bold, why not make a longer trip?"

"Not safe—yacht not big enough, my man. There, that will do: I want to think."

"I mean aboard ship, Sir Gordon. Why shouldn't we go as far as Australia? We've seen a deal of the world, Sir Gordon, but we haven't been there."

Tom Porter's master gave him a peculiar look, and then nodded towards the door, when the man made a nautical bow, with a very apologetic smile, and backed out.

"Went a bit too nigh the rocks that time. It warn't like me—but, lor! what a man will do when there's a woman in the way!"

He had hardly settled himself in his pantry when the bell rang, and he went up, expecting a severe talking to.

"Means a wigging!" he said, as he went up slowly, to find Sir Gordon pacing the room.

Tom Porter did not know it, but his words had fallen just at that time when his master was pondering upon the possibility of such a trip, and, though he would not have owned to it, his man's words had turned the balance.

"Pack up at once," he said.

"Long cruise or short, Sir Gordon?"

"Long."

"Ay, ay, Sir Gordon. Special dispatches, Sir Gordon?"

"No; longer cruise than usual, that's all."

"He's going! I'd bet ten hundred thousand pounds he's going!" said Tom Porter; "and I'm done for! She was a bit more easy last time we met; and I shall make a fool o' myself—I know I shall!"

He stood in the middle of his pantry, turning his right and left hands into a pestle and mortar, and grinding something invisible therein. Then, after a long silence:

"Its fate, that's about what it is!" said Tom Porter; "and that's a current that you can't fight agen."

After which philosophical declaration he began to pack, working well on into what he called the morning watch, and long after Sir Gordon had been comfortably asleep.

The next day Tom Porter had orders to go with his master to the Admiralty, where he waited for about a couple of hours; and two days later he was on his way to Plymouth with the sea-chests, as he termed them, perfectly happy, and with his shore togs, as he called his livery, locked up in one of the presses in the chambers in St. James's.

His sailing orders were brief, and he put into port at the chief hotel to wait for his master; and he waited. Meantime there had been the painful partings between those who loved, and who, in spite of hopeful words, felt that in all human probability the parting was final.

Through the interest of Sir Gordon, a passage had been obtained for Mrs Hallam and her daughter on board the *Sea King*, a fine ship, chartered by the Government to take out a large detachment of troops, as well as several important officials, bound to the Antipodes on the mission of trying to foster what promised to be one of our most important colonies.

"You will be more comfortable," Sir Gordon said. "There will be ladies on board, and I will get you some introductions to them, as well as to the Governor at Port Jackson."

Mrs Hallam gave Bayle a piteous look, as if asking him to intercede for her.

Bayle, however, seemed not to comprehend her look, and remained silent.

It was a painful task, but Millicent Hallam was accustomed to painful tasks, and, turning to Sir Gordon, she said, in a quiet, resigned way:

"You forget my position. I know how kindly all this is meant; but I must not be going out on false pretences. My fellow-passengers should not be deceived as to who and what I am. I may seem ungrateful to you, but it would have been far better for me to have gone out in some common ship."

"My dear child," cried Sir Gordon, wringing his hands, "don't be unreasonable! Do you suppose the womenkind on board the *Sea King* are going to be so contemptible as to visit the sins of—My dear Bayle, you have more influence than I!" he cried hastily; "tell Mrs Hallam everything is settled, and she must go, and—there, there, we've had knots and tangles enough, don't, pray, let us have any more!"

The old gentleman, who seemed terribly perplexed, turned away, but paused as he felt a little hand upon his arm.

"Don't speak angrily to mamma," whispered Julia; and the old man's countenance became wholly sunny again.

"No, no," he said; "but you two must leave matters to Mr Bayle and me. We are acting for the best, my child. You cannot conceive what it would have been to let you go out as your mother proposed. It was madness!"

"It is for Julie's sake," Mrs Hallam said to herself, when she consented to various little arrangements, though she shivered at the thought of being brought face to face with her fellow-passengers.

"Indeed, we are acting with all the foresight we can bring to bear," Bayle said, in answer to another remonstrance made in the hurry and bustle of preparation.

"Yes," she replied; "but you are doing too much. You make me tremble for the consequence."

Bayle smiled, and bade her take comfort. He was present with her almost daily, to report little matters that he had arranged for her as to money and baggage. Since he had accompanied her and Julia back to town he had been indefatigable, working with the most cheery good-humour, and smiling as he reported the success of the furniture sale; how capitally he had managed about the little investments of the wreck of Mrs Hallam's money; and how he had obtained letters of credit for her at the Colonial Bank.

Julia watched Bayle's countenance day by day with a curious, wistful look, that would at times be pitiful, at other times full of resentment; and one day she turned to the doctor—the old gentleman and Mrs Luttrell having insisted upon coming to town, and following their child to Portsmouth, where they were to embark.

"I believe, grandpa," she said half angrily, "that Mr Bayle is tired of us, and that he is glad to get us off his hands."

"Nothing would ever tire Mr Bayle, my dear," said Mrs Luttrell reprovingly.

Julia turned to her quickly and put her arms round the old lady's neck, the tears in her eyes brimming over.

"No; it was very unkind and ungenerous of me," she said. "He has always been so good."

In the midst of what was almost a wild excitement of preparation, mingled with fits of despondency, Millicent Hallam noticed this too, and found time to feel hurt.

"He is such an old friend," she said to herself. "He has been like a brother; and it seems hard that he should appear to be less moved at our approaching farewell than Mr Thickens and his wife."

For, instigated by the latter, Thickens had come up and followed them to Portsmouth.

"It would have about killed her, Mrs Hallam," he said in confidence, as he sat chatting with her aside in the hotel room on the eve of their sailing. "But now a bit of business. I've been trying ever since I came to get a few words with you alone, only Sir Gordon and Mr Bayle were always in the way."

"Business, Mr Thickens?"

"Yes, look here! I'm an actuary, you see, and money adviser, and that sort of thing. Now you are going out there on a long voyage, and you ought to be prepared for any little emergencies that may occur in a land that I find is not so barbarous as I thought, for I see they have a regular banking establishment there, and business regularly carried on in paper and bullion."

Mrs Hallam looked at him wonderingly.

"Ah, I see you don't understand me, so to be short," he continued, "fact is I talked it over with, madam, and we settled it between us."

"Settled what?" said Mrs Hallam, wonderingly.

"Well, the fact is, we've two hundred pounds fallen in. Been out on a good mortgage at five per cent, and just now I can't place it anywhere at more than four, and that won't do, you know, will it?"

"Of course it would not be so advantageous."

"No, to be sure not, so we thought we'd ask you to take it at five. Money's valuable out there. You could easily send us the dividend once a-year—ten pounds, you know, by credit note, and it would be useful to you, and doing your old friends a good turn. I hate to see money lying idle."

Mrs Hallam glanced across the room to see that little Mrs Thickens was watching them anxiously, and she felt the tears rise in her eyes as she darted a grateful look back, before turning to dry, drab-looking Thickens, who now and then put his hand up to his ear, as if expecting to find a pen there.

"It is very good and very generous of you," she said huskily, "and I can never be grateful enough for all this kindness. Believe me, I shall never forget it."

"That's right. I shall have it all arranged, so that you can draw at the Colonial Bank."

"No, no," cried Mrs Hallam with energy, "it is impossible. Besides, I have a sufficiency for our wants, ample for the present—the remains of my little property. Mr Bayle has managed it so well for me; my furniture brought in a nice little sum, and—"

"Your what?" said Thickens in a puzzled tone.

"My property. You remember what I had when—"

"When you were married? Why, my dear madam, you don't think any of that was left?"

"Mr Thickens!"

"Ah, I see," he cried with a good-humoured smile, for delicacy was not the forte of the bank clerk of the little country town. "Mr Bayle patched up that story. Why, my dear madam, when the crash came you hadn't a halfpenny. Here, quick, my dear! Mrs Hallam has turned faint!"

"No, it is nothing," she cried hastily. "I am better now, Mr Thickens. Go back to our friends, Julie—to grandma. It is past."

"I—I'm afraid I've spoken too plainly," said Thickens apologetically, as soon as they were alone once more. "I wish I'd held my tongue."

"I am very glad that you spoke, Mr Thickens," said Mrs Hallam in a low voice. "It was better that I should know."

"Then you will let me lend you that money?" eagerly.

"No. It is impossible. I am deeper in obligations than I thought. Pray spare me by not saying more."

"I want to do everything you wish," said Thickens uneasily.

"Then say no word about what you have told me to any one."

"Pooh! Mrs Hallam, as if I should. Money matters are always sacred with me. That comes of Mr Bayle banking in town. If he had trusted me with his money matters, I should never have spoken like this."

Volume Three—Chapter Eleven.

Millicent Hallam Learns a Little more of the Truth.

It was a painful evening that last. Every one was assuming to be light-hearted, and talking of the voyage as being pleasant, and hinting delicately at the possibility of seeing mother and daughter soon again, but all the while feeling that the farewells must in all probability be final.

Mr and Mrs Thickens retired early, for the latter whispered to her husband that she could bear it no longer.

"I feel, dear, as if it were a funeral, and we were being kept all this while standing by the open grave!"

"Hush!" whispered back Thickens; "it's like prophesying evil." And they hurriedly took leave.

Then Sir Gordon rose, saying that it was very late, and he, too, went, leaving mother and daughter exchanging glances, for the old man seemed cool and unruffled in an extraordinary degree.

Bayle remained a little longer, talking to Doctor and Mrs Luttrell, whose favourite attitudes all the evening had been seated on either side of Julia, each holding a hand.

"Good-night," said Bayle at last, rising and shaking hands with Julia in a cheery, pleasant manner. "No sitting up. Take my advice and have a good rest, so as to be prepared for the sea demon. Eleven punctually, you know, to-morrow. Everything ready?"

"Yes, everything is ready," replied Julia, looking at him with her eyes flashing and a feeling of anger at his cavalier manner forcing its way to the surface. It seemed so Cruel. Just at a time like that, when a few tender words of sympathy would have been like balm to the wounded spirit, he was as cool and indifferent as could be. She was right, she told herself. He really was tired of them.

Bayle evidently read her ingenuous young countenance and smiled, with the result that she darted an indignant glance at him, and then could not keep back her tears.

"Oh, no, no, no," he said, taking her hand and holding it, speaking the while as if she were a child. "Tears, tears? Oh, nonsense! Why, these are not the days of Christopher Columbus. You are not going to sail away upon an unknown sea. It is a mere yachting trip, and every mile of the way is known. Come, come: cheer up. That's nautical, you know, Julie. Good-night, my dear! good-night."

He shook hands far more warmly and affectionately with the Doctor and Mrs Luttrell, hesitating for a moment or two, and even taking poor weeping Mrs Luttrell in his arms, and kissing her tenderly again and again.

"Good-night, good-night, my dear old friend," he said. "You have been almost more than a mother to me. Good-night, good-night."

The old lady sobbed upon his shoulder for some time, the doctor holding Bayle's other hand, while Julia crossed to her mother, who was standing cold and statuesque near the door, and hid her face.

"Good-night and good-bye, my dear boy," said Mrs Luttrell, as she raised her head; and looked up in his face. "And you always have seemed as if you were our son."

Bayle's lip quivered, and his face was for a moment convulsed, but he was calm again in a moment.

"To be sure, doctor," he said. "I shall come down and see you again—some day. I want some gardening for a change. Good-night, good—"

His last word was inaudible, as he hurried towards the door, where Mrs Hallam was awaiting him.

"Go back to your grandmother, Julie," she said, in a low, stern voice. "Christie Bayle, I wish to speak to you."

"To me? To-night?" he said hastily. "No: to-morrow. I am not myself now, and you need rest."

"No," she said, in the same deep voice; "to-night," and she led the way into an inner room.

Julia made as if to follow, but stopped short, and stood watching till her mother and their old friend disappeared.

The room was lit only by the light that streamed in from the street lamp and a shop near the hotel, so that the faces of Millicent Hallam and Bayle were half in shadow as they stood opposite to each other.

Bayle was silent, for he had seen that Mrs Hallam was deeply moved. He had studied her face too many years not to be able to read its various changes; and now, on the eve of her departure, he knew that in spite of the apparent calmness of the surface a terrible storm of grief must be raging beneath, and feeling that perhaps she wished to say a few words of thanks to him, and while asking some attention towards the old people, she was about to take this opportunity to bid him farewell, he stood there in silence waiting for her to speak.

Twice over she essayed, but the words would not come. It was as if misery, indignation, and humiliation were contending in her breast, and each mood was uppermost when she opened her lips. How could she have been so unworldly—so blind all these years, as not to have seen that Christie Bayle had been impoverishing himself that she and her child might live?

As she thought this, she was moved to humility, and admiration of the gentleman who had hidden all this from them, always behaving with the greatest delicacy, and carefully hiding the part he had taken in her life.

"And I thought myself so experienced—so well taught by adversity," she said to herself.

"Did you wish to ask me something, Mrs Hallam!" said Bayle, at last. "Is it some commission you wish me to undertake?"

"Stop a moment," she said hoarsely. Then, as if by a tremendous effort over herself, she tried to steady her voice, and to speak indignantly, as she exclaimed:

"Christie Bayle, why have you humiliated me like this?"

He started, for he had not the remotest idea that she had learnt his secret.

"Humiliated you?" he said. "Oh, no, I could not have done that."

"I have trusted you so well—looked upon you as a brother, and now at the eleventh hour of my home life, I find that even you have not deserved my trust."

"Indeed!" he said, smiling. "What have I done?"

"What have you done?" she cried indignantly, her emotion begetting a kind of unreason, and making her bitter in her words. "What have I done in my misery and misfortune that you should take advantage of my position? That man to-night has told me all."

"I hardly understand you," he said gravely.

"Not understand? He has told me that when that terrible trouble came upon me, it did not come singly, and that I was left penniless to battle with the world. Is this true?"

Bayle refrained for a few moments before answering. "Is this wise?" he said at last. "For your own sake—for the sake of Julie, you have need of all your fortitude to bear up against a painful series of farewells. Why trouble about this trifle now?"

"Trifle!" she cried angrily. "Stop! Let me think." She stood with her hands pressed to her forehead, as if struggling to drag something from the past—from out of the mist and turmoil of those terrible days and nights, when her brain seemed to have been on fire, and she lay almost at the point of death.

"Yes," she cried, as if a flash had suddenly illumined her brain, "I see now. I know. Tell me: is what that man said true?"

He was slow to answer, but at last the words came, uttered sadly, and in a low voice:

"If he told you that at that terrible time you were left in distress, it is true."

"I knew it," she said, passionately. "Now tell me this—I will know. When my poor husband lay there helpless—in prison—yes, it all comes back clearly now—my illness seems to have covered it as with a mist, but I remember that there was powerful counsel engaged for his defence, and great efforts were made to save him. Who did this? I have kept it hidden away, not daring to drag these matters out into the light of the present, but I must know now. Who did this?"

He did not answer.

"Your silence convicts you," she cried, angrily. "It was you."

"Yes," he said, quietly, "it was I."

"Then we were left penniless, and it is to you we owe everything—for all these years?"

Again he was silent.

"Answer me," she cried imperiously.

"Did I not acknowledge it before," he said calmly. "Mrs Hallam, have I committed so grave a social crime, that you speak to me like this?"

"It was cruel—to me—to my child," she cried, indignantly. "You have kept us in a false position all these years. Man, can you not understand the degradation and shame I felt when I was enlightened here only an hour ago?"

He stood there silent again for a few moments, before speaking; and then took her hand.

"If I have done wrong," he said, "forgive me. When that blow fell, and in your position, all the past seemed to come back—that day when in my boyish vanity I—"

"Oh! hush!" she cried.

"Nay, let me speak," he said calmly. "I recalled that day when you bade me be friend and brother to you, and life seemed to be one blank despair. I remembered how I prayed for strength, and how that strength came, how I vowed that I would be friend and brother to you and yours; and when the time of tribulation came was my act so unbrotherly in your distress?"

She was silent.

"Millicent Hallam, do you think that I have not loved your child as tenderly as if she had been my own? Fate gave me money. Well, men, as a rule, spend their money in a way that affords them the most pleasure. I am only a weak man, and I have done the same."

"You have kept yourself poor that we might live in idleness."

"You are wrong," he said, with a quiet laugh. "I was never richer than during these peaceful years—that have now come to an end," he added sorrowfully; "and you would make me poor once more. There," he continued, speaking quickly, "I confess all. Forgive me. I could not see you in want."

"I should not have been in want," she said proudly. "If I had known that it was necessary I should work, the toil would have come easily to my hands. I should have toiled on for my child's sake, and waited patiently until my husband bade me come."

"But you forgive me?" he said, in his old tone.

For answer she sank upon the floor at his feet, covering her face with her hands; and he heard her sobbing.

"Good-night," he said at last. "I will send Julie."

He bent down and laid his fingers softly upon her head for a moment, and was turning to go, but she caught at his hand and held it.

"A moment," she cried; "best and truest friend. Forgive me, and mine—when we are divided, as we shall be—for life, try—pray for me—pray for him—and believe in him—as you do in me—my husband, Christie Bayle—my poor martyred husband."

"And I am forgiven?" he said.

"Forgiven!"

She said no more, and he passed quickly into the room where Julia was anxiously awaiting his return.

"Doctor—Mrs Luttrell," he said, "you must try and calm her, or she will not be able to undertake this journey. Julie, my child, try what you can do. Good-night. Good-night."

As the door closed after him, Mrs Hallam walked back into the room looking calm and stern; but her face softened as Julia clung to her and then seated herself at her mother's feet, the next hours passing so peacefully that it was impossible to believe that the time for parting was so near.

Volume Three—Chapter Twelve.

Over the Sea.

"Is—is it true, mother?" said Julia, as the town with its docks and shipping seemed to be growing less and less, while the Isle of Wight, and the land on their right looked dim and clouded over. The sun still shone, but it seemed to be watery and cold; there was a chill upon the sea, and though there was a great deal of hurrying to and fro among the sailors and soldiers as the cumbered decks were being cleared, it was to Mrs Hallam and her child as if a dead silence had fallen, and the noises of the ship and creaking of block and spar were heard from a distance.

Thisbe was seated near where they two stood by the bulwark, gazing towards the shore. Thisbe felt no desire to watch the retiring land, for her heart was very low, and she found rest and solace in shedding one salt tear now and then, and wiping it away with her glove.

Unfortunately, Thisbe's glove was black, and the dye in her glove not being fast, the effect was strange.

"I'm a fool to cry," she said to herself; "but he might have had as good manners as his master, and said 'good-bye.'"

Thisbe must have been deeply moved, or she would not have sat there upon a little box that she would not let out of her hands, probably on account of its insecurity, for it was tied up with two different kinds of string.

"It seems to me," continued Julia, "as if it were all some terrible dream."

"But one that is to have a happy waking, Julie."

"Poor grandma! she looked as if it would kill her," said Julia, sobbing gently.

"Hush!" cried Mrs Hallam, grasping her child's arm as a spasm of pain ran through her, and her face grew deadly pale. "We must think of one who, in pain and suffering, was dragged from his wife and child—forced to suffer the most terrible degradations. He is waiting for us, Julie—waiting as he has waited all these years. We must turn our backs upon these troubles, and think only of him. Be firm, my child, be firm." There was almost a savage emphasis in Mrs Hallam's words as she spoke.

"I'll try, dear; but, grandpa!" sobbed Julie, as she laid her arm upon the bulwark and her face upon it, that she might weep unseen; "shall we never see him and the pleasant old garden again?"

"Julie, this is childish," whispered Mrs Hallam. "Remember, you are a woman now."

"I do," cried the girl quickly; "but a woman must feel grief at parting from those she loves."

"Yes, but it must not overbear all, my child. Come, we must not give way now. Let us go below to our cabin."

"No," said Julia; "I must watch the shore till it is dark. Not yet, not yet. Mother, I thought Sir Gordon liked us—was a very, very great friend?"

"He is; he always has been."

"But he parted from us as if it was only for a day or two. He did not seem troubled in the least."

Mrs Hallam was silent.

"And Mr Bayle, mother—he quite checked me. I was so grieved, and felt in such despair at parting from him till he stood holding my hands. I wanted to throw my arms round his neck, and let him hold me to his breast, as he used years ago; but when I looked up in his face, he seemed so calm and cheerful, and he just smiled down at me, and it made me angry. Mamma, dear, men have no feeling at all."

"I think Mr Bayle feels our going deeply," replied Mrs Hallam, quietly.

"He did not seem to," said Julia pettishly.

"A man cannot show his sorrow as a woman may, my child," said Mrs Hallam, with a sigh.

She gazed back at the land that seemed to be growing more dim, minute by minute, as the great ship careened over to the press of sail, and sped on down Channel.

A wistful look came into the mother's eyes, as she thought of her child's words. In spite of resolutions and promises, the parting from the old people had been most painful; but, throughout all, there had seemed to her to be a curious indifference to her going, on the part of Bayle. He had been incessant in his attentions; a hundred little acts had been performed that were likely to make their stay on shipboard more pleasant; but there was a something wanting—a something she had felt deeply, and the pain became the more acute since she found that her feelings were shared.

They stood gazing at the grey and distant land, when the evening was falling. They were faint for want of food; but they knew it not, for the faintness was mingled with the sickness of the heart, and in spite of the glowing happy future Mrs Hallam tried to paint, a strange sense of desolation and despair seemed to overmaster her, and all her fortitude was needed to save her from bursting into a violent fit of sobbing.

On and on with the water rushing beneath them, as they leaned upon the bulwarks, gazing still at the fast receding shore. There had been a great deal of noisy bustle going on around; but so wrapt were they in their own feelings that sailors and passengers, officers and men, passed and repassed unheeded. They were in a little world of their own, blind to all beside, so that it was with quite a start that Mrs Hallam heard, for the second time, a voice say:

"Surely, ladies, you must be cold. Will you allow me to fetch shawls from the cabin?"

The first time these words were spoken, neither Mrs Hallam nor Julia moved; but, on their being repeated, they turned quickly round, to find that Thisbe had gone below, and that where she had been seated upon her box an officer in undress uniform was standing, cap in hand.

"I thank you, no," said Mrs Hallam coldly, as she returned the bow. "Julie, it is time we went below."

The officer drew back as mother and daughter swept slowly by towards the cabin stairs, and remained motionless even after they had disappeared.

He was roused from his waking dream by a hearty clap on the shoulders.

"What's the matter, Phil?" said a bluff voice, and a heavy-featured officer of about forty looked at him in a half-amused manner.

"Matter? Matter? Nothing; nothing at all."

"Bah! don't tell me. The old game, Phil. Is she nice-looking?"

"Beautiful!" cried the young officer excitedly.

"Ah! that's how I used to speak of Mrs Captain Otway," said the heavy-looking officer cynically; "but, my dear Phil, with all due respect to the sharer of my joys and the sorrows of going out to this horrible hole, Mrs Captain Otway does not look beautiful now."

"Otway, you are a brute to that woman. She is a thoroughly true-hearted lady, and too good for you."

"Much, Phil—much too good. Poor woman, it was hard upon her, with all her love of luxury and refinement, that she should be forced by fate to marry the poor captain of a marching regiment."

"Sent out to guard convicts in a penal settlement, eh?"

"Yes, to be sure. Oh, dear me! I shall be heartily glad when we are settled down and have had a week at sea."

"Oh, I don't know. I think time passes quite quickly enough. I say, Otway, do you think, if you asked her, Mrs Otway would lend a helping hand to those two ladies? They seem very strange and desolate on board here."

"My wife? Impossible, Phil; she is in her berth already, declaring that she is sea-sick, when all the time it is fancy."

"How do you know?"

"How do I know? Because she never is; it is so as to get out of the misery and confusion of the first day. Look here, boy, I'm always glad to help you, though. Shall I do?"

"You do? What for?"

"To go down and try and set your last enslavers at their ease."

"Don't be idiotic."

"Nice way for a subaltern to speak to his commanding officer, sir."

"I was not speaking to my commanding officer, but to my old companion, Jack Otway."

"Oh, I see! I say, Phil, which of the fair ones is it—Juno or Hebe?"

"Don't talk nonsense."

"All right. Who are they?"

"I can't find out yet. The captain gave me their names, that's all. Hist! here is their maid."

Just then Thisbe, who had been below, creeping off quietly to make things a bit comfortable, as she called it, came on deck, having missed Mrs Hallam and Julia, expecting to find them where she had left them, leaning over the bulwarks; and full of haste, as she had found that there was at last something like a pleasant meal spread in the principal cabin.

"It's very muddly," she muttered to herself, "and I'd give something for a snug little room where I could make them a decent cup of tea. And this is being at sea, is it?—sea that Tom Porter says is so lovely. Poor wretch!"

Thisbe impatiently dashed a tear from her eyes, the reason for whose coming she would not own; and then she stopped short, wondering at the presence of a couple of officers, where she had left Mrs Hallam and Julia, for, from some reason best known to himself, Philip Eaton, of His Majesty's —th Foot, was resting his arms where Julia had rested hers, and Captain Otway, in command of the draft on its way out to Port Jackson, had involuntarily taken Mrs Hallam's place.

"Looking for your ladies?" said Eaton.

"Yes. What have you done with—I mean where are they?"

"One moment," said the lieutenant in a confidential manner, as he slipped his hand into his pocket, "just tell me—"

He stopped astonished, for as she saw the motion of the young man's hand, and heard his insinuating words, Thisbe gave vent to a sound best expressed by the word "Wuff!" but which sounded exceedingly like the bark of some pet dog, as she whisked herself round and searched the deck before once more going below.

"Another of them," she muttered between her teeth. "Handsome as handsome, and ready to lay traps for my darling. But I'm not going to have her made miserable. I'm a woman now; I was a weak, watery, girlish thing then. I'm not going to have her life made a wreck."

Thisbe went below, little thinking that it would be a week before she again came on deck.

The weather turned bad that night, and the customary miseries ensued. It was so bad that the captain was glad that he had to run into Plymouth, but no sooner was he there than the weather abated, tempting him forth again to encounter a terrible gale off the Lizard, and more or less bad weather till they were well across the Bay of Biscay, and running down the west coast of Spain, when the weather changed all at once. The sky cleared, the sun came out warm and bright, the sea went down, and one by one the wretched passengers stole on deck.

Among them, pale and depressed by the long confinement in the cabins, Mrs Hallam and Julia were ready to hurry on deck to breathe the sweet, pure air.

"And is that distant shore Spain?" said Julia wonderingly, as she gazed at the faint grey line at which every eye and glass was being directed.

"Yes, Julie," said Mrs Hallam more cheerfully, "sunny Spain."

"And it seems just now that we were gazing at dear old England," said Julia, with a sigh.

"Yes," said Mrs Hallam, grasping her hand with feverish energy, "but now we are so many hundred miles nearer to him who is waiting our coming, Julie. Let us count the miles as he is counting the minutes before he can take his darling to his heart. Julie, my child, we must put the past behind us; it is the future for which we must live."

"Forget the past?" said Julia mournfully. "It was such a happy time."

"For you, Julie, but for me one long agonising time of waiting."

"Dearest mother," whispered Julia, pressing her hand, and speaking quickly, "I know—I know, and I will try so hard not to be selfish."

They had turned to the bulwarks the moment they came on deck, and, without casting a look round, had glanced at the distant coast, and then mentally plunged their eyes into the cloud ahead, beyond which stood Robert Hallam awaiting their coming.

"I had the pleasure of speaking to you before the storm, ladies," said a voice, and as they turned quickly, it was to find Lieutenant Eaton, cap in hand, smiling, and slightly flushed.

Mrs Hallam bowed.

"I sincerely trust that you have quite recovered," continued the young officer, directing an admiring gaze at Julia.

"Quite, I thank you," said Mrs Hallam coldly.

"Then we shall see you at the table, Mrs Hallam—and Miss Hallam?" he continued, with another bow.

Julia returned the bow, looking flushed and rather indignant.

"I hope you will excuse me," continued Eaton; "on shipboard you see we are like one family, all as it were in the same house."

Mrs Hallam bowed again, flushing as ingenuously as her daughter, for these advances troubled her greatly. She would have preferred being alone, and in a more humble portion of the vessel, but Sir Gordon and Bayle had insisted upon her occupying one of the best cabins, and it seemed to her that she was there under false pretences, and that it was only a question of days before there must come discovery which would put them to open shame.

Driven, as it were, to bay by the young officer's words, she replied hastily: "You must excuse me now; I have scarcely recovered."

"Pray forgive me," cried Eaton, giving Julia a look full of intelligence which made her shrink, "I ought to have known better. In a short time I hope, Mrs Hallam, that we shall be better acquainted."

He raised his cap again and drew back, while, excited and agitated beyond her wont, Mrs Hallam exclaimed:

"It cannot be, Julie. We must keep ourselves aloof from these people—from all the passengers; our course is alone—till we join him."

"Yes," said Julia, in a troubled way, "we must be alone."

"These people who make advances to us now," continued Mrs Hallam, "would master the object of our journey before we had gone far, and then we should be the pariahs of the ship."

"Would they be so unjust, mother?"

"Yes, for they do not know the truth. If they were told all, they would not believe it. My child, it was so that the world should never turn upon us and revile us for our misfortune that I have insisted all these years on living so reserved a life. And now we must go on in the same retired manner. If we are drawn into friendly relations with these people, our story will ooze out, and we shall have to endure the insult and misery of seeing them turn their backs upon us. Better that we should ostracise ourselves than suffer it at other hands; the blow will be less keen."

"I am ready to do all you wish, dear," said Julia, stealing her hand into her mother's.

"My beloved," whispered back Mrs Hallam, "it is our fate. We must bear all this, but our reward will be the more joyful, Julie: it is for your father's sake. Think of it, my child; there is no holier name under heaven to a child than that of father."

There was a pause, and then Julia, in a low, sweet voice, whispered: "Mother."

The two women stood there alone, seeming to gaze across the bright sea at the distant land. Passengers and sailors passed them, and the officers of the ship hesitated as they drew near about speaking, ending by respecting the reverie in which they seemed to be wrapt, and passing on. But Millicent and Julia Hallam saw neither sea, shore, nor the distant land: before each the face of Robert Hallam, as they had known it last, rose out of, as it were, a mist. And as they gazed into the future, the countenance of Julia seemed full of timid wonder, half shrinking, while that of Millicent grew more and more calm, as her eyes filled with a sweet subdued light, full of yearning to meet once more him who was waiting all those thousand miles away.

So intent were they upon their thoughts of the coming encounter, that neither of them noticed the quiet step that approached, and then stopped close at hand.

"Yes," said Mrs Hallam aloud, "we must accept our position, my child; better that we should be alone."

"Not quite!"

Julia started round with a cry of joy, and placed her hands in those of the speaker.

"Mr Bayle?" she cried excitedly; "what a surprise!"

"You here?" cried Mrs Hallam hoarsely.

"Yes," was the reply, given in the calmest, most matter-of-fact, half-laughing way, and as if it were merely a question of crossing a county at home. "Why, you two poor unprotected women, you did not think I meant to let you take this long voyage alone!"

Mrs Hallam drew a long breath and turned pale. She essayed to speak, but no words would come, and at last with a spasm seeming to contract her brow, she turned to gaze appealingly at her child.

"But you are going back?" said Julia, and she, too, seemed deeply moved.

He shook his head, and smiled.

"How good—how noble!" she began.

"Ah! tut! tut! little pupil; what nonsense!" cried Bayle merrily. "Why, here is Sir Gordon, who has done precisely the same thing." And the old baronet came slowly up, raising his straw hat just as Thisbe came hurriedly on deck to announce the discovery she had made, and found that she was too late.

Volume Three—Chapter Thirteen.

New Faces—New Friends.

"You may call it what you like, Mr Tom Porter, but I call it deceit."

"No," said Tom, giving his rough head a roll, as he stood with his legs very far apart, looking quite the sailor now, in place of the quiet body-servant of the St. James's pantry. "No, my lass, not deceit, reg'lar sea arrangement: sailing under sealed orders. Quite a reg'lar thing."

"It's the last thing I should have expected of Sir Gordon; and as to Mr Bayle, how he could keep it quiet as he did, and then all at once make his appearance off the coast of Spain—"

"After coming quietly on board at Plymouth, while you people were all shut up below out of the rough weather. Pooh! my lass, it was all meant well, so don't show so much surf."

"Reason?" said Bayle smiling, as he sat aft with Mrs Hallam and Julia, Sir Gordon having gone to his cabin. "I thought if I proposed coming it would agitate and trouble you both, and as to what you have said, surely I am a free agent, and if it gives me pleasure to watch over you both, and to render you up safely at our journey's end, you cannot wish to deny me that."

The subject dropped, and as the days glided on in the pleasant monotony of a life at sea, when the sky smiles and the wind is fair, the position seemed to be accepted by Mrs Hallam as inevitable. She tried hard to shut herself away with Julia, but soon found that she must yield to circumstances. She appealed to Sir Gordon and to Christie Bayle, but each smiled as he gave her a few encouraging words.

"You trouble yourself about an imaginary care," the latter said. "Bear in mind that you are on your way to a settlement where sins against the Government are often condoned, and you may rest assured that no one on board this vessel would be so cruel as to visit your unhappy condition upon your innocent heads."

"But I would far rather be content with Julie's company, and keep to our cabin."

"It is impossible," said Bayle. "It is like drawing attention to yourself. Be advised by me: lead the quiet regular cabin life, and all will be well."

Mrs Hallam shook her head.

"No," she said. "I am afraid. I am more troubled than I can say."

She gazed up in Bayle's eyes, and a questioning look passed between them. Each silently asked the other the same question: "Have you noticed that?"

But the time was not ripe for the question to be put in its entirety, and neither spoke.

The weather continued glorious from the time of the fresh grey dawn, when the tip of the sun gradually rose above the sea, on through the glowing heat of noon, when the pitch oozed from the seams, and outside the awnings the handrails could not be touched by the bare hand. Then on and on till the passengers assembled in groups to see sky and water dyed with the refulgent hues that dazzled while they filled with awe.

It was at these times that Mrs Hallam and Julia stole away from the other groups, to be followed at a distance by Bayle, who stood and watched them as they gazed at the setting sun. For it seemed to mother and daughter like a sign, a foretaste of the glory of the land to which they were going, and in the solemnity and silence of the mighty deep, evening by evening they stood and watched, their privacy respected by all on board, till lamps began to swing here and there beneath the awning, and generally Lieutenant Eaton came to ask Mrs Hallam to play or Julia to sing.

"Bayle," Sir Gordon would say, with the repetition of an elderly and querulous man, "you always seem to me like a watch-dog on the look-out for intruders."

"I am," said Bayle laconically.

"Then why, sir, confound you! when the intruders do come, don't you seize 'em, and shake 'em, and throw 'em overboard?"

"I'm afraid I should do something of the kind," replied Bayle, "only I must have cause."

"Cause? Well, haven't you cause enough, man?"

"Surely no. Everybody on board, from the captain to the humblest seaman, has a respectful smile for them as he raises his cap."

"Of course he has," cried Sir Gordon testily.

"Then why should the watch-dog interfere?"

"Why? Isn't that soldier fellow always making advances, and carrying them off to the piano of an evening?"

"Yes; and it seems, now the first trouble has worn off, to give them both pleasure. Surely they have had their share of pain!"

"Yes, yes," cried Sir Gordon; "but I don't like it; I don't like it, Bayle."

"I have felt the same, but we must not be selfish. Besides, we agreed that they ought to associate with the passengers during the voyage."

Sir Gordon's face grew full of puckers, as he drew out and lit a cheroot, which he smoked in silence, while Bayle went to the side and gazed at the black water, spangled with the reflected stars that burned above in the vast bejewelled arch of heaven.

"I don't like it," muttered Sir Gordon to himself, "and I don't understand Bayle. No," he continued after a pause, "I cannot ask him that. Time settles all these matters, and it will settle this."

From where he sat he could, by turning his head, gaze beneath the awning looped up like some great marquee. Here, by the light of the shaded lamps, the passengers and officers gathered night after night as they sailed on through the tropics. At times there would be a dance, more often the little tables would be occupied by players at some game, while first one lady and then another would take her place at the piano.

There were other eyes beside Sir Gordon's watching beneath the awning, and a signal would be given by a low whistle whenever Julia was seen to approach the instrument. Then a knot of the soldiers and sailors would collect to listen to her clear thrilling voice as she sang some sweet old-time ballad. It was always Philip Eaton who pressed her to sing, led her to the piano, and stood over her, holding a lamp or turning over the leaves. He it was, too, who was the first to applaud warmly; and often and often from where he leaned over the bulwarks listening, too, Bayle could see the ingenuous girlish face look up with a smile at the handsome young officer, who would stay by her side afterwards perhaps the greater part of the evening, or he would lead her to where Captain Otway was lolling back, talking to Mrs Captain Otway, a handsome, fashionable-looking woman, who seemed to win her way day by day more and more to the friendship of Millicent Hallam.

At such times Sir Gordon would sit alone and fume, while Bayle watched the black, starlit water, closing his eyes when Julia sang or Mrs Hallam played some old piece, that recalled the doctor's cottage at King's Castor.

Afterwards he would turn his head and look beneath the awning sadly—the warm, soft glow of the swinging lamp lighting up face after face, which then seemed to fade away into the shadow.

He was strangely affected at such times. Now it was the present, and they were at sea; anon it seemed that he was leaning over the rustic seat in the doctor's garden, and that was not the awning and the quarterdeck, but the little drawing-room with the open windows. Time had not glided on; and in a curious, dreamy fashion, that did not seem to be Julia, the child he had taught, but Millicent; and that was not Lieutenant Eaton leaning over her, but Robert Hallam.

Then one of the shadows on the awning would take a grotesque resemblance to little Miss Heathery, to help out the flights of fancy; and Bayle would listen for the tinkling notes of the piano again, and feel surprised not to hear a little bird-like voice piping "Gaily the troubadour."

Next there would be a burst of merry conversation, and perhaps a laugh; and as Bayle turned his head again to gaze half wonderingly, the lamp-light would fall, perhaps, upon the faces of mother and daughter, the centre of the group near the piano.

Christie Bayle would begin to study the stars once more, as if seeking to read therein his future; but in vain, for he gazed down where they were broken and confused in the dark waters, sparkling and gliding as they were repeated again below, deep down in the transparent depths, where phosphorescent creatures glowed here and there.

"I can't make him out," Sir Gordon would often say to himself.

No wonder! Christie Bayle could not analyse his own feelings, only that the old sorrow that was dead and buried years upon years ago seemed to be reviving and growing till it was becoming an agonising pang.

End of Volume Two.

Volume Three—Chapter Fourteen.

Lady Eaton's Son.

It was a long voyage, for in those days the idea of shortening a trip to the Antipodes had not been dreamed of, and the man who had suggested that the time would come when powerful steamers would run through the Mediterranean, down a canal, along the Red Sea, across the Indian Ocean, touch at Singapore, and after threading their way among the tropic Indian Islands, pass down the eastern side of the Australian continent within shelter of the Great Barrier Reef, would have been called a madman.

But long and tedious as it was made by calms, in what seemed to be a region of eternal summer, Christie Bayle prayed that the voyage might be prolonged.

And then, Julia—who had been to him as his own child, whose young life he had seen increase and develop till the bud was promising to be a lovely flower—seemed so happy. Everything was so new to the young girl, fresh from her life of retirement, and now thrust into a society where she was at once made queen. There was a smile and a pull at the forelock from every sailor, while every soldier of Captain Otway's company was ready to salute as soon as she came on deck.

The bluff old captain of the *Sea King* took her at once under his protection, and settled her place at table; while his officers vied with each other in their attentions. As for Philip Eaton, he was more than satisfied with the behaviour of Mrs Captain Otway, and he did not believe her when, in a free-and-easy way, she clapped him on the shoulder and said:

"It is not on your account, Phil Eaton—handsome youth, who falleth in love with every pretty woman he sees—but because I like the little lady. However, my boy, your flirtation is nearly over."

"Nearly over, Mrs Otway!" he cried warmly. "Flirtation? Don't call it by that wretched name."

"There, I told Jack so, and he laughed at me. It is serious, then?"

"Serious! I mean to be married this time."

"Pooh! nonsense, Phil. Absurd!"

"Was it absurd for you to make a runaway match with John Otway!"

"No; but then we loved each other passionately."

"Well, and do not we?"

"Hum! No, my dear boy. There, Phil, you see I am like a mother to you. You think you love the little thing desperately."

"And I do so. It is no thinking. I never saw a woman who moved me as she does with her sweet, innocent ways."

"Is it so bad as that?" said Mrs Otway, smiling.

"Bad! no, it's good. I'm glad I've seen the woman at last of whom I can feel proud. She is so different from any girl I ever met before."

"Don't singe your wings, my handsome butterfly," said Mrs Otway, laughing. "Why, my dear Phil, I don't think the girl cares for you a bit."

"But I am sure she does."

"Has she owned to it?"

"No," he said proudly. "I am in earnest now, and I reverence her so that I would not say a word until I have spoken to her mother and her friends."

"Humph! yes: her friends," said Mrs Otway. "What relatives are Sir Gordon Bourne and the Reverend Christie Bayle to the fair queen of my gallant soldier's heart?"

"I don't know," he said impatiently.

"Why are they all going out to Port Jackson?"

"I don't know. How should I?"

"Oh! they might have told you in conversation."

"I did not trouble myself about such things. Hang it all! Mrs Otway, how could I be so petty?"

"Is it not natural that a man should be anxious to know who and what are the relatives of the lady he thinks of as his future wife?"

"Oh, some sordid fellows would think of such things. I'm not going to marry her relations."

"In some sort a man must," said Mrs Otway coolly. "Look here," cried the young officer, "why do you talk to me like this?"

"Hullo! what's the matter?" cried Captain Otway, who had come up unobserved; "quarrelling?"

"No," said Mrs Otway, "I am only giving Phil Eaton a little of the common-sense he seems to have been losing lately. Why do I talk to you like this, my dear Phil? I'll tell you. Because the day before we sailed Lady Eaton came to me and said, 'You are a woman of experience, Mrs Otway; keep an eye upon my boy, and don't let him get entangled in any way.'"

"My mother said that to you?"

"Indeed she did; and now that you are running your head into a very pretty silken skein, and tangling yourself up in the most tremendous manner, I think it is time for me to act."

"Quite right, Phil," said the Captain. "You wanted checking. The young lady is delicious, and all that is innocent and nice; but you are not content with a pleasant chat."

"No," said the Lieutenant firmly; "I mean to marry her."

"Indeed!" said Otway dryly. "Who and what is she?"

"A lady of the greatest refinement and sweetness of character."

"Granted; but who is her mother?"

"Mrs Hallam, a lady whom, in spite of her sadness of disposition and distant ways, it is a privilege to know."

"Will you go on, Bel?" said Otway.

"No! Oh, Captain, you are talking grand sense! I'll listen."

"Well, then, here is another question. Who is Mr Hallam?"

"How should I know? Some merchant or official out at Port Jackson. They are going to join him. Julie—"

"Hullo!" cried Mrs Otway, "has it come to that?"

"Miss Hallam," continued the young officer, flushing, "told me she had not seen her father for years."

Captain Otway turned to his wife, and she exchanged glances with him in a meaning way.

Eaton looked sharply from one to the other, his eyes flashing, and his white teeth showing as he bit his lip.

"What do you two mean?" he cried angrily.

"Oh, nothing!" said Otway, shrugging his shoulders.

"I insist upon knowing!" cried Eaton. "You would not look like that without deep cause; and it is not fair to me. Look here, I can't bear it! You are thinking something respecting these people; and it is not like my old friends. Hang it all, am I a boy?"

"Yes," said Mrs Otway gently, "a foolish, hot-headed, impetuous boy. Now, my dear Phil, be reasonable. The young lady is sweet and gentle, and sings charmingly. She is a delicious little companion for the voyage, and at your wish Jack and I have been very friendly, not feeling ourselves called upon during a Voyage like this to inquire into people's antecedents so long as they were pleasant."

"But—"

"Hear me out."

"Yes, hear her out, Phil; and don't be a fool!" said Captain Otway.

"Mrs Hallam and Miss Hallam are both very nice, and we liked them, and I should like them to the end of the voyage if you were not beginning to make yourself very stupid."

"Stupid! Oh, shame upon you, Mrs Otway!"

"You say so now, my dear boy; but what would you say if we, your old friends, let you run blindly into an entanglement with a young lady whose antecedents would horrify Lady Eaton, your mother?"

"I say shame again, Mrs Otway!" cried Eaton. "Why, everything contradicts your ideas. Would Mrs and Miss Hallam have for friends and companions Sir Gordon Bourne and a clergyman? I had heard of Sir Gordon as an eccentric yachting baronet years ago."

"So had I," said Captain Otway; "but they have only become acquainted since they were on board ship. Sir Gordon and the parson came on board at Plymouth."

"Now I am going to show you how unjust you both are!" cried Eaton triumphantly. "Julie—I mean Miss Hallam—told me herself that she knew Sir Gordon Bourne when she was a little girl, and that Mr Bayle had acted as her private tutor ever since she could remember."

"And what did she say Mr Hallam was?" "She did not mention his name, and I did not ask her. Hang it, madam, what do you think he is?"

"I am not going to say, my dear Philip, because I should be sorry to misjudge any one; but please remember why we are going out to Port Jackson."

"Going out? Why, to join the regiment—from the dépôt."

"And when we join our regiment our duty is to—"

"Guard the convicts! Good heavens!"

The young man sprang from the chair in which he had been lounging, and turned white as paint, then he flushed with anger, turned pale again, and glared about the vessel.

Just then Mrs Hallam came out of the cabin with Julia and mounted to the after deck, going slowly to the vessel's side, as was her custom, to gaze away east and south, talking softly to her child the while.

"Oh, it is impossible!" said Eaton at last. "How dare you make such a charge!"

"My wife makes no charge, Phil," said Captain Otway firmly. "She only tells you what we think. Perhaps we are wrong."

"And now that you suspect this," said Eaton sarcastically, "are you both going to hold aloof from these ladies?"

"Certainly not!" said Mrs Otway warmly. "I have always found them most pleasant companions during our voyage, and I am the last woman to visit the sins of one person on the rest of his family."

"And yet you abuse me for doing as you do!" cried Eaton impetuously.

"There are different depths of shading in a picture, my dear Phil," said Mrs Otway, laying her hand upon the young man's arm. "Be friendly to these people, as Jack there and I are about to be, to the end, but don't go and commit yourself to an engagement with a convict's daughter."

"Oh, this is too much!" cried Eaton fiercely.

"No, it is not, Phil," said the Captain quietly. "I'm afraid my wife is right."

As he was speaking, Mrs Otway, who had left them, crossed the deck, and stood talking to Mrs Hallam and Julia, who soon went away, and Eaton saw her walk to where Sir Gordon was smoking the cigar just brought to him, and then leave him to go timidly up to where Christie Bayle was leaning over the bulwarks, book in hand, and seeming to read.

Volume Three—Chapter Fifteen.

Sir Gordon Gets out of Temper.

"Don't—pray don't look so agitated, dear, mother," whispered Julia, as they left the cabin one morning, after an announcement by the captain that before many hours had passed, a new phase in the long voyage would take place, for they would see land.

The news spread like lightning among the passengers, and was received with eager delight by those who had been cooped up gazing at sea and sky for months.

"I will try and be calm," said Mrs Hallam; "but it seems at times more than I can bear. Think, Julie; only a few more hours and we shall see him again."

Julia's fair young face contracted, and there was a strange fluttering about her heart. Mingled feelings troubled her. She was angry with herself that she did not share her mother's joy; and, strive how she would, *she* could not help feeling regret that the voyage was so near its end, and that they were to make a fresh plunge in life.

She had trembled and shrunk from the journey when it was first decided upon. There was so much of the unknown to encounter, and she had been so happy and contented in the simple home, that, unlike most young people of her age, novelty possessed for her few charms. But the voyage had proved, after the first few dreary days, one long succession of pleasant hours. Every one had been so kind—Mrs Otway almost loving, Captain Otway frank and manly, and—she coloured slightly as she thought of it all—Lieutenant Eaton so gentle and attentive to her every wish.

Yes, for months he had been ready to hurry to her side, to wait upon her, to read aloud, turn over her music, and join in the duets with an agreeable, manly voice. Yes, it had all been very, very pleasant; the only dark spots in the sunshine, the only clouds being that Sir Gordon had grown more testy and ready to say harsh things, and Mr Bayle had become strangely cold and distant—so changed. He who had been always so warm and frank looked at her gravely; the old playful manner had completely gone, and the change troubled her young breast sorely.

That morning, when Mrs Hallam took her old place by the bulwarks to gaze away into the distance, out of which the land she sought was to rise, Julia came to a determination, and, waiting her opportunity, she watched till Bayle had taken his place where he sat and read, and Sir Gordon was in his usual seat.

For, on ship-board, the nature of the vessel's management seems to communicate itself to the passengers. As they have special berths, so do they adopt special seats at the cabin table, and, when on deck, go by custom to regular places after their morning walk beneath the breeze-filled sails.

Sir Gordon was in his seat, and Tom Porter on his way with a cigar and light, when Julia intercepted him, took them from him, and walked up to Sir Gordon.

"Hullo!" he said shortly. "You?"

"Yes! I've brought you your cigar and light."

She held them out, and the old man took them, and lit the cheroot with all the careful dallying of an old smoker.

"Thankye," he said shortly; but Julia did not leave him, only stood looking down at the wrinkles of age and annoyance in the well-bred face.

"Well!" he said, "what are you waiting for, my child?" His voice was a little softer as the wreaths of smoke rose in the soft southern air.

"I want to talk to you," she said, looking at him wistfully.

"Sit down, then. Ah, there's no chair, and—where is our gay young officer to fetch one?"

Julia did not answer, but gazed up in his face as she seated herself upon the deck by his low lounge chair.

"Why do you speak to me so unkindly?" she said, with a naïve innocency of manner that made the old man wince and cease smoking.

"Unkindly?" he said at last.

"Yes," said Julia. "You have been so different. You are not speaking to me now as you used."

The old man frowned, looked from the upturned face at his side to where Mrs Hallam was gazing out to sea, and back again.

"Because I'm growing old and am chilly, and pettish, and jealous, my dear," he said at last warmly. "Julia!" he cried searchingly, "tell me; do you love this Lieutenant Eaton?"

The girl's face grew crimson, and her eyes flashed a look of resentment as she rose quickly to her feet.

"No, no! don't go, my dear," he cried; but it was too late even if the words could have stayed her. Julia was walking swiftly away, and Lieutenant Eaton, who was coming back from a morning parade of the company, increased his pace on seeing Julia, but she turned aside and walked towards Bayle.

"Yes, but if I had not just spoken to her," muttered Sir Gordon, "she would have stopped. Well, it is only natural, and I had no business to speak—no business to trouble myself about her. Tom Porter says the old maid is bitterly mad about it, and declares the poor child is going to wreck her life as her mother did. The old cat! How dare she think such a thing! The impudence! Wishes the ship may be wrecked first and that we may all be drowned. Ah! you're there, are you, sir?"

"Yes, Sir Gordon. Another cheroot?"

"Can't you see I haven't smoked this, fool? Here, give me a light!"

Tom Porter's mahogany face did not change as he produced a piece of tinder and held it for his testy master to ignite his cigar.

"Thank ye, Tom," said Sir Gordon, changing his tone. "Here, don't go away. What did that woman say?"

"Thisbe, Sir Gordon?"

"Yes; you know whom I mean. About Miss Hallam?"

"Wished we might all be wrecked and drowned before it came off."

"Before what came off?"

"A wedding with Lieutenant Eaton, Sir Gordon."

"Why?"

"Principally because she says he's so handsome, Sir Gordon. She hates handsome men."

"Humph! That's why she's so fond of you, Tom Porter."

"Which she ain't, Sir Gordon," said Tom Porter dolefully.

"You had been talking about weddings then?"

"Well, just a little, Sir Gordon," said Tom Porter, not a muscle of whose countenance moved. "I just said how nice it was to see two young folks so fond of each other."

"As whom?"

"As the Lufftenant and Miss Jooly, Sir Gordon; and that it would be just as nice for two middle-aged folks who had kept it all in store."

"And is she going to marry you, then, when we get to port?"

"No: Sir Gordon; it's all over. She ain't the marrying sort."

"Humph! Marry a black woman, then, to spite her, and then ask her to come and see your wife."

"No, Sir Gordon, beggin' your pardon, sir; I've been in the wrong, when I ought to have took you for an example. It's all over, and I'm settled down thorough. I have seen but one woman as I thought I'd like to splice."

"And that was Mrs Hallam's old maid?"

"Yes, Sir Gordon."

"Why? She isn't handsome."

"Not outside, Sir Gordon; and I don't rightly know why I took to her, unless it was that she seemed so right down like—such a stick-to-you-through-fair-weather-and-foul sort of woman. But it's all over now, Sir Gordon. Things won't turn out as one likes, and it's of no use to try."

"You're right, Tom Porter; you're a better philosopher than your master. There: that will do. When shall we see land?"

"Morrow morning, Sir Gordon. Daybreak; not afore. Any orders 'bout the shore?"

"Orders? What are we to do when we get there? Tom Porter, if you could tell me what we are to do, I'd give you a hundred pounds. There, give me a light, my cheroot's out again!"

Volume Three—Chapter Sixteen.

A Sore Place.

"Are you glad the voyage is nearly over?" said a soft little voice that made Bayle start.

"Glad?" he said, as he turned to gaze in Julia's plaintive-looking face. "No; I am sorry."

"Why?"

"Why? Because you have seemed so happy."

He paused a few moments, as if afraid that his voice would tremble.

"Because your mother has seemed so happy." And, he added to himself: "Because I tremble for all that is to come."

"Are you angry with me, Mr Bayle?" said Julia, after a pause.

"Angry with you, my child?" he said, with his eyes brightening, though there was a piteous look in his face. "Oh, no; how could I be?"

"I don't know," she replied; "but you have grown more and more changed. I have seen so little of you lately, and you have avoided me."

"But you have not been dull. You have had many companions and friends."

"Yes," she said quickly, "and they have been so kind; but I have seemed to regret the past days when we were all so quiet and happy together."

"Hush!" he said quickly. "Don't speak like that."

"Not speak like that? There, now you are angry with me again."

"Angry? No, no, my child," cried Bayle, whose voice trembled with emotion. "I am not angry with you."

"Yes; that's how I like to hear you speak," cried Julia. "That is how you used to speak to me, and not in that grave, measured way, as if you were dissatisfied."

"Julia," he said, hoarse with emotion, "how could I be dissatisfied when I see you happy? Has it not been the wish of my life?"

"Yes; I have always known it was. Now you make me happy again; and you will always speak so to me?"

"Always," he said, with his eyes lighting up with a strange fire. "Always, my child."

"That's right," she cried. "That is like my dear old teacher speaking to me again;" and her sweet, ingenuous eyes looked lovingly in his.

But they saw no response to their tenderness, for the fire died out of Bayle's gaze, the red spots faded from his cheeks, and an agonising pang made him shudder, and then draw in a long, deep breath.

At that moment Lieutenant Eaton approached, and Bayle saw the tell-tale colour come into Julia's cheeks.

"It is fate, I suppose," he said, drawing back to give place to Eaton.

Julia looked up at him quickly, as if she divined the words he had said to himself; but he did not speak, only smiled sadly, and walked towards where Mrs Hallam was gazing over the side.

He shuddered as he thought of the meeting that must take place, and walked up and down slowly, thinking of his position, unheeded by Mrs Hallam, whose face was irradiated by the joy that filled her breast.

He turned back to see that Eaton had led Julia to the other side of the vessel, and as she, too, stood with her hands resting on the bulwarks, Bayle could see that the young man's face was bright and animated; that he was talking quickly to the girl, whose head was slightly bent as though she was listening attentively to all he said.

Christie Bayle drew a long breath as he walked slowly on. His old, patient, long-suffering smile came upon his face, and now his lip ceased quivering, and he said softly:

"If it is for her happiness. Why not?"

"And after all I have said," he heard from a quick voice beyond the awning. "It's too bad, Jack. He is proposing to her now. What shall we do?"

"Nothing. Let him find all out for himself, and then cool down."

"And half break the poor girl's heart? I don't want that."

Bayle hurried away, feeling as if he could bear no more. The cabin seemed the best retreat, where he could take counsel with himself, and try and arrange some plan in which he could dispassionately leave out self, and act as he had vowed that he would—as a true friend to Millicent Hallam and her child.

But he was not to reach his cabin without another mental sting, for as he descended he came upon Thisbe, looking red-eyed as if she had been crying, and he stopped to speak to her.

"Matter, sir?" she answered; "and you ask me? Go back on deck, and see for yourself, and say whether the old trouble is to come all over again."

He felt as if he must speak angrily to the woman if he paused; and hurrying by her he shut himself in his cabin and stayed there for hours with the bustle of preparations for landing going on all around, the home of many months being looked upon now as a prison which every passenger was longing to quit, to gain the freedom of the shore.

Volume Three—Chapter Seventeen.

Communing with Self.

It was evening when Bayle went on deck again, his old calm having returned. He stopped short, and the elasticity of spirit that seemed to have come back—a feeling of hopefulness in keeping with the light champagny atmosphere, so full of life, died out again, even as the breeze that had wafted them on all day had now almost failed, and the ship glided very slowly through water that looked like liquid gold.

"A few short hours," he said to himself, as he gazed at Mrs Hallam standing with her arm round Julia, bathed in the evening light, watching the golden clouds upon the horizon that they were told were land—to them the land of hope and joy, but to Christie Bayle a place of sorrow and of pain.

"A few short hours," he said again, "and then the fond illusions must fall away, and they will be face to face with the truth."

He crept away sick at heart to the other side, where Lieutenant Eaton, who seemed to be hovering about mother and daughter, eager to join them but kept away by respect for their desire to be alone, passed him with a short nod, hesitated, as if about to speak, and then went on again.

Bayle waited hour after hour, ready should those in his charge require his services; but they did not move from their position, and it was Eaton who intercepted Thisbe, and took from her the scarves she was bringing to protect them from the night air; but only a few words passed, and he drew back to walk up and down till long after the Southern Cross was standing out among the glorious stars that looked so large and bright in the clear, dark sky above, when Mrs Hallam drew a deep breath and whispered a few words to Julia, and they descended to their cabin for the night, but not to sleep.

Then by degrees the deck was left to the watch, and a strange silence fell, for a change had come upon all on board. The first excitement that followed the look-out-man's cry of "Land ho!" had passed, and passengers and soldiers were gathered in groups after their busy preparation for the landing another day distant, and talked in whispers.

Lower and lower sank the weary spirit of Christie Bayle, as he stood leaning on the bulwark, gazing away into the starry depths of the glorious night, for it seemed to him that his task was nearly done, that soon those whom he had loved so well would pass out of his care, and as he thought of Millicent Hallam sharing the home of her convict husband he murmured a prayer on her behalf. Then his thoughts of the mother passed, and he recalled all that he had seen during the past months, above all, Julia's excited manner that day, and the conduct of Lieutenant Eaton. And as he pondered his thoughts took somewhat this form:

"Young, handsome, a thorough gentleman, what wonder that he should win her young love? but will he stand the test? A convict's daughter—an officer of the King. He must know; and if he does stand the test—"

Christie Bayle stood with his hands clasped tightly together, as once more a strange agony of soul pierced him to the core. He saw himself again the young curate entranced by the beauty of a fair young English girl in her happy home, declaring his love for her, laying bare his hopes, and learning the bitter lesson that those hopes were vain. He saw again the long years of peaceful friendship with a new love growing for the child who had been his principal waking thought. He saw her grow to womanhood, loving him as he had loved her— with a love that had been such as a father might bear his child, till the peaceful calm had been broken as he saw that Julia listened eagerly and with brightening eyes to the words of this young officer; and now it was that like a blow the knowledge came, the knowledge that beneath all this tenderness had been a love of a stronger nature, ready to burst forth and bloom when it was again too late.

"A dream—a dream," he said sadly. "How could she love me otherwise than as she said—as her dear teacher?"

"A dream," he said again. "'Thy will be done!'"

Volume Three—Chapter Eighteen.

"At Last!"

A busy day on ship-board, with the excitement growing fast, and officers and men cheerfully turning themselves into guides and describers of the scenery on either hand.

A glorious day, with a brisk breeze, and the white sails curving out, and the great vessel, that had borne them safely to their destination, careening gently over, with the white foam dividing and swelling away to starboard and to port.

The sky overhead might have been that of Italy, so gloriously bright and pure it seemed to all, as at last the vessel glided in between the guardian giants of the port, and then, as they stood well within the two grey rocky precipices, the swell upon which they had softly swayed died away, the breeze sank, and the great white sails flapped and filled and flapped, the ship slowly slackened its speed, and at last lay motionless, waiting for the tide that would bear them on to the anchorage within.

It was evening when the tantalising waiting was at an end, and the expectant groups saw themselves once more gliding on and on, past a long beach of white sand, into the estuary that, minute by minute, took more and more the aspect of some widening river.

Seen by the glory of the sinking sun, and after the long, monotonous voyage, it was like some glimpse of Eden, and with one consent the soldiers sent forth a hearty cheer, which died away into silence as the great ship glided on. Jutting promontories, emerald islands, golden waters, and a sky like topaz, as the sun slowly sank. Curving bays filled with roseate hues reflected from the sky, swelling hills in the distance of wondrous greyish green, with deepening slopes of softly darkening shadows. The harbour was without a ripple, and glistened as polished metal, and mirrored here and there the shore. Away in the distance, the soft greyish verdure stood out in the clear air; and as the wearied travellers drank in the glorious scene, there was a solemnity in its beauty that oppressed them, even unto tears.

Millicent Hallam stood in that self-same spot where she had so patiently watched for this her promised land, and as she bent forward with half-extended hands, Julia saw her lips part, and heard from time to time some broken utterances, as the tears of joy fell slowly from her dreamy eyes.

Time after time the most intimate of their fellow-passengers approached, but there was that in the attitude of mother and daughter which commanded respect, and they drew away.

On glided the ship, nearer and nearer, with the houses and rough buildings of the settlement slowly coming into sight, while, as the sun flashed from the windows, and turned the sand that fringed the shore for the time to tawny gold, the hearts of mother and daughter seemed to go out, to leap the intervening distance, and pour forth their longings to him who, they felt, was watching the ship that bore to him all he held dear.

Golden changing to orange, to amber, to ruddy wine. Then one deep glow, and the river-like harbour for a few minutes as if of molten metal cooling into purple, into black, and then the placid surface glistening with fallen stars.

And as Julia pressed nearer to the trusting woman, who gazed straight before her at the lights that twinkled in the scattered houses of the port, she heard a sweet, rich voice murmur softly:

"Robert, husband—I have come!" And again, soft as the murmur of the tide upon the shore:

"My God, I thank thee! At last—at last!"

Volume Three—Chapter Nineteen.

A Strange Encounter.

It had been hard work to persuade her, but Mrs Hallam had consented at last to rest quietly in the embryo hotel, while Bayle obtained the necessary passes for her and her daughter to see Hallam. This done, he took the papers and letters of recommendation he had brought and waited upon the governor.

There was a good deal of business going on, and Bayle was shown into a side room where a clerk was writing, and asked to sit down.

"Your turn will come in about an hour," said the official who showed him in, and Bayle sat down to wait.

As he looked up, he saw that the clerk was watching him intently; and as their eyes met, he said in a low voice:

"May I ask if you came out in the *Sea King?*"

"Yes; I landed this morning."

"Any good news, sir, from the old country?"

"Nothing particular; but I can let you have a paper or two, if you like."

"Thank you, sir, I should be very glad; but I meant Ireland. You thought I meant England."

"But you are not an Irishman?"

"Yes, sir. Have I forgotten my brogue?"

"I did not detect it."

"Perhaps I've forgotten it," said the man sadly, "as they seem to have forgotten me. Ten years make a good deal of difference."

"Have you been out here ten years?"

"Yes, sir, more."

"Do you know anything about the prisons?"

The clerk flushed, and then laughed bitterly.

"Oh, yes," he said; "I know something about them."

"And the prisoners?"

"Ye-es. Bah! what is the use of keeping it back? Of course I do, sir. I was sent out for the benefit of my country."

"You?"

"Yes, sir; I am a lifer."

Bayle gazed at the man in surprise.

"You look puzzled, sir," he said. "Why, almost every other man out here is a convict."

"But you have been pardoned?"

"Pardoned? No; I am only an assigned servant I can be sent back to the chain-gang at any time if I give offence. There, for heaven's sake, sir, don't look at me like that! If I offended against the laws, I have been bitterly punished."

"You mistake my looks," said Bayle gently; "they did not express my feelings to you, for they were those of sorrow."

"Sorrow?" said the man, who spoke as if he were making a great effort to keep down his feelings. "Ay, sir, you would say that if you knew all I had endured. It has been enough to make a man into a fiend, herding with the wretches sent out here, and at any moment, at the caprice of some brutal warder or other official ordered the lash."

Bayle drew his breath between his teeth hard.

"There, I beg your pardon, sir; but the sight of a face from over the sea, and a gentle word, sets all the old pangs stinging again. I'm better treated now. This governor is a very different man to the last."

"Perhaps you may get a full pardon yet," said Bayle; "your conduct has evidently been good."

"No. There will be no pardon for me, sir. I was too great a criminal."

"What—But I have no right to ask you," said Bayle.

"Yes, ask me, sir. My offence? Well, like a number of other hot-headed young men, I thought to make myself a patriot and free Ireland. That was my crime."

"Tell me," said Bayle, after a time, "did you ever encounter a prisoner named Hallam?"

"Robert Hallam—tall, dark, handsome man?"

"Yes; that answers the description."

"Sent over with a man named Crellock, for a bank robbery, was it not?"

"The same man. Where is he now?"

"He was up the country as a convict servant, shepherding; but I think he is back in the gangs again. Some of them are busy on the new road."

"Was he—supposed to be innocent out here?"

"Innocent? No. It was having to herd with such scoundrels made our fate the more bitter. Such men as he and his mate—"

"His mate?"

"Yes—the man Crellock—were never supposed to be very—"

He ceased speaking, and began to write quickly, for a door was opened, and an attendant requested Bayle to follow him.

He was ushered into the presence of an officer, who apologised for the governor being deeply engaged, consequent upon the arrival of the ship with the draft of men. But the necessary passes were furnished, and Bayle left.

As he was passing out with the documents in his hand he came suddenly upon Captain Otway and the Lieutenant, both in uniform.

The Captain nodded in a friendly way and passed on; but Eaton stopped.

"One moment, Mr Bayle," he said rather huskily. "I want you to answer a question."

Bayle bowed, and then met his eyes calmly, and without a line in his countenance to betoken agitation.

"I—I want you to tell me—in confidence, Mr Bayle—why Mrs Hallam and her daughter have come out here?"

"I am not at liberty, Lieutenant Eaton, to explain to a stranger Mrs Hallam's private affairs."

"Then will you tell me this? Why have you come here to-day? But I can see. Those are passes to allow you to go beyond the convict lines?"

"They are," said Bayle.

"That will do, sir," said the young man with his lip quivering; and hurrying on he rejoined Captain Otway, who was standing awaiting his coming in the doorway, in front of which a sentry was passing up and down.

Bayle went back to the hotel, where Mrs Hallam was watching impatiently, and Julia with her, both dressed for going out.

"You have been so long," cried the former; "but tell me—you have the passes?"

"Yes; they are here," he said.

"Give them to me," she cried, with feverish haste. "Come, Julia."

"You cannot go alone, Mrs Hallam," said Bayle in a remonstrant tone. "Try and restrain yourself. Then we will go on at once."

She looked at him half angrily; but the look turned to one of appeal as she moved towards the door.

"But are you quite prepared?" he whispered. "Do you still hold to the intention of taking Julia?"

"Yes, yes," she cried fiercely. "Christie Bayle, you cannot feel with me. Do you not realise that it is the husband and father waiting to see his wife and child?"

Bayle said no more then, but walked with them through the roughly marked out streets of the straggling port, towards the convict lines.

"I shall see you to the gates," he said, "secure your admission, and then await your return."

Mrs Hallam pressed his hand, and then as he glanced at Julia, he saw that she was trembling and deadly pale. The next minute, however, she had mastered her emotion, and they walked quickly on, Mrs Hallam with her head erect, and proud of mien, as she seemed in every movement to be wishing to impress upon her child that they should rather glory in their visit than feel shame. There was something almost triumphant in the look she directed at Bayle, a look which changed to angry reproach, as she saw his wrinkled brow and the trouble in his face.

Half-way to the prison gates there was a measured tramp of feet, and a quick, short order was given in familiar tones.

The next moment the head of a company of men came into sight; and Bayle recognised the faces. In the rear were Captain Otway and Lieutenant Eaton, both of whom saluted, Mrs Hallam acknowledging each bow with the dignity of a queen.

Bayle tried hard, but he could not help glancing at Julia, to see that she was deadly pale, but looking as erect and proud as her mother.

Captain Otway's company were on their way to their barracks. They had just passed the prison gates; and it was next to impossible for Mrs Hallam and her daughter to be going anywhere but to the large building devoted to the convicts.

Bayle knew that the two officers must feel this as they saluted; and, in spite of himself, he could not forbear feeling a kind of gratification. For it seemed to him that henceforth a gulf would be placed between them, and the pleasant friendship of the voyage be at an end.

Mrs Hallam knew it, but she did not shrink, and her heart bounded as she saw the calm demeanour of her child.

The measured tramp of the soldiers' feet was still heard, when a fresh party of men came into sight; and as he partly realised what was before him, Bayle stretched out his hand to arrest his companions.

"Come back," he said quickly; "we will go on after these men have passed."

"No," said Mrs Hallam firmly, "we will go on now, Christie Bayle, do you fancy that we would shrink from anything at a time like this?"

"But for her sake," whispered Bayle.

"She is my child, and we know our duty," retorted Mrs Hallam proudly.

But her face was paler, and she darted a quick glance at Julia, whose eyes dilated, and whose grasp of her mother's arm was closer, as from out of the advancing group came every now and then a shriek of pain, with sharp cries, yells, and a fierce volley of savage curses.

The party consisted of an old sergeant and three pensioners with fixed bayonets, one leading, two behind a party of eight men, in grotesque rough garments. Four of them walked in front, following the first guard, and behind them the other four carried a litter or stretcher, upon which, raised on a level with their shoulders, they bore a man, who was writhing in acute pain, and now cursing his bearers for going so fast, now directing his oaths against the authorities.

"It'll be your turn next," he yelled, as he threw an arm over the side of the stretcher. "Can't you go slow? Ah, the cowards—the cowards!"

Here the man rolled out a fierce volley of imprecations, his voice sounding hoarse and strange; but his bearers, morose, pallid-looking men, with a savage, downcast look, paid no heed, tramping on, and the guard of pensioners taking it all as a matter of course.

At a glance the difference between them was most marked.

The pensioner guard had a smart, independent air, there, was an easy-going, cheery look in their brown faces; while in those of the men they guarded, and upon whom they would have been called to fire if there were an attempt to escape, there were deeply stamped in the hollow cheek, sunken eye, and graven lines, crime, misery, and degradation, and that savage recklessness that seems to lower man to a degree far beneath the beast of the jungle or wild. The closely-cropped hair, the shorn chins with the stubble of several days' growth, and the fierce glare of the convicts' overshadowed eyes as they caught sight of the two well-dressed ladies, sent a thrill through Bayle's breast, and he would gladly have even now forced his companions to retreat, but it was impossible. For as they came up, the ruffian on the stretcher to which he was strapped, uttered an agonising cry of pain, and then yelled out the one word, "Water!"

Julia uttered a low sobbing cry, and, before Bayle or Mrs Hallam could realise her act, she had started forward and laid her hand upon the old sergeant's arm, the tears streaming down her cheeks as she cried:

"Oh, sir, do you not hear him? Is there no water here?"

"Halt!" shouted the sergeant; and with military precision the *cortège* stopped. "Set him down, lads." The convicts gave a half-turn and lowered the handles of the stretcher, retaining them for a moment, and then, in the same automatic way, placed their burden on the dusty earth. It was quickly and smoothly done, in silence, but the movement seemed to cause the man intense pain, and he writhed and cursed horribly at his bearers, ending by asking again for water.

"It isn't far to the hospital, miss," said the sergeant; "and he has had some once. Here, Jones, give me your canteen."

One of the guard unslung his water-tin and handed it to Julia, who seized it eagerly, while the sergeant turned to Bayle and said in a quick whisper:

"Hadn't you better get the ladies away, sir?"

By this time Julia was on her knees by the side of the stretcher, holding the canteen to the lips of the wretched man, who drank with avidity, rolling his starting eyes from side to side.

"Has there been a battle?" whispered Julia to the pensioner who had handed her the water-tin. "He is dreadfully wounded, is he not? Will he die?"

Julia's quickly following questions were heard by the eight convicts, who were looking on with heavy, brutal curiosity, but not one glanced at his companions.

"Bless your heart, no, miss. A few days in horspital will put him right," said the man, smiling.

"How can you be so cruel?" panted the girl indignantly. "Suppose you were lying there?"

"Well, I hope, miss," said the man good-humouredly, "that if I had been blackguard enough to have my back scratched, I should not be such a cur as to howl like that."

"Julia, my child, come away," whispered Bayle, taking her hand and, trying to raise her as the sergeant looked on good-humouredly. "The man has been flogged for some offence. This is no place for you."

"Hush!" she cried, as, drawing away her hand, she bent over the wretched man and wiped the great drops of perspiration from his forehead.

He ceased his restless writhing and gazed up at the sweet face bending over him with a look of wonder. Then his eyes dilated, and his lips parted. The next moment he had turned his eyes upon Mrs Hallam, who was bending over her child half-trying to raise her, but with a horrible fascination in her gaze, while a curious silence seemed to have fallen on the group—so curious, that when one of the convicts moved slightly, the clank of a ring he wore sounded strangely loud in the hot sunshine.

"By your leave, miss," said the sergeant, not unkindly. "I daren't stop. Fall in, my lads! Stretchers! Forward!"

As the man, who was perfectly silent now, was raised by the convicts to the level of their shoulders, he wrenched his head round that he might turn his distorted features, purple with their deep flush, and continue his wondering stare at Julia and Mrs Hallam.

Then the tramp and clank, tramp and clank went on, the guard raising each a hand to his forehead, and smiling at the group they left, while the old sergeant took off his cap, the sun shining down on a good manly English face, as he took a step towards Julia.

"I beg pardon, miss," he said; "I'm only a rough old pensioner—but if you'd let me kiss your hand."

Julia smiled in the sergeant's brown face as she laid her white little hand in his, and he raised it with rugged reverence to his lips.

Then, saluting Mrs Hallam, he turned quickly to Bayle:

"I did say, sir, as this place was just about like—you know what; but I see we've got angels even here."

He went off at the double after his men, twenty paces ahead, while Bayle, warned by Julia, had just time to catch Mrs Hallam as she reeled, and would have fallen.

"Mother, dear mother!" cried Julia. "This scene was too terrible for you."

"No, no! I am better now," said Mrs Hallam hoarsely. "Let us go on. Did you see?" she whispered, turning to Bayle.

"See?" he said reproachfully. "Yes; but I tried so hard to spare you this scene."

"Yes; but it was to be," she said in the same hoarse whisper, as, with one hand she held Julia from her, and spoke almost in her companion's ear. "You did not know him," she said. "I did; at once."

"That man?"

"Yes."

Then, after a painful pause, she added:

"It was Stephen Crellock."

"Her husband's associate and friend," said Bayle, as he stood outside the prison gates waiting; for, after the presentation of the proper forms, Millicent Hallam and her child had been admitted by special permission to see the prisoner named upon their pass, and Christie Bayle remained without, seeing in imagination the meeting between husband, wife, and child, and as he waited, seated on a block of stone, his head went down upon his hands, and his spirit sank very low, for all was dark upon the life-path now ahead.

Volume Three—Chapter Twenty.

In the Convict Barracks.

"Be firm, my darling," whispered Mrs Hallam; and as they followed their guide, hand in hand, Julia seemed to take strength and fortitude from the proud, pale face, and eyes bright with matronly love and hope.

"Mother!"

Only that word, but it was enough. Millicent Hallam was satisfied, for she read in the tone and in the look that accompanied it the fact that her teaching had not been in vain, and that she had come to meet her martyr husband with the love of wife and child.

The officer who showed them into a bare room, with its grated windows, glanced at them curiously before leaving: and then they had to wait through, what seemed to them, an age of agony, listening to the slow, regular tramp of a couple of sentries, one seeming to be in a passage close at hand, the other beneath the window of the room where they were seated upon a rough bench.

"Courage! my child," said Mrs Hallam, looking at Julia with a smile; and then it was the latter who had to start up and support her, for there was the distant sound of feet, and Mrs Hallam's face contracted as from some terrible spasm, and she swayed heavily sidewise.

"Heaven give me strength!" she groaned; and then, clinging together, the suffering women watched the door as the heavy tramp came nearer, and with it a strange hollow, echoing sound.

As Julia watched the door the remembrance of the stern, handsome face of her childhood seemed to come up from the past—that face with the profusion of well-tended, wavy black hair, brushed back from the high, white forehead; the bright, piercing eyes that were shaded by long, heavy lashes; the closely-shaven lips and chin, and the thick, dark whiskers—the face of the portrait in their little London home. And it seemed to her that she would see it again directly, that the old sternness would have given place to a smile of welcome, and as her heart beat fast her eyes filled with tears, and she was gazing through a mist that dimmed her sight.

The door was thrown open; the tramp of the footsteps ceased, and as the door was abruptly closed, mother and daughter remained unmoved, clinging more tightly together, staring wildly through their tear-blinded eyes at the gaunt convict standing there with face that seemed to have been stamped in the mould of the poor wretch's they had so lately seen: closely-cropped grey hair, stubbly, silvered beard, and face drawn in a half-derisive smile.

"Well!" he said, in a strange, hoarse voice that was brutal in its tones; and a sound issued from his throat that bore some resemblance to a laugh. "Am I so changed?"

"Robert! husband!"

The words rang through the cell-like room like the cry of some stricken life, and Millicent Hallam threw herself upon the convict's breast.

He bent over her as he held her tightly, and placed his mouth to her ear, while the beautiful quivering lips were turned towards his in their agony of longing for his welcoming kiss.

"Hush! Listen!" he said, and he gave her a sharp shake. "Have you brought the tin case?"

She nodded as she clung to him, clasping him more tightly to her heaving breast.

"You've got it safely?"

She nodded quickly again.

"Where is it?"

She breathed hard, and attempted to speak, but it was some time before she could utter the expected words.

"Why don't you speak?" he said in a rough whisper. "You have it safe?"

She nodded again.

"Where?"

"It—it is at—the hotel," panted Mrs Hallam.

"Quite safe?"

"Yes."

"Unopened?"

"Yes."

"Thank God!"

His manner seemed to change, his eyes brightened, and his brutalised countenance altogether looked less repellent, as he uttered those words. As he stood there at first, his head hung, as it were, forward from between his shoulders, and his whole attitude had a despicable, cringing, trampled-down look that now seemed to pass away. He filled out and drew himself up; his eyes brightened as if hope had been borne to him by the coming of wife and child. It was no longer the same man, so it seemed to Julia as she stood aloof, trembling and waiting for him to speak to her.

"Good girl! good wife!" said Hallam, in a low voice; and with some show of affection he kissed the quivering woman, who, as she clasped him to her heart and grew to him once more, saw nothing of the change, but closed her eyes mentally and really, the longing of years satisfied, everything forgotten, even the presence of Julia, in the great joy of being united once again.

"There!" he said suddenly; "that must do now. There is only a short time, and I have lots to say, my gal."

Millicent Hallam's eyes opened, and she quite started back from her love romance to reality, his words sounded so harsh, his language was so coarse and strange; but she smiled again directly, a happy, joyous smile, as nestling within her husband's left arm, she laid her cheek upon the coarse woollen convict garb, and clinging there sent with a flash from her humid eyes a loving invitation to her child.

She did not speak, but her action was eloquent as words, and bade the trembling girl take the place she had half-vacated, the share she offered—the strong right arm, and the half of her husband's breast.

Julia read and knew, and in an instant she too was clinging to the convict, looking piteously in his scarred, brutalised countenance, with eyes that strove so hard to be full of love, but which gazed through no medium of romance. Strive how she would, all seemed so hideously real—this hard, coarse-looking, rough-voiced man was not the father she had been taught to reverence and love; and it was with a heart full of misery and despair that she gazed at him with her lips quivering, and then burst into a wild fit of sobbing as she buried her face in his breast.

"There, there, don't cry," he said almost impatiently; and there was no working of the face, nothing to indicate that he was moved by the passionate love of his faithful wife, or the agony of the beautiful girl whose sobs shook his breast. "Time's precious now. Wait till I get out of this place. You go and sit down, Julie. By jingo!" he continued, with a look of admiration as he held her off at arm's length, "what a handsome gal you've grown! No sweetheart yet, I hope?"

Julia shrank from him with scarlet face, and as he loosed her hand she shrank back to the rough seat, with her eyes troubled, and her hands trembling.

"Now, Milly, my gal," said Hallam, drawing his wife's arm through his, and leading her beneath the window as he spoke in a low voice once more, "you have that case safe and unopened?"

"Yes."

"Then look here! Business. I must be rough and plain. You have brought me my freedom."

"Robert!"

Only that word, but so full of frantic joy.

"Quiet, and listen. You will do exactly as I tell you?"

"Yes. Can you doubt?"

"No. Now look here. You will take a good house at once, the best you can. If you can't get one—they're very scarce—the hotel will do. Stay there, and behave as if you were well off—as you are."

"Robert, I have nothing," she gasped.

"Yes, you have," he said with a laugh. "I have; and we are one."

"You have? Money?"

"Of course. Do you suppose a man is at work out here for a dozen years without making some? There! don't you worry about that: you're new. You'll find plenty of men, who came out as convicts, rich men now with land of their own. But we are wasting time. You have brought out my freedom."

"Your pardon?"

"No. Nonsense! I shall have to stay out here; but it does not matter now. Only go and do as I tell you, and carefully, for you are only a woman in a strange place, and alone till you get me out."

"Mr Bayle is here, and Sir Gordon—"

"Bayle!" cried Hallam, catching her wrist with a savage grip and staring in an angry way at the agitated face before him.

"Yes; he has been so helpful and true all through our trouble, and—"

"Curse Bayle!" he muttered. Then aloud, and in a fierce, impatient way: "Never mind that now, I shall have to go back to the gang directly, and I have not said half I want to say."

"I will not speak again," she said eagerly. "Tell me what to do."

"Take house or apartments at once; behave as if you were well off—I tell you that you are; do all yourself, and send in an application to the authorities for two assigned servants."

"Assigned servants?"

"Yes—convict servants," said Hallam impatiently. "There! you must know. There are so many that the Government are glad to get the well-behaved convicts off their hands, and into the care of settlers who undertake their charge. You want two men, as you have settled here. You will have papers to sign, and give undertakings; but do it all boldly, and you will select two. They won't ask you any questions about your taking up land, they are too glad to get rid of us. If they do ask anything, you can boldly say you want them for butler and coachman."

"But, Robert, I do not understand."

"Do as I tell you," he said sharply. "You will select two men—myself and Stephen Crellock."

"Yourself and Stephen Crellock?"

"Yes. Don't look so bewildered, woman. It is the regular thing, and we shall be set at liberty."

"At liberty?"

"Yes, to go anywhere in the colony. You are answerable to the Government for us."

"But, Robert, you would come as—my servant?"

"Pooh! Only in name. So long as you claim us as your servants, that is all that is wanted. Plenty are freed on these terms, and once they are out, go and live with their families, like any one else."

"This is done here?"

"To be sure it is. I tell you that once a man has been in the gangs here for a few years they are glad to get him off their hands, so as to leave room for others who are coming out. Why, Milly, they could not keep all who are sent away from England, and people are easier and more forgiving out here. Hundreds of those you see here were lags."

"Lags?"

"Bah! how innocent you are. Well, convicts. Now, quick! they are coming. You understand?"

"Yes."

"And you will do as I tell you?"

"Everything," said Mrs Hallam.

"Of course you cannot make this a matter of secrecy. It does not matter who knows. But the tin case; remember that is for me alone."

"But the authorities," said Mrs Hallam; "they will know I am your wife."

"The authorities will trouble nothing about it. I have a fairly good record, and they will be glad. As for Crellock—"

"That man!" gasped Mrs Hallam.

"Well?"

"We saw him—as we came."

Hallam's face puckered.

"Poor fellow," he said hastily. "Ah, that was a specimen of the cruel treatment we receive. It was unfortunate. But we can't talk about that. There they are. Remember!"

She pressed the coarse, hard hand that was holding hers as the door was thrown open, and without another word Hallam obeyed the sign made by the officer in the doorway, and, as the two women crept together, Julia receiving no further recognition, they saw him sink from his erect position, his head went down, his back rounded, and he went out.

Then the door shut loudly, and they stood listening, as the steps died away, save those of the sentries in the passage and beneath the window.

The silence, as they stood in that blank, cell-like room, was terrible; and when at last Julia spoke, her mother started and stared at her wildly from the confused rush of thought that was passing through her brain.

"Mother, is it some dreadful dream?"

Mrs Hallam's lips parted, but no words came, and for the moment she seemed to be sharing her child's mental shock, the terrible disillusioning to which she had been subjected.

The recovery was quick, though, as she drew a long breath.

"Dream? No, my child, it is real; and at last we can rescue him from his dreadful fate."

Whatever thoughts she may have had that militated against her hopes she crushed down, forcing herself to see nothing but the result of a terrible persecution, and ready to be angered with herself for any doubts as to her duty.

In this spirit she followed the man who had led them in back to the gates, where Bayle was waiting; and as he gazed anxiously in the faces of the two women it was to see Julie's scared, white, and ready to look appealingly in his, while Mrs Hallam's was radiant and proud with the light of her true woman's love and devotion to him she told herself it was her duty to obey.

That night mother and daughter, clasped in each other's arms, knelt and prayed, the one for strength to carry out her duty, and restore Robert Hallam to his place in the world of men; the other for power to love the father whom she had crossed the great ocean to gain—the man who had seemed to be so little like the father of her dreams.

Volume Four—Chapter One.

In the New Land—The Situation.

"Look here, Bayle, this is about the maddest thing I ever knew. Will you have the goodness to tell me why we are stopping here?"

Bayle looked up from the book he was reading in the pleasant room that formed their home, one which Tom Porter had found no difficulty in fitting up in good cabin style.

A year had glided by since they landed, a year that Sir Gordon had passed in the most unsatisfactory way.

"Why are we stopping here?"

"Yes. Didn't I speak plainly? Why are we stopping here? For goodness' sake, Bayle, don't you take to aggravating me by repeating my words! I'm irritable enough without that!"

"Nonsense, my dear old friend!" cried Bayle, rising.

"Hang it, man, don't throw my age in my teeth! I can't help being old!"

"May I live to be as old," said Bayle, smiling, and laying his hand on Sir Gordon's shoulder.

"Bah! don't pray for that, man! Why should you want to live? To see all your pet schemes knocked on the head, and those you care for go to the bad, while your aches and pains increase, and you are gliding down the hill of life a wretched, selfish old man, unloved, uncared for. There, life is all a miserable mistake."

"Uncared for, eh?" said Bayle. "Have you no friends?"

"Not one," groaned the old man, writhing, as he felt a twinge in his back. "Oh, this bitter south wind! it's worse than our north!"

"Shame! Why, Tom Porter watches you night and day. He would die for you."

"So would a dog. The scoundrel only thinks of how much money I shall leave him when I go."

Unheard by either, Tom Porter had entered the room, sailor fashion, barefoot, in the easy canvas suit he wore when yachting with his master. He had brought in a basin of broth of his own brewing, as he termed it—for Sir Gordon was unwell—a plate with a couple of slices of bread of his own toasting in the other hand, and he was holding the silver spoon from Sir Gordon's travelling canteen beneath his chin.

He heard every word as he stood waiting respectfully to bring in his master's "'levens," as he called it; and, instead of getting the sherry from the cellaret, he began screwing up his hard face, and showing his emotion by working about his bare toes.

As Sir Gordon finished his bitter speech, Tom Porter took a step forward and threw the basin of mutton broth, basin, plate, and all, under the grate with a crash, and stalked towards the door.

"You scoundrel!" roared Sir Gordon. "You, Tom Porter, stop!"

"Be damned if I do!" growled the man. "There's mutiny on, and I leave the ship."

Bang!

The door was closed violently, and Sir Gordon looked helplessly up at Bayle.

"You see!"

"Yes," said Bayle, "I see. Poor fellow! Why did you wound his feelings like that?"

"There!" cried Sir Gordon; "now you side with the scoundrel. Twenty-five years has he been with me, and look at my soup!"

Bayle laughed.

"Yes: that's right: laugh at me. I'm getting old and weak. Laugh at me. I suppose the next thing will be that you will go off and leave me here in the lurch."

"That is just my way, is it not?" said Bayle, smiling.

"Well, no," grumbled Sir Gordon, "I suppose it is not. But then you are such a fool, Bayle. I haven't patience with you!"

"I'm afraid I am a great trial to you."

"You are—a terrible trial; every one's a terrible trial—everything goes wrong. That blundering ass Tom Porter must even go and knock a hole in the *Sylph* on the rocks."

"Yes, that was unfortunate," said Bayle.

"Here: I shall go back. It's of no use staying here. Everything I see aggravates me. Matters are getting worse with the Hallams. Let's go home, Bayle."

Christie Bayle stood looking straight before him for some time, and then shook his head softly.

"No: not yet," he said at last.

"But I can't go back without you, man; and it is of no use to stay. As I said before—Why am I stopping here?"

Bayle looked at him in his quiet, smiling way for some moments before replying.

"In the furtherance of your old scheme of unselfishness, and in the hope of doing good to the friends we love."

"Oh, nonsense! Tush, man! Absurd! I wanted to be friends, and be helpful; but that's all over now. See what is going on. Look at that girl. Next thing we hear will be that she is married to one of those two fellows."

"I think if she accepted Lieutenant Eaton, and he married her, and took her away from this place, it would be the best thing that could happen."

"Humph! I don't!" muttered Sir Gordon. "Then look at Mrs Hallam."

Bayle drew in his breath with a low hiss.

"It is horrible, man—it is horrible!" cried Sir Gordon excitedly. "Bayle, you know how I loved that woman twenty years ago? Well, it was impossible; it would have been May and December even then, for I'm a very old man, Bayle—older than you think. I was an old fool, perhaps, but it was my nature. I loved her very dearly. It was not to be; but the old love isn't dead. Bayle, old fellow, if I had been a good man I should say that the old love was purified of its grosser parts, but that would not fit with me."

"Why judge yourself so harshly?"

"Because I deserve it, man. Well, well, time went on, and when we met again, I can't describe what I felt over that child. At times, when her pretty dark face had the look of that scoundrel Hallam in it, I hated her; but when her eyes lit up with that sweet, innocent smile, the tears used to come into mine, and I felt as if it was Millicent Luttrell a child again, and that it would have been the culmination of earthly happiness to have said, this is my darling child."

"Yes," said Bayle softly.

"I worshipped that girl, Bayle. It was for her sake I came over here to this horrible pandemonium, to watch over and be her guardian. I could not have stayed away. But I must go now. I can't bear it; I can't stand it any longer."

"You will not go," said Bayle slowly.

"Yes, I tell you, I must. It is horrible. I don't think she is ungrateful, poor child; but she is being brutalised by companionship with that scoundrel's set."

"No, no! For heaven's sake don't say that!"

"I do say it," cried the old man impetuously, "she and her mother too. How can they help it with such surroundings? The decent people will not go— only that Eaton and Mrs Otway. Bless the woman! I thought her a forward, shameless soldier's wife, but she has the heart of a true lady, and keeps to the Hallams in spite of all."

"It is very horrible," said Bayle; "but we are helpless."

"Helpless? Yes; if he would only kill himself with his wretched drink, or get made an end of somehow."

"Hush!" said Bayle, rather sternly; "don't talk like that."

"Now you are beginning to bully me, Bayle," cried the old man querulously. "Don't you turn against me. I get insults enough at that scoundrel Hallam's— enough to make my blood boil."

"Yes, I know, I know," said Bayle.

"And yet, old idiot that I am, I go there for the sake of these women, and bear it all—I, whom people call a gentleman, I go there and am civil to the scoundrel who robbed me, and put up with his insolence and his scowls. But I'm his master still. He dare not turn upon me. I can make him quail when I like. Bayle, old fellow," he cried, with a satisfied chuckle, "how the scoundrel would like to give me a dose!"

Bayle sat down with his brow full of the lines of care.

"I'm not like you," continued Sir Gordon, whom the relation of his troubles seemed to relieve, "I won't be driven away. I think you were wrong."

"No," said Bayle quietly, "it was causing her pain. It was plain enough that in his sordid mind my presence was a greater injury than yours. He was wearing her life away, and I thought it better that our intimacy should grow less and less."

"But, my boy, that's where you were wrong. Bad as the scoundrel is, he could never have had a jealous thought of that saint—there, don't call me irreverent—I say it again, that saint of a woman."

"Oh, no, I can't think that myself," said Bayle, "but my presence was a standing reproach to him."

"How could it be more than mine?"

"You are different. He always hated me from the first time we met at King's Castor."

"I believe he did," said Sir Gordon warmly; "but see how he detests the sight of me."

"Yes, but you expressed the feeling only a few minutes ago when you said you were still his master and you made him quail. My dear old friend, if I could ever have indulged in a hope that Robert Hallam had been unjustly punished, his behaviour towards you would have swept it away. It is always that of the conscience-stricken man—his unreasoning dislike of the one whom he has wronged."

"Perhaps you are right, Bayle, perhaps you are right. But there was no doubt about his guilt—a scoundrel, and I am as sure as I am that I live, the rascal made a hoard somehow, and is living upon it now."

"You think that? What about the sealing speculation?"

"Ah! he and Crellock have made some money *by* it, no doubt; but not enough to live as they do. I know that Hallam is spending my money and triumphing over me all the time, and I would not care if those women were free of him, but I'm afraid that will never be."

Bayle remained silent.

"Do you think she believes in his innocence still?"

Bayle remained silent for a time, and then said slowly: "I believe that Millicent Hallam, even if she discovered his guilt, and could at last believe in it, would suffer in secret, and bear with him in the hope that he would repent."

"And never leave him?"

"Never," aid Bayle firmly, "unless under some terrible provocation, one so great that no woman could bear; and from that provocation, and the deathblow it would be to her, I pray heaven she may be spared."

"Amen!" said Sir Gordon softly.

"Bayle," he added, after a pause, "I am getting old and irritable; I feel every change. I called you a fool!"

"The irritable spirit of pain within—not you."

"Ah! well," said Sir Gordon, smiling, "you know me by heart now, my dear boy. I want to say something ivery serious to you. I never said it before, though I have thought about it ever since those happy evenings we spent at Clerkenwell."

Bayle turned to him wonderingly.

"You will bear with me—I may hurt your feelings."

"If you do I know you will heal them the next time we meet," replied Bayle.

"Well, then, tell me this. When I first began visiting at Mrs Hallam's house there in London, had you not the full intention of some day asking Julie to be your wife?"

Christie Bayle turned his manly, sincere countenance full upon his old friend, and said, in a deep, low voice, broken by emotion:

"Such a thought had never entered my mind."

"Never?"

"Never, on my word as a man."

"You tell me that you have never loved Julie Hallam save as a father might love his child?"

Bayle shook his head slowly, and a piteous look came into his eyes.

"No," he said softly, "I cannot."

"Then you do love her?" cried the old man joyfully. "Now we shall get out of the wood. Why, my dear boy—"

"Hush!" said Bayle sadly, "I first learned what was in my heart when our voyage was half over."

"And you saw her chatting with that dandy young officer. Oh! pooh, pooh! that is nothing. She does not care for him."

Bayle shook his head again.

"Why, my dear boy, you must end all this."

"You forget," said Bayle sadly. "History is repeating itself. Remember your own affair."

"Ah! but I was an old man; you are young."

"Young!" said Bayle sadly. "No, I was always her old teacher; and she loves this man."

"I cannot think it," cried Sir Gordon, "and what is more, Hallam has outrageous plans of his own—look there."

There were the sounds of horses' feet on the newly-made Government road that passed the house Sir Gordon had chosen on account of its leading down on one side to where lay his lugger, in which he spent half his time cruising among the islands, and in fine weather out and along the Pacific shore; on the other side to the eastward of the huge billows that rolled in with their heavy thunderous roar.

As Bayle looked up, he saw Julia in a plain grey riding habit, mounted on a handsome mare, cantering up with a well-dressed, bluff-looking, middle-aged man by her side. He, too, was well mounted, and as Julia checked her mare to walk by Sir Gordon's cottage, the man drew rein and watched her closely. She bent forward, scanning the windows anxiously, but seeing no one, for the occupants of the room were by the fire as they passed on, and Bayle turned to Sir Gordon with an angry look in his eyes.

"Oh no! Impossible!" he exclaimed.

"There's nothing impossible out here in this horrible penal place," cried Sir Gordon, in a voice full of agitation.

"No," said Bayle, whose face cleared, and he smiled; "it is not even impossible that my old friend will go on enjoying his cruises about these glorious shores, and that the mutiny—Shall I call in Tom Porter?"

"Well, yes; I suppose you must," said Sir Gordon with a grim smile.

Bayle went to the door, and Tom Porter answered the call with an "Ay, ay, sir," and came padding over the floor with his bare feet like a man-o'-war's-man on a holy-stoned deck.

"Sir Gordon wants to speak to you, Porter," said Bayle, making as if to go.

"No, no, Bayle! don't go and leave me with this scoundrelly mutineer. He'll murder me. There, Tom Porter," he continued, "I'm an irritable old fool, and I'm very sorry, and I beg your pardon; but you ought to know better than to take offence."

Tom Porter, for answer, trotted out of the room to return at the end of a few moments with another basin of soup and two slices of toast already made.

Volume Four—Chapter Two.

Mrs Hallam's Servant.

Millicent Hallam had found that all her husband had said was correct. There was no difficulty at all in the matter, and few questions were asked, for the Government was only too glad to get convicts drafted off as assigned servants to all who applied, and so long as no complaints were made of their behaviour, the prisoners to whom passes were given remained free of the colony.

In many cases they led the lives of slaves to the settlers, and found that they had exchanged the rod for the scorpion; but they bore all for the sake of the comparative freedom, and even preferred life at some up-country station, where a slight offence was punished with the lash, to returning to the chain-gang and the prison, or the heavy work of making roads.

The cat was the cure for all ills in those days, when almost any one was appointed magistrate of his district. A., the holder of so many assigned men, would be a justice, and one of his men would offend. In that case, he would send him over to B., the magistrate of the next district. B. would also be a squatter and holder of assigned convict servants. There would be a short examination; A's man would be well flogged and sent back. In due time B. would require the same service performed, and would send an offender over to A. to have him punished in turn.

In the growing town, assigned servants were employed in a variety of ways; and it was common enough for relatives of the convicts to apply and have husband, son, or brother assigned to them, the ticket-of-leave-man finding no difficulty there on account of being a jail-bird, where many of the most prosperous traders and squatters had once worn the prison garb.

Robert Hallam was soon released, and at the end of a very short time Stephen Crellock followed; the pair becoming ostensibly butler and coachman to a wealthy lady who had settled in Sydney—but servants only in the Government books; for, unquestioned, Hallam at once took up his position as master of the house, and, to his wife's horror, Crellock, directly he was released, came and took possession of the room set apart for him as Hallam's oldest friend.

A strange state of society perhaps, but it is a mere matter of history; such proceedings were frequent in the days when Botany Bay was the dépôt for the social sinners of our land.

All the same though, poor Botany Bay, with its abundant specimens of Austral growth that delighted the naturalists of the early expedition, never did become a penal settlement. It was selected, and the first convict-ship went there to form the great prison; but the place was unsuitable, and Port Jackson, the site of Sydney, proved so vastly superior that the expedition went on there at once.

At home, in England, though, Botany Bay was spoken of always as the convicts' home, and the term embraced the whole of the penal settlements, including Norfolk Island, that horror of our laws, and Van Diemen's Land.

Opportunity had served just after Hallam was released, and had taken up his residence in simple lodgings which Mrs Hallam, with Bayle's help, had secured, for one of the best villas that had been built in the place—an attractive wooden bungalow, with broad verandahs and lovely garden sloping down towards the harbour—was to let.

Millicent Hallam had looked at her husband in alarm when he bade her take it; but he placed the money laughingly in her hands for furnishing; and, obeying him as if in a dream, the house was taken and handsomely fitted. Servants were engaged, horses bought, and the convicts commenced a life of luxurious ease.

The sealing business, he said with a laugh, was only carried on at certain times of the year, but it was a most paying affair, and he bade Mrs Hallam have no care about money matters.

For the first six months Hallam rarely stirred out of the house by day, contenting himself with a walk about the extensive grounds in an evening; but he made up for this abstinence from society by pampering his appetites in every way.

It was as if, these having been kept in strict subjection for so many years, he was now determined to give them full rein; and, consequently, he who had been summoned at early morn by the prison bell, breakfasted luxuriously in bed, and did not rise till midday, when his first question was about the preparations for dinner—that being the important business of his life.

His dinner was a feast at which good wine in sufficient abundance played a part, and over this he and Crellock would sit for hours, only to leave it and the dining-room for spirits and cigars in the verandah, where they stayed till bed-time.

Robert Hallam came into the house a pallid, wasted man, with sunken cheeks and eyes, closely-cropped hair and shorn beard; the villainous prison look was in his gaze and the furtive shrinking way of his stoop. His aspect was so horrible that when Millicent Hallam took him to her breast, she prayed for mental blindness that she might not see the change, while Julia's eyes were always full of a wondering horror that she was ever fighting to suppress.

At the end of four months, Robert Hallam was completely transformed; his cheeks were filled out, and were rapidly assuming the flushed appearance of the habitual drunkard's; his eyes had lost their cavernous aspect, and half the lines had disappeared, while his grizzled hair was of a respectable length, and his face was becoming clothed by a great black beard dashed with grey.

In six months, portly, florid and well-dressed, he was unrecognisable for the man who had been released from the great prison, and no longer confined himself to the house.

Stephen Crellock had changed in a more marked manner than his prison friend. Considerably his junior, the convict life had not seemed to affect him, so that when six months of his freedom had passed, he looked the bluff, bearded squatter in the full pride of his manhood, bronzed by the sun, and with a dash and freedom of manner that he knew how to restrain when he was in the presence of his old companion's wife and child, for he could not conceal from himself the fact that Mrs Hallam disliked his presence and resented his being there.

At first, in her eagerness to respond to Hallam's slightest wish, in the proud joy she felt in the change that was coming over his personal appearance, and which with the boastfulness of a young wife she pointed out to Julia, she made no objection to Crellock's presence.

"Poor fellow! he has suffered horribly," Hallam said. "He deserves a holiday."

How she had watched all this gradual change, and how she crushed down the little voices that now and then strove in her heart to make themselves heard!

"No, no, no," she said to them as it were half laughing, "there is nothing but what I ought to have pictured."

Then one day she found herself forced to make apology to Julia.

"You have hurt him, my darling, by your coldness," she said tenderly. "Julie, my own, he complains to me. What have you done?"

"Tried, dear mother—oh, so hard. I did not know I had been cold."

"Then you will try more, my child," said Mrs Hallam, caressing Julia tenderly, and with a bright, loving look in her eyes. "I have never spoken like this before. It seemed terrible to me to have to make what seems like an apology for our own, but think, dearest. He parted from us a gentleman—to be taken from his home and plunged into a life of horror, such as—no, no, no," she cried, "I will not speak of it. I will only say that just as his face will change, so will all that terrible corrosion of the prison life in his manner drop away, and in a few months he will be again all that you have pictured. Julie, he is your father."

Julia flung herself, sobbing passionately, into her mother's arms, and in a burst of self-reproach vowed that she would do everything to make her father love her as she did him.

Bravely did the two women set themselves to the task of blinding their eyes with love, passing over the coarse actions and speech of the idol they had set up, yielding eagerly to his slightest whim, obeying every caprice, and, while at times something was almost too hard to bear, Millicent Hallam whispered encouragement to her child.

"Think, my own, think," she said lovingly. "It is not his fault. Think of what he has suffered, and let us pray and thank Him that he has survived, for us to win back to all that we could wish."

There were times when despair looked blankly from Millicent Hallam's eyes as she saw the months glide by and her husband surely and slowly sinking into sensuality. But she roused herself to greater exertions, and was his veriest slave. Once only did she try by kindly resistance to make the stand she told herself she should have made when Crellock was first brought into the house.

It was when he had been out about six months, and Crellock, after a long debauch with Hallam and two or three chosen spirits from the town, had sunk in a brutal sleep upon the floor of the handsomely-furnished dining-room. The visitors had gone; they had dined there, Sir Gordon being of the party, and Mrs Hallam had smilingly done the honours of the table as their hostess, though sick at heart at the turn the conversation had taken before her child, who looked anxious and pale, while Sir Gordon had sat there very silent and grim of aspect. He had been the first to go, and had taken her hand in the drawing-room, as if about to speak, but had only looked at her, sighed, and gone away without a word.

"I must speak!" she had said. "Heaven help me! I must speak! This cannot go on!"

As soon as she could, she had hurried Julia to bed, and then sat and waited till the last visitor had gone, when she walked into the dining-room, where Hallam sat smoking, *heavy* with drink, but perfectly collected, scowling down at Crellock where he lay.

That look sent a thrill of joy through Millicent Hallam. He was evidently angry with Crellock, and disgusted with the wretched drinking scene that had taken place—one of many such scenes as would have excited comment now, but the early settlers were ready enough to smile at eccentricities like this.

"Robert—my husband! may I speak to you?"

"Speak, my dear? Of course," he said, smiling. "Why didn't you come in as soon as that old curmudgeon had gone? Have a glass of wine now.

Nonsense!—I wish it. You must pitch over a lot of that standoffish-ness with my friends. Julia, too—the girl sits and looks at people as glum as if she had no sense." Mrs Hallam compressed her lips, laid her hand upon her husband's shoulder, yielding herself to him as he threw an arm round her waist, but stood pointing to where Crellock lay breathing stertorously, and every now and then muttering in his sleep.

"What are you pointing at?" said Hallam. "Steve? Yes, the pig! Why can't he take his wine like a gentleman, and not like a brute?"

"Robert, dear," she said tenderly, "you love me very dearly?"

"Love you, my pet! why, how could a man love wife better?"

"And our Julia—our child?"

"Why, of course. What questions!"

"Will you do something to please me—to please us both?"

"Will I? Say what you want—another carriage—diamonds—a yacht like old Bourne's?"

"No, no, no, dearest; we have everything if we have your love, and my dear husband glides from the past misery into a life of happiness."

"Well, I think we are doing pretty well," he said with a laugh that sent a shudder through the suffering woman; he was so changed.

"I want to speak to you about Mr Crellock."

"Well, what about him? Make haste; it's getting late, and I'm tired."

"Robert, we have made a mistake in having this man here."

Hallam seemed perfectly sober, and he frowned.

"*I* would not mind if you wished him to be here, love," she said, with her voice sounding sweetly pure and entreating; "but he is not a suitable companion for our Julia."

"Stop there," said Hallam, sharply.

"No, no, darling; let me speak—this time," said Mrs Hallam, entreatingly. "I know it was out of the genuine goodness and pity of your heart that you opened your door to him. Now you have done all you need, let him go."

Hallam shook his head.

"Think of the past, and the terrible troubles he brought upon you."

"Oh, no! that was all a mistake," said Hallam, quickly. "Poor brute! he was as ill-treated as I was, and now you want him kicked out."

"No, no, dear; part from him kindly; but he was the cause of much of your suffering."

"No, he was not," said Hallam, quickly. "That was all a mistake. Poor Steve was always a good friend to me. He suffered along with me in that cursed hole, and he shall have his share of the comfort now."

"No, no, do not say you wish him to stay."

"But I do say it," cried Hallam, angrily. "He is my best friend, and he will stay. Hang it, woman, am I to be cursed with the presence of your friends who sent me out here and not have the company of my own?"

"Robert!—husband!—don't speak to me like that."

"But I do speak to you like that. Here is that wretched old yachtsman forcing his company upon me day after day, insisting upon coming to the house, and reminding me by his presence who I am, and what I have been."

"Darling, Sir Gordon ignores the past, and is grieved, I know, at the terrible mistake that brought you here. He wishes to show you this by his kindness to us all."

"Let him keep his kindness till it is asked for," growled Hallam. "He sits upon me like a nightmare. I don't feel that the place is my own when he is here. As for Bayle, he has had the good sense to stay away lately."

Mrs Hallam's eyes were full of despair as she listened.

"I hate Sir Gordon coming here. He and Bayle have between them made that girl despise me, and look down upon me every time we speak, while I am lavishing money upon her, and she has horses and carriage, jewels and dress equal to any girl in the colony."

"Robert, dear, you are not saying all this from your heart."

"Indeed, but I am," he cried angrily.

"No, no! And Julie—she loves you dearly. It is for her sake I ask this," and she pointed to Crellock where he lay.

"Let sleeping dogs lie," said Hallam, with a meaning laugh. "Poor Steve! I don't like him, but he has been a faithful mate to me, and I'm not going to turn round upon him now."

"But for Julie's sake!"

"I'm thinking about Julie, my dear," he said, nodding his head; "and as for Steve—there, just you make yourself comfortable about him. There's no harm in him; he is faithful as a dog to me, and if I behaved badly he might bite."

"You need not be unkind to Mr Crellock if he has been what you say. I only ask you for our child's sake to let him leave here."

"Impossible; he is my partner."

"Yes, you intimated that. In your business."

"Speculations," said Hallam quietly. "There, that will do."

"But, Robert—"

"That will do!" he roared fiercely. "Stephen Crellock must live here! Do you hear—*must*! Now *go* to bed."

"A woman's duty," she whispered softly, "is to obey," and she obeyed.

She obeyed, while another six months glided away, each month filling her heart more and more with despair as she shunned her child's questioning eyes and fought on, a harder battle every day, to keep herself in the belief that the pure gold was still beneath the blackening tarnish, and that her idol was not made of clay.

It was a terrible battle, for her eyes refused to be blinded longer by the loving veil she cast over them. The appealing, half-wondering looks of her child increased her suffering, while an idea, that filled her with horror, was growing day by day, till it was assuming proportions from which she shrank in dread.

Volume Four—Chapter Three.

Our Julia's Lover.

"What have we done, wifie, that we should be consigned to such quarters as these?" said Captain Otway one day with a sigh. "I don't think I'm too particular, but when I entered His Majesty's service I did not know that I should be expected to play gaoler to the occupants of the Government Pandemonium."

"It is a beautiful place," said Mrs Otway laconically. "It was till we came and spoiled it. It is one great horror, 'pon my soul; and it is degrading our men to set them such duty as this."

"Be patient. These troubles cure themselves."

"But they take such a long time over it," said the Captain. "It would be more bearable if Phil had not turned goose."

"Poor Phil!" said Mrs Otway, with a sigh.

"Poor Phil? Pooh! you spoil the lad! I can't get him out for a bit of shooting or hunting or fishing. Old Sir Gordon would often give us a cruise in his boat, but no: Phil must sit moonstruck here. The fellow's spoiled! Can't you knock all that on the head?"

"I perhaps could, but it must be a matter of time," said Mrs Otway, going steadily on with her work, and mending certain articles of attire.

"But he must be cured. It is impossible."

"Yes," sighed Mrs Otway, "so I tell him. I wish it were not."

"My dear Mary—a convict's daughter!"

"The poor girl was not consulted as to whose daughter she would like to be, Jack, and she is, without exception, the sweetest lassie I ever met."

"Yes, she is nice," said Otway. "Mother must have been nice too."

"*Is* nice," cried Mrs Otway, flushing. "I felt a little distant with her at first, but after what I have seen and know—by George, Jack, I do feel proud of our sex!"

"Humph!" ejaculated the Captain, with a smile at his wife's bluff earnestness. "Yes, she's a good woman; very ladylike, too. But that husband, that friend of his, Crellock! Poor creatures! it is ruining them."

"Yes," said Mrs Otway dryly. "That's one of the misfortunes of marriage; we poor women are dragged down to the level of our husbands."

"And when these husbands come out to convict settlements as gaolers they have to come with them, put up with all kinds of society, give up all their refinements, and make and mend their own dresses, and—"

"Even do their own chores, as the Americans call it," said Mrs Otway, looking up smiling. "It makes me look very miserable, doesn't it, Jack?"

She stopped her work, went behind her husband's chair, put her arms round his neck, and laid her cheek upon his head.

Neither spoke for a few minutes, but the Captain looked very contented and happy, and neither of them heard the step as Bayle came through the house, and out suddenly into the verandah.

"I beg your pardon!" he cried, drawing back.

"Ah, parson! Don't go!" cried the Captain, as Mrs Otway started up, and, in spite of her ordinary aplomb, looked disturbed. "Bad habit of ours acquired since marriage. We don't mind you."

Mrs Otway held out her hand to their visitor.

"Why, it is nearly a fortnight since you have been to see us. We were just talking about your friends—the Hallams."

"Have you been to see them lately?" said Bayle, eagerly.

"I was there yesterday. Quite well; but Mrs Hallam looks worried and ill. Julia is charming, only she too is not as I should like to see her."

She watched Bayle keenly, and saw his countenance change as she spoke.

"I am very glad they are well," he said.

"Yes, I know you are; but why don't you go more often?"

He looked at her rather wistfully, and made no reply. "Look here, Mr Bayle," she said, "I don't think you mind my speaking plainly, now do you? Come, that's frank."

"I will be just as frank," he replied, smiling. "I have always liked you because you do speak so plainly."

"That's kind of you to say so," she replied. "Well, I will speak out. You see there are so few women in the colony."

"Who are ladies," said Bayle quietly.

"Look here," said Otway, in a much ill-used tone, "am I expected to sit here and listen to my wife putting herself under the influence of the Church?"

"Don't talk nonsense, Jack!" said Mrs Otway sharply. "This is serious."

"I'm dumb."

"What I want to say, Mr Bayle, is this. Don't you think you are making a mistake in staying away from your friends yonder?"

He sat without replying for some minutes.

"No," he said slowly. "I did not give up my visits there till after I had weighed the matter very carefully."

"But you seemed to come out with those two ladies as their guardian, and now, when they seem most to require your help and guidance, you leave them."

"Have you heard anything? Is anything wrong?"

"I have heard nothing, but I have seen a great deal, because I persist in visiting, in spite of Mr Hallam's objection to my presence."

"I say, my dear, that man is always civil to you, I hope?" cried Otway sharply.

"My dear Jack, be quiet," said Mrs Otway. "Of course he is. I visit there because I have good reasons for so doing."

"Tell me," said Bayle anxiously.

"I have seen a great deal," continued Mrs Otway: "but it all comes to one point." Bayle looked at her inquiringly. "That it is very dreadful for those two sweet, delicate women to have come out here to such a fate. The man is dreadful!"

"They will redeem him," said Bayle huskily. "Poor wretch! he has had a terrible experience. This convict life is worse than capital punishment. We must be patient, Mrs Otway. The habits of a number of years are not got rid of in a few months. He will change."

"Will he?" said Mrs Otway shortly.

"Yes; they will, as I said before, redeem him. The man has great natural love for his wife and child."

"Do you think this?"

"Yes, yes!" he cried excitedly, as he got up and began to pace the verandah. "I stop away because my presence was like a standing reproach to him. The abstinence gives me intense pain, but my going tended to make them unhappy, and caused constraint, so I stop away."

"And so you think that they will raise him to their standard, do you?" said Mrs Otway dryly.

"Yes, I do," he cried fervently. "It is only a matter of time."

"How can you be so self-deceiving?" she cried quickly. "He is dragging them down to his level."

"Oh, hush!" cried Bayle passionately. Then mastering his emotion, he continued in his old, firm, quiet way: "No, no; you must not say that. He could not. It is impossible."

"Yes. You are wrong there, Bel," said the Captain. "Mrs Hallam is made of too good stuff."

"I give in," said Mrs Otway, nodding. "Yes, you two are right. He could not bring that sweet woman down to his level; but all this is very terrible. The man is giving himself up to a life of sensuality. Drinking and feasting with that companion of his. There is gambling going on too at night with friends of his own stamp. What a life this is for a refined lady and her child!"

Bayle spoke calmly, but he wiped the great drops of sweat from his brow.

"What can I do?" he said. "I am perfectly helpless."

"I confess I don't know," said Mrs Otway, with a sigh. "Only you and Sir Gordon must be at hand to help them in any emergency."

"Emergency! What do you mean?" anxiously.

"*I* don't know what may occur. Who knows? Women are so weak," sighed Mrs Otway; "once they place their faith in a man, they follow him to the end of the world."

"That's true, Bayle, old fellow—to convict stations, and become slaves," said the Captain.

"Mr Bayle," said Mrs Otway suddenly. "I am under a promise to my old friend, Lady Eaton, and I have done my best to oppose it all; but you have seen how deeply attached Phil Eaton has become to Miss Hallam?"

"Yes," said Bayle slowly, and he was very pale now, "I have seen it."

"He shall not marry her if I can prevent it, much as I love the girl, for it would be a terrible *mésalliance*; but he is desperately fond of her, and, as my husband here says, he has taken the bit in his teeth, and he will probably travel his own way."

"Don't you get fathering your coarse expressions on me," growled the Captain; but no one heeded him.

"As I say, he shall not marry her if I can stop it; but suppose he should be determined, and could get the father's consent, would you and Sir Gordon raise any opposition?"

"Lieutenant Eaton is an officer and a gentleman."

"He is a true-hearted lad, Mr Bayle, and I love him dearly," said Mrs Otway. "Only that he is fighting hard between love and duty he would have been carrying on the campaign by now; but you must allow Fort Robert Hallam is a terrible one to storm and garrison afterwards, for it has to be retained for life."

"I understand your meaning," said Bayle, speaking very slowly. "It is a terrible position for Mr Eaton to be in."

"Should you oppose it?"

"I have no authority whatever," said Bayle in the same low, dreamy tone. "If I had, I should never dream of opposing anything that was for Miss Hallam's good."

"And it would be, to get her away from such associations, Mr Bayle."

"Lady Eaton! Lady Eaton!" said the Captain in warning.

"Hush, Jack! pray."

"Yes," said Bayle; "it would be for Miss Hallam's benefit; but it would nearly break her mother's heart."

"She would have to make a sacrifice for the sake of the child."

"Yes," said Bayle softly. "Another sacrifice;" and then softly to himself, "how long? how long?"

He rose, and was gravely bidding his friends good-bye, when a sharp, quick step was heard, and Eaton came in, coloured like a girl on seeing Bayle, hesitated, and then held out his hand.

Bayle shook it warmly and left the verandah, Eaton walking with him to the gate.

"Jack," said Mrs Otway softly, "it's my belief that the parson loves Julia Hallam himself."

"You think so?"

"I'm sure of it."

"And will he marry her?"

"No. I'm about sure that she is desperately fond of our boy, and the parson is too true a man to stand in the way."

"Nonsense!" said the Captain. "Such men are not made now."

"But they were when Christie Bayle was born," she said, nodding her head quickly. "Yes," she said, after a pause, as they heard Eaton's returning steps; "it's a knot, Jack."

"Humph!" he replied. "For time to untie."

Volume Four—Chapter Four.

Stephen Crellock is Communicative.

"No hurry, Steve, my lad," said Hallam, as he turned over the newspaper that had come in by the last mail, and threw one of his booted legs upon a chair.

Crellock was leaning against the chimney-piece of the room Hallam called his study; but one, which in place of books was filled with fishing and shooting gear, saddles, bridles, and hunting whips, from that usually adopted for riding, to the heavy implement so terrible in a stockman's hands.

The man had completely lost all his old prison look; and the obedient, servile manner that distinguished him, when, years before, he had been Hallam's willing tool in iniquity, had gone. He had developed into a sturdy, independent, restless being, with whom it would be dangerous to trifle, and Robert Hallam had felt for some time that he really was master no longer.

Crellock had dressed himself evidently for a ride. He was booted and spurred; wore tightly-fitting breeches and jacket, and a broad-brimmed felt hat was thrust back on his curly hair, as he stood beating his boot with his riding-whip, and tucking bits of his crisp beard between his white teeth to bite.

"What do you say? No hurry?"

"Yes," said Hallam, rustling his paper. "No hurry, my lad: plenty of time."

"You think so, do you?"

"To be sure. There, go and have your ride. I've got some fresh champagne just come in by the *Cross*. We'll try that to-day."

"Hang your champagne! I've come to talk business," said Crellock, sternly. "You think there's no hurry, do you? Well, look here, I think there is, and I'm not going to wait."

"Nonsense! Don't talk like a boy."

"No: I'll talk like a man, Robert Hallam. A man don't improve by keeping. I shall do now; by-and-by perhaps I shan't. I'm double her age and more."

"Oh! yes, I know all about that," said Hallam, impatiently; "but there's plenty of time."

"I say there is not, and I'm going to have it settled. Your wife hates me. I'm not blind, and she'll set Julie against me all she can."

"I'm master here."

"Then show it, Rob Hallam, and quickly, before there's a row. I tell you it wants doing; she's easily led now she's so young; but I'm not blind."

"You said that before; what do you mean?"

"That soldier Eaton; he's hankering after her, and if we don't mind, she'll listen to him. It's only your being an old hand that keeps him back from asking for her."

"Well, well, let it go, and I'll see about it by-and-by," said Hallam. "Have patience."

"A man at my time of life can't have patience, Rob. Now come, you know I want the girl, and it will be like tying us more tightly together."

"And put a stop to the risk of your telling tales," said Hallam, bitterly.

"I'm not the man to tell tales," said Crellock, sturdily, "neither am I the man for you to make an enemy."

"Threatening?"

"No, but I'm sure you wouldn't care to go back to the gang and on the road, Robert Hallam. Such a good man as your wife and child think you are!"

"Hold your tongue, will you?" cried Hallam savagely.

"When I please," replied Crellock. "Oh! come, you needn't look so fierce, old chap. I used to think what a wonder you were, and wish I could be as cool and clever, and—"

"Well?" for the other stopped.

"Oh! nothing; only I don't think so now."

"Look here," said Hallam, throwing aside the paper impatiently, "what do you want?"

"Julia."

"You mean you want to try if she'll listen to you."

"No, I don't. I mean I want her, and I mean to have her, and half share."

"And if I say it's impossible?"

"But you won't," said Crellock coolly.

Hallam sat back, frowning and biting his nails, while the other slowly beat his boot with his whip.

At last Hallam's brow cleared, and he said in a quiet, easy way:

"She might do better, Steve; but I won't stand in your way. Only the thing must come about gently. Talk to the girl. You shall have chances. I don't want any scenes with her or her mother, or any flying to that old man or the parson to help her. It must be worked quietly."

"All right. Order the horses round, and let her go for a ride with me this morning."

Mrs Hallam was ready to object, but she gave way, and Julia went for a ride with Crellock, passing Sir Gordon's cottage, and then riding right away into the open country. The girl had developed into a splendid horsewoman, and at last, when she had forgotten her dislike to her companion in the excitement and pleasure of the exercise, and the horses were well breathed and walking up an ascent, Crellock, on the principle that he had no time to spare, tried to forward his position.

"I say, Miss Julia," he said, taking off his broad hat, and fanning his face, as they rode on in the bright sunshine, "do you remember when you first came over?"

"Oh, yes."

"And meeting me as I was carried out of the prison on the stretcher?"

Julia looked at him, her eyes dilating with horror as the whole scene came back.

"Don't," she said hoarsely, "it is too horrible to think of? Such cruelty is dreadful."

"I don't consider it too horrible to think of," he said smiling. "I'm always looking back on that day and seeing it all, every bit. That poor wretch shrieking out with pain."

"Mr Crellock!" cried Julia.

"Yes! me. Not hardly able to move himself, or bear his pain, and half mad with thirst."

"Oh, pray, hush!"

"Not I, my dear," continued Crellock, "and out of it all I can see coming through the sunshine a bright angel to hold water up to my lips, and wipe the sweat of agony off my brow."

"Mr Crellock! I cannot bear to listen to all this."

"But you could bear to look at it all, and do it, bless you!" said the man warmly. "That day I swore something, and I'm going to keep my oath."

"Don't talk about it any more, please," said Julia imploringly.

"If you don't wish me to, I won't," said Crellock smiling. "I do want to talk to you though about a lot of things, and one is about the drink."

Julia looked at him wonderingly.

"Yes, about the drink," continued Crellock; "the old man drinks too much."

Julia's face contracted.

"And I've been a regular brute lately, my dear. You see it has been such a temptation after being kept from it for years. I haven't been able to stop myself. It isn't nice for a young girl like you to see a man drunk, is it?"

Julia shook her head.

"Then I shan't never get drunk again. I'll only take a little."

"Oh! I am so glad," cried Julia with girlish eagerness.

"Are you?" he said smiling, "then so am I. That's settled then. I want to be as decent as I can. You see you're such a good religious girl, Miss Julia, while I'm such a bad one."

"But you could be better."

"Could I? I don't like being a hypocrite. I'm not ashamed to own that I was a bad one, and got into all that trouble in the old country."

"Oh! hush, please. You did wrong, and were punished for it. Now all that is passed and forgiven."

"I always said you were an angel," said Crellock earnestly, "and you are."

"Nonsense! Let us talk of something else."

"No: let's talk about that. I want to stand fair and square with you, and I don't want you to think me a humbug and a hypocrite."

"Mr Crellock, I never thought so well of you before," said Julia warmly. "Your promise of amendment has made me feel so happy."

"Has it?" he cried eagerly, but with a rough kind of respect mingled with his admiration. "So it has me. I mean it—that I do. You shall never see me the worse for drink again."

"And you will attend more to the business, then?"

"What business?" he said.

"The business that you and my father carry on."

"The business that I and your father carry on?"

"Yes, the speculations about the seals and the oil."

Crellock stared at her. "Why, what have you got in your pretty little head?" he said at last.

"I only alluded to the business in which you and my father are partners."

"Pooh!" cried Crellock, with a sort of laugh. "What nonsense it is of him! Why, my dear, you are not a child now. After all the trouble you and your mother went through. You are a clever, thoughtful little woman, and he ought to have taken you into his confidence."

"What do you mean?" cried Julia, for she felt dazed.

"Your father! What's the use of a man like him—an old hand—setting himself up as a saint, and playing innocent? It isn't my way. As you say, when one has done wrong and suffered punishment, and is whitewashed—"

"Mr Crellock," said Julia, flushing, "I cannot misunderstand your allusions; but if you dare to insinuate that my poor father was guilty of any wrong-doing before he suffered, it is disgraceful, and it is not true."

Crellock looked at her admiringly.

"Bless you!" he said warmly. "I didn't think you had so much spirit in you. Now be calm, my dear; there's nothing worse than being a sham—a hypocrite. I never was. I always owned up to what I had done. Your father never did."

"My father never did anything wrong!" cried Julia.

Crellock smiled.

"Come, I should like us to begin by being well in each other's confidence," he said as he leaned over and patted the arching neck of Julia's mare. "You must know it, so what's the use of making a pretence about it to me?"

"I do not understand you," said Julia indignantly.

"Not understand me? Why, my dear girl, you know your father was transported for life?"

"Do I know it?" cried Julia, with an indignant flash of her eyes.

"Yes, of course you do. Well, what was it for?"

"Because appearances were cruelly against him," cried Julia.

"They were," said Crellock dryly.

"Because his friends doubted him, consequent upon the conduct of a man he trusted," said Julia bitterly.

"I never knew your father trust any one, Miss Julia, and I knew him before he went to King's Castor. We were clerks in the same office."

"He trusted you," cried Julia indignantly; "and you deceived him, and he suffered for your wicked sin."

She struck the mare with her whip, and it would have dashed off, but Crellock was smoothing her mane above the reins, and as they tightened they came into his hand, and he checked the little animal which began to rear.

"Quiet! quiet!" cried Crellock fiercely; and he held the mare back with ears twitching and nostril quivering.

"Let my rein go," cried Julia.

"Wait a bit; I've a lot to say to you yet, my dear," cried Crellock indignantly. "Look here. Did your father say that?"

"Yes; and you know it is true."

"I say again, did your father say that to your mother?"

"Yes," indignantly.

"Then that's why she has always shown me such a stiff upper lip, and been so bitter against me. I wouldn't have stopped in her house a day, she was so hard on me, only I wanted to be near you, and to think about that day coming out of the prison. Well, of all the mean, cowardly things for a man to do!"

"My father is no coward. You dare not speak to him like that."

"I dare say a deal more to him, and I will if he runs me down before you and your mother, when I wanted to show you I wasn't such a bad one after all. It's mean," he cried, working himself up. "It's cowardly. But it's just like him. When that robbery took place before, he escaped and I took the blame."

"Loose my rein!" cried Julia. "Man, you are mad."

"See here," cried Crellock, catching her arm, and looking white with rage. "I'll take my part; but I'm not going to have the credit of the Dixons' business put on to my shoulders. I'm not a hypocrite, Miss Julia. I've done wrong, as I said before, and was punished. There, it's of no use for you to struggle. I mean you to hear. I want to stand well with you. I always did after you gave me that drink of water, and now I find I've been made out to be a regular bad one, so as some one else may get off."

"Will you loose my rein?" cried Julia.

"No, I won't. Now you are going to call out for help?"

"No," cried Julia. "I'm not such a coward as to be afraid of you."

"That you are not," he said admiringly, in spite of the passion he was in. "Now once more tell me this. I'll believe you. You never told a lie, and you never would. Is this a sham to back up your father?"

She did not answer, only gave him a haughtily indignant look.

"Do you mean to tell me you don't know that your father did all that Dixons' business himself?"

"I know it is false."

"And that I only did what he told me, and planted the deeds at the different banks?"

"It is false, I tell you."

"You're making me savage," he cried in his blundering way. "I tell you I'm not such a brute. Look here once more. Do you mean to tell me that you don't know that we have all been living on what he—your father—got from Dixons' bank?"

"How dare you!" cried Julia, scarlet with anger.

"And that you and your mother brought over the plunder when you came?"

For answer, Julia struck his hand with her whip, giving so keen a cut that he loosened his hold, and she went off like the wind towards home.

"What a fool I was to talk like that!" he cried biting his lips, as he set spurs to his horse and galloped off in pursuit. "I've been talking like a madman. It all comes of being regularly in love."

Volume Four—Chapter Five.

"You are my Wife."

Stephen Crellock was fifty yards behind, with his horse completely blown, when Julia quickly slipped from her saddle, threw the rein over the hook at the door-post, and ran upstairs to the room where her mother loved to sit gazing over the beauties of the cove-marked estuary.

Mrs Hallam started up in alarm, and she had evidently been weeping.

"What is it, my child?" she cried, as Julia threw herself sobbing in her arms.

"That man—that man!" cried Julia. "Has he dared to insult you?" cried Mrs Hallam, with her eyes flashing, and her motherly indignation giving her the mien of an outraged queen.

"Yes—you—my father," sobbed Julia; and in broken words she panted out the story of the ride.

Mrs Hallam had been indignant, and a strange shiver of horror had passed through her, as it seemed as she listened that she was going to hear in form of words the dread that had been growing in her mind for a long time past.

It was then at first with a sense of relief that she gathered from her child's incoherent statement that Crellock had uttered few words of love. When, however, she thoroughly realised what had passed, and the charge that Crellock had made, it came with such a shock in its possibility, that her brain reeled.

"It is not true," she cried, recovering herself quickly. "Julia, it is as false as the man who made it."

"I knew—I knew it was, dear mother," sobbed Julia. "My father shall drive him from the house."

"Stay here," said Mrs Hallam sternly. Then, more gently, "My child, you are flushed, and hot. There, there! we have been so happy lately. We must not let a petty accusation like this disturb us."

"So happy, mother," cried Julia piteously, "when our friends forsake us; and Mr Bayle is as good as forbidden the house?"

"Hush, my darling?" said Mrs Hallam agitatedly. "There, go to your room."

She hurried Julia away, for she heard the trampling of the horses' feet as they were led round to the stables, and then a familiar step upon the stairs.

"I was coming to speak to you," she said as Hallam opened the door.

"And I was coming to you," he said roughly. "What has that little idiot been saying to Crellock to put him in such a rage?"

"Sit down," she said, pushing a chair towards him, and there was a look in her eyes he had never seen before.

"Well, there. Now be sharp. I don't care to be bothered with trifles; I've had troubles enough. Has that champagne been put to cool?"

She looked, half wonderingly, in the heavy, sensual face, growing daily more flushed and changed.

"Come, go on," he said, as if the look troubled him. "Now, then, what is it? Crellock is half mad. She has offended him horribly."

"She has been defending her father's honour," said Mrs Hallam slowly.

"Defending my honour?" he said, smiling. "Ah!" Mrs Hallam clasped her hands, and a sigh full of the agony of her heart escaped her lips. The scales seemed to be falling from her eyes, but she wilfully closed them again in her passion of love and trust.

But it was in vain. Something seemed to be tearing these scales away— something seemed to be rending that thick veil of love, and the voices she had so long quelled were clamouring to be heard, and making her ears sing with the terrible tale they told.

She writhed in spirit. She denied it all as a calumny, but as she walked to and fro there the tiny voices in her soul seemed to be ringing out the destruction of her idol, and to her swimming eyes it seemed tottering to its fall.

"You are very strange," he said roughly. "What's the matter? I thought you were going to tell me about Julia and Steve."

"I am," she cried at last, as if mastering herself after some terrible spasm. "Robert, I have been told something to-day that makes me tremble."

"Some news?" he said coolly.

"Yes, news—terrible news."

"Let's have it—if you like," he said. "I don't care. It don't matter, unless it will do you good to tell it."

Her face was wrung by the agony of her soul as she heard his callous words. The veil was being terribly rent now; and as her eyes saw more clearly, she tried in vain to close her mental sight; but no, she seemed forced to gaze now, and the idol that was tottering began to show that it was indeed of clay.

"Well, don't look like that," he said. "A man who has been transported is pretty well case-hardened. There *is* no worse trouble in life."

"No worse?" she panted out in a quick, angry way, as words had never before left her lips; "not if he lost the love and trust of wife and child?"

"Well, that would be unpleasant," he said coolly. "Perhaps the poor wretch would be able to get over it in time. What is your news?"

"I have heard you freshly accused to-day of that old crime, of which you were innocent."

"Of which I was innocent, of course," he said coolly. "Is that all?"

She did not answer for a few minutes, and then as he half rose impatiently, as if to go, she said excitedly: "That case I brought over, Robert."

"Case?" he said with a slight start.

"From the old house."

"Well—what about it?"

"Tell me at once, or I shall go mad. What did it contain?"

"Papers. I told you when I wrote."

"That would set him free," the voices in her heart insisted.

"Who has been setting you to ask about that, eh?" She did not reply.

"You did not keep faith with me," he cried angrily. "You have been telling Sir Gordon, or that Bayle."

"I told no one," she said hoarsely.

"Hah!" he ejaculated with a sigh of relief.

"Stephen Crellock has told Julia what she—and I—declare is false."

"Stephen Crellock is a fool," he cried quickly. "Go and fetch Julia here. She must be talked to."

"Robert! my husband," cried Mrs Hallam, throwing herself upon her knees and catching his hands, "you do not speak out. Why do you not passionately say it is false? How dare he accuse you of such a crime! You do not speak!"

She gazed up at him wildly.

"What do you want me to say?" he cried angrily. "Do you think me mad, woman? Here, let's have an end of all this nonsense. What does Crellock say?" She could not speak for a few minutes, so overladen was her heart; and when she did, the words were hoarse that fell upon his ears.

"He said—he told our simple, loving girl, whom I have taught to trust in and reverence her martyred father's name; whose faith has been in your innocency of the crime for which you were sent here—the girl I taught to pray that your innocence might be proved—"

"Will you go on?" he cried brutally. "I'm sick of this. Now, what did he say?"

"That—Oh, Robert, my husband, I cannot say it! His words cannot be true!"

"Will you speak?" he cried. "Out with it at once! When will you grow to be a woman of the world, and stop this childishness? Now what did the chattering fool say?"

"That the box I brought over contained the proceeds of the bank robbery— money that you had hidden away."

Millicent Hallam started up and gazed about her with a dazed look, as if she were startled by the words she heard—words that seemed to have come from other lips than hers; and then she pressed her hands to her heaving bosom as her husband spoke.

"Stephen Crellock must be getting tired of his leave," he said coolly. "An idiot! He had better have kept his tongue between his teeth. How came he to be chattering about that? If he don't mind—" He did not finish the sentence, and his wife's eyes dilated as she gazed at him in a horrified way.

"You do not deny it!" she said at last. "You do not declare that this is all cruelly false!"

"No," he said slowly, "I am not going to worry myself about his words. He can't prove anything."

"But it is a charge against your honour," she cried; "against me. Robert! you will not let this go uncontradicted for an hour longer?"

"Stephen Crellock had better mind," said Hallam, slowly and thoughtfully, as if he had not heard his wife.

"But, Robert—my husband! you will speak for your own sake—for your child's sake—for mine?"

There was a growing intensity in the words, whose tones rose to one of passionate appeal.

He made an impatient motion that implied a negative, and she threw herself once more upon her knees at his feet.

"You will deny this atrocious charge?"

"If I am asked I shall deny it of course," he said coolly; "but you don't suppose I am going to talk about it without?"

"But—but—that man believes it to be true!"

"Well, let him."

"Robert—dear Robert," she cried, "you must not, you shall not treat it like that! It is as if you were indifferent to this dreadful statement."

"Because it is better to let it rest, madam, so let it be."

"No!" she cried, with a wave as it were of her old trust sweeping all before it; "I cannot let it rest. If you will not speak in your own defence, I must!"

"What do you mean?" he said hastily.

"That if for his child's sake, Robert Hallam will not defend himself against such a vile and cruel lie, his wife will!"

"What will you do?" he said, with an ugly sneer upon his lip.

"See this man myself, and force him to deny it—to declare that it is not true. My husband cannot sit down patiently with that charge flung against his wife's honour and his own."

Me sat gazing at her from beneath his thick eyebrows for a few minutes as she paced the room, agitated almost beyond bearing; and then he spoke in the most matter-of-fact way.

"You'll do nothing of the kind."

"Not speak?"

"No; I forbid it."

"Forbid it?"

"Yes. Do you suppose I want my leave stopped? Do you want to send me back to the gang who are chained like dogs?"

"Hush!" she cried, with a shudder; and she covered her face, as if to shut out some terrible sight. "Do you not feel that you are running risks by remaining silent?"

"I should run greater risks by having the matter talked about. That great fool, Steve, must be warned to be more cautious in what he says, for all our sakes."

"Robert!" in a tone of horror.

"There, there, wife, that will do! Let's talk it over without sentiment; I haven't a bit of romance left in me, my dear. Life out here has cleared it off. You may as well know the truth as at any future time. Bah! Let's throw away all this flimsy foolery. You've known it all along, only you've been too brave to show it."

"I—known the truth?" she faltered. "You believe this?"

"Yes," he said, without reading the horror and despair in her eyes; and the brutal callousness of his manner seemed to grow. "What's the use of shamming innocence? You knew what was in the box."

"I knew what my husband told me; that there were papers to prove his innocence," she replied.

"You knew that?"

"They were my husband's words; and in my wifely faith I said that they were true."

He looked at her mockingly.

"You play your part well, Millicent," he said; "but remember we are in Sydney, both twenty years older than when we first met at King's Castor. Is it not time we talked like man and woman, and not, after all that we have gone through, like a sentimental boy and girl?"

"Robert!"

"There, that will do," he said. "You understand now why you must hold your tongue."

It was as if once more she had snatched at the veil and thrust it over her eyes, to gaze at him in the old, old way, as if it were impossible to give up the faith to which she had clung for so many years.

"No," she said softly, "I cannot. Some things are too hard to understand, and this is one."

"Then I'll make you understand," he said, almost fiercely. "If another word is uttered about this it will go like wildfire. Some meddling fool in the Government service will take it up; everything will be seized, and I shall be sent back to the gang through you. Do you hear? through you!"

She stood now gazing at him with her eyes contracting. Her lips parted several times as if she were about to speak, and as if her brain were striving, indeed, to comprehend this thing that she had declared to be too hard. At last she spoke.

"You shall say," she cried hoarsely. "Tell me what it was I brought over to you."

"What, again!" he cried. "Well, then, what I had saved up for the rainy day that I knew was coming. My fortune, that I have been waiting all these years to spend; notes that would change at any time; diamonds that would always fetch their price. You did not guess all this? You did not see through it all? Bah! I'm sick of this miserable mock sentiment and twaddle about innocence!"

She drew her breath hard.

"I had to fight the world when I was unlucky in my speculations, and the world got me down. Now my turn has come, and I can laugh at the world. Let's have no more fooling. You have understood it all from the beginning, and have played your part well. Let me play mine in peace."

An angry reply rose to her lips, but it died away, and she caught at his hand.

"It is true, then?" she whispered.

"True? Yes, of course," he said brutally.

"That money, then? Robert, husband, it is not ours. You will give it up—everything?"

"Give it up!" he said, laughing. "Not a shilling. They hounded me down most cruelly!"

"For the sake of our old love, Robert," she whispered, as she clung to him. "Let us begin again, and I will work for you. Let us try, in a future of toil, to wash away this clinging disgrace. My husband, my husband! for the sake of our innocent child!"

"Give up what I have!" he cried. "Now that I have schemed till success is mine! Not a shilling if it were to save old Sir Gordon's life."

"But, Robert, for the sake of our child. I am your wife, and I will bear this blow; but let her go on believing in him whom I have taught her to love. Let the past be dead; begin a new life—repentance for that which has gone. Robert, my husband, I have loved you so dearly, and so long."

"Pish!" he cried, impatiently. "You don't know what you're saying. Lead a new life—a life of repentance! I have had a fine preparation for it here. Why, I tell you they would turn a saint here into a fiend! I sinned against their laws, and they sent me here, herded with hundreds, some of whom might have been brought to better lives; but it has been one long course of brutal treatment, and the lash. Hope was dead to us all, and we had to drag on our lives in misery and despair. I tell you I've had to do with people who sought to make us demons, and you talk to me now of repentance for the past."

"Yes, and you shall repent!" she cried, wildly.

"Silence!" he said, fiercely. "You are my wife, and it is your duty to obey. Not a word of this to Julie. I will speak to her; and as to Crellock—oh, I can manage him."

He thrust her aside, and strode out of the room without another word, leaving her standing with her hands clasped together, gazing into vacancy, as if stunned by the blow that had fallen—as if the savage acceptance of the truth of the charges by her husband had robbed her of her reason.

During her long trial, whenever a shadowy doubt had crept into her sight, she had slain it. Always he had been her martyr, and she had been ready, in fierce resentment, to turn upon those who would have cast the slightest reflection upon his fame. He, the idol of her young life, her first love, had suffered through misfortune, through an ugly turn of fate, and she had gone on waiting for the day when he would be cleared.

In that spirit, she had crossed the wide ocean, bearing with her his freedom, as she believed; and now, after fighting a year against the terrible disillusions that had been showing Robert Hallam in his true light, the veil that she had so obstinately held was rent in twain, torn away for ever. By his own confession, the husband of her love was a despicable thief; and as she realised how she had been made his accomplice in bringing over the fruits of his theft, the blow seemed now greater than she could bear, the future one terrible void.

Volume Four—Chapter Six.

The Shadow across the Path.

What to do? How to bear it? How far she—woman of purest thought—had sinned in participating as she had in Hallam's crime?

It was as if the shock had blunted and confused her understanding, so that she could not think clearly or make out any plan for her future proceeding. And all the time she was haunted as by a great horror.

Now light would come, and she would seem to see her course clearly and wonder that she should have hesitated before. It was all so simple. Sir Gordon was there in Sydney, her oldest friend. He it was who had been the sufferer by her husband's defalcations, and of course it was her duty to go straight to him and tell him all.

No sooner had she arrived at this than she shrank from the idea with horror. What could she have been thinking! To go to Sir Gordon was to denounce her husband as a criminal, and the result would be to send him back to the prison lines and the hideous convict life that had changed him from a man of refinement to a brutal sensualist, from whom in future she felt that she must shrink with horror.

Those last thoughts distracted her. Shrink with horror from him whom she had so dearly loved, from him whom she had believed a martyr to a terribly involved chain of evidence! It was too terrible!

But what was she to do? She could not lead this life of luxury, purchased by the money she had so innocently brought; that was certain. She and Julia must leave there at once. They could not stay.

She shivered as she thought of the difficulties that would rise up. For where were they? Out here, in this half-civilised place, penniless; and what defence had she to bring forward if Robert Hallam, her husband and master, said no, she should stay, and claimed her and her child as his?

There was light again. She could appeal to the governor, for Hallam had forfeited his social rights, and she would be free.

Down came the darkness and shut out that light, closing her in with a blackness so terrible that she shuddered.

It was impossible—impossible!

"He is my husband," she moaned, "and were he ten times the sinner, I could not take a step that would injure the man I loved—the father of my child!"

Christie Bayle!

Yes; Christie Bayle, truest and most faithful of friends, who in the days of his boyish love had resigned himself to her wishes, and promised to be her brother through life.

How good he had been; and how she had in her agony of spirit reviled him, and called him her husband's enemy! How his conduct seemed to stand out now, bright and shining! How full of patient self-denial! Brother, indeed, through all, while she had been—she knew it now, and shivered in her agony—so obstinately blind.

Christie Bayle would help her and protect Julia, whom he loved as if she were his child. He would—yes, she reiterated the thought with a strange feeling of joy—he would help her, as he had helped her before, in this time of anguish, and protect Julia from that man.

For now came, in all its solid horror, the reality of that which had only been cast, so far, as a shadow across her path.

This man, Crellock, who had seemed like Hallam's evil genius from the first, but whom she saw now as her husband's willing tool, had conceived a passion for her darling child. More—he was her husband's chosen companion in pleasure and in guilt, and Hallam would—if he had not done so already—accept him.

"And I sit here bemoaning my suffering," she cried passionately, "when such a blow is impending for my darling. Shame! shame! Am I ever to be so weak a woman, so mere a puppet in others' hands? Heaven give me strength to be forgetful of self, and strong in defence of my child!"

She pressed back her hair from her brow, which became full of lines, and, resting her elbows upon her knees, her chin upon her hands, she sat there gazing as it were into the future, as she told herself that her own sufferings must be as nought, but that she must save Julia from such a fate.

Sir Gordon? Bayle? No! no! Only as a last resource. Not even then; they must be left. They had known the truth from the first—she saw it now—and in pity for her had borne all she had said, and helped her.

No! to ask their aid was to punish her husband. That could not be. She must act alone, weak woman as she was. She must be strong now, and she and Julia must leave this man at once. They must take some cottage or lodging in the town, and work for a living. That must be the first step.

Then came the black cloud again, to shut out the hope. Hallam would not allow them to go; and if they could steal away they were absolutely penniless.

She sat gazing before her, feeling as if old age had come suddenly to freeze her faculties and render her helpless; but, starting from her blank sense of misery, she forced herself to think.

What should she do? Julia should not be a convict's wife; she felt that she would rather see her dead.

Once more a ray of hope—a thin, bright ray of light piercing the cloud of darkness ahead.

Lieutenant Eaton!

He loved her child, and it had seemed as if Julia cared for him, but in her maiden innocency she had always shrunk from anything more than a friendly show of attachment.

"But he is manly, and evidently devoted to her," said Mrs Hallam in a low voice. "She would soon learn to love him."

She ran over in her own mind all that had passed since the acquaintance on ship-board began. Eaton's attentions, the pleasant hours Julia had seemed to spend in his company, the young officer's manner—everything pointed to its being on his part more than the gallant attention of one of his stamp. Then there was the life here since they had landed. His occasional calls; his evident hesitancy. It was all so plain. He loved Julia dearly, but he was kept back from proposing for her by her connections.

"But he will ignore them for her sake," she cried at last joyously. "He must be learning day by day how true and good she is. He will forget everything, and she will be saved."

Mrs Hallam started up with the ray of hope cutting its way more and more brightly through the dark cloud ahead; and then her senses seemed to reel, a terrible fit of giddiness came over her as she tottered, caught at a chair, and then fell heavily upon the floor.

Volume Four—Chapter Seven.

"To the Better Way."

When Mrs Hallam came to herself, she was in bed, where she had lain, talking incoherently at times, during the greater part of a week.

It was evening, and the sun was shining in at the open window, lighting up Julia's dark hair as she sat with her face in the shadow, careworn and evidently suffering deeply.

Mrs Hallam lay for some time feeling restful and calm. The fevered dream was at an end, and she had slept long, to wake now with that pleasurable sensation upon her that is given to the sick when an attack is at an end, and nature is tenderly repairing the damages of the assault. She was lying there; Julia, her beloved child, was by her side. A veil was between her and the past, and there was nothing but the peaceful sensation of rest.

Then, as her eyes wandered slowly about the room and rested at last upon her child, her mind began to work; the mother's quick instinct awoke, and she read trouble in Julia's face. The memories that were slumbering came back, and she tried to rise in her bed but sank back.

"Mother!"

"My child! Tell me quickly: have I been ill?"

"Yes; very, very ill. But you are better now, dear mother. I am so lonely! Ah! at last, at last!"

Worn out and weak with constant watching, Julia threw herself sobbing by the bedside, but only to hurriedly dry her eyes and try to be calm.

She succeeded, and answered the questions that came fast; and as she replied, Mrs Hallam trembled, for she could see that Julia was keeping something back.

"Have I been delirious?" she said at last.

"Yes, dear; but last night you slept so peacefully, and all through to-day. There, let me call Thisbe."

"No, not yet," said Mrs Hallam, clinging to her child's arm, as a great anxiety was longing to be satisfied. "Tell me, Julia, did I talk—talk of anything while I was like that?"

Julia nodded quickly, and the despairing look deepened in her eyes.

"Not—not of your father, my child?" panted the suffering woman.

"Yes, mother, dear mother," sobbed Julia, with a passionate cry that she could not withhold, and she buried her face in the sick woman's breast.

The sun sank lower, and Julia's low sobs grew more rare, but she did not rise from her knees—she did not lift her tear-stained face, while clasped about her neck, and her fingers joined above the glossy head, as if in prayer, Mrs Hallam's hands, thin and transparent from her illness, seemed bathed in the orange glow of the sweet, calm eve.

All was still and restful on the hill-slope above the beautiful Paramatta River, and from the window there was a scene of peace that seemed to hinder the possibility of trouble existing on this earth.

"Julia," said Mrs Hallam at length; "have you thought of all this—since—since I have been lying here?"

"Yes, dear, till I could think no more."

"It has come at last," said Mrs Hallam, as she lay with closed eyes.

"It has come, dear?" said Julia, starting up, and gazing at her mother with dilating eyes.

"Yes, my child, our path. I could not see it before in the wild confusion of my thoughts, but I know our duty now. You will help me, dear?"

"Help you, mother? Oh, yes. What shall I do?"

Mrs Hallam did not answer for a few minutes, and then said softly:

"You know all, you say. It has come to you with as great a shock as to me; but I can see our duty now. Julia, he must love us dearly; we are his wife and child, and we must lead him back to the better way."

Volume Four—Chapter Eight.

A Convict Rising.

"Ah, Mr O'Hara," said Bayle, holding out his hand, "I have not seen you for months. Why do you not give me a call?"

"Because I am a convict, sir," said the young Irishman, paying no heed to the extended hand.

"Oh, yes; but that is past now," said Bayle. "One doesn't look upon you as one would upon a thief or a swindler, and even if you had been both these worthies, a man of my cloth comes to preach forgiveness, and is ready to hold out the right hand to every man who is sorry for the past."

"But I am not sorry for the past, sir," said O'Hara firmly.

"I've studied it all," said Bayle quietly, "and the rising was a mistake."

"Don't talk about it, please, sir," said O'Hara hotly. "You are an Englishman. You could not gaze upon that trouble, for which I was transported, from an Irishman's point of view."

"Then we will not talk about it," said Bayle; "but come, I am no enemy of your country."

"I should say, sir, that you were never any man's enemy but your own," said O'Hara dryly.

Bayle smiled.

"There, shake hands," he said. "How has the world been using you?"

"Better lately, sir. I am comfortable enough in the Government office, and now I am helping the commission that is investigating the prison affairs. And you, sir?"

"Oh, I am busy enough, and happy enough. Then it was you I caught sight of in the prison yard a month ago? I thought it was; but it gave me such a chill that I would not look."

"Why, sir?"

"I was afraid that you had gone backwards, and were there again."

O'Hara's hard, care-lined face relaxed, and there was a pleasant smile on his countenance when he spoke again. "I heard about you, sir, in the lines."

"Indeed!"

"The men talked a good deal about you."

"Yes?" said Bayle good-humouredly. "I'm afraid they laugh at me and my notions."

"They do," said O'Hara thoughtfully. "Poor wretches! But you have made more impression and gained more influence, sir, than you think."

"I wish I could feel so," said Bayle with a sigh.

"If you will take my opinion, sir, you will feel so," said O'Hara. "I'm glad I met you, sir, for I have been a great deal in the prison lately, and I can't help thinking there is something wrong."

"Something wrong?"

"Yes, sir. I believe the men are meditating a rising."

"A rising? In Heaven's name, what do they expect to do?"

"Obtain the mastery, sir, or seize upon a vessel or two, and escape to some other land."

"But have you good reason for suspecting this?"

"No other reason than suspicion—the suspicion that comes from knowing their ways and habits. Such a rising took place when I was there years ago."

"Well?"

"It was suppressed, and the poor wretches who were in it made their case worse, as they would now."

"But the authorities must be warned."

"They have been warned," said O'Hara quietly. "I am not one of them now, and knowing what I do of the musket and bayonet and the lash, I lost no time in laying my suspicions before my superiors. Yes," he said, "I was right, was I not?"

"Right? Unquestionably. Such men, until they have been proved, have no right to be free. Then that is the meaning of the extra sentries I have seen."

"That is it, sir; but if the sentries were doubled again, I'm afraid the mistaken men would carry out their notions, unless some strong influence were brought to bear. Why don't you try to get hold of the ringleaders, sir, and show them the madness of the attempt?"

"I will," said Bayle quickly, and they parted; but they were not separated a hundred yards before there was a shout, and Bayle turned to see O'Hara running after him swiftly.

"What is it?" he asked.

"I'm afraid I have spoken too late, sir. I heard a shot out yonder, beyond that house where the new road is being made. A strong gang has been at work there for a fortnight past. Do you hear that?"

Two distant shots in quick succession were heard, and Christie Bayle turned pale, for the sounds came from beyond the house pointed out, and that house was Hallam's.

"We had better go and give the alarm at the governor's office."

"No, no," said Bayle. "We may be in time to help up here. Come quickly, man; run!"

It seemed madness to O'Hara; but there was a decision in Bayle's order that did not seem to brook contradiction, and being a quick, lithe man, he ran step for step with his companion, as they made their way amongst the park-like growth of the hill-side in the direction of the spot whence the sounds had come.

Bayle had a very misty idea of what he meant to do, and once or twice the thought came that, after all, this might be only some one amusing himself with a gun after the beautifully-plumaged birds that were common enough in the neighbourhood then.

These ideas were quickly overthrown, for soon they could see the uniforms of the convict guard in the distance, and the gleam of a bayonet, followed by another shot, and some figures running down the side of one of the valleys leading to the shore.

It was now that Bayle realised his intentions, and they were to go to the help of those who were at Hallam's house, in case it should be attacked.

As they came nearer, though, it was evident that the fight which was in progress was more to the right of the house, and becoming fiercer, for some half-dozen shots were fired in a volley from a ravine down amongst some trees, the hills being occupied by a swarm of men.

All at once three figures came out of the house on the slope, and as he advanced Bayle made out that they were Hallam, Crellock, and one who was unmistakable from his undress uniform.

When they came out it was evident that the latter was urging his companions to follow him; but they stopped back, and he dashed on, down into the ravine.

It was heavy running for Bayle, and the young officer was far ahead of him; but he hurried on, O'Hara keeping well up to his side, and together they saw him meet a couple of the retreating guard, who stopped at his command, faced round, and accompanied him, the three plunging down among the bushes and disappearing from the sight of Bayle and his companion.

"The men will be very dangerous," said O'Hara. "We shall find them armed with picks, spades, and hammers."

"They will not hurt me," panted Bayle, "and we may save bloodshed."

"I don't think they will hurt me," said the young Irishman grimly. "Are you going on, sir?"

"Of course."

"Good. Then I will risk it, too."

They were going forward all the time, hurrying down into the valley, and leaving Hallam's house away to the left, with Hallam and Crellock watching the proceedings, they having a view from their commanding position of that which was hidden from Bayle and his friend.

As they ran on, though, they heard another shot or two, and a loud shouting, while a couple of hundred yards on ahead they could see four of the guard retreating along the slope, pursued by about a dozen of the convicts, another party coming towards them, a glimpse of a bayonet showing that others of the guard were being driven back towards Hallam's house, while in another minute it was plain that Eaton had not been able to join forces with the men.

In fact the convicts had divided into two parties, and these, going in opposite directions, were driving their guards before them with furious shouts.

A little army of two pensioners, led by an officer armed with a cane, had but a poor chance of success against some five-and-twenty savage men, whose passions had been raised to volcanic point by seeing a couple of their number shot down at the beginning of the fray, when they had risen against the sergeant and eight men who had them in charge. Of these they had beaten down the sergeant and two of his men, and were apparently determined upon taking revenge upon those who had fired upon them, before trying to escape.

The bushes hindered the view, but at last Bayle came in full sight of Eaton and the two men just as a stone was hurled, hitting one of them in the chest, so that he went down as if shot. His companion turned to fly, but a furious shout from Eaton stopped him, and he faced the enemy again as the young officer reached over the fallen guard, took his musket, with its fixed bayonet, and stood his ground, to protect the poor fellow who was down.

It was only a matter of moments, and before Bayle could get up the convicts had made a rush, yelling furiously.

It was hard to see what took place; but as Bayle ran down the slope, his heart beating fast with apprehension, the man dropped, and Bayle had just time to strike one blow on the young officer's behalf, as the convicts closed him in, and bore him back against the scarped face of the little ravine.

It was only one blow, but it was given with the full force of a strong arm and had the weight of a well-built man rushing down a steep slope to give it additional force.

The result was that the man Bayle struck, and another behind him, went rolling over—the former just as he had raised a spade to strike at Eaton's defenceless head.

"You cowardly dogs!" roared Bayle, as, failing another weapon, he caught up a spade one of the convicts had let fall.

The attack was so sudden and unexpected that the men gave way, and stood glaring for a few moments, till one of their number shouted:

"It's only the parson, boys. Down with 'em!"

But they did not come on, and, taking advantage of their hesitation, Bayle turned to Eaton.

"Quick!" he said, "get away from here."

"No," said the young officer hoarsely. "I can't leave my men. Ah!"

He uttered a sharp cry, and sank down, for a piece of stone had been hurled at him with force enough to dislocate his shoulder, half stunning him with the violence of the blow.

As the young man fell the convicts uttered a yell of delight, all three of their adversaries being now *hors de combat*; but they were not satisfied, one of their number rushing forward to deliver a cowardly blow with the stone-hammer he bore.

Bayle did not realise for the moment that so brutal an act could be committed upon a fallen adversary, and he was so much off his guard that he only had time to make a snatch at the handle, and partly break the force of the blow, which fell on Eaton's cap.

Then there was a quick struggle, and the convict staggered, tripped over a loose block of stone, and fell with a crash. There was an ominous murmur here, and the men stood hesitating, each disposed to make a rush and revenge the fall of his companion; but there was no leader to combine the force and lead them on, and, taking advantage of their hesitation, Bayle stooped down, lifted the insensible man, and strode away.

The convicts were taken by surprise at this act, and some were for fetching him back, but the remainder were for letting him go.

"Take the swaddy's guns, lads, and let's be off at once," said one of the party, and the two muskets were seized, a convict presenting the bayonet of the piece he had secured at the breast of one of the fallen men, both of whom lay half-stunned and bleeding on the rough ground.

"Shall I, boys?" he said.

"No; hold hard," cried a voice, and a member of the party who had been in pursuit of the other portion of the guard came up. "Tie them hand and foot, and leave them so as they can't give warning. Who's that going up the hill?"

"Parson and the orficer," said one of the men.

"And who's that running yonder?"

"That Irishman who was in with us—O'Hara."

"Can any one shoot and bring him down? Give me a musket."

He snatched the piece offered to him, took careful aim by resting the musket on the edge of the scarped bank, and fired.

There was the sharp report, the puff of white smoke,

(This page missing.)

Volume Four—Chapter Nine.

Lieutenant Eaton is in the Way.

(This page missing.)

Panting, and with his throat dry with excitement as much as with exertion, he toiled on, feeling as if every few paces had brought him nearly to a haven of refuge, but only on raising his eyes to see the house apparently as far off as ever, and to hear the voices of the convicts close at hand, the gully acting as a kind of tube to convey the sound. He paused for a moment to get a better hold of his burden, and Eaton uttered a low groan, but he managed to get him in an easier position, and started off once more, toiling on till the gully opened on his left, and he saw O'Hara rise from behind some bushes, where he had been creeping, and begin to run. Then his blood seemed to turn cold, his heart to stop beating, for quicker than it can be told, there was a shout, a dead silence, and then the sharp report of a musket, as O'Hara went down, and rolled out of his sight as well.

Bayle ground his teeth, and a chill of despair came over him as he realised that the Irishman had been making for the town to give the alarm and bring help, while now the news might not reach Sydney till the hour when the draft and their guard should return.

"Those poor fellows!" moaned Eaton, piteously, as Bayle toiled on with him, seeing now that Hallam and Crellock were outside the verandah, looking curiously towards him, but not taking a step to his aid.

"I can't ask their help if they do not offer it," muttered Bayle, as he staggered on, growing weaker with his exertion, and finally stopping for a moment or two so as to get his breath.

Then came the confused murmur of voices, when, looking back, he saw that he was pursued; and as he pressed forward again the horrible thought flashed through his brain that he was leading the savage band of utterly reckless men right to the house where two tender women might even then be trembling witnesses of what was going on. The agony he suffered at this thought was so great that he stopped short, his brain swimming; and, in spite of the fact that the convicts were close behind, he would have staggered off to the left, had not a white figure suddenly appeared on the side farthest from where Hallam and Crellock had backed close to the window, and ran swiftly to meet him.

It was like some episode in a dream to Bayle, as that white figure flew to his side.

"Quick, Mr Bayle, quick!" and, catching at Eaton in the belief that she was helping to bear him, Julia pressed towards the house.

"Julie! are you mad?" roared Hallam, as soon as she was seen; and Crellock started out after her.

"Quick! help! help!" she cried in a sharp imperious manner; and, as is so often the case where one quick order is given, those who would not, if they had time to think, stir a finger in a cause, feel themselves moved by some irresistible influence, and obey. So Crellock seized Eaton, and helped bear him into the dining-room, Hallam banging to the window and fastening it as Eaton was thrown upon the couch.

"You are mad!" cried Hallam passionately. "They'll wreck the place now."

"They won't hurt us," said Crellock coolly; and to Julia's horror he threw open the window as the convicts came up at the double and rushed into the room.

"Steady, mates, steady!" shouted Hallam. "You know us."

The leading men hesitated a moment, and then one of them made a dash at Eaton.

"Now, boys, have him out," he cried.

Julia shrieked, and threw herself before the helpless man, when the convict rudely caught her by the arms to swing her aside, but was sent staggering sideways from a blow dealt by Bayle.

"Save him, Mr Bayle," shrieked Julia, as she clung to Eaton. "Father! oh, father, help!"

Neither Hallam nor Crellock stirred as the man whom Bayle had struck uttered an oath which was echoed by his companions, who seized Bayle and held him as others of the party dragged out Eaton, fortunately insensible to all that was going on.

In their insensate fury believing that they had a long list of injuries to repay the convict guard, who in guarding them had only done their duty, in another minute Eaton's life would have been sacrificed, when there was the tramp of feet, an order given in a loud voice, and a party of soldiers led by Captain Otway dashed up with bayonets fixed. And then two wounded convicts were lying on the floor, the others were in full flight down the gully, pursued by the troops, a shot every now and then breaking the silence that had fallen upon the group.

Hallam was the first to speak, and he turned angrily upon Bayle.

"Were you mad to bring him here?" he snarled.

"Father!" cried Julia with a reproachful look, as she knelt down beside Eaton to hold her handkerchief to his wounded head.

Bayle made no reply to the question, but said sternly:

"Mr Hallam, you had better send for medical aid. My dear Julia, you must go."

"No," she cried with a quick, imperious look; "send for help."

Bayle's brow contracted, but he concealed the pain he suffered as he saw Julia bending over Eaton, and was hurrying out, but was met by Captain Otway, who came in breathless, followed by O'Hara, and a couple of his men.

"Is he much hurt?" he cried anxiously. "Carry out these two, my lads."

He bent down over Eaton as Julia sobbed out, "He is killed! he is killed!"

"Oh, no: not so bad as that; only stunned. Here, you two," he continued sharply, turning to Hallam and Crellock, "don't stand there staring. Lift this gentleman on to the sofa."

Years of slavish obedience to authority had left their traces, and as if moved by one impulse, they sprang to where Eaton was lying and lifted him to the couch. The moment this was done though, Hallam gave an impatient stamp of the foot and gazed at Crellock, who ground out something between his teeth.

"Now fetch water—a sponge," said Otway, sheathing his sword, throwing off his cap, and turning up his sleeves.

"This is my house—"

Hallam said no more. He had begun in a fierce, loud voice, and then he stopped as Captain Otway turned upon him with an imperious—

"What's that you say?" Then he seemed to recall where he was, for he glanced at Julia and Bayle. "Look here," he said quietly, and he took a step or two towards Hallam to whisper something in his ear.

Hallam made no reply, but left the room, and did not return, Thisbe hurrying in directly after with basin and towels, and helping eagerly.

"Oh, come, come, my dear Miss Hallam," said Otway, after cleverly bandaging the wound. "You must not take on like that. I can't do anything to the shoulder—at least, I will not. Our doctor will soon put him right. There, see! he is coming to."

"I have been trying very hard," said Julia with a gasp; "but it is so dreadful."

"No, no, no! Why, my wife would have seen it all without shedding a tear. It's only dreadful when some one is killed, and, thank heaven! I don't think one of the men has met that fate."

"I wish I could feel the same about the convicts," said Bayle softly.

"The convicts? Well, I wish so, too, Mr Bayle; but law and order must be maintained, and they know their lives are forfeit if they attempt to escape."

Bayle nodded in acquiescence as he glanced at where Julia knelt beside Eaton, crying softly, and fanning his face.

"There, you have nothing to fear, Miss Hallam," continued the Captain kindly. "Eaton has only had a few hard knocks—soldier's salary, I call them. As to the rising, the poor wretches are, I expect, all taken by this time. Yes, here they come."

He had walked to the window and gazed out to see the greater part of the convict gang, hot, bleeding some of them, and dejected, coming along, guarded by the soldiers under the command of a boyish-looking ensign.

"Ah, Mr O'Hara," he said, stepping out, and laying his hand on the young Irishman's shoulder, "I think we may thank you for getting up in time. Your message set us off, and we met you just in the nick. Why, man, you are hurt."

"Not much, sir. They shot at me, and the bullet grazed my arm."

"Come in," he said, "and let me see."

O'Hara followed unwillingly, but had to submit to have his wound dressed.

"Where is your master?" said the Captain at last, turning to Thisbe.

"In his room, sir."

"Fetch him."

Hallam uttered a furious oath when the message was given, and swore he would not come. Then, rising from his chair, he followed Thisbe to the dining-room like one compelled to obey.

"I am going to leave my brother officer in your charge, Mr Hallam," said the Captain in the quick manner of one giving an order. "You will see that he has every attention! The regimental surgeon will be up in an hour or so. Miss Hallam, thank you for your kindness," he continued, turning his back on Hallam. "Good-morning, Mr Bayle. I'm sorry you have had such an upset. You stay here, I suppose?"

"No," said Bayle quietly; "I am going back to the town."

"Come with me, then."

He stepped out, and Bayle followed, but turned to look at Julia, who gave him one quick look that seemed to say "Good bye," and then as he stepped out into the verandah he saw her bending over Eaton again.

"Nice little girl that," said the Captain, as they marched down behind the guards and the wretched men they drove before them almost at the bayonet's point.

Bayle bowed.

"Sweet and innocent, and all that. Really, Mr Bayle, I agree with my wife."

"Indeed!" said Bayle.

"Yes; she thinks that at any cost her friends ought to have kept her in England, and not brought her here."

Christie Bayle made no reply, for he was thinking of Philip Eaton lying wounded up at the house, and Julia installing herself as his nurse.

But she was not bending over him at that time, for no sooner had the last of the party gone, than Crellock said something fiercely to Hallam.

"No, no, never mind," the latter said, savagely.

"I tell you I won't have it," cried Crellock. "Ah, you needn't scowl like that. I'm not afraid of your looks. Will you go and fetch her out?"

"No, I shall not interfere."

"Then I will," cried Crellock, passionately. "I've been played with too long."

"Played with!" cried Hallam. "Look here, Steve, if I put up with the bullying of that officer fellow, don't you think I'm going to let you say and do what—"

He stopped short and literally flinched, as if he expected a blow, for Crellock turned upon him sharply, but merely looked him full in the face.

"Well, I—that is—I—"

He faltered and stopped. The old days of his domination had gone by; Crellock had ceased to be slave to the self-indulgent man, who had become servant, first to the strong drinks in which he indulged, and then, as his nerve failed, the obedient tool of him who had once trembled before him, worshipped him almost as the very perfection of what a man should be, and now made him tremble before him in his turn.

"Do you want to quarrel and get rid of me?" said Crellock, sharply.

"Don't talk like that, my lad," said Hallam, piteously. "You know how my health's going, and how nervous I am. It makes me irritable when you are so unreasonable."

"Yes, very unreasonable to bear what I do," snarled Crellock. "But reasonable or no, I'm not going to back out of it, and I am not going to let you."

Hallam's flushed face turned of a sodden white.

"I'd just as soon be back with the gang," continued Crellock, "as be trifled with in this way by a man who used to be one to say a thing and do it. Now he's becoming a miserable, feeble driveller, afraid of every one who speaks to him."

"So were you just now, when that Otway gave his orders."

"Force of habit," said Crellock, with a grim smile. "Anyhow, I'm not afraid of you, and if you have not strength of mind enough to carry out what I say, I shall do it without you."

"No, no, Steve; you are so hasty," said Hallam, in a feeble, whimpering tone.

"Hasty!"

"Well, as I keep telling you, there's plenty of time."

"And I keep telling you there is not. Look here, Hallam. I'm not blind. That miserable parson wants her."

"Now you are getting ridiculous."

"And this officer fellow will be making such way with her, if I don't mind, that I shall have no chance."

"You're frightening yourself with bogies, Steve."

"You're playing such a double game, Robert Hallam, that either I shall have to take the reins in my own hands, or we shall come to a breakdown."

"Nonsense! What's the use of talking like that?"

"What's the use of a man setting his mind upon something, and then letting a weak thing like you play with him? I'll have no more of it. Now you have to do as I say or break, and that means—"

"Hush, Steve!" cried Hallam, looking sharply round; but Crellock paid no heed to his words, and swung out of the study to walk straight into the room where Julia was kneeling by Eaton, with Thisbe on the other side.

"Come here, Julia," he said roughly; "I want you."

"Hush! Not so loud," she whispered, raising her hand.

"Come here!" he cried, with a stamp of the foot, "at once."

Julia started to her feet with an angry look flashing from her eyes; and as she faced him, her countenance full of resentment, Thisbe rose, thinking of her mistress in bygone days.

"What do you want?" she said firmly.

"Your father wants you in the study at once."

Julia flushed slightly, and glanced at Thisbe, whose face looked as hard as if cut in stone, while the resemblance was increased by the position of her eyelids, which were drawn down, as if to veil the anger that was burning in her breast.

Then, without a word Julia left the room, closely followed by Crellock, and Thisbe was left with the wounded man alone.

Volume Four—Chapter Ten.

In the Night.

Julia escaped the interview that she dreaded; for, just as they entered the hall, there was the thudding of horses' feet coming over the road, and Hallam came out of his room with a curious startled look in his face, to catch Crellock by the arm.

"There's something wrong, Steve," he whispered hoarsely; "a stranger coming up, and the Captain with him."

"Bah! You shivering coward," said Crellock, with a look of contempt which made Julia bite her lip, though she could not hear the words. "You have drunk bad brandy till you see a warder in every man who comes to the house. Have a little pluck in you, if you can."

The door was opened directly without ceremony by Captain Otway, who held it back for his companion, who had just dismounted, to enter.

"Sorry to intrude so unceremoniously, Miss Hallam," said the Captain, ignoring the presence of the two men, "but I met my friend here coming up, Mr Woodhouse, our doctor."

Julia bowed, and the doctor, a little, rubicund-looking man, took off his cap.

"I'm a bit of a vulture in my way," he said pleasantly. "I always mount and come out to see whenever anything of this kind goes on. Which room, please?" he added quickly. "I want to get back."

Julia hastily opened the door, and was about to follow them, but the doctor said quietly:

"No, no. You shall hear how he is afterwards."

Julia coloured, for the visitor spoke in a very meaning tone; and, leaving the hall, she hurried to her mother's side, while Hallam angrily backed into his room, followed by Crellock.

"They treat me as if I were nobody," he cried, grinding his teeth; and then going to a cupboard he took out a bottle and glass, poured out some liquid and drank it off with a sigh of relief.

"Yes," said Crellock slowly; "they don't forget about our past, old fellow. Never mind. No, thank you: I promised Julie to leave the stuff alone;" and he thrust back the offered glass.

"You promised her that?" said Hallam.

"Yes, and I'm going to keep my word. Hang it, Bob Hallam, I wouldn't drink myself into such a wreck as you're getting to be for the whole world."

The spirit was rapidly giving Hallam temporary confidence, and he turned upon his companion sharply.

"Don't speak to me like that," he said, "or you'll regret it."

"Don't speak to you like that?" retorted Crellock, scornfully. "Bah! I shall speak as I please. Look here, Robert Hallam, some of us must be masters, some servants. You've made yourself servant, so keep your place. I'm not going to be turned out of my purpose by a little Dutch courage."

Hallam came at him furiously, but Crellock took him by the shoulders and thrust him back into his chair, and then stood over him.

"It won't do, old fellow," he said; "the nerve has gone, and the more you drink to get it up, the weaker it grows. Now then, we understand each other, so let's settle this matter quietly, and get it over. No more excuses; no more shuffling. Understand me, I don't mean to wait. What's that?"

It was the voice of Captain Otway summoning some one to come; and Julia, who had been anxiously waiting, hastened down at the same time as Thisbe hurried to the room.

"The doctor wants to give a few instructions," he said. "Eaton is going on all right, but he thinks he had better not be moved to-night, Miss Hallam, so we must beg your hospitality till to-morrow."

"And there is no danger?" said Julia eagerly.

"Not if he is kept quiet," said the doctor, putting on his gloves. "Let him sleep all he can. Some one ought to sit up with him to-night."

"I'll do that," said Crellock, who had been standing in the doorway.

Julia started slightly, but Crellock's countenance was quite unmoved.

"That will do," said the doctor. "Come, Otway."

The latter raised his cap, and they left the house.

"I don't much like leaving Eaton with a ticket-of-leave man for nurse," said the Captain, as they descended the hill towards their quarters.

"Oh, he'll be right enough there," replied the doctor chuckling. "The young lady will take care of him. I say, does Phil mean to marry her?"

"I don't know," said Otway shortly. "Let's get on."

They hurried away, and for the next two hours the doctor was busy with the injured people; the convicts being safe in the prison, groaning over their wounds and the ill-success of their attempt.

Julia felt a strange anxiety about their patient, as the night drew near; and her anxiety was increased by the behaviour of Mrs Hallam, who, after keeping her room for some days, declared herself well enough to come down.

Opposition from Thisbe and her child was useless, and she descended to sit with the latter, watching by Eaton's couch, which was made up for him in the dining-room, where he lay apparently insensible to all that was going on around.

It was a strange afternoon and evening, the excitement of the early portion of the day having unnerved every one in the house. The meals were partaken of hastily, and the attention of all was centred on the sleeping man in the dining-room.

Julia, in her anxiety, was for staying with Thisbe and continuing the watch; but Crellock showed that he had not forgotten his promise, and a nameless dread took possession of the girl's breast.

She told herself that it was absurd—that in spite of his roughness there seemed to be something genuine about her father's companion; but, all the same, her dread increased, and it was the more painful, that she did not dare to communicate it to Mrs Hallam.

In fact, she was at a loss to explain her reasons for feeling alarmed to herself. Eaton seemed to be sleeping comfortably, and Crellock, when he came into the room, was gentle and respectful, more than was his wont.

"You two had better go to bed," said Hallam at last roughly; and, pale and troubled looking, Mrs Hallam rose without a word, took Julia's hand, and they left the room, but not to sleep; while Crellock's watch began by his taking a candle, snuffing it, and holding it down close to Eaton's face, scanning his features well before setting it on the chimney-piece, lighting a cigar, and going out into the verandah, to walk up and down, thinking deeply.

Sometimes he stopped to lean his arms on the wooden rail, and stare up at the great mellow stars that burned in the deep purple sky; but only to start as from a dream, to go back into the room, and see if the wounded man had moved.

When in the verandah he ground his teeth and clenched his hands.

"The fools!" he muttered; "they might have hit a little harder, and then— Pooh! what does he matter?"

At the end of an hour he stole back softly into the room to look at the sleeping man again.

"He's not much hurt," he muttered. "Who's there?"

"Only me," said Hallam, in a hoarse whisper. "Just coming to see how you were getting on."

"No, you were not. You were watching me," said Crellock, in an angry whisper. "Did you think I was going to kill him—to get him out of the way?"

"No, no. Nothing of the kind, my dear boy," whispered Hallam. "There, I'll go back to my room."

"You'll go up to bed," said Crellock firmly. "You've been drinking too much."

"Indeed, no. Just a little to steady me."

"You go up to bed," said Crellock, taking him by the shoulder. "I'm not going to have my dear father-in-law elect drive himself mad with brandy. Come, no nonsense! Bed!"

Hallam made a few feeble protests, and then suffered himself to be led up to his bedroom, Julia and Mrs Hallam sitting trembling in the next, and watching the light flash beneath their door, as they listened to the ascending and descending steps, followed by a rustling in Hallam's room, the low angry muttering he indulged in, and then there was silence once again.

A quarter of an hour passed, and they were listening to the heavy, stertorous breathing, when a soft tap came at their door, the handle was turned, and Thisbe appeared.

"I only came to see if you were both quite safe," she said. "I could not sleep."

"Dear old Thisbe," said Julia, kissing her.

"Do, do, please go to bed, my dears," said Thisbe. "I'll sit and watch by you;" and at last, in obedience to her prayer, mother and daughter lay down, but not to sleep, for the dread of some impending calamity that they fancied was about to befall them.

Meanwhile Crellock had returned to the dining-room and examined the wounded man again.

"It wouldn't be hard," he said to himself, with a laugh. "He is half killed, so it would only be half a murder. Why shouldn't I? He would be out of his misery; and that drunken wretch gave me the credit of being about to do it."

He stood gazing down at the sleeping face faintly seen by the candle-light; and then turned away to go out through the glass door, and pace the verandah again.

"I wonder whether that's what they call a temptation," he thought. "It would be very easy, and then—"

He stopped to lean over the rails again, and gaze before him out into the night.

"No," he said softly. "I told the little lass I wouldn't drink again, so as to be more fit to come nigh her, and I don't think I should do to go nigh her if I killed that spark of a fellow so as to be sure of getting a wife. It's curious what a woman can do," he went on musing. "They can make anything of a man— go through fire and water to get her, but it must be fire and water such as she'd be glad to see me go through. A year or so ago I'd got to that state with the prison life and the lash, that I'd have given any soldier or warder a crack on the head and killed him, and felt the happier for doing it. Since I've been nigh her—since that day she hung over me, and gave me water, and wiped the sweat from my face, I've seemed as if I must make myself cleaner about the heart; and I have, all but the drink, and that was his fault, for he was never happy when he wasn't forcing it on one.

"No, my fine fellow," he said with a sigh, "you're safe enough for me. I won't hurt you; and as to her liking you—bah! If she does, I'll soon make her forget that."

He took a cigar from his pocket, and was in the act of placing it between his lips when his gaze became fixed, and he stood staring straight before him.

"Who's there?" he said in a quick, sharp whisper. "I can see you. You there!"

He sprang over the rail, and his hand went by old habit into his pocket in search of a weapon; but the answer that came disarmed him.

"It is I."

"What are you doing here in the middle of the night?" cried Crellock.

"I am watching," said Bayle.

"Yes," cried Crellock wearily. "Me, I suppose. Well, what have you seen? Do you think I was going to finish young Eaton? There—speak out."

"I came up because I could not sleep," said Bayle quietly. "I was anxious about my friends. How is Mr Eaton?"

"Go in and see," said Crellock roughly; and he led the way through the verandah.

Bayle made no reply, but walked straight to the couch, after taking the candle from the chimney-piece, and examined the injured man.

"He is sleeping comfortably and well," he said in a whisper, as he replaced the candle.

"Of course he is," sneered Crellock. "You seem very fond of him." Bayle paid no heed to his manner, but stood as if thinking. "Well, are you going to stop? Have a cigar?"

"I will stay and watch with you if you are tired, and relieve you for an hour or two," said Bayle, at last.

"I'm not tired. You can stop if you like. You won't find me very good company." Bayle walked to the couch again, and stood looking down at the handsome dimly-seen face for a few minutes, while, with an impatient gesture, Crellock walked back into the verandah. At the end of a few minutes Bayle joined him. "You are going to stay then?" said Crellock.

"No," replied Bayle, "I am going home."

"Better stop," sneered Crellock. "He'll be safer if you do. I might do him some mischief."

"No, Stephen Crellock," said Bayle calmly, "I am not afraid of that; bad as you are. Good-night."

Crellock started at the words "Bad as you are," but the friendly sound of the "good-night" checked him.

"Good-night," he said, hoarsely; and he stood watching the dark figure till it disappeared amongst the trees, and then paced the verandah, and sat and smoked till morning.

Volume Four—Chapter Eleven.

The Doctor Gives Way.

The doctor was up there soon after sunrise to find Mrs Hallam and Julia by Eaton's couch, they having come down to take Crellock's place shortly after daybreak.

"Good-morning. How is he?" said the doctor, quickly. "Mrs Hallam, you look ill yourself."

"Nervous excitement. This trouble," said Mrs Hallam, quietly; and she left the room with Julia, after answering a few questions.

The doctor examined the injury to the head, which was sufficiently grave, and then proceeded to re-bandage the shoulder that had been dislocated, watching the young man's face, however, the while.

He felt the strained sinews, pressed on this bone, then on that, causing intense pain, and making his patient wince again and again; but though the muscles of his face twitched, and his lips involuntarily tightened, he did not even moan till, passing one hand beneath his shoulder, the doctor pressed on the bones again, when, with a sharp cry, Eaton drew in his breath.

"Hang it, doctor," he whispered, quickly, "it's like molten lead."

"Ah, I thought that would make you speak, Phil. You confounded young humbug! I saw you were shamming."

"No, no, doctor, not shamming. My head aches frightfully, and I can't move my arm."

"But you could get up and walk down to barracks to breakfast?"

"No, indeed I couldn't, doctor."

"It's a lie, sir. If the enemy were after you, I'll be bound to say you would get up and run."

"By George, I wouldn't!" whispered Eaton.

"Well, get up and have a go at them, my boy."

"Perhaps I might do that," said the young man, with the blood coming in his white face.

"Pretty sort of a soldier, lying here because you've had your shoulder out, and a crack on the head. Why I've seen men behave better after a bullet wound, or a bayonet thrust."

"But there is no need for me to behave better, as you call it, and one gets well so much more quickly lying still."

"With a couple of women paddling about you, and making you gruel and sop. There, get up, and I'll make you a sling for that arm."

"No, no, doctor. Pray, don't."

"Get up, sir."

"Hush! Don't speak so loudly," whispered Eaton.

"Ah-h-h! I see," said the doctor, "that's it, is it? Why how dense I am! Want to stop a few days, and be nursed, eh?"

Eaton nodded.

"Fair face to sympathise. White hands to feed you with a spoon. Oh, I say, Phil Eaton! No, no! I've got my duty to do, and I'm not going to back up this bit of deceit."

"I wouldn't ask you if there was anything to call for me, doctor," pleaded Eaton; "but I am hurt, there's no sham about that."

"Well, no; you are hurt, my lad. That's a nasty crack on the head, and your shoulder must be sore."

"Sore!" said Eaton. "You've made it agonising."

"Well, well, a few days' holiday will do you good. But no; I'm not going to be dragged up here to see you."

"I don't want to see you, doctor. I'm sure I shall get well without your help. Pray don't have me fetched down."

"I say, Phil," said the doctor; "look me in the face."

"Yes."

"Is it serious? You know—with her."

"Very, doctor."

"But it's awkward. The young lady's father!"

"Miss Hallam is not answerable for her father's sins," said Eaton warmly.

"But the young lady—does she accept?"

Eaton shook his head.

"Not yet," he said; "and now that the opportunity serves to clinch the matter you want to get me away. Doctor, for once—be human."

Doctor Woodhouse sat with his chubby face pursed up for a few minutes, gazing down in the young man's imploring countenance without speaking.

"Well, well," he said, "I was a boy myself once, and horribly in love. I'll give you a week, Phil."

"And I'll give you a life's gratitude," cried the young man joyfully.

"Why, by all that's wonderful," cried the doctor, with mock surprise, "I've cured him on the spot! Here, let me take off your bandages, so that you may get up and dance. Eh? Poor lad, he is a good deal hurt though," he continued, as he saw the colour fade from the young man's face, and the cold dew begin to form. "A few days will do him good, I believe. He is, honestly, a little too bad to move."

He bathed his face, and moistened his lips with a few drops of liquid from a flask, and in a few minutes Eaton looked wonderingly round.

"Easier, boy? That's it. Yes, you may stay, and you had better be quiet. Feel so sick now?"

"Not quite, doctor. Oh! I am so glad I really am ill."

The doctor smiled, and summoned Mrs Hallam, who came in with Julia.

"I must ask you to play hostess to my young friend here. He shan't die on your hands."

Julia turned pale, and glanced from one to the other quickly.

"Mr Eaton shall have every attention we can give him," said Mrs Hallam, smiling; and the doctor looked with surprise at the way her pale, careworn face lit up with tenderness and sympathy as she laid her hand upon the young man's brow.

"I'm sure he will," said the doctor, "and I'll do my best," he added, with a quick look at his patient, "to get him off your hands, for he will be a deal of trouble."

"It will be a pleasure," said Mrs Hallam, speaking in all sincerity. "English women are always ready to nurse the wounded," she added with a smile.

"I wish I could always have such hands to attend my injured men, madam," said the doctor with formal politeness. "There, I must go at once. Good-bye, Eaton, my boy. You'll soon be on your legs. Don't spoil him, ladies; he is not bad. I leave him to you, Mrs Hallam."

She followed the doctor to the door to ask him if he had any directions, received his orders, and then, with a bright, hopeful light in her eyes, she went softly back towards the dining-room. A smile began to glisten about her lips, like sunshine in winter, as she laid her hand upon the door. Then she looked round sharply, for in the midst of that dawning hope of safety for her child there was a heavy step, and the study-door opened.

She turned deadly pale, for it was Stephen Crellock's step; and the words that came from the study were in her husband's voice.

Volume Four—Chapter Twelve.

Mrs Otway on Love.

"Ah! Phil, Phil, Phil!" exclaimed Mrs Otway as she sat facing Eaton some mornings later, while he lay back in a Chinese cane chair, propped up by pillows. "Come, this will not do."

He met her gaze firmly, and she went on.

"This makes five days that you have been here, tangling yourself more and more in the net. It's time I took you by the ears and lugged you out."

"But you will not?" he said, lifting his injured arm very gently with his right hand, sighing as he did so, and rearranging the sling.

Mrs Otway jumped up, went behind him, untied the handkerchief that formed the sling, and snatched it away.

"I won't sit still and see you play at sham in that disgraceful way, Phil," she cried. "It's bad enough, staying here as you do, without all that nonsense."

"You are too hard on me."

"I'm not," she cried. "I've seen too many wounded men not to know something about symptoms. I knew as well as could be when I was here yesterday, but I would not trust myself, and so I attacked Woodhouse about you last night, and he surrendered at once."

"Why, what did he say?"

"Lit a cigar, and began humming, 'Oh, 'tis love, 'tis love that makes the world go round!'"

Eaton clapped his hands upon the arms of his chair, half raised himself, and then threw himself back, and began beating the cane-work with his fingers, frowning with vexation.

"There, you see what a lot of practice it takes to make a good impostor," said Mrs Otway.

"What do you mean?"

"How bad your arm seems!"

"Pish!" exclaimed the young man, beginning to nurse it, then ceasing with a gesture of contempt, and looking helplessly at his visitor. "The pain's not there," he said dolefully.

"Poor boy! What a fuss about a pretty face! There, I'm half ready to forgive you. It was very tempting."

"And I've been so happy: I have indeed."

"What, with those two men?"

"Pish!—nonsense! It's dreadful that those two sweet ladies should be placed as they are."

"Amen to that!"

"Mrs Hallam is the sweetest, tenderest-hearted woman I ever met."

"Indeed."

"No mother could have been more gentle and loving to me."

"Except Lady Eaton," said Mrs Otway dryly.

"Oh! my mother, of course; but then she was not here to nurse me."

"I'd have nursed you, Phil, if you had been brought into quarters."

"Oh, I know that!" cried Eaton warmly; "but, you see, I was brought on here."

"Where mamma is so tender to you, and mademoiselle sits gazing at you with her soft, dark eyes, thinking what a brave hero you are, how terribly ill, and falling head-over-ears more in love with you. Phil, Phil, it isn't honest."

"What isn't honest?" he said fiercely. "No man could have resisted such a temptation."

"What, to come here and break a gentle girl's heart?"

"But I'm not breaking her heart," said Eaton ruefully.

"I've written and told your mother how things stand."

"You have?"

"Yes; and that you have taken the bit in your teeth, and that I can't hold you in."

"Well, it doesn't matter," said Eaton gloomily. "I don't want to hurt my dear mother's feelings; but when she knows Julia and Mrs Hallam—"

"And the convict father and his friend."

"For Heaven's sake don't!" cried Eaton, striking the chair and wincing hard, for he hurt his injured shoulder.

"I must, my dear boy. Marriage is a terrible fact, and you must look at it on all sides."

"I mean to get them both away from here," said Eaton firmly. "Their present life is horrible."

"Yes; it is, my boy."

"My gorge rises every time I hear that drinking scoundrel of a father speak to Julia, and that other ruffian come and fetch her away."

"Not a very nice way of speaking about the father of your intended," said Mrs Otway dryly—"about your host."

"No, and I would not speak so if I did not see so much. The man has served part of his time for his old crime, of which he swears he was innocent, and I'd forget all the past if I saw he was trying to do the right thing."

"And he is not?"

"He's lost," said Eaton bitterly. "The greatest blessing which could happen to this house would be for him to be thrown back into the gang. He'd live a few years then, and so would his wife. As it is he is killing both. As for poor Julia—ah! I should be less than man, loving her as I do, if I did not determine to throw all thoughts of caste aside and marry her, and get her away as soon as I can."

"I wish she were not so nice," said Mrs Otway thoughtfully.

"Why?"

"Because, like the silly, stupid woman I am, I can't help sympathising with you both."

"I knew you did in your heart," cried Eaton joyfully.

"Gently, gently, my dear boy," continued Mrs Otway. "I may sympathise with the enemy, but I have to fight him all the same. Have you spoken to the young lady—definitely offered marriage?"

"No, not yet."

"But you've taught her to love you?"

"I don't know—yet—"

"Judging from appearances, Phil, I'm ready to say I do know. What about mamma?"

"Ah! there I feel quite satisfied."

"What, have you spoken to her?"

"No, but she sits and talks to me, and I talk to her."

"About Julia?"

"Yes; and it seems as if she can read my heart through and through. Don't think me a vain coxcomb for what I am about to say."

"I make no promises: say it."

"I think she likes me very much."

"Why?"

"She comes into the room sometimes, looking a careworn woman of sixty; and when she has been sitting here for a few minutes, there's a pleasant smile on her face, as if she were growing younger; her eyes light up, and she seems quite at rest and happy."

"Poor thing!" said Mrs Otway sadly. "But, there, I can't listen to any more. I am on your mother's side."

"And you are beaten, so you may give up. It's fate. My mother must put up with it. So long as I am happy she will not care. And, besides, who could help loving Julie? Hush!"

There was a tap at the door, and Julia entered.

"Not I, for one," said Mrs Otway aside, as she rose and held out her hands, kissing the young girl warmly. "Why, my dear, you look quite pale. This poor bruised boy has been worrying you and your mother to death."

"Indeed, no," cried Julia eagerly. "Mr Eaton has been so patient all the time, and we were so glad to be able to be of service. Sir Gordon Bourne is in the other room with mamma. May he come in and see you?"

"I shall be very glad," said Eaton, looking at her fixedly; and Mrs Otway noted the blush and the downcast look that followed.

"Phil's right. He has won her."

"He proposes driving you home with him, and taking you out in his boat. He thinks it will help your recovery."

"Oh no, I couldn't move yet," said Eaton quickly.

"I think it would do you good," said Mrs Otway. "What do you say, Miss Hallam?"

"We should be very sorry to see Mr Eaton go," said Julia quietly; "but I think you are right."

"Phil's wrong," said Mrs Otway to herself.

At this moment Sir Gordon entered the room with Mrs Hallam and proposed that Eaton should return with him, but only to find, to his annoyance, that the offer was declined.

"You will have to make the offer to my husband, Sir Gordon," said Mrs Otway merrily. "You will not find him so ungrateful." And then she turned to Eaton, leaving the old man free to continue a conversation begun with Mrs Hallam in another room.

"I do not seem to find much success in my offers," he said, in a low voice; "but let me repeat what I have said. Should necessity arise, remember that I am your very oldest friend, and that I am always waiting to help Millicent Hallam and her child."

"I shall not forget," said Mrs Hallam, smiling sadly.

"If I am away, there is Bayle ready to act for me, and you know you can command him."

"I have always been the debtor of my friends," replied Mrs Hallam; "but no such emergency is likely to arise. I have learnt the lesson of self-dependence lately, Sir Gordon."

"But if the emergency did occur?"

"Then we would see," replied Mrs Hallam.

"Well, Philip, my dear boy," cried Mrs Otway loudly, "in three days we shall have you back."

"Yes, in three days," he replied, glancing at Julia, who must have heard, but who went on with a conversation in which she was engaged with Sir Gordon, unmoved.

"Then good-bye," she cried, "Mrs Hallam, Miss Hallam, accept my thanks for your kindness to my boy here. Lady Eaton appointed me her deputy, but I'm tired of my sorry task. Good-bye. Are we to be companions back, Sir Gordon?"

"Yes—yes—yes," said the old gentleman, "I am coming. Remember," he said, in a low tone to Mrs Hallam.

"I never forget such kindness as yours, Sir Gordon," she replied.

"Good-bye, Julia, my child," he said, kissing her hands. "If ever you want help of any kind, come straight to me. Good-bye."

"If she would only make some appeal to me," he muttered. "But I can't interfere without. Poor things! Poor things!"

"*I* beg your pardon, Sir Gordon," said Mrs Otway. "What are poor things?"

"Talking to myself, ma'am—talking to myself."

"You don't like Philip Eaton," she said quickly.

"Eh? Well, to be frank, ma'am, no: I don't."

"Because he likes your little *protégée*?"

"I'm sorry to say, madam, that she is not my *protégée*. Poor child!"

"Hadn't we better be frank, Sir Gordon? Suppose Philip Eaton wanted to marry her—what then?"

"Confound him! I should like to hand him over to the blacks!"

"What if she loved him?"

"If she loved him—if she loved him, Mrs Otway?" said the old man dreamily. "Why, then—dear me! This love's one of the greatest miseries of life. But, there, ma'am, I have no influence at all. You must *go* to her father, not come to me."

Volume Four—Chapter Thirteen.

In the Toils.

"So he goes to-day, eh?" said Crellock.

"Yes; I've seen him, and he's going to-day."

"Lucky for him, for I've got into a state of mind that does not promise much good for any one who stands in my way," said Crellock, with an unpleasant look in his eyes. "And now, mind this: as soon as he is gone, and we are alone, the matter is to be pressed home. Here, I'll be off. I don't want to say good-bye." He picked up his whip and stepped out into the verandah, walking along past the dining-room window, which was open, and through it came the voice of Julia in measured cadence, reading aloud.

Crellock ground his teeth and half stopped; but he gave his whip a sharp crack and went on.

"A row would only frighten her, and I don't want to *do* that. The coast will be clear this afternoon."

He went on round to the stable, saddled and mounted his horse, and turned off by the first track for the open country.

"A good ride will calm me down," he said; and he went off at a gallop for a few miles, but with his head down, seeing neither green tree with its tints of pearly grey and pink, nor the curious tufts of grass in his path. A mob of kangaroos started before him and went off with their peculiar bounds; flock after flock of parrots, with colours bright as the most gorgeous sunset, flew screaming away; and twice over he passed spear-armed blacks, who ceased their task of hunting for grubs to stare at the man riding so recklessly through the bush.

All at once he dragged his horse back upon its haunches with a furious tug at the reins, and sat staring before him as in imagination he pictured a scene in the dining-room at the Gully House.

"I'm a fool," he cried savagely; "a fool! I've got the fruit ready to my hand, and I'm getting out of the way so as to let some one else pluck it. Now perhaps I shall be too late."

Dragging his horse's head round, he set spurs to its flanks, and in the same reckless manner began to gallop back. This time he was less fortunate, though. As he went he left the horse to itself, and the careful beast avoided rough parts or leaped them, carrying his rider in safety. On the return Crellock was bent upon one thing only, getting back to the Gully House at the earliest moment possible. Twice over the horse swerved at an awkward depression or piece of rock, either of them sufficient to bring both to grief, but for reward there was a savage jerk at the bit, a blow over the head from the heavy whip, and a dig from the spurs. The result was that the poor brute went on as the crow flies at a hard gallop, rushed at an awkward clump of bush, rose, caught its hoofs, and fell with a crash, sending Crellock right over its head to lie for a few minutes half-stunned, and when he did gather himself up, with the scene seeming to sail round him, the horse was standing with its head hanging, snuffing at the coarse herbage, and stamping angrily with its off hind hoof.

"You awkward brute!" cried Crellock, catching at the rein, and then lashing the poor animal across the flank.

The horse started to the full length of the rein, but only on three legs; one had had a terrible sprain.

"My luck!" said Crellock savagely, and, taking off the bridle, he hobbled the horse's legs, and started off to walk.

Julia went on reading, with Philip Eaton drinking in every word she uttered, and at last, leaning forward from the couch upon which he lay, he felt that the time had come, and, no matter who and what her relatives might be, here was the wife of his choice.

"Julia," he said in a low voice made husky with the emotion from which he suffered.

She raised her eyes from the book and coloured, for it was the first time he had called her by her Christian name.

"Have you thought," he said, "that I am going to-morrow?"

"I thought it was to-day," she said naïvely.

"To-day? Yes, I suppose it is to-day, but I cannot think of anything but the one great fact that all this pleasant intercourse is to be at an end."

Julia half rose.

"No, no," he cried, trying to reach her hand, and then uttering a petulant ejaculation, for Mrs Hallam entered the room, looked eagerly from one to the other, and came forward, while Julia gave her a beseeching look, and went out.

For a few minutes neither spoke, and then Eaton placed a chair for Mrs Hallam, and as she took it gazing at him searchingly, he hastily thought over what he should say, and ended by saying something else, for in a quick, blundering way, he cried:

"Mrs Hallam, I cannot say what I wish. You know how I love her."

Mrs Hallam drew a long sighing breath, full of relief, and her eyes became suffused with tears.

"Yes," she said at last; "I felt that you did love her. Have you told Julie so?"

"Not in words," he cried. "She disarms me. I want to say so much, but I can only sit and look. But you will give your consent?"

"Have you thought all this over?" said Mrs Hallam gravely. "You know everything—why we came here?"

"Yes, yes," he cried quickly. "I know all. I have known it from your first landing."

"Such a union would not be suitable for you," she said gravely.

"Not suitable! Mrs Hallam, I am not worthy of your child. But you are playing with me," he cried, his words coming fast now. "You will not oppose it. You see I know all. Give me your consent."

She sat looking at him in silence for some moments, and then laid her hand in his.

"Yes," she said. "If Julie loves you I will not withhold my consent."

"And Mr Hallam, may I speak to him now? Of course he will not refuse me. You will tell him first. And Julia, where is she?"

In his eagerness his words came hurriedly, and he caught Mrs Hallam's hands to his lips and kissed them.

"I will fetch Julie here," she said gently, and with a strange look of repose coming over her troubled face.

She left the room and sought her child, who looked at her wonderingly.

"Come," she said with her voice sounding broken and strange; "Mr Eaton wishes to speak to you."

"Mother!" exclaimed Julia, shrinking.

At that moment they heard Hallam's steps as he passed across the hall.

Mrs Hallam's countenance changed, and she shuddered.

"Come," she said; "you are not afraid of him?"

"Of Mr Eaton? Oh, no," cried Julia with animation; "but—"

"Hush, my child! I will not leave you. Hear what he has to say before you speak."

Julia's eyes seemed to contract, and there was a shrinking movement, but directly after she drew herself up proudly, laid her hand in her mother's, and suffered herself to be led into the room.

"At last!" cried Eaton, flushing with pleasure. "Julie, I dare speak to you now. I love you with all my heart."

He stopped short, for the window was darkened by the figure of Stephen Crellock, who looked in for a moment, and then beckoned with his hand to some one in the verandah. Hallam came forward looking flushed and angry, and the two men entered the room.

"We are just in time," said Crellock with a half laugh, but with a savage flash of the eye at Eaton. "Mr Lieutenant Eaton is bidding the ladies good-bye."

Eaton gave him an indignant look, and turned to Hallam.

"Mr Hallam," he said proudly, "Mr Crellock is wrong. I have been speaking to Mrs Hallam and—"

"Mr Crellock is right," said Crellock in a voice of thunder, "and Mr Eaton is wrong. He is saying good-bye; and now, Robert Hallam, will you tell him why?"

"Yes," said Hallam firmly; "Mr Eaton should have spoken to me, and I would have explained at once that Mr Stephen Crellock has proposed for my daughter's hand, and I have promised that she shall be his wife."

"But this is monstrous!" cried Eaton furiously. "Julie, I have your mother's consent. You will be mine?"

Julia looked at him pityingly and shook her head.

"Speak! for heaven's sake, speak!" cried Eaton.

"No," she said in a low pained voice. "You have mistaken me, Mr Eaton. I could never be your wife."

Eaton turned to Mrs Hallam to meet her agonised, despairing eyes, and then without a word he left the room.

For the blow had fallen; the shadow Millicent Hallam had seen athwart her daughter's life had assumed consistency, and as the thought of her own fate came with its dull despairing pain, she caught Julia to her breast to protect her from Crellock, and faced him like some wild creature standing at bay in defence of her young.

Volume Four—Chapter Fourteen.

For Julie.

"Where are you going?" said Crellock roughly, as prowling about the verandah, in pursuance of a determination to take care that there should be no further interference with his plans, he carefully watched the place, ready to refuse entrance, in Hallam's name, to every one who came till he had made sure of his prize.

It was very early in the morning, and he had come suddenly upon Thisbe, dressed for going out, and with a bundle under her arm.

"Into town," she said sharply.

"What for?"

"To stay."

"It's a lie!" he said. "You are going to take a message to that parson, or the lieutenant. You have a letter."

"No, I haven't," said Thisbe, looking harder than ever.

"What's in that bundle?"

"Clothes. Want to see 'em? You can look."

"Come, no nonsense, Thisbe! You don't like me, I know."

"I hate the sight of you!" said the woman stoutly. "So you may; but look here, you may as well understand that in future I shall be master here, and for your own sake you had better be friends. Now then, where are you going?"

"Into town, I tell you; and I shall send for my box. It's corded up in my room."

"Why, what do you mean?" he said.

"That I'm going, and I'm not coming back; and you two may drink yourselves to death as soon as you like."

She brushed by him, and before he had recovered from his surprise, she was going down the path towards the gate.

A thought struck Crellock, and he ran upstairs to the room Thisbe had occupied, and, sure enough, there was the big chest she had brought with her, corded up tightly, and with a direction-card tacked on, addressed, "Miss Thisbe King. To be called for."

"So much the better," he said joyously; "that woman had some influence with Mrs Hallam, and might have been unpleasant."

That day he went down the town to one of his haunts, and after a good deal of search found out that Thisbe was in the place, and had taken a small cottage in one of the outskirts. So, satisfied with his discovery, he returned, to find a man with a pony and dray on his way up to the house, where he claimed the box for its owner, and soon after bore it away.

Hallam was in his room, half dozing by the open window, ready to give him a friendly nod as he entered, threw down his riding-whip, and took up his usual position, with his back to the fireplace.

"Well," said Hallam, "what news?"

"Oh, she has gone, sure enough."

"So much the better," said Hallam. "I always hated that woman."

"What news have you?"

"None at all."

"Have you told your wife that I wish the marriage to take place at once?"

"No."

"Then go and tell her."

Hallam shifted uneasily in his chair, but did not stir. "Look here!" cried Crellock fiercely, "do you want me to go through all our old arguments again? There it is—the marriage or the gang."

"You would have to go too!" said Hallam angrily.

"Oh, no! Don't make a mistake. I did not bring over the plunder; and not a single note you have changed can be brought home to me. Your leg is in the noose, or in the irons again, if you like it better. No nonsense! Go and see her while I prepare Julia." Hallam rose, went to the cupboard, poured a quantity of brandy into a tumbler, gulped it down, and went to the drawing-room. Mrs Hallam, who was looking white and hollow of cheek, was seated alone, with Julia, half-way down the garden slope, gazing pensively towards the town.

Mrs Hallam rose quickly, as if in alarm, but Hallam caught her hand, and then softly closed the window, in spite of her weak struggle, as she saw Crellock crossing the garden to where Julia was standing.

"Now, no nonsense!" he said. "There, sit down."

Mrs Hallam took the chair he led her to, and gazed up at him as if fascinated by his eyes.

"I may as well come to the point at once," said Hallam. "You know what I said the other night about Crellock?"

"Yes," she replied hoarsely.

"Well, he wishes it to take place at once, so we may as well get it over."

"It is impossible!"

"It is not impossible!" he said, flashing into anger. "It is necessary for my comfort and position that the wedding should take place at once."

"No, no, Robert!" she cried in a last appeal; "for the sake of our old love, give up this terrible thought. If you have any love left for me spare our child this degradation!"

She threw herself upon her knees and clasped his hands.

"Don't be foolish and hysterical," he said coldly; "and listen to reason, unless you want to make me angry with you. Get up!"

She obeyed him without a word.

"Now, listen. I shouldn't have chosen Crellock for her husband, but he is very fond of her, and I cannot afford to offend him, so it must be."

"It would kill her!" panted Mrs Hallam. "Our child! Robert—husband—my own love! don't, don't drive me to do this!"

"I'm going to drive you to obey me in this sensible matter, which is for the good of all. There, you see the girl is listening to him quietly enough."

"It would kill her! For the sake of all the old times do not drive me to this— my husband!" pleaded Mrs Hallam again.

"You will prepare her for it; you will tell her it must be as soon as the arrangements can be made; you will stop all communications with Bayle and old Sir Gordon, and do exactly as I bid you. Look here, once let Julia see that there is no other course, and she will be quiet and sensible enough."

"Once more!" cried Mrs Hallam passionately, "spare me this, Robert, and I will be your patient, forgiving wife to the end! I tell you it would break her heart!"

"You understand!" he said. "There, look at her!" he cried, pointing. "Why, the girl loves him after all."

Julia was coming slowly up the path, with Crellock bending down and talking to her earnestly, till he reached the window, which Hallam unfastened, shrinking back and leaving the room, as if he could not face his child.

As Julia entered, Crellock seemed to have no wish to encounter Mrs Hallam, and he drew back and went round the house to the study window, where he stopped leaning on the verandah-rail and gazing in, as Hallam stood at the cupboard, pouring himself out some more brandy.

He had the glass in one hand, the bottle in the other, when he caught sight of the figure at the window, and with a start and cry of horror he dropped bottle and glass.

"Bah! where is your nerve, man?" cried Crellock with a laugh of contempt. "Did you think it was a sergeant with a file of men to fetch you away?"

"You—you startled me," cried Hallam angrily. "All that brandy gone!"

"A good thing too! You've had plenty. Well, have you told her?"

"Yes."

"What did she say?"

"The old thing."

"But you made her understand?"

"Yes. What did Julia say?"

"Oh, very little. Told me she could never love me, of course; but she's a clever, sensible girl."

"And she has consented?"

"Well, not exactly; but it's all right. There will be no trouble there."

Meanwhile Julia had gone straight to her mother and knelt down at her feet, resting her hands upon her knees, in her old child-like position, and gazing up in the pale, wasted face for some minutes without speaking.

"There is no hope, mother," she said at last; "it must be."

Mrs Hallam sat without replying for some minutes; then, taking her child's face between her thin hands she bent down and pressed her lips upon the white forehead.

"Julie," she whispered, "I was wrong. I thought you loved Mr Eaton, and I believed that if you married him it would have cut this terrible knot."

Julia smiled softly, and with her eyes half closed. There was a curious, rapt expression in her sweet face, as if she were dreaming of some impossible joy. Then, as if rousing herself to action, she gave her dark curls a shake, and said quietly:

"If I had loved Mr Eaton it would only have cut the knot as far as I was concerned. Mother, he would have broken my heart."

"No, no; he loved you dearly."

"But he would have taken me from you. No: I did not love him, but I liked him very much. But there, we must think and be strong, for there is no hope, dear mother, now. You are right. And you will be firm and strong?"

"Yes," said Mrs Hallam, rising. "For your sake, my child—my child!"

Volume Four—Chapter Fifteen.

Crellock on Guard.

That night, after the roughly-prepared meal that topic the place of dinner, and at which mother and daughter resumed their places as of old, Hallam sat for some time with Crellock talking in a low tone, while Mrs Hallam returned to the drawing-room with Julia, both looking perfectly calm and resigned to their fate.

At last Hallam rose, and followed by Crellock, crossed the hall and opened the drawing-room door, where his wife and child were seated with the light of the candles shining softly upon their bended heads.

"It will be all right," he muttered; and he turned round and faced Crellock, who smiled and nodded.

"Nothing like a little firmness," he said, smiling.

Then Crellock went into the verandah to smoke his cigar and play the part of watch-dog in case of some interruption to his plans; and, while Hallam employed himself in his old fashion, drinking himself drunk in the house of Alcohol his god, the dark calm evening became black night, and a moist, soft wind from the Pacific sighed gently among the trees.

Crellock walked round the house time after time, peering in at the windows, and each time he looked there was the heavy stolid face of Hallam staring before him at vacancy; on the other side of the house Julia gazing up into her mother's face as she knelt at her feet.

It must have been ten o'clock when, as Crellock once more made his round, he saw that Hallam was asleep, and that Mrs Hallam had taken up the candle still burning, and with Julia holding her hand, was looking round the room as if for a last good-night.

Then together they went to the door, hand in hand; the door closed; the light shone at the staircase window, then in their bedroom, where he watched it burn for about a quarter of an hour before it was extinguished, and all was dark.

"I shan't feel satisfied till I have her safe," he said, as he walked slowly back to his old look-out that commanded the road.

The wind came in stronger gusts now, for a few minutes, and then seemed to die quite away, while the clouds that overspread the sky grew so dense that it was hard to distinguish the trees and bushes a dozen yards from where he stood.

He finished his cigar, thinking out his plans the while, and at last coming to the conclusion that it was an unnecessary task this watching, he was about to make one more turn round the verandah, and then enter by the window and go to bed, when he fancied he heard a door close, as if blown by the wind that was once more sighing about the place.

"Just woke up, I suppose," he said, and he walked towards the study window and looked in.

Hallam had not moved, but was sleeping heavily in his old position.

Crellock listened again, but all was perfectly still. It could not have been fancy. Certainly he had heard a door bang softly, and the sound seemed to come from this direction.

He stood thinking, and then went round and tried the front door.

"Fast."

He walked round to the back door, following the verandah all the way, and found that door also fast.

"I couldn't have been mistaken," he said, as he listened again.

Once more the wind was sighing loudly about the place, but the noise was not repeated, and he walked on to the dining-room window; but as he laid his hand upon the glass door and thrust it open, a current of air rushed in, and there was the same sound: a door blew to with a slight bang.

Crellock closed and fastened the glass door as he stepped out and ran quickly round to the drawing-room, where it was as he suspected: the glass door similar to that he had just left was open, and blew to and fro.

"There's something wrong," he said excitedly, his suspicions being aroused; and, dashing in, he upset a chair in crossing the room, and it fell with a crash, but he hurried on into the hall, through to the study, and caught Hallam by the arm.

"Wake up!" he said excitedly. "Hallam! Wake up, man."

He had to shake him heavily before the drink stupefaction passed off, and then Hallam stood trembling and haggard, trying to comprehend his companion's words.

"Wrong?" he said. "Wrong? What's wrong?"

"I don't know yet. Look sharp! Run up to your wife's room. Take the candle. Quick, man; are you asleep?"

In his dazed state Hallam staggered, and his hand trembled so that he could hardly keep the light anything like steady. There was the knowledge, though faintly grasped, that something was terribly wrong. He gathered that from his companion's excited manner, and, stumbling on into the hall, blundered noisily up the stairs while Crellock stood breathing hard and listening.

"Here, Millicent! Julie!" he cried hoarsely; "what's the matter?"

Crellock heard the lock handle turn, and the door thrown open so violently that it struck against the wall, but there was no reply from the voices of frightened women.

"Do you hear? Milly—Julie! Why don't you answer?" came from above, and Crellock's harsh breathing became like the panting of some wild beast.

For a few moments there was absolute silence; then the sound of stumbling, heavy steps, and Hallam came out on to the landing.

"Steve!" he cried excitedly, perfectly sober now, "what is it? What does it mean? They've gone!"

"I knew it," cried Crellock with a furious cry. "I might have seen it if I had not been a fool. Come down quick! They've not gone far."

Candle in hand, Hallam came staggering down the stairs with his eyes staring and his face blotched with patches of white.

"They've gone," he stammered hoarsely. "What for? Where have they gone?"

"Out into the dark night," cried Crellock furiously. "There is only one way that they could go, and we must have them before they reach the town."

"Town!" faltered Hallam; "town!" for in the horror of his waking and the conscience hauntings of the moment, he seemed to see two ghastly white faces looking up at him from the black waters of the harbour.

"Yes, come along, follow me as quickly as you can," roared Crellock; and going swiftly through the dining-room he crossed the verandah and dashed out into the thick darkness that seemed to rise up as a protecting wall on behalf of those whom he pursued.

Volume Four—Chapter Sixteen.

The Flight.

"I am so weak, my child," sighed Mrs Hallam, "that my heart fails me. What shall I do?"

Julia stood over her dressed for flight, and a chill of despair seized her.

"Oh, mother, try—try," she whispered.

"I am trying, Julie. I am fighting so hard, but you cannot realise the step I am trying to take; you cannot see it, my child, as it is spread before me."

"Let us stay then," whispered Julie, "and to-morrow I will appeal to Sir Gordon to come to our help."

"No," said Mrs Hallam, firmly, as if the words of her child had given her strength, "we can ask help of no one in such a strait as this, Julie; the act must be mine and mine alone; but now the time has come, my child, I feel that it is too much."

"Mother!" sobbed Julie, "that man horrifies me. You heard all that my father said. I would sooner die than become his wife."

Mrs Hallam caught her arm with a sharp grip, and remained silent for a few moments. "Yes," she said at last, "and much as I love you, my own, I would sooner see you dead than married to such a man as he. You have given me the courage I failed in, my darling. For myself, I would live and bear until the end; but I am driven to it—I am driven to it. Come."

They were standing in the dark, and now for the time being Mrs Hallam seemed transformed. Gathering her cloak about her, she went quickly to the door and listened, and then turned and whispered to Julia.

"Come at once," she said. "Follow me down." Julia drew a long breath and followed her, trembling, the boards of the lightly-built house cracking loudly as she passed quickly to the stairs. And again in the silence and darkness these cracked as they passed down.

In the hall Mrs Hallam hesitated for a moment, and then, putting her lips to Julia's ear:

"Stop!" she whispered.

Julia stood listening, and with her eyes strained towards where a light shone beneath the ill-fitting study-door from which, in the stillness, the heavy stertorous breathing of Hallam could be heard. She could hear, too, the faint rustle of Mrs Hallam's dress as she paced along the hall; and as Julia gazed in the direction she had taken, the light that streamed from beneath, and some faint rays from the side, showed indistinctly a misty figure which sank down on its knees and remained for a few moments.

The silence was awful to the trembling girl, who could not repress a faint cry as she heard a loud cough coming from beyond the dining-room.

But she, too, drew her breath hard, and set her teeth as if the nearness of her enemy provoked her to desperate resistance, and she stood waiting there firmly, but wondering the while whether they would be able to escape or be stopped in the act of flight by Crellock, whom she knew to be watching there.

She dare not call, though she felt that her mother was again overcome by the terrors of the step they had resolved to take, and the moments seemed interminable before there was a change in the light beneath the door, and a faint rustle mingled with the heavy breathing. Then her hand was clasped by one like ice in its coldness, and, as if repeating the prayer she had been uttering, Julia heard her mother say in a faint whisper:

"It is for her sake—for hers alone."

Julia drew her into the drawing-room as they had planned, and closed the door. Then Mrs Hallam seemed to breathe more freely.

"The weakness has passed," she said softly. "We must lose no time."

They crossed the room carefully to where a dim light showed the French window to be, and Mrs Hallam laid her hand upon it firmly, and turned the fastening after slipping the bolt.

"Keep a good heart, my darling," she said. "You are not afraid?"

"Not of our journey, mother," said Julia in agitated tones; "but of—a listener."

"Hist!" whispered Mrs Hallam, drawing back; and the window which she had opened swung to with a faint click, as the firm pace of Crellock was heard coming along the verandah; and as they stood there in the darkness they could see the dim figure pass the window.

Had he stretched forth a hand, he would have felt the glass door yield, and have entered and found them there; and, knowing this, they stood listening to the beating of their hearts till the figure passed on and they heard the step of the self-constituted sentry grow faint on the other side of the house.

"Julie, are you ready?"

"Yes, mother; let us go—anywhere, so that I may not see that man again."

Mrs Hallam uttered a sigh of relief, for her child's words had supplied her once more with the power that was failing.

"It is for her sake," she muttered again. Then, in a low whisper: "Quick! your hand. Come." And they stepped out into the verandah, drew the door to without daring to stop to catch it, and the next minute they were threading their way amongst the trees of the garden, and making for the gate.

The darkness was now intense, and though the faint twinkling of lights showed them the direction of the town, they had not gone far before they found themselves astray from the path, and after wandering here and there for a few minutes, Mrs Hallam paused in dread, for she found that there was now another enemy in her way upon which she had not counted.

She spoke very calmly, though, as Julia uttered a gasp.

"The wind is rising," she said, "and it will soon grow lighter. Let us keep on."

They walked on slowly and cautiously in and out among the trees of what was, in the darkness, a complete wilderness. At times they were struggling through bushes that impeded their progress, and though time after time the track seemed to be found, they were deceived. It was as if Nature were fighting against them to keep them within reach of Hallam and his friend, and, though they toiled on, a second hour had elapsed and found them still astray.

But now, as they climbed a steep slope, the wind came with a gust, the clouds were chased before it, there was the glint of a star or two, and Mrs Hallam uttered an exclamation.

"There!" she cried, "to the left. I can see the lights now."

Catching Julia's hand more firmly, she hurried on, for the night was now comparatively light, but neither uttered a word of their thoughts as they gave a frightened glance back at a dim object on the hill behind, for they awoke to the fact that they had been wandering round and about the hill and gully, returning on their steps, and were not five hundred yards away from their starting-point.

At the end of a quarter of an hour the stars were out over half the vault of heaven, and to their great joy the path was found—the rough track leading over the unoccupied land to the town.

"Courage! my child," whispered Mrs Hallam; "another hour or two and we shall be there."

"I am trying to be brave, dear," whispered back Julia as the track descended into another gully; "but this feeling of dread seems to chill me, and—oh! listen!"

Mrs Hallam stopped, and plainly enough behind them there was the sound of bushes rustling; but the sound ceased directly.

"Some animal—that is all," said Mrs Hallam, and they passed on.

Once more they heard the sound, and then, as they were ascending a little eminence before descending another of the undulations of the land, there came the quick beat of feet, and mother and daughter had joined in a convulsive grasp.

"We are followed," panted Mrs Hallam. "We must hide."

As she spoke they were on the summit of the slope, with their figures against the sky-line to any one below, and in proof of this there was a shout from a short distance below, and a cry of "Stop!"

"Crellock!" muttered Mrs Hallam, and she glanced from side to side for a place of concealment, but only to see that the attempt to hide would be only folly.

"Can you run, Julie?" she whispered.

For answer Julia started off, and for about a hundred yards they ran down the slope, and then stopped, panting. They could make no further effort save that of facing their pursuer, who dashed down to them breathless.

"A pretty foolish trick," he cried. "Mercy I found you gone, and came. What did you expect would become of you out here in the night?"

"Loose my hand," cried Julia angrily; "I will not come back."

"Indeed, but you will, little wifie. There, it's of no use to struggle; you are mine, and must."

"Julia, hold by me," cried Mrs Hallam frantically. "Help!"

"Hah!"

That ejaculation was from Crellock, for as Mrs Hallam's appeal for help rang out amongst the trees of the gully into which they had descended, there was the dull sound of a heavy blow, and their assailant fell with a crash amongst the low growth of scrub.

"This way," said a familiar voice. "Do you want to join Thisbe King?"

"Yes, yes," cried Julia, sobbing now; "but how did you know?"

"How did I know!" was the reply, half sadly, half laughingly. "Oh, I have played the spy: waiting till you wanted help."

"Christie Bayle!" wailed Mrs Hallam; "my friend in need."

He did not answer. He hardly heard her words as Mrs Hallam staggered on by his side, for two little hands were clinging to his arm, Julia's head was resting against him, as she nestled closer and closer, and his heart beat madly, for it seemed to him as if it was in his breast that Julia Hallam would seek for safety in her time of need.

Volume Four—Chapter Seventeen.

In Sanctuary.

"Let them come if they dare, my dear," said Thisbe stoutly. "I've only waited for this. You know how I've never said word against him, but have seen and borne everything."

"Yes, yes," sighed Mrs Hallam.

"For, I said to myself, the day will come when she will see everything in its true light, and then—"

Thisbe said no more, but cut her sentence in half by closing her lips more tightly than they had ever been closed before, as, with a smile, she busied herself about Julia and her mother.

"I was in a way last night," she said cheerily, as she straightened first one thing and then another in the modest lodgings she had secured, "but I daren't come away for fear you might get here while I was looking for you. You don't know the relief I felt when Mr Bayle knocked at the door with you two poor tired things. There, you needn't say a word, only be quiet and rest."

Thisbe nodded from one to the other, and smiled as if there was not a trouble in the world. Then she stood rolling up her apron, and moistening her lips, as if there was something she wanted to say but hesitated. At last she went to Mrs Hallam's side, and took hold of the sleeve of her dress.

"Let me go and ask Mr Bayle to take berths for you on board the first ship that's going to sail, and get taken away from this dreadful place."

Mrs Hallam gazed at her wistfully, but did not answer for a few moments.

"I must think, Thibs," she said. "*I* must think; and now I cannot, for I feel as if I am stunned."

"Then lie down a bit, my dear Miss Milly. Do, dear. She ought to, oughtn't she, Miss Julie? There, I knew she would. It's to make her strong."

It was as if old girlish days had come back, for Mrs Hallam yielded with a sigh to the stronger will of the faithful old servant, letting her lift and lay her down, and closing her eyes with a weary sigh.

"Now I may go to Mr Bayle, mayn't I?"

"No," said Mrs Hallam sternly.

"Then to Sir Gordon, and ask him to help us?"

"No," said Mrs Hallam again; "I must work alone in this—and I will."

She closed her eyes, and in a few minutes seemed to have dropped off asleep, when Thisbe signed to Julia to accompany her out of the room.

"Don't you fret and trouble yourself, my darling," she whispered. "I'll take care no one comes and troubles you. She's worn out with suffering, and no doctor would do her good, or we'd soon have the best in the town. What she wants is rest and peace, and your dear loving hands to hold her. If anything will ease her that's it."

She kissed Julia, and the next moment the girl's arms were clasped about her neck, and she sobbed upon her breast.

"It's so terrible," she cried. "I can't bear it! I can't bear it! I tried so hard to love him, but—but—"

"An angel with wings couldn't have loved such a father as that, my dear."

"Thibs!"

"Well, there, then, I won't say much, my darling; but don't you fret. You've both done quite right, for there's a pynte beyond which no one can go."

"But if we could win him back to—"

"Make you marry that man Crellock! Oh, my darling, there's no winning him back. I said nothing and stood by you both to let you try, and I was ready to forgive everything; but oh, my pet! I knew how bad it all was from the very first."

"No, no, Thibs, you didn't think him guilty when he was sent out here."

"Think, my dear! No: I knew it, and so did Sir Gordon and Mr Bayle, but for her sake they let her go on believing in him. Oh! my dear, only that there's you here, I want to know why such a man was ever allowed to live."

"Thibs, he is my father," cried Julia angrily.

"Yes, my dear, and there's no changing it, much as I've thought about it."

Julia stood thinking.

"I shall go to him," she said at last, "with you, and tell him why we have left him. I feel, Thibs, as if I must ask him to forgive me, for I am his child."

"You wait a bit, my dear, and then talk about forgiveness by-and-by. You've got to stay with your poor mother now. Why, if you left her on such an errand as that, what would happen if he kept you, and wouldn't let you come back?"

Julia's eyes dilated, and her careworn face grew paler.

"He would not do that."

"He and that Crellock would do anything, I believe. There, you can't do that now. You've got to sit and watch by her."

"Julia!" came in an excited voice from the next room.

"There, what did I tell you, my dear?" said Thisbe; and she hurried Julia back and closed the door.

"They'll go back and forgive him if he only comes and begs them to, and he'll finish breaking her heart," said Thisbe, as she went down. "Oh, there never was anything so dreadful as a woman's weakness when once she has loved a man. But go back they shall not if I can help it, and what to do for the best I don't know."

She went into the little sitting-room, seated herself, and began rolling her apron up tightly, as she rocked herself to and fro, and all the time kept on biting her lips.

"I daren't," she said. "She would never forgive me if she knew. No, I couldn't."

She went on rocking herself to and fro.

"I will—I will do it. It's right, for it's to save them; it's to save her life, poor dear, and my darling from misery."

She started from her chair, wringing her hands, and with her face convulsed, ending by falling on her knees with clasped hands.

"Oh, please God, no," she cried, "don't—don't suffer that—that darling child to be dragged down to such a fate. I couldn't bear it. I'd sooner die! For ever and ever. Amen."

She sobbed as she crouched lower and lower, suffering an agony of spirit greater than had ever before fallen to her lot, and then rose, calm and composed, to wipe her eyes.

"I'll do it, and if it's wicked may I be forgiven. I can't bear it, and there's only that before he puts the last straw on."

There was a loud tap at the door just then, evidently given by a hard set of knuckles.

"It's them!" cried Thisbe excitedly; "it's them!" The door was locked and bolted, and she glanced round the room as if in search of a weapon. Then going to the window, she looked sidewise through the panes, and her hard, angry face softened a little, and she opened the window.

"How did you know I was wanting you to come?"

Tom Porter's hard brown face lit up with delight. "Was you?" he cried; "was you, Thisbe? Lor'! how nice it looks to see you in a little house like this, and me coming to the door; but you might let me in. Are you all alone?"

"Don't you get running your thick head up against a wall, Tom Porter, or you'll hurt it. And now, look here, don't you get smirking at me again in that way, or off you go about your business, and I'll never look at you again."

"But Thisbe, my dear, I only—"

"Don't only, then," she said, in a fierce whisper; "and don't growl like that, or you'll frighten them as is upstairs into thinking it's some one else."

"All right, my lass; all right. Only you are very hard on a man. You was hard at King's Castor, you was harder up at Clerkenwell, while now we're out here rocks is padded bulkheads to you."

"I can't help it, Tom; I'm in trouble," said Thisbe more gently.

"Are you, my lass? Well, let me pilot you out."

"Yes, I think you shall," she said, "I wanted you to come."

"Now, that's pleasant," said Tom Porter, smiling; "and it does me good, for the way in which I wants to help you, Thisbe, is a wonder even to me."

"Oh, yes, I know," she said grimly. "Now then, why did you come?"

"You said you wanted me."

"Yes; but tell me first why you came."

"The Admiral sent me to say that he was waiting for the missus's commands, and might he come down and see her on very partic'lar business? He couldn't write, his hand's all a shake, and he ain't been asleep all night."

"Tell him, and tell Mr Bayle, too, that my mistress begs that she may be left alone for the present. She says she will send to them if she wants their help."

"Right it is," said Tom Porter. "Now then, what did *you* want along o' me?"

Thisbe's face hardened and then grew convulsed, and the tears sprang to her eyes. Then it seemed to harden up again, and she took hold of Tom Porter's collar and whispered to him quickly.

"Phe-ew!" whistled Sir Gordon's man.

She went on whispering in an excited way.

"Yes, I understand," he said.

She whispered to him again more earnestly than ever.

"Yes. Not tell a soul—and only if—"

"Yes."

"Only if—"

"Yes, yes," whispered Thisbe. "Mind, I depend upon you."

"If Tom Porter's a living soul," he replied, "it's done. But you do mean it?"

"I mean it," said Thisbe King. "Now go."

"One moment, my lass," he said. "I've been very humble, and humble I am; but when this trouble's over and smooth water comes, will you?"

Thisbe did not answer for a few moments, and then it was in a softened voice.

"Tom Porter," she said, "there's one upstairs half dead with misery, and her darling child suffering more than words can tell. My poor heart's full of them; don't ask me now."

Tom Porter gave his lips a smart slap and hurried down the street, while Thisbe closed the window and went back to her chair, to rock herself to and fro again, with her hands busily rolling and unrolling her apron.

"I've done it," she said; "but it all rests on him. It's his own doing."

Then, after a pause:

"How long will it be before they find out where we are? Not long. Hah!"

Thisbe King passed her hands up and down her bare brawny arms, and her face tightened for the encounter which she felt must come before long.

Volume Four—Chapter Eighteen.

The Blow Falls.

It was close upon evening before the trouble Thisbe expected came. Tom Porter had been again, tapped at the door, and when Thisbe went to the window he had contorted his face in the most horrible manner, closing his left eye, and then walked off without a word.

Thisbe watched till he was out of sight, and then returned to her chair.

"He's to be trusted," she said to herself. "It's a pity he wants to marry me. We're much better as we are; and who knows but what he might turn wild? There's only one thing in his favour, he ain't a handsome man."

Now Tom Porter at fifty looked to be about the last person in the world to turn wild, but Thisbe's experiences had done much to harden her virgin heart.

At least a dozen times over she had slipped off her shoes and ascended the stairs to find that, utterly exhausted, Mrs Hallam and Julia were sleeping heavily, the latter on a chair, with her arms clasped about her mother's neck.

"Poor dears!" said Thisbe, as she descended; "I daren't wake them, but they ought to have a cup of tea."

"Ah," she exclaimed softly, "what would she say? I shall never dare to look her in the face again."

At last the trouble came.

"I knew it," said Thisbe, as she heard the steps at the door. "He was bound to find us. Yes, they're both there. Well, it's his own work and not mine. What shall I do?"

She rose from her chair, looking very resolute. "I'll face them bold. It's the only way."

She heard the murmur of men's voices, and then there was a rap at the door given with the handle of a whip. She went to the door, unfastened and threw it open.

"What is it?" she said.

Hallam and Crellock were on the threshold, and the latter exclaimed, as soon as he saw her:

"I thought so."

They stepped in quickly, and Thisbe's lips tightened as she was forced to back before them, and the door swung to.

"Where is your mistress?" said Hallam sharply.

"Asleep. Worn out and ill."

"Where's my daughter?"

"With her mother: upstairs."

"I'll soon have an end of this fooling," he exclaimed; and as Thisbe stood with her arms folded, she seemed to see a flash of the old look she remembered—the look she hated—when they were at Castor years before.

Hallam threw open the door at the foot of the narrow staircase, while Crellock seated himself astride a chair with his hat on and beat his boot with his whip.

"Millicent! Julie!" cried Hallam fiercely, and there were footsteps heard above, for the arrival had awakened those who slept. "Come down at once."

He let the door swing to and began to pace the little room, muttering to himself, and evidently furious with rage at his wife's desertion.

Crellock watched him from the corner of his eyes, and from time to time unconsciously applied his hand to a great discolouration on the cheek. He was evidently quite satisfied, for Hallam needed no egging on to the task, and he felt that this episode would hasten his marriage.

"Are you coming?" cried Hallam, after a few minutes, and as he flung back the door, that of the bedroom was heard to open, and Mrs Hallam and Julia came down, both very pale, but with a firmness in their countenances that sent a thrill of joy through Thisbe.

"There you are then," cried Hallam, as they stood before him. "Ah! I've a good mind to—"

He raised his hand and made a feint as if to strike the pale, suffering woman. With a cry of horror, Julia flung herself between them, her eyes flashing, her dread gone, and in its place, indignant horror sweeping away the last feeling of pity and compunction for the brutalised man to whom she owed her birth.

"Now then," cried Hallam. "You've both had your fool's game out, so put on your bonnets and come home." Mrs Hallam passed her hand round Julia and remained silent.

"Do you hear?" cried Hallam. "I say, put on your things and come home. As for you, madam, you shall have a home of your own, and a husband, before you know where you are. Come; stir!" he cried, with a stamp. "This is my home," said Mrs Hallam, sternly. "What!"

"Robert Hallam, the last thread that bound me to you is broken," she continued, in a calm, judicial voice. "We are separated for ever."

"You're mad," cried Hallam, with a laugh. "Come, no nonsense, ma'am! Don't make a scene, for I'm not in the humour to put up with much. Come out of this house or—"

He made a step or two towards the door, for Thisbe had thrown it open, having seen Bayle pass the window with Sir Gordon. Then he seized the door to fling it in their faces; but Thisbe held it firmly, and they walked in, Hallam himself giving way.

"Coward!" snarled Crellock in his ear, as he started up, whip in hand.

"Mrs Hallam," said Sir Gordon, "you must forgive this intrusion. I am sure we are wanted here."

"Wanted here!" cried Hallam savagely; "no, you are not wanted here. I'll have no more interferences from such as you; you've both been the curse of my life."

Sir Gordon turned upon him with a calm look of disgust and contempt, which at another time would have made him quail; but, fevered with brandy as he was, the effect was to make him more beside himself.

"As you are here, both of you, let me tell you this: that I don't kick you out because one of you is a weak, doddering old idiot, the other—oh, his cloth must protect Mr Bayle. Now what do you want?"

"Be calm, Julia," whispered Bayle. "No harm shall befall either of you."

Crellock advanced menacingly, but Sir Gordon interposed.

"Mrs Hallam, as your father's old friend, I must interfere for your protection now."

"Must you?" cried Hallam fiercely, "then I tell you that you won't. This is my house, taken by my wife. That is my wife. That is my child, and in a few days she will be the wife of this gentleman, my oldest friend. Now go. Millicent—Julie—get on your things, and come, or, by all that's holy, we'll drag you through the streets."

Julia clung to Bayle, and turned her flushed face to him as if asking help; while, with a look of calm contempt, he patted the hand he held, and glanced at Mrs Hallam, for something seemed to warn him that the crisis had arrived.

"I have told you, Robert Hallam," she said, in a calm, firm voice, that grew in strength as she went on, "that from this hour we are separated, never to be man and wife again. I clung to you in all a woman's proud faith in her husband. I loved you as dearly as woman could love. When you were condemned of all, I defended you, and believed you honest."

"Bah!" he exclaimed; "enough of this!" and he took a step forward, but quailed before her gaze.

"You crushed my love. You made me your wretched innocent tool and slave when you brought me here, and at last you brutally told me all the cruel truth. Even then, heartbroken, I clung to you, and suffered in silence. God knows how I tried to bring you to penitence and a better life. I forgave all for the sake of our child; and in my love for her I would have gone on bearing all."

"Have you nearly done?" he said mockingly.

"Nearly," she said, in the same firm, clear tones; and she seemed to tower above him, pale and noble of aspect, while he, drink-brutalised and blotched, seemed to shrink.

"I say I would have borne everything, even if you had beaten me like a dog. But when—oh, my God, judge between us and forgive me if I have done wrong!—when I am called upon to see my innocent child dragged down by you to the fate of being the wife of the villain who has been your partner in all your crimes, my soul revolts, and I say—from this hour all between us is at an end."

"And I say," he yelled, "that you are my wife, this my child, and you shall obey me. Come; I am master here."

He made a snatch at her arm, but she raised it before him, with outstretched palm, and her voice rang out with a cry that made him shrink and cower.

"Stop!"

There was a moment's utter silence, broken by the softly heard tramp of feet.

"Husband no longer, father of my child no more. Robert Hallam, you are my convict servant! I discharge you. Leave this house!"

Hallam took a step back, literally stunned by the words of the outraged woman, who for so long a time had been his slave, while Bayle uttered a long sighing sound as if relieved of some terrible weight.

For a time no one spoke, but all turned from gazing on the prominent figure of that group, to Hallam, who stood clenching and unclenching his hands, and gasping as if trying to recover from the shock he had received.

He essayed to speak as he glared at Mrs Hallam, and scowled at her as if each look were an arrow to wound and bring her to his feet humbled and appealing as of old; but the arrows glanced from the armour of indignant maternal love with which she was clothed; and, drawn up to her full height, scornful and defiant as she seemed, her look absolutely made him quail.

Tramp—tramp—tramp—tramp.

The regular march of disciplined men coming nearer and nearer, but heard by none within that room, as Crellock, with a coarse laugh, bent forward, and whispered in his companion's ear:

"Why, man, are you going to submit to this?"

"No!" roared Hallam, as if his gang-companion's words had broken a spell. "No! The woman's mad! Julia, you are my child. Come here!"

Julia met the eyes that were fixed fiercely upon her, and stepped forward.

Bayle tried to arrest her, but she raised her hand to keep him back, and then placed it on her father's arm, trembling and looking white. Then she reached up, and kissed him solemnly upon the cheek.

"There, gentlemen," he cried triumphantly. "You see. Now, wife—my wife, come to your convict servant—come—home."

He passed his arm round Julia's waist, and signed to Crellock to come forward, but his child glided from his grasp.

"Good-bye—father—good-bye—for ever."

He made a snatch at her hand; but she had gone, and was clinging to Bayle.

Hallam uttered a fierce oath, and then listened: stopped short with his head wrenched round to gaze at the door.

For at that moment the tramp of feet reached the entrance, and a voice rang out:

"Halt!"

There was the rattle of muskets on the path, and as, ghastly of face, and with starting eyes, Robert Hallam saw in imagination the interior of the prison, the grim convict dress, the chains, and the lash, the door was thrown open, and Captain Otway entered, followed by a sergeant and a file of the convict guard, a squad remaining outside, drawn up before the house.

Otway glanced round, his brow furrowed, and his lips tightened, as his eyes fell on Mrs Hallam and her child.

It was but a momentary emotion. Then the stern military precision asserted itself, and he said quickly:

"Robert Hallam, number 874, assigned servant, I arrest you for breaking the terms of your pass. Sergeant, remove this man."

Two men stepped to Hallam's side on the instant.

"Curse you," he yelled, as he started forward to reach his wife, but a strong hand on either arm stayed him. "This is your work."

She shook her head slowly, and Julia darted to her side, for the firmness that had sustained her so far was failing fast.

"No," she said slowly; "it is no work of mine."

"Then I have to thank my dear friend the Baronet here," he cried with a vindictive look at Sir Gordon.

"No, Hallam. I have known for months past that you have been living in wild excess on the money you stole from me, but I spared you for others' sake."

"Oh, I see, then," cried Hallam, turning to Bayle; "it was you—you beggarly professor of—"

"Stay your reproaches," cried Bayle sternly. "I could not have taken steps against you had I wished."

"If it'll make it easier for Mr Hallam to know who gave information again him," said a voice at the door, "it was me."

"Tom Porter!" cried Sir Gordon.

"Ay, ay, sir."

"Remove your prisoner," said Captain Otway sternly. Crellock stepped forward with a blustering swagger.

"Am I included in this?" he said.

"No, sir," said Captain Otway sternly. "I have no orders about you—at present. Take my advice and go." Crellock made a step toward Julia, but she shrank from him in horror, and the next minute he was literally forced out by the soldiers with their prisoner, the door closed, and a low, wailing voice arose:

"Julia!"

"Mother, dear mother, I am here," cried Julia, kneeling and supporting the stricken woman on her breast.

"Hold me, my darling, tightly," she moaned. "It is growing dark—is this the end?"

Volume Four—Chapter Nineteen.

The Good that was in him.

"Hi! Sir Gordon!"

The old gentleman turned as a big-bearded man cantered up over the rough land by the track, some six months after the prison gates had closed upon Robert Hallam.

"Oh, it's you!" said Sir Gordon, shading his eyes from the blazing sun. "Well?"

"Don't be rough on a fellow, Sir Gordon. I've been a big blackguard, I know, but somehow I never had a chance from the first. I want to do the right thing now."

"Humph! Pretty well time," said the old man. "Well, what is it?"

The man hesitated as if struggling with shame, and he thought himself weak, but he struck his boot heavily with his whip, and took off his broad felt hat.

"I'll do it," he said sharply to himself. Then, aloud: "Look here, sir, I'm sick of it."

"Humph! then you'd better leave it," said the old man with an angry sneer. "Go and give yourself up, and join your old companion."

"That's rough!" said Crellock with a grim smile. "How hard you good people can be on a fellow when he's down!"

"What have you ever done to deserve anything else, you scoundrel?" cried Sir Gordon fiercely. "Twenty thousand pounds of my money you and your rogue of a companion had, and I'm tramping through this blazing sun, while you ride a blood horse."

"Take the horse then," said Crellock good-humouredly. "I don't want it!"

"You know I'm too old to ride it, you dog, or you wouldn't offer it."

"There, you see, when a fellow does want to turn over a new leaf you good people won't let him."

"Won't let him? Where's your book and where's your leaf?"

"Book? Oh, I'm the book, Sir Gordon, and you won't listen to what's on the leaf."

Sir Gordon seated himself on a great tussock of soft grass, took out his gold-rimmed glasses, put them on deliberately and stared up at the great, fine-looking, bronzed man.

"Hah!" he said at last. "You, a man who can talk like that! Why, you might have been a respectable member of society, and here you are—"

"Out on pass in a convict settlement. Say it, Sir Gordon. Well, what wonder? It all began with Hallam when I was a weak young fool, and thought him with his good looks and polished ways a sort of hero. I got into trouble with him; he escaped because I wouldn't tell tales, and I had to bear the brunt, and after that I never had a chance."

"Ah, there was a nice pair of you."

Crellock groaned and seemed about to turn away, but the man's good genius had him tightly gripped that day, and he smiled again.

"Don't be hard on me, Sir Gordon. I want to say something to you. I was going to your friend, Mr Christie Bayle, but—I couldn't do that."

Sir Gordon watched him curiously.

"You haven't turned bushranger, then? You're not going to rob me?"

"No," said Crellock grimly. "Haven't I robbed you enough!"

"Humph! Well?"

"Ah, that's better," said Crellock; "now you'll listen to me. The fact is, sir, I've been thinking, since I've been living all alone, that forty isn't too old for a man to begin again."

"Too old? No, man. Why, I'm—there, never mind how old. Older than that, and I'm going to begin again. Forty! Why, you're a boy!"

"Well, Sir Gordon, I'm going to begin the square. I gave up the drink because—there, never mind why," he said huskily. "I had a reason, and now I'm going to make a start."

"Well, go and do it, then. What are you going to do?"

"Oh, get up the country, sir, stockman or shepherding."

"Wolfing, you mean, sir."

"Oh, no, I don't, Sir Gordon," said Crellock, laughing. "There's plenty of work to be got, and I like horses and cattle better than I do men now."

"Well, look here," said Sir Gordon testily; "I don't believe you."

"Eh?"

"I don't believe you, sir. If you meant all this you'd have gone and begun it instead of talking. There, be off. I'm hot and tired, and want to be alone." Crellock frowned again, but his good genius gave him another grip of the shoulder, and the smile came back. "You don't understand me yet, Sir Gordon," he said. "No, I never shall."

"I wanted to tell you, sir, that since Hallam was taken, I've been living up in the Gully House. I'd nowhere else to go, and I was desperate like. I thought every day that you or somebody would come and take possession, but no one did. Law seems all anyhow out here. Then the days went on. This horse had been down—sprained leg from a bad jump."

"Confound your horse, sir! I don't want to hear your stable twaddle," cried Sir Gordon.

Crellock seemed to swallow a lump in his throat, and paused, but he went on after a while:

"The poor brute was a deal hurt, and tending and bandaging his leg seemed to do me good like. Then I used to send one of the blacks to town for food."

"And drink?" said Sir Gordon acidly.

"No—for tea; and I've lived up there with the horses ever since. There's—"

"Well, why don't you go on, man?"

"Give me time," said Crellock, who had stopped short. "There's Miss Hallam's mare there, too. She was very fond of that mare," he added huskily.

Sir Gordon's eyes seemed half shut, as he watched the man and noted the changes in his voice.

"Well, sir, I've lived there six months now, and nobody has taken any notice. There's the furniture and the house, and there's a whole lot of money left yet of what Mrs Hallam brought over."

"Well?"

"Well! why, Sir Gordon, it's all yours, of course, and I've been waiting for weeks to have this talk to you. I couldn't come to the cottage."

"Why not?"

Crellock shook his head.

"No, I couldn't come there. I've laid in wait for you when you were going down to your boat for a sail, but that Tom Porter was always with you; and I didn't want to write. I didn't think you'd come if I did. You'd have thought it was a plant, and set the authorities after me, and I didn't want that because I've had enough of convict life."

"Humph! Well, what do you want me to do?"

"Come and take possession, Sir Gordon, and have the house taken care of. There's her mare there, you see. Then there's the money; no one but Hallam and me knows where it's hidden. I shouldn't like the place to fall into anybody's hands."

"But you? You want to give all this up to me?"

"Of course, sir. It's all yours. It was the bank money that bought everything."

"And what are you going to do?"

"Oh, I'm sick of it all, sir, and I want to start clear. I shall go up the country. I think I'm a clever stockman."

"And you give up everything?"

The man set his teeth.

"Yes, sir," he said, firmly, as he turned and patted the horse's neck as it stood close by, cropping the tender shoots of a bush; and it raised its head and laid its muzzle in his hand. "I should like you to see that Joey here had a good master. I threw him down once, and doctoring seemed to make him fond of me. He's a good horse. It's a pity you're too old to ride."

"Confound you! how dare you?" cried Sir Gordon.

"I'm not too old to ride, sir. I—I—" he started up with his lip quivering. "Here! here! sit down, Crellock. Confound you, sir, I never met with such a scoundrel in all my life!"

Crellock looked at him curiously, and then, throwing the bridle on the ground, he sat down, while Sir Gordon paced up and down in a quick, fidgety walk.

"Have you got anything more to say, sir?" he cried at last.

Crellock was silent for a few moments, and then, drawing a long breath, he said:

"How is Mrs Hallam, sir?"

"Dying," said Sir Gordon, shortly. "It is a matter of days. Well, is that all?"

There was another interval before Crellock spoke.

"Will you take a message for me, sir, to those up yonder?"

"No!—Yes."

The words would not come for some moments, and when they did come they were very husky.

"I want you to ask Mrs Hallam to forgive me my share of the past."

"Is that all?"

"No, Sir Gordon. Tell Miss Julia that for her sake I did give up the drink; that I'm going up now into the bush; that for her sake I'm doing all this; and that I shall never forget the gentle face that bent over me outside the prison walls."

He turned to go, and had gone a score of yards, walking quickly, but with the horse following, when Sir Gordon called out:

"Stop!"

Crellock stood still, and Sir Gordon walked up to him slowly.

"You are right, Crellock," he said in a quiet, changed tone. "I believe you. You never had a chance."

He held out his hand, which the other did not take.

"Shake hands, man."

"I am a convict, sir," said Crellock proudly.

"Shake hands," cried Sir Gordon firmly; and he took the strong, brown hand, slowly raised.

"There is my forgiveness for the past—and—yes—that of the truest, sweetest woman I ever knew. Now, as to your future, do as you say, go into the bush and take up land—new land in this new country, and begin your new life. I shall touch nothing at the Gully House—place, horses, money, they are yours."

"Mine?" exclaimed Crellock.

"Yes; I have more than ever I shall want; and as to that money which I had always looked upon as lost, if it makes you into what you say you will strive to be, it is the best investment I ever made."

"But—"

"Good-bye."

Volume Four—Chapter Twenty.

Overheard.

Sir Gordon Bourne looked ten years younger as he walked towards the cottage on the bluff. The hill was steep to climb, and the sun was torrid in its heat; but he forgot the discomfort and climbed higher and higher till he reached the rough fence that surrounded the grounds, and there stood, with his hat off, wiping his brow and gazing at the glorious prospect of sea and land.

"I feel almost like a good fairy this morning," he said, with a laugh. "Ah! how beautiful it all is, and what a pity that such an Eden should be made the home of England's worst."

He opened the rough gate and entered the grounds, that were admirably kept by a couple of convict servants, watched over by Tom Porter, crossed a patch of lawn, and was about to go up to the house, but a pleasantly-placed rustic seat, beneath the shelter of a gum-tree, and nearly surrounded by Austral shrubs, emitting their curious aromatic scent in the hot sunshine, tempted him to rest; and in a few minutes, overcome by the exertions of the morning, his head bowed down upon his breast, and he dropped into a light doze.

He was aroused by voices—one low, deep, and earnest, the other low and deep, but silvery and sweet, and with a tender ring in it that brought up memories of a little, low-roofed drawing-room in the quiet Lincolnshire town; and a curious dimness came over the old man's eyes.

The speakers were behind him, hidden by a veil of soft grey-green leaves; and as Sir Gordon involuntarily listened, one voice said in trembling tones:

"I dared not even look forward to such an end."

"But ever since others began to set me thinking of such things, I have waited, for I used to say, some day he will ask me to be his wife."

"And you loved me, Julie?"

"Loved you? Did you not know?"

"But like this?"

"Like this? Always; for when you came, all trouble seemed to go, and I felt that I was safe."

The voices paused, and Sir Gordon sat up, leaning upon his stick and thinking aloud.

"Well, I have always hoped it would be so—no, not always; and now it seems as if he were going to rob me of a child."

He sat gazing straight before him, seeing nothing of the soft blue sea and sky, nor the many shades of grey and green that rolled before his eyes, for they were filled with the face of Julia Hallam.

"Yes," he said at last. "Why not? Ah, Bayle! Where is Julie?"

"With her mother now. Sir Gordon—"

"Hush! I know. I've nought to say but this: God bless you both!"

Volume Four—Chapter Twenty One.

Rest.

There had been some talk of a speedy return to the old country, but the doctor shook his head.

"Let her live her few hours in rest and peace," he said. "It would be madness to attempt such a thing." And so all thought of the journey home was set aside, and Mrs Hallam was borne up to the cottage.

In her weakness she had protested, but Sir Gordon had quietly said:

"Am I your father's oldest friend?" And then: "Have I not a right to insist—for Julie's sake?"

She yielded, and the cottage for the next few months became their home, Bayle going down into the town, spending much of his time amongst the convicts and seeing a good deal of the Otways.

"That's how it's going to be," said Mrs Otway. "I always said so, Jack."

"Nonsense! he's old enough to be her father."

"Perhaps so in years; but he's about the youngest man in his ways I ever knew, while she is old and staid for her age."

"Time proves all things," said Captain Otway. "Phil won't get her, that's certain."

"No; that's all over, and he is not breaking his heart about her, in spite of all the fuss at first. Well, I'm glad for some things; I shall be able to look Lady Eaton in the face."

"A task you would very well have fulfilled, even if he had married Julia Hallam. It would take a very big Lady Eaton to frighten you, my dear. Been up to see Mrs Hallam to-day?"

The lady nodded.

"No hope?"

"Not the slightest," said Mrs Otway quietly. Then after a pause: "Jack," she said, "do you know, I think it would be wrong to wish her to live. What has she to live for?"

"Child—her child's husband—their children."

Mrs Otway shook her head.

"No; I don't think she would ever be happy again. Poor thing! if ever woman's heart was broken, hers was. I don't like going up to see her, but I feel obliged. There are so few women here whom one like her would care to see. Ah, it's a sad case!"

"Does she seem to suffer much?"

"She does not seem to, but who knows what a quiet, patient creature will bear without making a sign?"

The months glided on, and still Millicent Hallam lingered as if loth to leave the beautiful world spread before her, and on which she loved to gaze.

She had half-expected it, but it was still a surprise when Julia whispered to her, as she sat beside her couch, that she was going to be the wife of Christie Bayle.

Mrs Hallam's eyes dilated.

"He has asked you to be his wife?" she said, in her low, sweet voice.

"No, mother," said Julia, as she laid her head beside her, and gazed dreamily before her; "I don't think he asked me."

"But, my child—you said—"

"Yes, mother dear," said Julia innocently, "I hardly know how it came about. It has always seemed to me that some day I should be his wife. Why, I have always loved him! How could I help it?"

Mrs Hallam laid her hand upon her child's glossy hair, and closed her eyes, wondering in herself at the simple, truthful words she had heard. One moment she felt pained, and as if it ought not to be; the next, a flood of joy seemed to send a wave through her breast, as she thought of the days when Julia would be alone in the world, and in whose charge would she rather have left her than in that of Christie Bayle?

The battle went on at intervals for days; but at last it was at an end, and she lay back calmly as she said to herself:

"Yes, it is right. Now I can be at rest!"

Another month passed. Doctor Woodhouse came, as was his custom, more as a friend than from the belief that his knowledge could be of any avail. One particular morning he stopped to lunch, and went up again afterwards to see Mrs Hallam, staying some little time. He left Julia with her, and came down to where Sir Gordon was seated on the lawn with Bayle.

The latter started up, as he saw the doctor's face, and his eyes asked him mutely for an explanation of his look.

The doctor answered him as mutely, while Sir Gordon saw it, and rose to stand agitatedly by his chair.

"Bayle," he whispered; "I thought I was prepared, but now it has come it seems very hard to bear!"

Bayle glided away into the house, to go upstairs, meeting Thisbe on the way wringing her hands, and blinded with her tears.

"I couldn't bear to stop, sir—I couldn't bear to stop," she whispered. "It's come—it's come at last."

Bayle entered the room softly, steeling his heart to bear with her he loved some agonising scene. But he paused on the threshold, almost startled by the look of peace upon the wasted face, full in the bright Southern light.

Mrs Hallam smiled as she saw him there; and as he crossed the room and knelt by her side, she laid her hand in his, and feebly took Julia's and placed them together.

"The rest is coming now," she said.

Julia burst into a passion of weeping.

"Mother! Mother! If you could but live!" she sobbed.

"Live? No, my darling, no. I am so tired—so worn and weary. I should faint now by the way."

She closed her eyes, smiling at them tenderly, and for the space of an hour they watched her sleeping peacefully and well.

And as Julia sat there with her hands clasped in Christie Bayle's strong palms, a feeling of hopefulness and peace, to which she had long been a stranger, came into her heart. The doctor had once said that there might be a change for the better if his patient's mind were at rest, and that rest seemed to have come at last.

The afternoon had passed away, and the fast-sinking sun had turned the clear sky to gold; and as the great orb of day descended to where a low bank of clouds lay upon the horizon, it seemed to glide quickly from their view. The room, but a few moments before lit up by the refulgent glow, darkened and became gloomy; but as the glorious light streamed up in myriad rays from behind the clouds, there was still a soft flush upon the sick woman's face.

A wondrous stillness seemed to have come upon the watchers, for the hope that had been warm in Julia's breast was now chilled as if by some unseen presence, and she turned her frightened eyes from her mother to Bayle, and back.

"Christie!" she cried suddenly.

"Hush!"

One softly-spoken, solemn-sounding word, as Christie Bayle held fast the hand of his affianced wife, and together they sank upon their knees.

The glowing purple clouds opened slowly, and once more as from the dazzling golden gates of the great city on the farther shore, a wondrous light streamed forth, filling the chamber and brightening the features of the dying woman.

The pain and agony of the past with their cruel lines had gone, and the beautiful countenance shone with that look of old that he who knelt there knew so well. But it was etherealised in its sweet calm, its restfulness, as the still, bright eyes gazed calmly and trustfully far out to sea.

Julia's fingers tightened on her mother's chilling hand, and she gazed with awe at the rapt look and gentle smile that flickered a few moments on the trembling lips.

Then, as the clouds closed in once more and the room grew dark, the passionate yearning cry of the young heart burst forth in that one word, "Mother?"

But there was no response—no word spoken, save that as they knelt there in the ever darkening room Christie Bayle's lips parted to whisper, in tones so low, that they were like a sigh:

"'Come unto Me all ye that are weary and are heavy laden, and I will give you rest.'"

Volume Four—Chapter Twenty Two.

The Doctor's Garden.

The place the same. Not a change visible in all those years. The old church with its mossed tiles and lichened walls; the familiar tones of the chiming clock that gave notice of the passing hours, and at the top of the market-place the old Bank—Dixons' Bank, at whose door that drab-looking man stood talking for a few minutes—talking to Mr Trampleasure before going home to feed his fishes in the waning light, and then take Mrs Thickens up to the doctor's house to spend the evening.

And that evening. The garden unchanged in the midst of change. The old golden glow coming through the clump of trees in the west beyond the row of cucumber-frames—those trees that Dr Luttrell told his wife he must cut down because they took off so much of the afternoon sun. But he had not cut them down. He would as soon have thought of lopping off his own right hand.

Everything in that garden and about and in that house seemed the same at the first glance, but there had been changes in King's Castor in the course of years.

There was a stone, for instance, growing very much weather-stained, relating the virtues of one Daniel Gemp; and there was the same verse cut in the stone that had been sent round on the funeral cards with some pieces of sponge cake, one of which cards was framed in the parlour at Gorringe's, his crony, who still cut up cloth as of old.

Mrs Pinet, too, had passed away, and the widow who now had the house, and let lodgings, painted her pots green instead of red, and robbed the dull old place of one bit of colour.

But the doctor's garden was the same, and so thought Christie Bayle, as he stood in the gathering gloom six months after his return to England, and shortly after his acceptance of the vicarage of King's Castor—at his old friend's wish.

There were the old sweet scents of the dewy earth, that familiar one of the lately cut grass; there was the old hum of a beetle winging its way round and round one of the trees; and there before him were the open French windows, and the verandah, showing the lit-up drawing-room furniture, the old globe lamps, and the candles on the piano just the same.

Had he been asleep and dreamed? and was he still the boyish curate who fell in love and failed?

Yes; there was little Miss Heathery going to the piano and laying down the reticule bag, with the tail of her white handkerchief hanging out. And there was Thickens with his hands resting on his drab trousers; and there was the doctor, and little pleasant Mrs Luttrell, going from one to the other, and staying longest by, and unable to keep her trembling hands off that tall, dark, beautiful woman, who smiled down upon her in answer to each caress.

No change, and yet how changed! How near the bottom of the hill that little grey old man, and that rosy little white-haired woman! How querulous and thin sounded Mrs Thickens's voice in her old trivial troubadour Heathery song! The years had gone, and in spite of its likeness to the past, what a void there was—absent faces!

No; that carefully dressed old gentleman was half behind the curtain, and he has risen to cross to the doctor, pausing to pat the tall, graceful woman on the arm, and nod at her affectionately by the way. There is another familiar face, too, that of Thisbe's in a most wonderful cap, carrying in tea, to hand round, and Tom Porter obediently "following in his commodore's wake," his own words, and handing bread-and-butter, sugar and cream.

And still Christie Bayle gazes on, half expecting to see the tall, dark, handsome man who cast so deep a shadow across so many lives; but instead of that the graceful figure that is so like Millicent Hallam of the past, appears framed in the window to stand there gazing out into the dark garden.

Then she turns back sharply, to answer some remark made in the little drawing-room, and looks quickly out again with hands resting on the door.

It is very dark out there, and her eyes are accustomed to the light of the drawing-room; but in a minute or so she sees that which she sought, and half runs over the dewy lawn to where she is clasped in two strong arms.

"You truant!" she says playfully, as she nestles close to him. "Come in and sing; we want you to make the place complete. Why, what are you thinking about?"

"I was thinking of the past, Julie," he says.

She looks up at him in the starlight; and he gazes down in her glistening eyes.

"The past? Let me think of it too. Are we not one?"

And as they stand together the little English interior before them seems to fade away, and the light they gaze upon to be the glowing sunshine of the far South, blazing down in all its glory upon the grassy grave and glistening stone that mark the resting-place of This Man's Wife.

The End.

Milton Keynes UK
Ingram Content Group UK Ltd.
UKHW031044120324
439302UK00006B/603